The Carrie Diaries

CANDACE BUSHNELL

The Carrie Diaries

HarperCollins*Publishers*

First published in hardback in the USA by Balzer + Bray,

an imprint of HarperCollins*Publishers* Inc. in 2010

First published in the UK by HarperCollins*Publishers* Ltd in 2010

The Carrie Diaries

www.harpercollins.co.uk

HB ISBN: 978-0-00-731206-1

TPB ISBN: 978-0-00-735842-7

Typography by Sarah Hoy

10 8 6 4 2 1 3 5 7 9

Mixed Sources
Product group from well-managed
forests and other controlled sources
www.fsc.org Cert no. SW-COC-001806
© 1996 Forest Stewardship Council

FSC is a non-profit international organisation established to promote the
responsible management of the world's forests. Products carrying the FSC
label are independently certified to assure consumers that they come
from forests that are managed to meet the social, economic and
ecological needs of present and future generations.

Find out more about HarperCollins and the environment at
www.harpercollins.co.uk/green

For Calvin Bushnell

CHAPTER ONE

A Princess on Another Planet

They say a lot can happen in a summer.

Or not.

It's the first day of senior year, and as far as I can tell, I'm exactly the same as I was last year.

And so is my best friend, Lali.

"Don't forget, Bradley, we have to get boyfriends this year," she says, starting the engine of the red pickup truck she inherited from one of her older brothers.

"Crap." We were supposed to get boyfriends last year and we didn't. I open the door and scoot in, sliding the letter into my biology book, where, I figure, it can do no more harm. "Can't we give this whole boyfriend thing a rest? We already know all the boys in our school. And—"

"Actually, we don't," Lali says as she slides the gear stick into reverse, glancing over her shoulder. Of all my friends, Lali is the best driver. Her father is a cop and insisted she learn to drive when she was twelve, in case of an emergency.

"I hear there's a new kid," she says.

"So?" The last new kid who came to our school turned out to be a stoner who never changed his overalls.

"Jen P says he's cute. Really cute."

"Uh-huh." Jen P was the head of Leif Garrett's fan club in sixth grade. "If he actually is cute, Donna LaDonna will get him."

"He has a weird name," Lali says. "Sebastian something. Sebastian Little?"

"Sebastian Kydd?" I gasp.

"That's it," she says, pulling into the parking lot of the high school. She looks at me suspiciously. "Do you know him?"

I hesitate, my fingers grasping the door handle.

My heart pounds in my throat; if I open my mouth, I'm afraid it will jump out.

I shake my head.

We're through the main door of the high school when Lali spots my boots. They're white patent leather and there's a crack on one of the toes, but they're genuine go-go boots from the early seventies. I figure the boots have had a much more interesting life than I have. "Bradley," she says, eyeing the boots with disdain. "As your best friend, I cannot allow you to wear those boots on the first day of senior year."

"Too late," I say gaily. "Besides, someone's got to shake things up around here."

"Don't go changing." Lali makes her hand into a gun

shape, kisses the tip of her finger, and points it at me before heading for her locker.

"Good luck, Angel," I say. *Changing.* Ha. Not much chance of that. Not after the letter.

Dear Ms. Bradshaw, it read.

Thank you for your application to the New School's Advanced Summer Writing Seminar. While your stories show promise and imagination, we regret to inform you that we are unable to offer you a place in the program at this time.

I got the letter last Tuesday. I reread it about fifteen times, just to be sure, and then I had to lie down. Not that I think I'm so talented or anything, but for once in my life, I was hoping I was.

I didn't tell anyone about it, though. I didn't even tell anyone I'd applied, including my father. He went to Brown and expects me to go there, too. He thinks I'd make a good scientist. And if I can't hack molecular structures, I can always go into biology and study bugs.

I'm halfway down the hall when I spot Cynthia Viande and Tommy Brewster, Castlebury's golden Pod couple. Tommy isn't too bright, but he is the center on the basketball team. Cynthia, on the other hand, is senior class president, head of the prom committee, an outstanding member of the National Honor Society, and got all the Girl Scout badges by the time she was ten. She and Tommy have been dating for three years. I try not to give them much thought, but alphabetically, my last name comes right before Tommy's, so I'm stuck with the locker next to his and stuck sitting next to him in assembly, and therefore basically stuck seeing him—and Cynthia—every day.

"And don't make those goofy faces during assembly," Cynthia scolds. "This is a very important day for me. And don't forget about Daddy's dinner on Saturday."

"What about my party?" Tommy protests.

"You can have the party on Friday night," Cynthia snaps.

There could be an actual person inside Cynthia, but if there is, I've never seen it.

I swing open my locker. Cynthia suddenly looks up and spots me. Tommy gives me a blank stare, as if he has no idea who I am, but Cynthia is too well brought up for that. "Hello, Carrie," she says, like she's thirty years old instead of seventeen.

Changing. It's hard to pull off in this little town.

"Welcome to hell school," a voice behind me says.

It's Walt. He's the boyfriend of one of my other best friends, Maggie. Walt and Maggie have been dating for two years, and the three of us do practically everything together. Which sounds kind of weird, but Walt is like one of the girls.

"Walt," Cynthia says. "You're just the man I want to see."

"If you want me to be on the prom committee, the answer is no."

Cynthia ignores Walt's little joke. "It's about Sebastian Kydd. Is he really coming back to Castlebury?"

Not again. My nerve endings light up like a Christmas tree.

"That's what Doreen says." Walt shrugs as if he couldn't care less. Doreen is Walt's mother and a guidance counselor at Castlebury High. She claims to know everything, and passes all her information on to Walt—the good, the bad, and the completely untrue.

"I heard he was kicked out of private school for dealing drugs," Cynthia says. "I need to know if we're going to have a problem on our hands."

"I have no idea," Walt says, giving her an enormous fake smile. Walt finds Cynthia and Tommy nearly as annoying as I do.

"What kind of drugs?" I ask casually as we walk away.
"Painkillers?"

"Like in *Valley of the Dolls*?" It's my favorite secret book, along with the *DSM-III*, which is this tiny manual about mental disorders. "Where the hell do you get painkillers these days?"

"Oh, Carrie, I don't know," Walt says, no longer interested.
"His mother?"

"Not likely." I try to squeeze the memory of my one-and-only encounter with Sebastian Kydd out of my head but it sneaks in anyway.

I was twelve and starting to go through an awkward stage. I had skinny legs and no chest, two pimples, and frizzy hair. I was also wearing cat's-eye glasses and carrying a dog-eared copy of *What About Me?* by Mary Gordon Howard. I was obsessed with feminism. My mother was remodeling the Kydds' kitchen, and we'd stopped by their house to check on the project. Suddenly, Sebastian appeared in the doorway. And for no reason, and completely out of the blue, I sputtered, "Mary Gordon Howard believes that most forms of sexual intercourse can be classified as rape."

For a moment, there was silence. Mrs. Kydd smiled. It was the end of the summer, and her tan was set off by her pink and green shorts in a swirly design. She wore white eye shadow and pink lipstick. My mother always said Mrs. Kydd was considered a great beauty. "Hopefully you'll feel differently about it once you're married."

"Oh, I don't plan to get married. It's a legalized form of prostitution."

"Oh my." Mrs. Kydd laughed, and Sebastian, who had paused on the patio on his way out, said, "I'm taking off."

"Again, Sebastian?" Mrs. Kydd exclaimed with a hint of annoyance. "But the Bradshaws just got here."

Sebastian shrugged. "Going over to Bobby's to play drums."

I stared after him in silence, my mouth agape. Clearly Mary Gordon Howard had never met a Sebastian Kydd.

It was love at first sight.

In assembly, I take my seat next to Tommy Brewster, who is hitting the kid in front of him with a notebook. A girl in the aisle is asking if anyone has a tampon, while two girls behind me are excitedly whispering about Sebastian Kydd, who seems to become more and more notorious each time his name is mentioned.

"I heard he went to jail—"

"His family lost all their money—"

"No girl has managed to hold on to him for more than three weeks—"

I force Sebastian Kydd out of my thoughts by pretending Cynthia Viande is not a fellow student but a strange species of bird. Habitat: any stage that will have her. Plumage: tweed skirt, white shirt with cashmere sweater, sensible shoes, and a string of pearls that is probably real. She keeps shifting her papers from one arm to the other and tugging down her skirt, so maybe she's a little nervous after all. I know I would be. I wouldn't want to be, but I would. My hands would be shaking and my voice would come out in a squeak, and afterward, I'd hate myself for not taking control of the situation.

The principal, Mr. Jordan, goes up to the mike and says a bunch of boring stuff about being on time for classes and something about a new system of demerits, and then Ms. Smidgens informs us that the school newspaper, *The Nutmeg*, is looking for reporters and how there's some earthshaking story about cafeteria food in this week's issue. And finally, Cynthia walks up to the mike. "This is the most important year of our lives. We are poised at the edge of a very great precipice. In nine months, our lives will be irreparably altered," she says, like she thinks she's Winston Churchill or something.

I'm half expecting her to add that all we have to fear is fear itself, but instead, she continues: "So this year is all about senior moments. Moments we'll remember forever."

Suddenly Cynthia's expression changes to one of annoyance as everyone's head starts swiveling toward the center of the auditorium.

Donna LaDonna is coming down the aisle. She's dressed like a bride, in a white dress with a deep V, her ample cleavage accentuated by a tiny diamond cross hanging from a delicate platinum chain. Her skin is like alabaster; on one wrist, a constellation of silver bracelets peal like bells when she moves her arm. The auditorium falls silent.

Cynthia Viande leans into the mike. "Hello, Donna. So glad you could make it."

"Thanks," Donna says, and sits down.

Everyone laughs.

Donna nods at Cynthia and gives her a little wave, as if signaling her to continue. Donna and Cynthia are friends in that weird way that girls are when they belong to the same clique but don't really like each other.

"As I was saying," Cynthia begins again, trying to recapture the crowd's attention, "this year is all about senior moments. Moments we'll remember forever." She points to an AV guy, and the song "The Way We Were" comes over the loudspeaker.

I groan and bury my face in my notebook. I start to giggle along with everyone else, but then I remember the letter and get depressed again.

But every time I feel bad, I try to remind myself about what this little kid said to me once. She was loaded with personality—so ugly she was cute. And you knew she knew it too. "Carrie?" she asked. "What if I'm a princess on another planet? And no one on this planet knows it?"

That question still kind of blows me away. I mean, isn't it the truth? Whoever we are here, we might be princesses somewhere else. Or writers. Or scientists. Or presidents. Or whatever the hell we want to be that everyone else says we can't.

CHAPTER TWO

The Integer Crowd

"Who knows the difference between integral calculus and differential calculus?"

Andrew Zion raises his hand. "Doesn't it have something to do with how you use the differentials?"

"That's getting there," Mr. Douglas, the teacher, says. "Anyone else have a theory?"

The Mouse raises her hand. "In differential calculus you take an infinitesimal small point and calculate the rate of change from one variable to another. In integral calculus you take a small differential element and you integrate it from one lower limit to another limit. So you sum up all those infinitesimal small points into one large amount."

Jeez, I think. How the hell does The Mouse know *that*?

I'm never going to be able to get through this course. It will be the first time math has failed me. Ever since I was a kid, math was one of my easiest subjects. I'd do the homework and ace the tests, and hardly have to study. But I'll have to study now, if I plan to survive.

I'm sitting there wondering how I can get out of this course, when there's a knock on the door. Sebastian Kydd walks in, wearing an ancient navy blue polo shirt. His eyes are hazel with long lashes, and his hair is bleached dark blond from seawater and sun. His nose, slightly crooked, as if he was punched in a fight and never had it fixed, is the only thing that saves him from being too pretty.

"Ah, Mr. Kydd. I was wondering when you were planning to show up," Mr. Douglas says.

Sebastian looks him straight in the eye, unfazed. "I had a few things I needed to take care of first."

I sneak a glance at him from behind my hand. Here is someone who truly does come from another planet—a planet where all humans are perfectly formed and have amazing hair.

"Please. Sit down."

Sebastian looks around the room, his glance pausing on me. He takes in my white go-go boots, slides his eyes up my light blue tartan skirt and sleeveless turtleneck, up to my face, which is now on fire. One corner of his mouth lifts in amusement, then pulls back in confusion before coming to rest on indifference. He takes a seat in the back of the room.

"Carrie," Mr. Douglas says. "Can you give me the basic equation for movement?"

Thank God we learned that equation last year. I rattle it off like a robot: "X to the fifth degree times Y to the tenth degree minus a random integer usually known as N."

"Right," Mr. Douglas says. He scribbles another equation on the board, steps back, and looks directly at Sebastian.

I put my hand on my chest to keep it from thumping.

"Mr. Kydd?" he asks. "Can you tell me what this equation represents?"

I give up being coy. I turn around and stare.

Sebastian leans back in his chair and taps his pen on his calculus book. His smile is tense, as if he either doesn't know the answer, or does know it and can't believe anyone would be so stupid as to ask. "It represents infinity, sir. But not any old infinity. The kind of infinity you find in a black hole."

He catches my eye and winks.

Wow. Black hole indeed.

"Sebastian Kydd is in my calculus class," I hiss to Walt, cutting behind him in the cafeteria line.

"Christ, Carrie," Walt says. "Not you, too. Every single girl in this school is talking about Sebastian Kydd. Including Maggie."

The hot meal is pizza—the same pizza our school system has been serving for years, which tastes like barf and must be the result of some secret school-system recipe. I pick up a tray, then an apple and a piece of lemon meringue pie.

"But Maggie is dating you."

"Try telling Maggie that."

We carry our trays to our usual table. The Pod People sit

at the opposite end of the cafeteria, near the vending machines. Being seniors, we should have claimed a table next to them. But Walt and I decided a long time ago that high school was disturbingly like India—a perfect example of a caste system—and we vowed not to participate by never changing our table. Unfortunately, like most protests against the overwhelming tide of human nature, ours goes largely unnoticed.

The Mouse joins us, and she and Walt start talking about Latin, a subject in which they're both better than I am. Then Maggie comes over. Maggie and The Mouse are friendly, but The Mouse says she would never want to get too close to Maggie because she's overly emotional. I say that excessive emotionality is interesting and distracts one from one's own problems. Sure enough, Maggie is on the verge of tears.

"I just got called into the counselor's office—again. She said my sweater was too revealing!"

"That's outrageous," I say.

"Tell me about it," Maggie says, squeezing in between Walt and The Mouse. "She really has it out for me. I told her there was no dress code and she didn't have the right to tell me what to wear."

The Mouse catches my eye and snickers. She's probably remembering the same thing I am—the time Maggie got sent home from Girl Scouts for wearing a uniform that was too short. Okay, that was about seven years ago, but when you've lived in the same small town forever, you remember these things.

"And what did *she* say?" I ask.

"She said she wouldn't send me home this time, but if she sees me in this sweater again, she's going to suspend me."

Walt shrugs. "She's a bitch."

"How can she discriminate against a sweater?"

"Perhaps we should lodge a complaint with the school board. Have her fired," The Mouse says.

I'm sure she doesn't mean to sound sarcastic, but she does, a little. Maggie bursts into tears and runs in the direction of the girls' room.

Walt looks around the table. "Which one of you bitches wants to go after her?"

"Was it something I said?" The Mouse asks innocently.

"No." Walt sighs. "There's a crisis every other day."

"I'll go." I take a bite of my apple and hurry after her, pushing through the cafeteria doors with a bang.

I run smack into Sebastian Kydd.

"Whoa," he exclaims. "Where's the fire?"

"Sorry," I mumble. I'm suddenly hurtled back in time, to when I was twelve.

"This is the cafeteria?" he asks, gesturing toward the swinging doors. He peeks in the little window. "Looks heinous. Is there any place to eat off campus?"

Off-campus? Since when did Castlebury High become a campus? And is he asking me to have lunch with him? No, not possible. Not me. But maybe he doesn't remember that we've met before.

"There's a hamburger place up the street. But you need a car to get there."

"I've got a car," he says.

And then we just stand there, staring at each other. I can feel the other kids walking by but I don't see them.

"Okay. Thanks," he says.

"Right." I nod, remembering Maggie.

"See ya," he says, and walks away.

Rule number one: Why is it that the one time a cute guy talks to you, you have a friend who's in crisis?

I run into the girls' room. "Maggie? You won't believe what just happened." I look under the stalls and spot Maggie's shoes next to the wall. "Mags?"

"I am totally *humiliated*," she wails.

Rule number two: Humiliated best friend always takes precedence over cute guy.

"Magwitch, you can't let what other people say affect you so much." I know this isn't helpful, but my father says it all the time and it's the only thing I can think of at the moment.

"How am I supposed to do that?"

"By looking at everyone like they're a big joke. Come on, Mags. You know high school is absurd. In less than a year we'll be out of here and we'll never have to see any of these people ever again."

"I need a cigarette," Maggie groans.

The door opens and the two Jens come in.

Jen S and Jen P are cheerleaders and part of the Pod clique.

Jen S has straight dark hair and looks like a beautiful little dumpling. Jen P used to be my best friend in third grade. She was kind of okay, until she got to high school and took up social climbing. She spent two years taking gymnastics so she could become a cheerleader, and even dated Tommy Brewster's best friend, who has teeth the size of a horse. I waver between feeling sorry for her and admiring her desperate determination. Last year, her efforts paid off and she was finally admitted to the Pod pack, which means she now rarely talks to me.

For some reason, she does today, because when she sees me, she exclaims, "Hi!" as if we're still really good friends.

"Hi!" I reply, with equally false enthusiasm.

Jen S nods at me as the two Jens begin taking lipsticks and eye shadows out of their bags. I once overheard Jen S telling another girl that if you want to get guys, you have to have "a trademark"—one thing you always wore to make you memorable. For Jen S, this, apparently, is a thick stripe of navy blue eyeliner on her upper lid. Go figure. She leans in to the mirror to make sure the eyeliner is still intact as Jen P turns to me.

"Guess who's back at Castlebury High?" she asks.

"Who?"

"Sebastian Kydd."

"Re-e-e-ally?" I look in the mirror and rub my eye, pretending I have something in it.

"I want to date him," she says, with complete and utter

confidence. "From what I've heard, he'd be a perfect boyfriend for me."

"Why would you want to date someone you don't know?"

"I just do, that's all. I don't need a reason."

"Cutest boys in the history of Castlebury High," Jen S says, as if leading a cheer.

"Jimmy Watkins."

"Randy Sandler."

"Bobby Martin."

Jimmy Watkins, Randy Sandler, and Bobby Martin were on the football team when we were sophomores. They all graduated at least two years ago. *Who cares?* I want to shout.

"Sebastian Kydd," Jen S exclaims.

"Hall of Famer for sure. Right, Carrie?"

"Who?" I ask, just to annoy her.

"Sebastian Kydd," Jen P says in a huff as she and Jen S exit.

"Maggie?" I ask. She hates the two Jens and won't come out until they've left the bathroom. "They're gone."

"Thank God." The stall door opens and Maggie heads for the mirror. She runs a comb through her hair. "I can't believe Jen P thinks *she* can get Sebastian Kydd. That girl has no sense of reality. Now, what were you going to tell me?"

"Nothing," I say, suddenly sick of Sebastian. If I hear one more person mention his name, I'm going to shoot myself.

"What was that business with Sebastian Kydd?" The Mouse asks a little later. We're in the library, attempting to study.

"What business?" I highlight an equation in yellow, thinking about how useless it is to highlight. It makes you think you're learning, but all you're really learning is how to use a highlighter.

"He winked at you. In calculus class."

"He did?"

"Bradley," The Mouse says, in disbelief. "Don't even try to tell me you didn't notice."

"How do I know he was winking at me? Maybe he was winking at the wall."

"How do we know infinity exists? It's all a theory. And I think you should go out with him," she insists. "He's cute and he's smart. He'd be a good boyfriend."

"That's what every girl in the school thinks. Including Jen P."

"So what? You're cute and you're smart, too. Why shouldn't *you* date him?"

Rule number three: Best friends always think you deserve the best guy even if the best guy barely knows you exist.

"Because he probably only likes cheerleaders?"

"Faulty reasoning, Bradley. You don't know that for a fact." And then she gets all dreamy and rests her chin in her hand. "Guys can be full of surprises."

This dreaminess is not like The Mouse. She has plenty of guy friends, but she's always been too practical to get romantically involved.

"What does that mean?" I ask, curious about this new

Mouse. "Have you encountered some surprising guys recently?"

"Just one," she says.

And rule number four: Best friends can also be full of surprises.

"Bradley." She pauses. "I have a boyfriend."

What? I'm so shocked, I can't speak. The Mouse has never had a boyfriend. She's never even had a proper date.

"He's pretty nifty," she says.

"Nifty? *Nifty?*" I croak, finding my voice. "Who is he? I need to know all about this nifty character."

The Mouse giggles, which is also very un-Mouse-like. "I met him this summer. At the camp."

"Aha." I'm kind of stunned and a little bit hurt that I haven't heard about this mysterious Mouse boyfriend before, but now it makes sense. I never see The Mouse during the summer because she always goes to some special government camp in Washington, D.C.

And suddenly, I'm really happy for her. I jump up and hug her, popping up and down like a little kid on Christmas morning. I don't know why it's such a big deal. It's only a stupid boyfriend. But still. "What's his name?"

"Danny." Her eyes slide away and she smiles dazedly, as if she's watching some secret movie inside her head. "He's from Washington. We smoked pot together and—"

"Wait a minute." I hold up my hands. "Pot?"

"My sister Carmen told me about it. She says it relaxes you before sex."

Carmen is three years older than The Mouse and the most proper girl you've ever seen. She wears pantyhose in the summer. "What does Carmen have to do with you and Danny? Carmen smokes pot? Carmen has sex?"

"Listen, Bradley. Even smart people get to have sex."

"Meaning *we* should be having sex."

"Speak for yourself."

Huh? I pull The Mouse's calculus book away from her and bang it shut. "Listen, Mouse. What are you talking about? Did you have *sex*?"

"Yup," she says, nodding, as if it's no big deal.

"How can you have sex and I haven't? You're supposed to be a nerd. You're supposed to be inventing the cure for cancer, not doing it in the backseat of some car filled with marijuana smoke."

"We did it in his parents' basement," The Mouse says, taking her book back.

"You did?" I try to imagine The Mouse naked on some guy's cot in a damp basement. I can't picture it. "How was it?"

"The basement?"

"The sex," I nearly scream, trying to bring The Mouse back down to earth.

"Oh, that. It was good. Really fun. But it's the kind of thing you have to work at. You don't just start doing it. You have to experiment."

"Really?" I narrow my eyes in suspicion. I'm not sure how

to take this news. All summer, while I was writing some stupid story to get into that stupid writing program, The Mouse was losing her virginity. "How did you even figure out how to do it in the first place?"

"I read a book. My sister told me everyone should read an instructional manual before they do it so they know what to expect. Otherwise it might be a big disappointment."

I squint, adding a sex book to my image of The Mouse and this Danny person getting it on in his parents' basement. "Do you think you're going to . . . continue?"

"Oh, yes," The Mouse says. "He's going to Yale, like me." She smiles and goes back to her calculus book, as if it's all settled.

"Hmph." I fold my arms. But I suppose it makes sense. The Mouse is so organized, she would have her romantic life figured out by the time she's eighteen.

While I have nothing figured out at all.

CHAPTER THREE

Double Jeopardy

"I don't know how I'm going to get through this year," Maggie says. She takes out a pack of cigarettes, which she stole from her mother, and lights up.

"Uh-huh," I say, distracted. I'm still shocked The Mouse is having sex. *What if* everyone *is having sex?*

Crap. I absentmindedly pick up a copy of *The Nutmeg*. The headline screams: YOGURT SERVED IN CAFETERIA. I roll my eyes and shove it aside. With the exception of the handful of kids who actually work on *The Nutmeg*, no one reads it. But someone left it on the old picnic table inside the ancient dairy barn that sits just outside school property. The table's been here forever, scratched with the initials of lovers, the years of graduating classes, and general sentiments toward Castlebury High, such as "Castlebury sucks." The teachers never come out here, so it's also the unofficial smoking area.

"At least we get yogurt this year," I say, for no particular reason. *What if I never have sex? What if I die in a car accident before I have the chance to do it?*

"What's that supposed to mean?" Maggie asks.

Uh-oh. Up next: the dreaded body discussion. Maggie will say she thinks she's fat, and I'll say I think I look like a boy. Maggie will say she wishes she looked like me and I'll say I wish I looked like her. And it won't make a bit of difference, because two minutes later, we'll both be sitting here in our same bodies, except we'll have managed to make ourselves feel bad over something we can't change.

Like not getting into the damn New School.

What if some guy wants to have sex with me and I'm too scared to go through with it?

Sure enough, Maggie says, "Do I look fat? I do look fat, don't I? I *feel* fat."

"Maggie. You're not fat." Guys have been drooling over Maggie since she was thirteen, a fact that she seems determined to ignore.

I look away. Behind her, in the dark recesses at the far end of the barn, the glowing tip of a cigarette moves up and down. "Someone's in here," I hiss.

"Who?" She spins around as Peter Arnold comes out of the shadows.

Peter is the second-smartest boy in our class and kind of a jerk. He used to be a chubby-faced short kid with pasty skin, but it appears something happened to Peter over the summer. He grew.

And apparently took up smoking.

Peter is good friends with The Mouse, but I don't really know him. When it comes to relationships, we're all like little planets with our own solar system of friends. Unwritten law states that the solar systems rarely intersect—until now.

"Mind if I join you?" he asks.

"Actually, we do. We're having girl talk here." I don't know why I'm like this with boys, especially boys like Peter. Bad habit, I guess. Worse than smoking. But I don't want boring old Peter to ruin our conversation.

"No. We don't mind." Maggie kicks me under the table.

"By the way, I don't think you're fat," Peter says.

I smirk, trying to catch Maggie's eye, but she's not looking at me. She's looking at Peter. So I look at Peter too. His hair is longer and he's shed most of his zits, but there's something else about him.

Confidence.

Jeez. First The Mouse and now Peter. Is everyone going to be different this year?

Maggie and Peter keep ignoring me, so I pick up the paper and pretend to read. This gets Peter's attention.

"What do you think of *The Nutmeg*?" he asks.

"Drivel," I say.

"Thanks," he says. "I'm the editor."

Nice. Now I've done it again.

"If you're so smart, why don't you try writing for the paper?" Peter asks. "I mean, don't you tell everyone you want to be a writer? What have you ever written?"

Maybe he doesn't mean to sound aggressive, but the question catches me off guard. Does Peter somehow know about the rejection letter from The New School? But that would be impossible. Then I get angry. "What does it matter, what I've written or not?"

"If you say you're a writer, it means you write," Peter says smugly. "Otherwise you should go and be a cheerleader or something."

"And you should stick your head in a barrel of boiling oil."

"Maybe I will." He laughs good-naturedly. Peter must be one of those obnoxious types who's so used to being insulted he's not even offended when he is.

But still, I'm shaken. I grab my swim bag. "I've got practice," I say, as if I can hardly be bothered with this conversation.

"What's the matter with her?" Peter asks as I storm out.

I head down the hill toward the gym, scuffing the heels of my boots in the grass. Why is it always like this? I tell people I want to be a writer, and they roll their eyes. It drives me crazy. Especially since I've been writing since I was six. I have a pretty big imagination, and for a while I wrote stories about a pencil family called "The Number 2's," who were always trying to get away from a bad guy called "The Sharpener." Then I wrote about a little girl who had a mysterious disease that made her look like she was ninety. And this summer, in order to get into that stupid writing program, I wrote a whole book about a boy who turned into a TV, and no one in his family noticed until he used up all the electricity in the house.

If I'd told Peter the truth about what I'd written, he would have laughed. Just like those people at The New School.

"Carrie!" Maggie calls out. She hurries across the playing fields to catch up. "Sorry about Peter. He says he was joking about the writing thing. He has a weird sense of humor."

"No kidding."

"Do you want to go to the mall after swim practice?"

I look across the grounds to the high school and the enormous parking lot beyond. It's all exactly the same as it always was.

"Why not?" I take the letter out of my biology book, crumple it up, and stick it in my pocket.

Who cares about Peter Arnold? Who cares about The New School? Someday I'll be a writer. Someday, but maybe not today.

"I am so effing sick of this place," Lali says, dropping her things onto a bench in the locker room.

"You and me both." I unzip my boots. "First day of swim practice. I hate it."

I pull one of my old Speedos out of my bag and hang it in the locker. I've been swimming since before I could walk. My favorite photo is of me at five months, sitting on a little yellow float in Long Island Sound. I'm wearing a cute white hat and a polka-dot suit, and I'm beaming.

"You'll be *fine*," Lali says. "I'm the one with the problems."

"Like what?"

"Like Ed," she says with a grimace, referring to her father.

I nod. Sometimes Ed is more like a kid than a dad, even though he's a cop. Actually, he's more than a cop, he's a detective—the only one in town. Lali and I always laugh about it because we can't figure out exactly what he detects, as there's never been a serious crime in Castlebury.

"He stopped by the school," Lali says, stripping off her clothes. "We had a fight."

"What's wrong now?" The Kandesies fight like Mongolians, but they always make up, cracking jokes and doing outrageous things, like waterskiing in their bare feet. For a while, they kind of took me in, and sometimes I'd wish I'd been born a Kandesie instead of a Bradshaw, because then I'd be laughing all the time and listening to rock 'n' roll music and playing family baseball on summer evenings. My father would die if he knew, but there it is.

"Ed won't pay for college." Lali faces me, naked, her hands on her hips.

"What?"

"He won't pay," she repeats. "He told me today. He never went to college and he's just fine," she says mockingly. "I have two choices. I can go to military school or I can get a job. He doesn't give jack shit about what *I* want."

"Oh, Lali." I stare at her in shock. How can this be? There are five kids in Lali's family, so money has always been tight.

But Lali and I assumed she'd go to college—we'd both go, and then we'd do something big with our lives. In the dark, tucked into a sleeping bag on the floor next to Lali's bunk bed, we'd share our secrets in excited whispers. I was going to be a writer and Lali was going to win the gold medal in freestyle. But now I've been rejected from The New School. And Lali can't even go to college.

"I guess I'm going to be stuck in Castlebury forever," Lali says furiously. "Maybe I can work at Ann Taylor and earn five dollars an hour. Or maybe I could get a job at the supermarket. Or"—she smacks her hand on her forehead—"I could work at the bank. But I think you need a college degree to be a teller."

"It's not going to be like that," I insist. "Something will happen—"

"What?"

"You'll get a swimming scholarship—"

"Swimming is not a profession."

"You could still go to military school. Your brothers—"

"Are both in military school and they hate it," Lali snaps.

"You can't let Ed ruin your life," I say with bravado. "Find something you want to do and just do it. If you really want something, Ed can't stop you."

"Right," Lali says sarcastically. "Now all I need to do is figure out what that 'something' is." She holds out her suit, sliding her legs through the openings. "I'm not like you, okay? I don't know what I want to do for the rest of my life. I mean, why should I? I'm only seventeen. All I know is that I don't want someone telling me what I *can't* do."

She turns and makes a grab for her swim cap, accidentally knocking my clothes to the floor. I bend over to pick them up, and as I do, I see that the letter from The New School has slid out of my pocket, coming to rest next to Lali's foot. "I'll get that," I say, making a grab for it, but she's too fast.

"What's this?" she asks, holding up the crumpled piece of paper.

"Nothing," I say helplessly.

"Nothing?" Her eyes widen as she looks at the return address. "Nothing?" she repeats as she smoothes out the letter.

"Lali, *please.*"

Her eyes move back and forth, scanning the brief missive.

Crap. I knew I should have left the letter at home. I should have torn it up into little pieces and thrown it away. Or burned it, although it's not that easy to burn a letter, no matter how dramatic it sounds in books. Instead, I keep carrying it around, hoping it will act as some kind of perverse incentive to try harder.

Now I'm paralyzed by what must be my own stupidity.

"Lali, don't," I whisper.

"Just a minute," she says, reading the text one more time. She looks up, shakes her head, and presses her lips together in sympathy. "Carrie. I'm sorry."

"So am I." I shrug, trying to make light of it. My insides feel like they're filled with broken glass.

"I mean it." She folds the letter and hands it back to me, busying herself with her swim goggles. "Here I am, complaining about Ed. And you're being rejected by The New School. That's got to suck."

"Sort of."

"Looks like we're both going to be hanging around here for a while," she says, putting her arm around my shoulder. "Even if you do go to Brown, it's only forty-five minutes away. We'll still see each other all the time."

She pulls open the door to the pool, enveloping us in a chemical steam of chlorine and cleaning fluid. I consider asking her not to tell anyone about the rejection. But that will only make it worse. If I act like it's not a big deal, Lali will forget about it.

Sure enough, she flings her towel into the bleachers and runs across the tiles. "Last one in is a rotten egg," she shouts, doing a cannonball into the water.

CHAPTER FOUR

The Big Love

I return home to bedlam.

A puny kid with a punk haircut is running across the yard, followed by my father, who is followed by my sister Dorrit, who is followed by my other sister Missy. "Don't ever let me catch you on this property again!" my father shouts as the kid, Paulie Martin, manages to jump on his bike and pedal away.

"What the hell?" I ask Missy.

"Poor Dad."

"Poor Dorrit," I say, shifting my books. As if in mockery of my situation, the letter from The New School falls out of my notebook. *Enough.* I pick it up, march into the garage, and throw it away.

I immediately feel lost without it and fish it out of the trash.

"Did you see that?" my father says proudly. "I just ran

that little thug off the property." He points to Dorrit. "You— get back in the house. And don't even think about calling him."

"Paulie's not that bad, Dad. He's only a kid," I say.

"He's a little S-H-I-T," says my father, who prides himself on rarely swearing. "He's a hoodlum. Did you know he was arrested for buying beer?"

"Paulie Martin bought beer?"

"It was in the paper," my father exclaims. "*The Castlebury Citizen.* And now he's trying to corrupt Dorrit."

Missy and I exchange a look. Knowing Dorrit, the opposite is true.

Dorrit used to be the sweetest little kid. She would go along with anything Missy and I told her to do, including crazy stuff like pretending she and our cat were twins. She was always making things for people—cards and little scrapbooks and crocheted pot holders—and last year, she decided she wanted to be a vet and spent practically all her time after school holding sick animals while they got their shots.

But now she's nearly thirteen, and lately, she's become a real problem child, crying and having temper tantrums and yelling at me and Missy. My father keeps insisting she's in a stage and will grow out of it, but Missy and I aren't so sure. My father is this very big scientist who came up with a formula for some new kind of metal used in the *Apollo* space rockets, and Missy and I always joke that if people were theories instead of actual human beings, Dad would know everything about us.

But Dorrit isn't a theory. And lately, Missy and I have found little things missing from our rooms—an earring here or a tube of lip gloss there—the kinds of things you might easily lose or misplace on your own. Missy was going to confront her, but then we found most of our things stuffed behind the cushions in the couch. Nevertheless, Missy is still convinced that Dorrit is on the path to becoming a little criminal, while I'm worried about her anger. Missy and I were both brats at thirteen, but neither one of us can remember being so pissed off all the time.

True to form, in a couple of minutes Dorrit appears in the doorway of my room, aching for a fight.

"What was Paulie Martin doing here?" I ask. "You know Dad thinks you're too young to date."

"I'm in eighth grade," Dorrit says stubbornly.

"That's not even high school. You have years to have boyfriends."

"Everyone else has a boyfriend." She picks a flake of polish from her nail. "Why shouldn't I?"

This is why I hope never to become a mother. "Just because everyone else is doing something, it doesn't mean you should too. Remember," I add, imitating my father, "we're Bradshaws. We don't have to be like everyone else."

"Maybe I'm *sick* of being a stupid old *Bradshaw*. What is so great about being a Bradshaw anyway? If I want to have a boyfriend, I'll have a boyfriend. You and Missy are just jealous because you don't have boyfriends." She glares at me, runs to her room, and slams the door.

I find my father in the den, sipping a gin and tonic and staring at the TV. "What am I supposed to do?" he asks helplessly. "Ground her? When I was a boy, girls didn't act like this."

"That was thirty years ago, Dad."

"Doesn't matter," he says, pressing on his temples. "Love is a holy cause." Once he goes off on one of these spiels, it's hopeless. "Love is spiritual. It's about self-sacrifice and commitment. And discipline. You cannot have true love without discipline. And respect. When you lose the respect of your spouse, you've lost everything." He pauses. "Does this make any sense to you?"

"Sure, Dad," I say, not wanting to hurt his feelings.

A couple of years ago, after my mother died, my sisters and I tried to encourage my father to find someone else, but he refused to entertain the idea. He wouldn't even go on a date. He said he'd already had the one big love of his life, and anything less would feel like a sham. He felt blessed, he said, to have had that kind of love once in his life, even if it didn't last forever.

You wouldn't think a hard-boiled scientist like my father would be such a romantic, but he is.

It worries me sometimes. Not for my father's sake, but for my own.

I head up to my room, sit down in front of my mother's old Royale typewriter, and slide in a piece of paper. *The Big Love*, I write, then add a question mark.

Now what?

I open the drawer and take out a story I wrote a few years ago, when I was thirteen. It was a stupid story about a girl who rescues a sick boy by donating her kidney to him. Before he got sick, he never noticed her, even though she was pining away for him, but after she gives him her kidney, he falls madly in love with her.

It's a story I would never show anyone, because it's too sappy, but I've never been able to throw it away. It scares me. It makes me worry that I'm secretly a romantic too, just like my father.

And romantics get burned.

Whoa. Where's the fire?

Jen P was right. You can fall in love with a guy you don't know.

That summer when I was thirteen, Maggie and I used to hang out at Castlebury Falls. There was a rock cliff where the boys would dive into a deep pool, and sometimes Sebastian was there, showing off, while Maggie and I sat on the other side of the river.

"Go on," Maggie would urge. "You're a better diver than those boys." I'd shake my head, my arms wrapped protectively around my knees. I was too shy. The thought of being seen was terrifying.

I didn't mind watching, though. I couldn't take my eyes off Sebastian as he scrambled up the side of the rock, sleek and sure-footed. At the top, there was horseplay between the boys, as they jostled one another and hooted dares, demanding increasing feats of skill. Sebastian was always the bravest, climbing higher than the other boys and launching himself into the water with a fearlessness that told me he had never thought about death.

He was free.

He's the one. The Big Love.

And then I forgot about him.

Until now.

I find the soiled rejection letter from The New School and put it in the drawer with the story about the girl who gave away her kidney. I rest my chin in my hands and stare at the typewriter.

Something good has to happen to me this year. It just does.

CHAPTER FIVE

Rock Lobsters

"Maggie, get out of the car."

"I can't."

"Please—"

"What's wrong now?" Walt asks.

"I need a cigarette."

Maggie, Walt, and I are sitting in Maggie's car, which is parked in the cul-de-sac at the end of Tommy's street. We've been in the car for at least fifteen minutes, because Maggie is paranoid about crowds and refuses to get out of the car when we go to parties. On the other hand, she does have the best car. It's a gigantic gas-guzzling Cadillac that fits about nine people and has a quadraphonic stereo and a glove compartment filled with her mother's cigarettes.

"You've smoked three cigarettes already."

"I don't feel good," Maggie moans.

"Maybe you'd feel better if you hadn't smoked all those

cigarettes at once," I say, wondering if Maggie's mother notices that every time Maggie gives the car back, about a hundred cigarettes are missing. I did ask Maggie about it once, but she only rolled her eyes and said her mother was so clueless, she wouldn't notice if a bomb blew up in their house. "Come on," I coax her. "You know you're just scared."

She frowns. "We're not even invited to this party."

"We're not *not* invited. So that means we're invited."

"I can't stand Tommy Brewster," she mutters, and crosses her arms.

"Since when do you have to like someone to go to their party?" Walt points out.

Maggie glares and Walt throws up his hands. "I've had enough," he says. "I'm going in."

"Me too," I say suddenly. We slide out of the car. Maggie looks at us through the windshield and lights up another cigarette. Then she pointedly locks all four doors.

I make a face. "Do you want me to stay with her?"

"Do you want to sit in the car all night?"

"Not really."

"Me neither," Walt says. "And I don't plan to indulge in this ridiculousness for the rest of senior year."

I'm surprised by Walt's vehemence. He usually tolerates Maggie's neuroses without complaint.

"I mean, what's going to happen to her?" he adds. "She's going to back into a tree?"

"You're right." I look around. "There aren't any trees."

We start walking up the street to Tommy's house. The one good thing about Castlebury is that even if it's boring, it's beautiful in its own way. Even here, in this brand-new development with hardly any trees, the grass on the lawns is bright green and the street is like a crisp black ribbon. The air is warm and there's a full moon. The light illuminates the houses and the fields beyond; in October, they'll be full of pumpkins.

"Are you and Maggie having problems?"

"I don't know," Walt says. "She's being a huge pain in the ass. I can't figure out what's wrong with her. We used to be fun."

"Maybe she's going through a phase."

"She's been going through a phase all summer. And it's not like I don't have my own problems to worry about."

"Like what?"

"Like everything?" he says.

"Are you guys having sex too?" I ask suddenly. If you want to get information out of someone, ask them unexpectedly. They're usually so shocked by the question, they'll tell you the truth.

"Third base," Walt admits.

"That's it?"

"I'm not sure I want to go any further."

I hoot, not believing him. "Isn't that all guys think about? Going further?"

"Depends on what kind of guy you are," he says.

Loud music—Jethro Tull—is threatening to shake Tommy's house down. We're about to go in, when a fast yellow car roars up the street, spins around in the cul-de-sac, and comes to rest at the curb behind us.

"Who the hell is that?" Walt asks, annoyed.

"I have no idea. But yellow is a much cooler color than red."

"Do we know anyone who drives a yellow Corvette?"

"Nope," I say in wonder.

I love Corvettes. Partly because my father thinks they're trashy, but mostly because in my conservative town, they're glamorous and a sign that the person who drives one just doesn't care what other people think. There's a Corvette body shop in my town, and every time I pass it, I pick out which Corvette I'd drive if I had the choice. But then one day my father sort of ruined the whole thing by pointing out that the body of a Corvette is made of plastic composition instead of metal, and if you get into an accident, the whole car shatters. So every time I see a Corvette now, I picture plastic breaking into a million pieces.

The driver takes his time getting out, flashing his lights and rolling his windows up, down, and back up again as if he can't decide if he wants to go to this party either. Finally, the door opens and Sebastian Kydd rises from behind the car like the Great Pumpkin himself, if the Great Pumpkin were eighteen years old, six-foot-one, and smoked Marlboro cigarettes. He looks up at the house, smirks, and starts up the walk.

"Good evening," he says, nodding at me and Walt. "At least

I hope it's a good one. Are we going inside?"

"After you," Walt says, rolling his eyes.

We. My legs turn to jelly.

✧ ✳ CB ✳ ✧

Sebastian immediately disappears into a throng of kids as Walt and I weave our way through the crowd to the bar. We snag a couple of beers, and then I go back to the front door to make sure Maggie's car is still at the end of the street. It is. Then I run into The Mouse and Peter, who are backed up against a speaker. "I hope you don't have to go to the bathroom," The Mouse shouts, by way of greeting. "Jen P saw Sebastian Kydd and freaked out because he's so cute she couldn't handle it and started hyperventilating, and now she and Jen S have locked themselves in the toilet."

"Ha," I say, staring carefully at The Mouse. I'm trying to see if she looks any different since she's had sex, but she seems pretty much the same.

"If you ask me, I think Jen P has too many hormones," The Mouse adds, to no one in particular. "There ought to be a law."

"What's that?" Peter asks loudly.

"Nothing," The Mouse says. She looks around. "Where's Maggie?"

"Hiding in her car."

"Of course." The Mouse nods and takes a swig of her beer.

"Maggie's here?" Peter says, perking up.

"She's still in her car," I explain. "Maybe you can get her out. I've given up."

"No problem," Peter shouts. He hurries away like a man on a mission.

The bathroom scene sounds too interesting to miss, so I head upstairs. The toilet is at the end of a long hall and a line of kids are snaked behind it, trying to get in. Donna LaDonna is knocking on the door. "Jen, it's me. Let me in," she commands. The door opens a crack and Donna slips inside. The line goes crazy.

"Hey! What about us?" someone shouts.

"I hear there's a half-bath downstairs."

Several annoyed kids push past as Lali comes bounding up the stairs. "What the hell is going on?"

"Jen P freaked out over Sebastian Kydd and locked herself in the bathroom with Jen S and now Donna LaDonna went in to try to get her out."

"This is ridiculous," Lali declares. She goes up to the door, pounds on it, and yells, "Get the hell out of there, you twits. People have to pee!" When several minutes pass in which Lali does more knocking and yelling to no avail, she gives me an exaggerated shrug and says loudly, "Let's go to The Emerald."

"Sure," I say, full of bluster, like we go there all the time.

The Emerald is one of the few bars in town with—according to my father—a reputation for being full of shady characters: i.e. alcoholics, divorcées, and drug addicts. I've only been three times, and each time I looked around desperately for these so-called degenerates but was never able to spot any patrons that fit the bill. In fact, I was the one who looked suspicious—I was shaking like a Slinky, terrified that someone was going to ask for my ID and, when I couldn't produce it, call the police.

But that was last year. This year I'll be seventeen. Maggie and The Mouse are nearly eighteen, and Walt is already legal, so they can't kick him out.

Lali and I find Walt and The Mouse and they want to go too. We troop out to Maggie's car, where she and Peter are deep in conversation. I find this slightly irritating, although I don't know why. We decide that Maggie will drive Walt to The Emerald, while The Mouse will take Peter, and I'll go with Lali.

Thanks to Lali's speedy driving, we're the first to arrive. We park the truck as far away from the building as possible in order to avoid detection. "Okay, this is weird," I say, while we wait. "Did you notice how Maggie and Peter were having some big discussion? It's very strange, especially since Walt says he and Maggie are having problems."

"Like that's a surprise." Lali snorts. "My father thinks Walt is gay."

"Your father thinks everyone is gay. Including Jimmy Carter. Anyway, Walt can't be gay. He's been with Maggie for two years. And I know they definitely do more than make out because he told me."

"A guy can have sex with a woman and still be gay," Lali insists. "Remember Ms. Crutchins?"

"Poor Ms. Crutchins," I sigh, conceding the argument.

She was our English teacher last year. She was about forty years old and she'd never been married and then she met "a wonderful man" and couldn't stop talking about him, and after three months they got married. But then, one month later, she announced to the class that she'd annulled her marriage. The rumor was that her husband turned out to be gay. Ms. Crutchins never came right out and admitted it, but she would let revealing tidbits drop, like, "There are just some things a woman can't live with." And after that, Ms. Crutchins, who was always full of life and passionate about English literature, seemed to shrink right into herself like a deflated balloon.

The Mouse pulls up next to us in a green Gremlin, followed by the Cadillac. It's terrible what they say about women drivers, but Maggie really is bad. As she's trying to park the car, she runs the front tires over the curb. She gets out of the car, looks at the tires, and shrugs.

Then we all do our best to stroll casually into The Emerald, which isn't really seedy at all—at least not to look at. It has red leather banquettes and a small dance floor with a disco ball, and a hostess with bleached blond hair who appears to be the definition of the word "blousy."

"Table for six?" she asks, like we're all absolutely old enough to drink.

We pile into a banquette. When the waitress comes over, I order a Singapore Sling. Whenever I'm in a bar I always try to order the most exotic drink on the menu. A Singapore Sling has several different kinds of alcohol in it, including something called "Galliano," and it comes with a maraschino cherry and an umbrella. Then Peter, who's ordered a whiskey on the rocks, looks at my drink and laughs. "Not too obvious," he says.

"What are you talking about?" I ask innocently, sipping my cocktail through a straw.

"That you're underage. Only someone who's underage orders a drink with an umbrella and fruit. And a straw," he adds.

"Yeah, but then I get to take the umbrella home. And what do you get to take home besides a hangover?"

The Mouse and Walt think this is pretty funny, and decide to only order umbrella drinks for the rest of the night.

Maggie, who usually drinks White Russians, orders a whiskey on the rocks, instead. This confirms that something is definitely going on between Maggie and Peter. If Maggie likes a guy, she does the same thing he does. Drinks the same drink, wears the same clothes, suddenly becomes interested in the same sports he likes, even if they're totally wacky, like whitewater rafting. All through sophomore year, before Maggie and Walt started going out, Maggie liked this weird boy who went whitewater rafting every weekend in the fall. I can't tell you how many hours I had to spend freezing on top of a rock, waiting for him to pass by in his canoe. Okay— I knew it wasn't really a canoe, it was a kayak, but I insisted on calling it a canoe just to annoy Maggie for making me freeze my butt off.

And then the door of The Emerald swings open and for

a moment, everyone forgets about who's drinking what.

Standing by the hostess are Donna LaDonna and Sebastian Kydd. Donna has her hand on his neck, and after he holds up two fingers, she puts her other hand on his face, turns his head, and starts kissing him.

After about ten seconds of this excessive display of affection, Maggie can't take it anymore. "Gross," she exclaims. "Donna is such a slut. I can't believe it."

"She's not so bad," Peter counters.

"How do you know?" Maggie demands.

"I helped tutor her a couple of years ago. She's actually kind of funny. And smart."

"That still doesn't mean she should be making out with some guy in The Emerald."

"He doesn't look like he's resisting much," I murmur, stirring my drink.

"Who is that guy?" Lali asks.

"Sebastian Kydd," The Mouse volunteers.

"I know his name," Lali sniffs. "But who *is* he? Really?"

"No one knows," I say. "He used to go to private school."

Lali can't take her eyes off him. Indeed, no one in the bar seems to be able to tear themselves away from the spectacle. But now I'm bored with Sebastian Kydd and his attention-getting antics.

I snap my fingers in Lali's face to distract her. "Let's dance."

Lali and I go to the jukebox and pick out some songs. We're not regular boozers, so we're both feeling the giddy effects of being a little bit drunk, when everything seems funny. I pick out my favorite song, "We Are Family" by Sister Sledge, and Lali picks "Legs" by ZZ Top. We take to the dance floor. I do a bunch of different dances—the pony, the electric slide, the bump, and the hustle, along with a lot of steps I've made up on my own. The music changes and Lali and I start doing this crazy line dance we invented a couple of years ago during a swim meet where you wave your arms in the air and then bend your knees and shake your butt. When we straighten up, Sebastian Kydd is on the dance floor.

He's a pretty cool dancer, but then, I expected he would be. He dances a little with Lali, and then he turns to me and takes my hand and starts doing the hustle. It's a dance I'm good at, and at a certain point one of his legs is in-between mine, and I'm kind of grinding my hips, because this, after all, is a legitimate part of the dance.

He says, "Don't I know you?"

And I say, "Yes, actually you do."

Then he says, "That's right. Our mothers are friends."

"Were friends," I say. "They both went to Smith." And then the music ends and we go back to our respective tables.

"That was hilarious." The Mouse nods approvingly. "You should have seen the look on Donna LaDonna's face when he was dancing with you."

"He was dancing with both of us," Lali corrects her.

"But he was mostly dancing with Carrie."

"That's only because Carrie is shorter than I am," Lali remarks.

"Whatever."

"Exactly," I say, and get up to go to the bathroom.

The restroom is at the end of a narrow hall on the other side of the bar. When I come out, Sebastian Kydd is standing next to the door as if he's waiting to go in. "Hello," he says. He delivers this in a sort of fakey way, like he's an actor in a movie, but he's so good-looking, I decide I don't mind.

"Hi," I say cautiously.

He smiles. And then he says something astoundingly ridiculous. "Where have you been my whole life?"

I almost laugh, but he appears to be serious. Several responses run through my head, and finally I settle on: "Excuse me, but aren't you on a date with someone else?"

"Who says it's a date? She's a girl I met at a party."

"Sure looks like a date to me."

"We're having fun," he says. "For the moment. You still live in the same house?"

"I guess so—"

"Good. I'll come by and see you sometime." And he walks away.

This is one of the oddest and most intriguing things that has ever happened to me. And despite the bad-movie-ish quality to the scene, I'm actually hoping he meant what he said.

I go back to the table, full of excitement, but the atmosphere has changed. The Mouse looks bored talking to Lali, and Walt appears glum, while Peter impatiently shakes the ice cubes in his glass. Maggie suddenly decides she wants to leave. "I guess that means I'm going," Walt says with a sigh.

"I'll drop you first," Maggie says. "I'm going to drive Peter home, too. He lives near me."

We get into our respective vehicles. I'm dying to tell Lali about my encounter with the notorious Sebastian Kydd, but before I can say a word, Lali announces that she's "kind of mad at The Mouse."

"Why?"

"Because of what she said. About that guy, Sebastian Kydd. Dancing with you and not me. Couldn't she see he was dancing with both of us?"

Rule number five: Always agree with your friends, even if it's at your own expense, so they won't be upset. "I know," I say, hating myself. "He *was* dancing with both of us."

"And why would he dance with you, anyway?" Lali asks. "Especially when he was with Donna LaDonna?"

"I have no idea." But then I remember what The Mouse said. Why *shouldn't* Sebastian dance with me? Am I so bad? I don't think so. Maybe he thinks I'm kind of smart and interesting and quirky. Like Elizabeth Bennet in *Pride and Prejudice*.

I dig around in my bag and find one of Maggie's cigarettes. I light up, inhale briefly, and whoosh the smoke out the window.

"Ha," I say aloud, for no particular reason.

CHAPTER SIX

Bad Chemistry

I've had boyfriends before, and frankly, each one was a disappointment.

There was nothing horribly wrong with these boys. It was my fault. I'm kind of a snob when it comes to guys.

So far, the biggest problem with the boys I've dated is that they weren't too smart. And eventually I ended up hating myself for being with them. It scared me, trying to pretend I was something I wasn't. I could see how easily it could be done, and it made me realize that was what most of the other girls were doing as well—pretending. If you were a girl, you could start pretending in high school and go on pretending your whole life, until, I suppose, you imploded and had a nervous breakdown, which is something that's happened to a few of the mothers around here. All of a sudden, one day something snaps and they don't get out of bed for three years.

But I digress. Boyfriends. I've had two major ones: Sam,

who was a stoner, and Doug, who was on the basketball team. Of the two I liked Sam better. I might have even loved him, but I knew it couldn't last. Sam was beautiful but dumb. He took woodworking classes, which I had no idea existed until he gave me a wooden box he'd made for Valentine's Day. Despite his lack of intelligence—or perhaps, more disturbingly, because of it—when I was around him I found him so attractive I thought my head would explode. I'd go by his house after school and we'd hang in the basement with his older brothers, listening to *Dark Side of the Moon* while they passed around a bong. Then Sam and I would go up to his room and make out for hours. Half the time, I worried I shouldn't be there, that I was wasting precious time engaging in an activity that wouldn't lead to anything (in other words, I wasn't using my time "constructively," as my father would say). But on the other hand, it felt so good I couldn't leave. My mind would be telling me to get up, go home, study, write stories, advance my life, but my body was like a boneless sea creature incapable of movement on land. I can't remember ever having a conversation with Sam. It was only endless kissing and touching in a bubble of time that seemed to have no connection with real life.

Then my father took me and my sisters away for two weeks on an educational cruise to Alaska and I met Ryan, who was tall and smooth like polished wood and was going to Duke, and I fell in love with him. When I got back to Castlebury, I could barely look at Sam. He kept asking if I'd met someone else. I was a coward and said no, which was partly true because Ryan lived in Colorado and I knew I'd never see him again. Still, the Sam bubble had been punctured by Ryan, and then Sam was like a little smear of wet soap. That's all bubbles are anyway—a bit of air and soap. So much for the wonders of good chemistry.

With bad chemistry, though, you don't even get a bubble. Me and Doug? Bad chemistry.

Doug was a year older, a senior when I was a junior. He was one of the jocks, a basketball player, friends with Tommy Brewster and Donna LaDonna and the rest of the Pod crowd. Doug wasn't too bright, either. On the other hand, he wasn't so good-looking that a lot of other girls wanted him, but he was good-looking *enough*. The only thing that was really bad about him was the zits. He didn't have a lot of them, just one or two that always seemed to be in the middle of their life cycle. But I knew I wasn't perfect either. If I wanted a boyfriend, I figured I would have to overlook a blemish or two.

Jen P introduced us. And sure enough, at the end of the week, he came shuffling around my locker and asked if I wanted to go to the dance.

That was all right. Doug picked me up in a small white car that belonged to his mother. I could picture his mother from the car: a nervous woman with pale skin and tight curls who was an embarrassment to her son. It made me kind of depressed, but I told myself I had to complete this experiment. At the dance, I hung around with the Jens and

Donna LaDonna and some older girls, who all stood with one leg out to the side, and I stood the same way and pretended I wasn't intimidated.

"There's a great view at the top of Mott Street," Doug said, after the dance.

"Isn't that the place next to the haunted house?"

"You believe in ghosts?"

"Sure. Don't you?"

"Naw," he said. "I don't even believe in God. That's girl stuff."

I vowed to be less like a girl.

It was a good view at the top of Mott Street. You could see clear across the apple orchards to the lights of Hartford. Doug kept the radio on; then he put his hand under my chin, turned my head, and kissed me.

It wasn't horrible, but there was no passion behind it. When he said, "You're a good kisser," I was surprised. "I guess you do this a lot," he said.

"No. I hardly do it at all."

"Really?" he said.

"Really," I said.

"Because I don't want to go out with a girl who every other guy has been with."

"I haven't been with anyone." I thought he must be crazy. Didn't he know a thing about me?

More cars pulled in around us, and we kept making out. The evening began to depress me. This was it, huh? This was dating, Pod-style. Sitting in a car surrounded by a bunch of other cars where everyone was making out, seeing how far they could go, like it was some kind of *requirement*. I started wondering if anyone else was enjoying it as little as I was.

Still, I went to Doug's basketball games and I went by his house after school, even though there were other things I wanted to do more, like read romance novels. His house was as dreary as I'd imagined—a tiny house on a tiny street (Maple Lane) that could have been in Any Town, U.S.A. I guess if I were in love with Doug it wouldn't have mattered. But if I had been in love with Doug it would have been worse, because I would have looked around and realized that this would be my life, and that would have been the end of my dream.

But instead of saying, "Doug, I don't want to see you anymore," I rebelled.

It happened after another dance. I'd barely let Doug get to third base, so maybe he figured it was time to straighten me out. The plan was to go parking with another couple: Donna LaDonna and a guy named Roy, who was the captain of the basketball team. They were in the front seat. We were in the back. We were going someplace we'd never get caught, a place where no one would find us: a cemetery.

"Hope you don't still believe in ghosts," Doug said, squeezing my leg. "If you do, you know they'll be watching."

I didn't answer. I was studying Donna LaDonna's profile. Her hair was a swirl of white cotton candy. I thought she looked like Marilyn Monroe. I wished I looked like Marilyn Monroe. Marilyn Monroe, I figured, would know what to do.

When Doug unzipped his pants and tried to push my head down, I'd had enough. I got out of the car. "Charade" was the word I was thinking over and over again. It was all a charade. It summed up everything that was wrong between the sexes.

Then I was too angry to be frightened. I started walking along the little road that wound through the headstones. I might have believed in ghosts, but I wasn't scared of them per se. It was people who were troubling. Why couldn't I just be like every other girl and give Doug what he wanted? I pictured myself as a Play-Doh figure; then a hand came down, squeezing and squeezing until the Play-Doh oozed through the fingers into ragged clumps.

To distract myself, I started looking at the headstones. The graves were pretty old, some more than a hundred years. I started looking for one type in particular. It was macabre but that's the kind of mood I was in. Sure enough, I found one: *Jebediah Wilton. 4 mos. 1888.* I started thinking about Jebediah's mother and the pain she would have felt putting that little baby into the ground. I bet it felt worse than childbirth. I got down on my knees and screamed into my hands.

I guess Doug figured I would come right back, because he didn't bother looking for me for a while. Then the car pulled up and a door opened. "Get in," Doug said.

"No."

"Bitch," Roy said.

"Get in the car," Donna LaDonna ordered. "Stop making a scene. Do you want the cops to come?"

I got into the car.

"See?" Donna LaDonna said to Doug. "I told you it was useless."

"I'm not going to have sex with some guy just to impress you," I said.

"Whoa," Roy said. "She really is a bitch."

"Not a bitch," I said. "Just a woman who knows her own mind."

"You're a woman now?" Doug said, sneering. "That's a laugh."

I knew I should have been embarrassed, but I was so relieved it was over, I couldn't be bothered. Surely, Doug wouldn't dare ask me out again.

He did though. First thing Monday morning, I found him standing by my locker. "I need to talk to you," he said.

"So talk."

"Not now. Later."

"I'm busy."

"You're a prude," he hissed. "You're frigid." When I didn't reply, he added, "It's okay," in a creepy tone. "*I* know what's wrong with you. I *understand*."

"*Good,*" I said.

"I'm coming by your house after school."

"Don't."

"You don't need to tell me what to do," he said, spinning an imaginary basketball on his finger. "You're not my *mother*." He shot the imaginary basketball into an imaginary hoop and walked away.

Doug did come by my house that afternoon. I looked up

from my typewriter and saw the pathetic white car pull hesitantly into the driveway, like a mouse cautiously approaching a piece of cheese.

A discordant phrase of Stravinsky came from the piano followed by the soft taps of Missy running down the stairs. "Carrie," Missy called from below. "Someone's here."

"Tell him I'm not."

"It's *Doug*."

"Let's go for a drive," Doug said.

"I can't," I begged. "I'm busy."

"Listen," he said. "You can't do this to me." He was pleading, and I started to feel sorry for him. "You *owe* me," he whispered. "It's only a drive in the car."

"Okay," I relented. I figured maybe I did owe him for embarrassing him in front of his friends.

"Look," I said when we were in the car and driving toward his house. "I'm sorry about the other night. It's just that—"

"Oh, I know. You're not ready," Doug said. "I understand. With everything you've been through."

"No. It isn't that." I knew it had nothing to do with my mother's death. But I couldn't bring myself to tell Doug the truth—that my reluctance was due to the fact that I didn't find him the least bit attractive.

"It's okay," he said. "I forgive you. I'm going to give you a chance to make it up to me."

"Ha," I said, hoping he was making a joke.

Doug drove past his house and kept going, down the dirt track that led to the river. Between his sad little street and the river were miles and miles of mud-flat farmland, deserted in November. I began to get scared.

"Doug, stop."

"Why?" he asked. "We have to talk."

I knew then why boys hated that phrase, "We have to talk." It gave me a tired, sick feeling. "Where are we going? There's nothing out here."

"There's the Gun Tree," he said.

The Gun Tree was all the way down by the river, so named because a lightning strike had split the branches into the shape of a pistol. I began calculating my chances for escape. If we got all the way to the river, I could jump out of the car and run along the narrow path that led through the trees. Doug couldn't follow in his car, but he could certainly outrun me. And then what would he do? Rape me? He might rape me and kill me afterward. I didn't want to lose my virginity to Doug Haskell, for Christ's sake, and definitely not like that. I decided he'd have to kill me first.

But maybe he did only want to talk.

"Listen, Doug, I'm sorry about the other night."

"You are?"

"Of course. I just didn't want to have sex in a car with other people. It's kind of gross."

We were about half a mile from civilization.

"Yeah. Well, I guess I can understand that. But Roy is the

captain of the basketball team and—"

"Roy is disgusting. Really, Doug. You're much better than he is. He's an asshole."

"He's one of my best buds."

"You should be captain of the basketball team. I mean, you're taller and better looking. And smarter. If you ask me, Roy's taking advantage of you."

"You think?" He took his eyes off the road and looked at me. The road was becoming increasingly bumpy, made for tractors not cars, and Doug had to slow down.

"Well, of course," I said smoothly. "Everyone knows that. Everyone says you're a better player than Roy—"

"I am."

"And—" I took a quick peek at the speedometer. Twenty miles an hour. The car was bucking like an old bull. If I was going to make a break for it, I had to do it now. "And, Doug, I *need* to go home." I rolled down the window. A cold blast of air hit my face like a slap. "The car's covered with mud. Your mother's going to kill you."

"My mother won't care."

"Come on, Doug. Stop the car."

"We'll go to the Gun Tree. Then I'll take you home." But he didn't sound so sure.

"I'm getting out." I grabbed the door handle.

Doug tried to pull my hand away as the car veered off the track and slid into a pile of dried cornstalks.

"Christ, Carrie. Why the hell d'you do *that*?"

We got out of the car to inspect the damage. It wasn't too bad. Mostly straw caught in the bumper. "If *you* hadn't . . ." I said, relief and anger burning the back of my throat. "Because you wanted to prove to your stupid friends that you aren't a *loser*—"

He stared at me, his breath steaming the air around him like a mysterious dry ice.

Then he smacked his hand on the hood of the car. "I wouldn't fuck you if you paid me," he shouted, pausing for breath. "You're lucky . . . lucky I even considered having sex with you. Lucky I even took you out in the first place. I only did it because I felt *sorry* for you."

What else could he say?

"Good. Then you should be *happy*."

"Oh, I'm happy all right." He gave the front tire a good kick. "I'm happy as *hell*."

I turned and started walking up the road. My back was a firestorm of nerves. When I got about fifty feet away, I started whistling. When I was a hundred feet away, I heard the puttering sound of the car engine, but I kept going. Eventually, he passed me, looking straight ahead as if I didn't exist. I picked up a strand of dried grass and tore it with my fingers, watching the pieces blow away.

I did tell this story to The Mouse and Maggie. I even told it to Walt. I told it again and again, but I made it funny. I made it so funny, The Mouse couldn't stop laughing. Funny always makes the bad things go away.

CHAPTER SEVEN

Paint the Down Red

"Carrie, you're not going to be able to joke your way out of this," Mrs. Givens says, pointing to the can of paint.

"I wasn't planning to make a joke," I insist, as if I'm completely innocent. I have a problem with authority. I really do. It turns me into mush. I'm a real jellyfish when it comes to facing adults.

"What were you planning to do with the paint, then?" Mrs. Givens is one of those middle-aged ladies who you look at and think, If I ever end up like her, shoot me. Her hair is teased into a dried bush that looks like it could self-ignite at any moment. I suddenly picture Mrs. Givens with a conflagration on her head, running through the halls of Castlebury High, and I nearly crack up.

"Carrie?" she demands.

"The paint is for my father—for one of his projects."

"This is not like you, Carrie. You've never been in trouble before."

"I swear, Mrs. Givens. It's nothing."

"Very well. You can leave the paint with me and pick it up after school."

"Givens confiscated my paint can," I whisper to The Mouse as we enter calculus.

"How did she find it?"

"She saw me trying to shove it into my locker."

"Damn," The Mouse says.

"I know. We're going to have to go to plan B."

"What is plan B?"

"Action must be taken," I say. "I'll think of something."

I sit down and look out the window. It's October now. Time to find a perfect red leaf and iron it between two pieces of waxed paper. Or stick cloves into a crisp apple, the juice running all over your fingers. Or scoop the slimy guts out of a pumpkin and roast the seeds until they nearly explode. But mostly, it's time to paint the year of our high school graduation on the roof of the dairy barn.

It's a grand tradition around here. Every fall, a few members of the graduating class scrawl their year on the roof of the barn behind the school. It's always some boys who do it. But this year, The Mouse and I decided we should do it. Why should the boys have all the fun? Then we got Lali involved. Lali was going to bring the ladder, and The Mouse and I would get the paint. Then Maggie wanted to come. Maggie is fairly useless in these kinds of situations, but I figured she'd be good for booze and cigarettes. Then Maggie spilled the beans to Peter. I told her to un-tell Peter, but she said she couldn't do that, and now Peter's all excited about it even though he says he won't actually be participating. Instead, he plans to stand there and direct.

After calculus, I head out to the barn, where I take a good look at the structure. It's at least a hundred years old, and though it looks sturdy enough, the roof is higher and steeper than I'd imagined. But if we chicken out, next week the boys will probably do it, and I don't want that to happen. No more missed opportunities. I want to leave some mark on Castlebury High, so when I'm old, I can say, "I did it. I painted the year of our graduation on the old barn out back." Lately, high school hasn't been bugging me as much as usual and I've been in a pretty good mood. Today, I'm wearing overalls, Converse sneakers, and a red and white checked shirt that I got at a vintage store in honor of the occasion. I also have my hair in braids, and I'm wearing a strip of rawhide around my head.

I'm standing there, staring up at the roof, when I'm suddenly overcome by a mysterious happiness and I have to start doing my best John Belushi *Animal House* imitation. I run all the way around the barn and when I get back to where I started, Sebastian Kydd is there, looking at me curiously while he shakes a cigarette out of a pack of Marlboro Reds.

"Having fun?" he asks.

"Sure," I say. I should be embarrassed, but I'm not. I hate the way girls are supposed to be embarrassed all the time and I decided a long time ago that I just wouldn't do it. "What about you? Are you having fun?"

"Relatively."

I'm sure he is having fun, but not with me. After that night at The Emerald—nothing. He never called, never came by my house—all I get are bemused looks from him when he sees me in calculus or in the halls or occasionally hanging out here at the barn. I tell myself it's just as well; I don't need a boyfriend anyway—but it doesn't prevent my mind from veering out of control every time I sense he's in the vicinity. It's almost as bad as being twelve—worse, I remind myself, because I ought to know better by now.

I glance at Sebastian, thinking it's a good thing he can't read my mind, but he's no longer paying attention. He's looking over my shoulder at the two Jens, who are carefully picking their way up the hill in high heels, like they've never walked on grass before. Their appearance is not surprising. The two Jens have taken to following Sebastian everywhere, like two small, cheery tugboats. "Ah," I say. "Your fan club is here."

He looks at me quizzically but says nothing. In my fantasy, Sebastian is a person of great and perceptive thought. But in reality, I don't know a thing about him.

Lali picks me up in the truck at nine o'clock that evening. We're dressed in black turtlenecks, black jeans, and sneakers.

There's an enormous harvest moon. Lali hands me a beer and I crank up the radio and we scream over the music. I'm pretty sure this is going to be the best thing we've ever done. I'm pretty sure this is going to be a real Senior Moment— A Moment to Remember. "Fuck Cynthia Viande," I scream, for no good reason.

"Fuck Castlebury High," Lali says. "Fuck the Pods."

We pull into the driveway of the high school going about eighty miles an hour and drive right over the grass. We try to drive straight up the hill, but the truck gets stuck, so we decide to park it in a dark corner of the parking lot. While we're struggling to get the ladder out of the back, I hear the telltale sputter of a fully loaded V-eight engine, and sure enough, Sebastian Kydd pulls up beside us.

What the hell is he doing here?

He rolls down the window. "You girls need some help?"

"No."

"Yes," Lali says. She gives me the shut-up look. I give her the shut-up look right back.

Sebastian gets out of the car. He's like a panther getting up from a nap. He even yawns. "Slow night?"

"You could say that," Lali says.

"Or you could get off your keister and help us. Since you don't appear to be leaving," I add.

"Can we trust you?" Lali asks.

"Depends on what you want to trust me *with*," he says.

Eventually, we get the ladder up against the barn, and then

The Mouse shows up with the paint and a large brush. Two enormous cone-shaped lights play over the parking lot, indicating Maggie's arrival in the Cadillac. Maggie insists she can't keep track of her high and low beams and usually blinds her fellow motorists. She parks the car and meanders up the hill with Walt and Peter in tow. Peter busies himself by examining the paint. "Red?" he says, and then, as if we didn't hear him the first time, *"Red?"*

"What's wrong with red?"

"It's not the traditional Castlebury color for this exercise. It should be blue."

"We wanted *red*," I counter. "Whoever does the painting gets to pick the color."

"But it's not right," Peter insists. "For the rest of the year, I'm going to be looking out the window seeing the year of our graduation painted in red instead of blue."

"Does it really matter?" Sebastian asks.

"Red is a statement. It's a fuck-you to tradition," Walt says. "I mean, isn't that the point?"

"Right on, brother." Sebastian nods.

Maggie hugs her arms around her chest. "I'm scared."

"Have a cigarette," Walt remarks. "That will calm your nerves."

"Who's got the booze?" Lali asks. Someone hands her a bottle of whiskey, and she takes a swig, wiping her mouth on her shirt sleeve.

"Okay, Bradley. Get on up there," The Mouse commands.

In unison, we tip our heads back and look skyward. The orange moon has come up behind the roof, casting a boxlike black shadow below. In the spooky light, the peak appears as high as Mount Everest.

"*You're* going up?" Sebastian asks, astonished.

"Bradley used to be very good in gymnastics," The Mouse says. "*Very good*. Until she was about twelve, anyway. Remember when you did that jump onto the balance beam and landed right on your—"

"I'd rather not," I say, sneaking a glance at Sebastian.

"I'd do it, but I'm scared of heights," Lali explains. Heights, indeed, are the only thing she admits to being scared of, probably because she thinks it makes her more interesting. "Every time I cross the bridge to Hartford, I have to get down on the floor so I don't get dizzy."

"What if you're the one who's driving?" asks The Mouse.

"Then she has to stop in the middle of traffic and sit there shaking until the police come and tow her car," I say, finding this vision hysterical.

Lali gives me a dirty look. "That is so not true. If I'm driving, it's different."

"Uh-huh," Walt says.

Maggie takes a gulp of whiskey. "Maybe we should go to The Emerald. I'm getting cold."

Oh no. Not after we've made all this effort. "*You* go to The Emerald, Magwitch. I'm going to do this," I say, with what I hope sounds like gutsy determination.

Peter rubs Maggie's shoulders, a gesture not lost on Walt. "Let's stay. We can go to The Emerald later."

"All right," The Mouse says pointedly. "Anyone who doesn't want to be here should go now. Anyone who wants to stay should just shut up."

"I'm staying," Walt says, lighting up a cigarette. "And I'm not shutting up."

The plan is simple: Lali and Peter will hold the ladder while I go up. Once I'm at the top, Sebastian will climb up after me with the can of paint. I place my hand on a rung. The metal is cold and grooved. Look up, I remind myself. The future is ahead of you. Don't look down. Never look back. Never let 'em see you sweat.

"Go on, Carrie."

"You can do it."

"She's at the top. Ohmigod. She's on the roof!" That's Maggie.

"Carrie?" Sebastian says. "I'm right behind you."

The harvest moon has transformed into a bright white orb surrounded by a million stars. "It's beautiful up here," I shout. "You should all have a look."

I slowly rise, testing my balance, and take a few steps to get my footing. It's not so hard. I remind myself of all the kids who have done this in the past. Sebastian's at the top of the ladder with the paint. With the can in one hand and the brush in the other, I make my way to the side of the roof.

I begin painting, as the group takes up a chant below.

"One . . . Nine . . . Eight . . ."

"NINETEEN. EIGHTY—" And just as I'm about to paint the last number, my foot slips.

The can flies out of my hand, bounces once, and rolls off the roof, leaving a huge splotch of paint behind. Maggie screams. I drop down to my knees, scrambling to get a handhold on the wooden shingles. I hear a soft thud as the can hits the grass. Then . . . nothing.

"Carrie?" The Mouse says tentatively. "Are you all right?"

"I'm fine."

"Don't move," Peter shouts.

"I'm not."

And it's true. I'm not moving. But then, with excruciating slowness, I begin to slide. I try to jam my toe into the shingles to stop, but my sneaker glides right over the slick spill of red paint. I reassure myself that I will not die. It's not my time. If I were going to die, I'd know it, right? Some part of my brain is aware of the scraping of skin, but I have yet to feel the pain. I'm picturing myself in a body cast, when suddenly a firm hand grabs my wrist and drags me up to the peak. Behind me I see the tips of the ladder fall away from the edge, followed by a whomp as it clatters into the bushes.

Everyone is screaming.

"We're okay. We're fine. No injuries," Sebastian shouts as the wail of a police siren rips the air.

"There goes Harvard," Peter says.

"Hide the ladder in the barn," Lali commands. "If the cops

ask we're just up here smoking cigarettes."

"Maggie, give me the booze," Walt says. There's a crash as he throws the bottle into the barn.

Sebastian tugs on my arm. "We need to get to the other side."

"Why?"

"Don't ask questions. Just do it," he orders as we scramble over the peak. "Lie flat on your back with your knees bent."

"But now I can't see what's happening," I protest.

"I've got a record. Don't move and don't say a word, and pray the cops don't find us."

My breath is as loud as the pounding of a drum.

"Hello, Officers," Walt says when the police arrive.

"What are you kids up to?"

"Nothing. Just smoking some cigarettes," Peter says.

"Have you been drinking?"

"Nope." A group answer.

Silence, followed by the sound of feet squelching around in the wet grass. "What the hell's this?" demands one of the cops. The beam from his flashlight slides up the roof and into the sky. "You kids painting the barn? That's a misdemeanor. Violation of private property."

"Yo, Marone," Lali says to one of the cops. "It's me."

"Whoa," Marone says. "Lali Kandesie. Hey, Jack. It's Lali, Ed's girl."

"You want to take a look around?" Jack asks cautiously, now that he's being confronted by the boss's daughter.

"Nah. Looks okay to me," says Marone.

Jack snorts. "Okay, kids. Party's over. We're going to make sure you get to your cars and get home safely."

And they all leave.

Sebastian and I lie frozen on the roof. I stare up at the stars, intensely aware of his body a few inches from mine. If this isn't romance, I don't know what is.

Sebastian peers over the side. "I think they're gone."

Suddenly, we look at each other and laugh. Sebastian's laugh—I've never heard anything like it—is deep and throaty and slightly sweet, like ripe fruit. I imagine the taste of his mouth as being slightly fruity too, but also sharp, with a tang of nicotine. Boys' mouths are never what you think they're going to be anyway. Sometimes they're stiff and sharp with teeth, or like soft little caves filled with down pillows.

"Well, Carrie Bradshaw," he says. "What's your big plan now?"

I hug my knees to my chest. "Don't have one."

"You? Without a plan? That must be a first."

Really? Is that how he thinks of me? As some nerdly, uptight, efficient *planner*? I've always thought of myself as the spontaneous type. "I don't *always* have a plan."

"But you always seem to know where you're going."

"I do?"

"Sure. I can barely keep up with you."

What does *that* mean? Is this a dream? Am I actually having this conversation with Sebastian Kydd?

"You could always try calling—"

"I did. But your phone's perennially busy. So tonight I was going to stop by your house, but then I saw you getting in Lali's truck and followed you. I figured you were up to something interesting."

Is he saying he *likes* me?

"You're definitely a character," he adds.

A character? Is that good or bad? I mean, what kind of guy falls in love with a *character*?

"I guess I can be . . . sort of funny sometimes."

"You're funny a lot. You're very entertaining. It's good. Most girls are boring."

"They are?"

"Come on, Carrie. You're a girl. You must know that."

"I think most girls are pretty interesting. I mean, they're a lot more interesting than boys. *Boys* are the ones who are boring."

"Am I boring?"

"You? You're not boring at all. I just meant—"

"I know." He moves a little closer. "Are you cold?"

"I'm okay."

He takes off his jacket. As I put it on, he notices my hands. "Christ," he says. "That must hurt."

"It does—a little." The palms of my hands are stinging like hell where I've scraped the skin. "It's not the worst thing that's happened to me though. One time, I fell off the back of the Kandesies' truck and broke my collarbone. I didn't know it was broken until the next day. Lali made me go to the doctor."

"Lali's your best friend, huh?"

"Pretty much. I mean, she's been my best friend since we were ten. Hey," I ask. "Who's your best friend?"

"Don't have one," he says, staring out at the trees.

"I guess that's the way guys are," I say musingly. I check my hands. "Do you think we're ever going to get off this roof?"

"Do you want to get off this roof?"

"No."

"So don't think about it. Someone will come and get us eventually. Maybe Lali, or your friend The Mouse. She's cool."

"Yeah." I nod. "She's got her life all figured out. She's applying early admission to Yale. And she'll definitely get in."

"That must be nice," he says with a hint of bitterness.

"Are you worried about your future?"

"Isn't everyone?"

"I guess . . . But I thought . . . I don't know. I thought you were going to Harvard or something. Weren't you in private school?"

"I was. But I realized I didn't necessarily want to go to Harvard."

"How could anyone not want to go to Harvard?"

"Because it's a crock. Once I go to Harvard, that's it. Then I'll have to go to law school. Or business school. Then I'll be a suit, working for a big corporation. Taking the commuter train to New York City every day. And then some girl will get me to marry her, and before you know it, I'll have kids and a mortgage. Game over."

"Hmph." It's not exactly what a girl wants to hear from a guy, but on the other hand, I have to give him points for being honest. "I know what you mean. I always say I'm never getting married. Too predictable."

"You'll change your mind. All women do."

"I won't. I'm going to be a writer."

"You look like a writer," he says.

"I do?"

"Yeah. You look like you've always got something going on in your head."

"Am I that transparent?"

"Kind of." He leans over and kisses me. And suddenly, my life splits in two: before and after.

CHAPTER EIGHT

The Mysteries of Romance

"Tell me *exactly* what he said."

"He said I was interesting. And a character."

"Did he say he liked you?"

"I think it was more that he liked the idea of me."

"Liking the *idea* of a girl is different from actually *liking* a girl," Maggie says.

"I think if a guy says you're interesting and a character, it means you're *special*," The Mouse counters.

"But it doesn't mean he wants to be with you. Maybe he thinks you're special—and *weird*," Maggie says.

"So what happened after we left?" The Mouse asks, ignoring her.

"Lali came and rescued us. He went home. He said he'd had enough excitement for one evening."

"Has he said anything since?" Maggie asks.

I scratch a nonexistent itch. "Nope. But it doesn't matter."

"He'll call," The Mouse says with confidence.

"Of course he'll call. He *has* to call," Maggie says, with too much enthusiasm.

Four days have passed since the barn-painting incident and we're dissecting the event for about the twentieth time. After Lali rescued us, apparently The Mouse and Walt did come back, but we were gone along with the ladder, so they figured we got away okay. On Monday when we showed up at school, we couldn't stop laughing. Every time one of us looked out the window and saw *198* and that big red splotch, we'd crack up. At assembly that morning, Cynthia Viande referred to the incident, saying the vandalism to private property had not gone unnoticed, and the perpetrators, if caught, would be prosecuted.

We all snickered like little cats.

All of us, that is, except for Peter. "Can the cops really be *that* dumb?" he kept asking. "I mean, they were right *there*. They *saw* us."

"And what did they see? A few kids standing around an old dairy barn."

"That Peter guy—geez," Lali said. "He's so paranoid. What the hell was he doing there anyway?"

"I think he likes Maggie."

"But Maggie's with Walt."

"I know."

"She has two boyfriends now? How can you have two boyfriends?"

"Listen," Peter said the next day, sidling up to me in the hall. "I'm not sure we can trust Sebastian. What if he rats us out?"

"Don't worry. He's the last person who's going to tell."

Hearing Sebastian's name was like a skewer to the gut.

Ever since the kiss, Sebastian's presence has been like an invisible shadow sewn to my skin. I cannot go anywhere without him. In the shower, he hands me the shampoo. His face floats up behind the words in my textbooks. On Sunday, Maggie, Walt, and I went to a flea market, and while I pawed through piles of sixties T-shirts, all I could think about was what Sebastian would like.

Surely he'll call.

But he hasn't.

A week passes, and on Saturday morning, I reluctantly pack a little suitcase. I look at the clothes I've laid out on the bed, perplexed. They're like the random, disjointed thoughts of a thousand strangers. What was I thinking when I bought that beaded fifties sweater? Or that pink bandanna? Or the green leggings with yellow stripes? I have nothing to wear for this interview. How can I be who I'm supposed to be with these clothes?

Who am I supposed to be again?

Just be yourself.

But who am I?

What if he calls while I'm gone? Why hasn't he called already?

Maybe something happened to him.

Like what? You saw him every day at school and he was fine.

"Carrie?" my father calls out. "Are you ready?"

"Almost." I fold a plaid skirt and the beaded sweater into the suitcase, add a wide belt, and throw in an old Hermès scarf that belonged to my mother. She bought it on the one trip to Paris she took with my father a few years ago.

"Carrie?"

"Coming." I bang down the stairs.

My father is always nervous before a trip. He gathers maps and estimates time and distance. He's only comfortable with the unknown or the unexpected if it's a number in an equation. I keep reminding him that this is not a big deal. It's his alma mater, and Brown is only forty-five minutes away.

But he fusses. He takes the car to the car wash. He withdraws cash. He inspects his travel comb. Dorrit rolls her eyes. "You're going to be gone for less than twenty-four hours!"

It rains during the drive. As we head east, I notice the leaves are already beginning to flee their branches, like flocks of birds heading south for the winter.

"Carrie," my father says. "Don't sweat the small stuff. Don't beat yourself up about things." He can usually sense when something is wrong, although he's rarely able to pinpoint the cause.

"I'm not, Dad."

"Because when you do," he continues, warming up to one of his favorite topics, "you lose twice. You've lost what you've lost, but then you also lose your perspective. Because life happens to people. Life is bigger than people. It's all about nature. The life cycle . . . It's out of our control."

It shouldn't be, though. There ought to be a law that says every time a boy kisses a girl, he has to call within three days.

"So in other words, old man, shit happens and then you die."

I say this in a way that makes my father laugh. Unfortunately, I can hear Sebastian in the backseat, laughing too.

"Carrie Bradshaw, right?"

The guy named George shifts my file from one arm to another and shakes my hand. "And you, sir, must be Mr. Bradshaw."

"That's right," my father says. "Class of 1958."

George looks at me appraisingly. "Are you nervous?"

"A little."

"Don't be." He smiles reassuringly. "Professor Hawkins is one of the best. He has PhD's in English literature and physics. I see on your application that you're interested in science and writing. Here at Brown, you can do both." He reddens a little, as if he realizes he's being quite the salesman, and suddenly adds, "Besides, you look great."

"Thanks," I murmur, feeling a bit like a lamb being led to slaughter.

I immediately realize I'm being silly and overly dramatic. George is right: Everything about Brown is perfect, from the charming redbrick buildings of the Pembroke College campus, to College Green, dotted with voluptuous elms that still have their leaves, to the glorious columned John Carter Brown Library. I need only insert my mannequin self into this picture-postcard scene.

But as the day progresses from the interview in the artfully messy professor's office—"What are your goals, Ms. Bradshaw?" "I'd like to make an impact on society. I'd like to contribute something meaningful"—to the tour of the campus, chem labs, the computer room, a first-year dorm room, and finally to dinner with George on Thayer Street, I begin to feel more and more flimsy, like a doll constructed of tissue paper. Halfway through dinner, when George mentions there's a rock 'n' roll band playing at the Avon Theatre, I feel like I can't refuse, even though I'd prefer to lie in my hotel room and think about Sebastian instead.

"Go," my father urges. He's already informed me that George is the kind of young man—intelligent, well-mannered, thoughtful—that he's always pictured me dating.

"You're going to love Brown," George says in the car. He drives a Saab. Well engineered, slightly expensive, with European styling. Like George, I think. If I weren't obsessed with Sebastian, I probably would find George attractive.

"Why do you love Brown so much?" I ask.

"I'm from the city, so this is a nice break. Of course, I'll be in the city this summer. That's the great thing about Brown. The internships. I'm going to be working for *The New York Times*."

George suddenly becomes much more interesting. "I've always wanted to live in New York City," I say.

"It's the best place in the world. But Brown is right for me now." He gives me a hesitant smile. "I needed to explore a different side of myself."

"What were you like before?"

"Tortured," George says, and grins. "What about you?"

"Oh, I'm a little tortured too," I say, thinking of Sebastian. But when we pull up to the theater, I vow to put Sebastian out of my mind. Clusters of college kids, drinking beer and flirting, are seated outside at tiny French tables. As we push through the crowd, George puts his hand on my shoulder and squeezes. I look up at him and smile.

"You're awfully cute, Carrie Bradshaw," he says into my ear.

We stay out until closing time, and when we get back in the car, George kisses me. He kisses me again in the driveway of the hotel. It's a clean and tentative kiss, the kiss of a man who thinks in straight lines. He takes a pen out of the glove compartment. "May I ask for your number?"

"Why?" I ask, giggling.

"So I can call you, dummy." He tries to kiss me again, but I turn my head.

I'm feeling a little woozy, and the beer hits me full force

when I lie down. I ask myself if I would have given George my number if I weren't so drunk. I probably wouldn't have let him kiss me either. But surely Sebastian will call now. Guys always call as soon as another man is interested. They're like dogs: They never notice if you've changed your hair, but they can sense when there's another guy sniffing around their territory.

We're back in Castlebury by mid-afternoon on Sunday, but my theory proves wrong. Sebastian hasn't called. Maggie, on the other hand, has. Several times. I'm about to call her when she calls me. "What are you doing? Can you come over?"

"I just got back," I say, suddenly deflated.

"Something happened. Something big. I can't explain it on the phone. I have to tell you in person." Maggie sounds very dire and I wonder if her parents are getting divorced.

Maggie's mother, Anita, opens the door. Anita looks stressed, but you can tell that a long time ago she was probably pretty. Anita is really, really nice—too nice, in fact. She's so nice that I always get the feeling the niceness has swallowed up the real Anita, and someday she's going to do something drastic, like burn down the house.

"Oh, Carrie," Anita says. "I'm so glad you're here. Maggie won't come out of her room and she won't tell me what's wrong. Maybe you can get her to come downstairs. I'd be so grateful."

"I'll take care of it, Mrs. Stevenson," I say reassuringly. Hiding in her room is something Maggie's been doing for as long as I've known her. I can't tell you how many times I've had to talk her out.

Maggie's room is enormous with floor-to-ceiling windows on three sides and a closet the length of one wall. Nearly everyone in town is familiar with the Stevenson house, because it was designed by a famous contemporary architect and is mostly comprised of glass. The inside of the house is pretty sparse, though, because Maggie's father can't abide clutter. I crack open the door to Maggie's room as Anita stands anxiously to the side. "Magwitch?"

Maggie is lying in her bed, wearing a white cotton nightgown. She rises from beneath the covers like a ghost, albeit a rather churlish one. "Anita!" she scolds. "I told you to leave me alone." The expression on Anita's face is startled, guilty, and helpless, which is pretty much her usual demeanor around Maggie. She scurries away as I go in.

"Mags?" I caution. "Are you okay?"

Maggie sits cross-legged on the bed and puts her head in her hands. "I don't know. I did something terrible."

"What?"

"I don't know how to tell you."

I can tell, however, that I'm going to have to wait for this terrible revelation, so I sit on the padded stool-y thing Maggie uses as a chair. According to her father, it's a Swedish-designed ergonomically correct sitting contraption that prevents backaches. It's also sort of bouncy, so I bob up and down a bit. But then I'm suddenly tired of everyone else's problems.

"Listen, Mags," I say firmly. "I don't have much time. I have to pick up Dorrit at the Hamburger Shack." This is true, sort of. I probably will have to pick her up eventually.

"But Walt will be there!" she cries out.

"So?" Walt's parents insist that Walt have an after-school job to make money for college, but the only job Walt's ever had is working at the Hamburger Shack for four dollars an hour. And it's only part-time, so it's hard to see how Walt will be able to save enough money for even one semester.

"That means you'll see him," Maggie gasps.

"And?"

"Are you going to tell him you saw me?"

This is becoming more and more irritating. "I don't know. Should I tell him I saw you?"

"No!" she exclaims. "I've been avoiding him all weekend. I told him I was going to see my sister in Philadelphia."

"Why?"

"Don't you get it?" She sighs dramatically. "Peter."

"Peter?" I repeat, slightly appalled.

"I had sex with him."

"What?" My legs are all tangled up in the Swedish sitting device and I bounce so hard the whole thing falls over, taking me with it.

"Shhhhh!" Maggie says.

"I don't get it," I say, trying to detach myself from the stool. "You had *sex* with Peter?"

"I had *intercourse* with him."

And another one bites the dust.

"When?" I ask, once I manage to get off the floor.

"Last night. In the woods behind my house." She nods. "You remember? The night we painted the barn? He was all over me. Then he called yesterday morning and said he *had* to see me. He said he'd secretly been in love with me for, like, three years but was afraid to talk to me because he thought I was so gorgeous I wouldn't talk to him. Then we went for a walk, and we immediately started making out."

"And then what? You just did it? Right in the woods?"

"Don't act so surprised." Maggie sounds slightly hurt and superior at the same time. "Just because you haven't done it."

"How do you know I haven't?"

"Have you?"

"Not yet."

"Well then."

"So you just did it. On top of the leaves? What about sticks? You could have gotten a stick stuck in your butt."

"Believe me, when you're doing it, you don't notice things like sticks."

"Is that so?" I have to admit, I'm immensely curious. "What did it feel like?"

"It was amazing." She sighs. "I don't know exactly how to describe it, but it was the best feeling I've ever had. It's the kind of thing that once you do it, all you want is to do it again and again. And"—she pauses for effect—"I think I had an orgasm."

My mouth hangs open. "That's incredible."

"I know. Peter says girls almost never have orgasms their first time. He said I must be highly sexed."

"Has Peter done it before?" If he has, I'm going to shoot myself.

"Apparently," Maggie says smugly.

For a minute, neither one of us speaks. Maggie picks dreamily at a thread on her bedspread while I look out the window, wondering how I got so left behind. Suddenly, the world seems divided into two kinds of people—those who have done it and those who haven't.

"Well," I say finally. "Does this mean you and Peter are dating?"

"I don't know," she whispers. "I think I'm in love with him."

"But what about Walt? I thought you were in love with Walt."

"No." She shakes her head. "I thought I was in love with Walt two years ago. But lately, he's been more like a friend."

"I see."

"We used to go to third base. But then Walt never wanted to go any further. And it made me think. Maybe Walt didn't really love me after all. We were together for two years. You'd think a guy would want to do it after two years."

I want to point out that maybe he's saving himself, but the truth is, it is pretty strange. "So you were willing and he wasn't?" I ask just to clarify.

"I wanted to do it on my birthday, and he wouldn't."

"Weird," I say. "Definitely weird."

"And that really tells you something."

Not necessarily. But I don't have the energy to contradict her.

All of a sudden, even though I know this isn't really about me, I feel a thundering sense of loss. Maggie and Walt and I were a unit. For the past couple of years, we went everywhere together. We'd sneak into the country club at night and steal golf carts, and cooling off a six-pack of beer in a stream, we'd talk and talk and talk about everything from quarks to who Jen P was dating. What's going to happen to the three of us now? Because somehow I can't imagine Peter taking Walt's place in our corny adventures.

"I guess I have to break up with Walt," Maggie says. "But I don't know how. I mean, what am I supposed to say?"

"You could try telling him the truth."

"Carrie?" she asks in a wheedling tone. "I was wondering if maybe you could—"

"What? Break up with him? You want me to break up with Walt for you?"

"Just kind of prepare him," Maggie says.

Maggie and Peter? I can't think of two people who belong together less. Maggie is so flighty and emotional. And Peter is so serious. But maybe their personalities cancel each other out.

I pull into the parking lot of the Hamburger Shack, turn off the car, and think, Poor Walt.

The Hamburger Shack is one of the few restaurants in

town, known for its hamburgers topped with grilled onions and peppers. That's pretty much considered the height of cuisine around here. People in Castlebury are mad for grilled onions and peppers, and while I do love the smell, Walt, who has to man the onion and pepper grill, says the stench makes him sick. It gets into his skin and even when he's sleeping, all he dreams about are onions and peppers.

I spot Walt behind the counter by the grill. The only other customers are three teenage girls with hair dyed in multiple hues of pink, blue, and green. I nearly walk past them when suddenly I realize that one of these punks is my sister.

Dorrit is eating an onion ring as if everything is perfectly normal. "Hi, Carrie," she says. Not even a "Do you like my hair?" She picks up her milk shake and drains the glass with a loud slurp.

"Dad's going to kill you," I say. Dorrit shrugs. I look at her friends, who are equally apathetic. "Get out to the car. I'll deal with you in a minute."

"I'm not done with my onion rings," she says with equanimity. I hate the way my sister won't listen to authority, especially my authority.

"Get in the car," I insist, and walk away.

"Where are you going?"

"I have to talk to Walt."

Walt's wearing a stained apron and there's sweat on his hairline. "I hate this job," he says, lighting up a cigarette in the parking lot.

"But the hamburgers are good."

"When I get out of here, I never want to see another hamburger in my life."

"Walt," I say. "Maggie—"

He cuts me off. "She didn't go to her sister's in Philadelphia."

"How do you know?"

"Number one, how many times does she visit her sister? Once a year? And number two, I know Maggie well enough to know when she's lying."

I wonder if he knows about Peter, as well. "What are you going to do?"

"Nothing, I guess. I'll wait for her to break up with me and that'll be it."

"Maybe *you* should break up with *her.*"

"Too much effort." Walt tosses his cigarette into the bushes. "Why should I bother when the result will be the same either way?"

Walt, I think, is sometimes a bit passive.

"But maybe if you did it first—"

"And save Maggie from feeling guilty? I don't think so."

My sister walks by with her new Day-Glo hair. "You'd better not let Dad catch you smoking," she says.

"Listen, kid. First of all, I wasn't smoking. And secondly, you've got bigger things to worry about than cigarettes. Like your hair."

As Dorrit gets into the car, Walt shakes his head. "My little brother's just like her. The younger generation—they've got no respect."

CHAPTER NINE

The Artful Dodger

When Dorrit and I get home, my poor father takes one look at Dorrit's hair and nearly passes out. Then he goes into her room to have a talk with her. That's the worst, when my father comes into your room for a talk. He tries to make you feel better, but it never quite works that way. He usually goes into some long story about something that happened to him when he was a kid, or else makes references to nature, and sure enough, that's what he does with Dorrit.

Dorrit's door is closed, but our house is a hundred and fifty years old, so you can hear every word of any conversation if you stand outside the door. Which is exactly what Missy and I do.

"Now, Dorrit," my dad says. "I suspect your actions concerning your, ah, *hair* are indirectly related to overpopulation, which is something that is increasingly becoming a problem on our planet. Which was not meant to sustain these vast clusters of people in limited spaces . . . and tends to result in these mutilations of the human body—piercings, dyeing the hair, tattoos . . . It's human instinct to want to stand out, and it manifests itself in more and more extreme measures. Do you understand what I'm saying?"

"No."

"What I mean," he continues, "is that you must do all you can to resist these unwarranted instincts. The successful human being is able to conquer his unwanted and unwise desires. Am I making myself clear?"

"Sure, Dad," Dorrit says sarcastically.

"In any event, I still love you," my father says, which is the way he ends all his talks. And then he usually cries. And then you feel so horrible, you vow never to upset him again.

This time, however, the crying bit is interrupted by the ringing of the phone. Please, let it be Sebastian, I pray, while Missy grabs it. She puts her hand slyly over the receiver. "Carrie? It's for you. It's a *guy*."

"Thanks," I say coolly. I take the phone into my room and close the door.

It has to be him. Who else could it be?

"Hello?" I ask casually.

"Carrie?"

"Yes?"

"It's George."

"*George*," I say, trying to keep the disappointment out of my voice.

"You got home okay?"

"Sure."

"Well, I had a great time on Saturday night. And I was wondering if you'd like to get together again."

I don't know. But he's asked too politely to refuse. And I don't want to hurt his feelings. "Okay."

"There's a nice country inn between here and Castlebury. I thought maybe we could go next Saturday."

"Sounds great."

"I'll pick you up around seven. We'll have dinner at eight and I can get you home by eleven."

We hang up and I go into the bathroom to examine my face. I have a sudden desire to radically alter my appearance. Maybe I should dye my hair pink and blue like Dorrit's. Or turn it into a pixie cut. Or bleach it white blond. I pick up a lip pencil and begin outlining my lips. I fill in the middle with red lipstick and turn the corners of my mouth down. I draw two black tears on my cheeks and step back to check the results.

Not bad.

I take my sad-clown face into Dorrit's room. Now she's on the phone. I can tell by her side of the conversation that she's comparing notes with one of her friends. She bangs down the receiver when she spots me.

"Well?" I ask.

"Well what?"

"What do you think about my makeup? I was thinking of wearing it to school."

"Is that supposed to be some kind of comment about my hair?"

"How would you feel if I showed up at school tomorrow looking like this?"

"I wouldn't care."

"Bet you would."

"Why are you being so mean?" Dorrit shouts.

"How am I being mean?" But she's right. I *am* being mean. I'm in a mean, foul mood.

And it's all because of Sebastian. Sometimes I think all the trouble in the world is caused by men. If there were no men, women would always be happy.

"C'mon, Dorrit. I was only *kidding*."

Dorrit puts her hands on top of her head. "Does it really look that bad?" she whispers.

My sad-clown face no longer feels like a joke.

When my mother first got sick, Dorrit would ask me what was going to happen. I'd put on a smiley face because I read somewhere that if you smile, even if you're feeling bad, the action of the muscles will trick your brain into thinking you're happy. "Whatever happens, we're all going to be fine," I'd tell Dorrit.

"Promise?"

"Of course, Dorrit. You'll see."

"Someone's here," Missy calls out now. Dorrit and I look at each other, our little tiff forgotten.

We clatter down the stairs. There, in the kitchen, is

Sebastian. He looks from my sad-clown face to Dorrit's pink and blue hair. And slowly, he shakes his head.

"If you're going to be around Bradshaws, you have to be *prepared*. There could be craziness. Anything might happen."

"No kidding," Sebastian says. He's wearing a black leather jacket, the same one he was wearing at Tommy Brewster's party and on the night we painted the barn—the night we first kissed.

"Do you always wear that jacket?" I ask as Sebastian downshifts on the curve leading to the highway.

"Don't you like it? I got it when I lived in Rome."

I suddenly feel like I've been swept under a wave. I've been to Florida and Texas and all around New England, but never to Europe. I don't even have a passport. I sure wish I had one now, though, so I'd know how to deal with Sebastian. They should make passports for relationships.

A guy who's lived in Rome. It sounds so romantic.

"What are you thinking?" Sebastian asks.

I'm thinking that you probably won't like me because I've never been to Europe and I'm not sophisticated enough. "Have you ever been to Paris?" I ask.

"Sure," he says. "Haven't you?"

"Not really."

"That sounds like being a little bit pregnant. You either have been or you haven't."

"I haven't been there in person. That doesn't mean I haven't been there in my mind."

He laughs. "You are a very strange girl."

"Thank you." I look out the window to hide my tiny smile. I don't care if he thinks I'm strange. I'm just so happy to see him.

I don't ask him why he hasn't called. I don't ask him where he's been. When I found him in my kitchen, leaning against the counter like he belonged there, I pretended it was perfectly natural, not even a surprise. "Am I interrupting something?" he asked, like it wasn't odd that he suddenly decided to show up.

"Depends on what you call interrupting." My insides were filled with diamonds, suddenly illuminated by the sun.

"Do you want to go out?"

"Sure." I ran upstairs and scrubbed off my clown face, knowing all the while I should have said no, or at least allowed myself to be convinced, because what girl agrees to go on a date spur of the moment like that? It sets a bad precedent, makes the guy think he can see you whenever he wants, treat you however he wants. But I didn't have it in me to refuse. As I pulled on my boots, I wondered if I'd come to regret being so easy.

I'm not regretting it now, though. Who makes up those rules about dating, anyway? And why can't I be exempt?

He puts his hand on my leg. Casually. Like we've been dating for a long time. If we were, I wonder if his hand on my leg would always produce the reaction I'm having now, which is a confused sort of divine giddiness. I decide it would.

I can't imagine ever not feeling like this when I'm with him.

I'm losing it.

"It's not that great, you know," he says.

"Huh?" I turn back to him, my happiness pitching into inexplicable panic.

"Europe," he says.

"Oh," I breathe. "Europe."

"Two summers ago when I lived in Rome, I went all around—France, Germany, Switzerland, Spain—and when I got back here, I realized this place is just as beautiful."

"Castlebury?" I gasp.

"It's as beautiful as Switzerland," he says.

Sebastian Kydd actually likes Castlebury? "But I always imagined you"—I falter—"living in New York. Or London. Or someplace exciting."

He frowns. "You don't know me that well." And just as I'm about to expire from fear that I've insulted him, he adds, "But you will.

"In fact," he continues, "since I figured we ought to get to know each other better, I'm taking you to see an art exhibit."

"Ah," I say, nodding. I don't know a damn thing about art either. Why didn't I take art history when I had the chance?

I'm a goner.

Sebastian will figure it out and dump me before we've even had a proper first date.

"Max Ernst," he says. "He's my favorite artist. Who's yours?"

"Peter Max?" It's the only name I can think of at the moment.

"You *are* funny," he says, and laughs.

He takes me to the Wadsworth Atheneum Museum of Art in Hartford. I've been there a million times on field trips, holding the sticky hand of another little classmate so no one got lost. I hated the way we were marched around, scolded by a teacher's aide who was always somebody's mother. Where was Sebastian back then? I wonder as he takes my hand.

I look down at our intertwined fingers and see something that shocks me.

Sebastian Kydd bites his nails?

"Come on," he says, pulling me along beside him. We stop in front of a painting of a boy and a girl on a marble bench on a fantasy lake in the mountains. Sebastian stands behind me, resting his head on top of mine and wrapping his arms around my shoulders. "Sometimes I wish I could go into that painting. Close my eyes and wake up there. I'd stay there forever."

But what about me? screams a voice in my head. I suddenly don't like being left out of his fantasy. "Wouldn't you get bored?"

"Not if you were there with me."

I just about fall over. Guys aren't supposed to say these things. Or rather, they're supposed to but never do. I mean, who actually says things like that?

A guy who is crazily, madly in love with you. A guy who

sees how incredible and amazing you are, even though you're not the cheerleader or even close to the prettiest girl in the school. A guy who thinks you're beautiful, just the way you are.

"My parents are in Boston," he says. "Want to go to my house?"

"Sure." I figure I'd go just about anywhere with him.

✧ ✳ CB ✳ ✧

I have this theory that you can tell everything about a person by their room, but in Sebastian's case, it isn't true. His room is more like a guestroom in an antique boardinghouse than an actual boy's lair. There's a black and red handmade quilt, and an old wooden captain's wheel hangs on the wall. No posters, photographs, albums, baseballs—not even a dirty sock. I stare out the window at the view of a fading brown field and past that, the stark yellow brick of a convalescent home. I close my eyes and try to pretend I'm with Sebastian in the Max Ernst painting under an azure blue sky.

Now that I'm actually in his room—with him, for real— I'm a little uneasy.

Sebastian takes my hand and leads me to the bed. He puts his hands on either side of my face and kisses me.

I can barely breathe. Me—and Sebastian Kydd. It's really happening.

After a while, he raises his head and looks at me. He's so close I can see the tiny flecks of dark green around his irises. He's so close I could count them if I tried.

"Hey," he says. "You never asked why I didn't call."

"Was I supposed to?"

"Most girls would have."

"Maybe I'm not most girls." This sounds kind of arrogant but I'm certainly not going to tell him how I spent the last two weeks in an emotional panic, jumping every time the phone rang, giving him sidelong glances in class, promising myself I would never, ever do any bad thing ever again if he would only talk to me the way he had that night at the barn . . . and then hating myself for being so stupid and girlish about the whole thing.

"Did you think about me?" he asks slyly.

Oh boy. A trick question. If I say no, he'll be insulted. If I say yes, I'll sound pathetic.

"Maybe a little."

"I thought about you."

"Then why didn't you call?" I ask playfully.

"I was afraid."

"Of me?" I laugh, but he seems oddly sincere.

"I was worried that I could fall in love with you. And I don't want to be in love with anyone right now."

"Oh." My heart drops to my stomach.

"Well?" he asks, running his finger along my jaw.

Aha. I smile. It's only another one of his trick questions.

"Maybe you just haven't met the right girl," I murmur.

He brings his lips close to my ear. "I was hoping you'd say that."

CHAPTER TEN

Rescue Me

My parents met in a library.

After college, my mother was a librarian. My father came in to borrow some books, saw my mother, and fell in love.

They were married six months later.

Everyone says my mother used to look like Elizabeth Taylor, but in those days they told every pretty girl she looked like Elizabeth Taylor. Nevertheless, I always picture Elizabeth Taylor sitting demurely behind an oak desk. My father, bespectacled and lanky, his blond hair modeled into a stiff crew cut, approaches the desk as my mother/Elizabeth Taylor stands up to help him. She is wearing a poodle skirt flourished with fuzzy pink pom-poms.

The skirt is somewhere up in the attic, zipped away in a garment bag with the rest of my mother's old clothes, including her wedding gown, saddle shoes, ballet slippers, and the megaphone embossed with her name, Mimi, from her days as a high-school cheerleader.

I almost never saw my mother when she wasn't beautifully dressed and had completed her hair and makeup. For a period, she sewed her own clothes and many of ours. She prepared entire meals from the Julia Child cookbook. She decorated the house with local antiques, had the prettiest gardens and Christmas tree, and still surprised us with elaborate Easter baskets well past the time when we had ceased to believe in the Easter Bunny.

My mother was just like all the other mothers, but a little better, because she felt that presenting one's home and family in the best possible light was a worthy pursuit, and she made everything look easy.

And even though she wore White Shoulders perfume and thought jeans were for farmers, she also assumed that women should embrace this wonderful way of being called feminism.

The summer before I started second grade, my mother and her friends started reading *The Consensus*, by Mary Gordon Howard. It was a heavy novel, lugged to and from the club in large canvas bags filled with towels and suntan lotion and potions for insect bites. Every morning, as they settled into their chaises around the pool, one woman after another would pull *The Consensus* out of her bag. The cover is still etched in my brain: a blue sea with an abandoned sailboat, surrounded by the black-and-white college photographs of eight young women. On the back was a photograph of Mary Gordon Howard herself, taken in profile, a patrician woman who, to my young mind, resembled George Washington wearing a tweed suit and pearls.

"Did you get to the part about the pessary?" one lady would whisper to another.

"Shhhh. Not yet. Don't give it away."

"Mom, what's a pessary?" I asked.

"It's not something you need to worry about as a child."

"Will I need to worry about it as an adult?"

"Maybe. Maybe not. There might be new methods by then."

I spent the whole summer trying to find out what it was about that book that so managed to hold the attention of the ladies at the club that Mrs. Dewittle didn't even notice when her son David fell off the diving board and needed ten stitches in his head.

"Mom!" I said later, trying to get her attention. "Why does Mary Gordon Howard have two last names?"

My mother put down the book, holding her place with her finger. "Gordon is her mother's maiden name and Howard is her father's last name."

I considered this. "What happens if she gets married?"

My mother seemed pleased by the question. "She is married. She's been married three times."

I thought it must be the most glamorous thing in the world to be married three times. Back then, I didn't know one adult who had been divorced even once.

"But she never takes her husbands' names. Mary Gordon Howard is a very great feminist. She believes that women should be able to define themselves and shouldn't let a man take their identity."

I thought it must be the most glamorous thing in the world to be a feminist.

Until *The Consensus* came along, I'd never thought much about the power of books. I'd read a ton of picture books, and then the Roald Dahl novels and the *Chronicles of Narnia* by C. S. Lewis. But that summer, the idea that a book could change people began to flutter around the edges of my consciousness. I thought that I, too, might want to become a writer and a feminist.

On Christmas of that year, as we sat around the table eating the Bûche de Noël that my mother had spent two days assembling, she made an announcement. She was going back to school to get her architecture degree. Nothing would change, except that Daddy would have to make us dinner some nights.

Years later, my mother got a job with Beakon and Beakon Architects. I loved to go to her office after school, which was in an antique house in the center of town. Every room was softly carpeted, perfumed with the gentle scent of paper and ink. There was a funny slanted desk where my mother did her work, drawing elegant structures in a fine, strict hand. She had two people working for her, both young men who seemed to adore her, and I never thought you couldn't be a feminist if you wore pantyhose and high heels and pulled your hair back in a pretty barrette.

I thought being a feminist was about how you conducted your life.

When I was thirteen, I saw in the local paper that Mary Gordon Howard was coming to speak and sign books at our public library. My mother was no longer well enough to leave the house, so I decided to go on my own and surprise her with a signed book. I braided my hair into pigtails and tied the ends with yellow ribbons. I wore a yellow India print dress and a pair of wedge sandals. Before I left, I went in to see my mother.

She was lying in her bed with the blinds half-closed. As always, there was the mechanical *tick, tick, tick* of the grandfather clock, and I imagined the little teeth in the mechanism biting off a tiny piece of time with each inexorable movement.

"Where are you going?" my mother asked. Her voice, once mellifluous, was reduced to a needle scratch.

"To the library," I said, beaming. I was dying to tell her my secret.

"That's nice," she said. "You look pretty." She took a heavy breath and continued. "I like your ribbons. Where did you get them?"

"From your old sewing box."

She nodded. "My father brought those ribbons from Belgium."

I touched the ribbons, unsure if I should have taken them.

"No, no," my mother said. "You wear them. That's what they're there for, right? Besides," she repeated, "you look pretty."

She began to cough. I dreaded the sound—high and weak, it was more like the futile gasping of a helpless animal than an actual cough. She'd coughed for a year before they discovered she was sick. The nurse came in, pulling the top off a syringe with her teeth while tapping my mother's forearm with two fingers.

"There you go, dear, there you go," she said reassuringly, smoothly inserting the needle. "Now you'll sleep. You'll sleep for a bit and when you wake up, you'll feel better."

My mother looked at me and winked. "I doubt it," she said as she began to drift away.

I got on my bike and rode the five miles down Main Street to the library. I was late, and as I pedaled, an idea began to form in my head that Mary Gordon Howard was going to rescue me.

Mary Gordon Howard was going to *recognize* me.

Mary Gordon Howard was going to see me and know, instinctively, that I, too, was a writer and a feminist, and would someday write a book that would change the world.

Standing atop my pedals to pump more furiously, I had high hopes for a dramatic transformation.

When I reached the library, I threw my bike into the bushes and ran upstairs to the main reading room.

Twelve rows of women sat on folding chairs. The great Mary Gordon Howard, the lower half of her body hidden behind a podium, stood before them. She appeared as a woman dressed for battle, in a stiff suit the color of armor enhanced by enormous shoulder pads. I caught an undercurrent of hostility in the air, and slipped behind a stack.

"Yes?" she barked at a woman in the front row who had raised her hand. It was our next-door neighbor, Mrs. Agnosta. "What you're saying is all very well and good," Mrs. Agnosta began carefully. "But what if you're not unhappy with your life? I mean, I'm not sure my daughter's life *should* be different than mine. In fact, I'd really like my daughter to turn out just like me."

Mary Gordon Howard frowned. On her ears were enormous blue stones. As she moved her hand to adjust her earring, I noticed a rectangular diamond watch on her wrist. Somehow, I hadn't expected Mary Gordon Howard to be so bejeweled. Then she lowered her head like a bull and stared straight at Mrs. Agnosta as if she were about to charge. For a second, I was actually afraid for Mrs. Agnosta, who no doubt had no idea what she'd wandered into and was only looking for a little culture to enhance her afternoon.

"That, my dear, is because you are a classic narcissist," Mary Gordon Howard declared. "You are so in love with yourself, you imagine that a woman can only be happy if she is 'just like you.' You are exactly what I'm talking about when I refer to women who are a hindrance to the progress of other women."

Well, I thought. That was probably true. If it were up to Mrs. Agnosta, all women would spend their days baking cookies and scrubbing toilets.

Mary Gordon Howard looked around the room, her mouth drawn into a line of triumph. "And now, if there are no more questions, I will be happy to sign your books."

There were no more questions. The audience, I figured, was too scared.

I got in line, clutching my mother's copy of *The Consensus* to my chest. The head librarian, Ms. Detooten, who I'd known since I was a kid, stood next to Mary Gordon Howard, handing her books to sign. Mary Gordon Howard sighed several times in annoyance. Finally she turned to Ms. Detooten and muttered, "Unenlightened housewives, I'm afraid." By then I was only two people away. "Oh no," I wanted to protest. "That isn't true at all." And I wished I could tell her about my mother and how *The Consensus* had changed her life.

Ms. Detooten shrank and, flushed with embarrassment, turned away and spotted me. "Why, here's Carrie Bradshaw," she exclaimed in a too-happy, nudging voice, as if I were a person Mary Gordon Howard might like to meet.

My fingers curled tightly around the book. I couldn't seem to move the muscles in my face, and I pictured how I must look with my lips frozen into a silly, timid smile.

The Gorgon, as I'd now begun to think of her, glanced my way, took in my appearance, and went back to her signing.

"Carrie's going to be a writer," Ms. Detooten gushed. "Isn't that so, Carrie?"

I nodded.

Suddenly I had The Gorgon's attention. She put down her pen. "And why is that?" she asked.

"Excuse me?" I whispered. My face prickled with heat.

"Why do *you* want to be a writer?"

I looked to Ms. Detooten for help. But Ms. Detooten only looked as terrified as I did. "I . . . I don't know."

"If you can't think of a very good reason to do it, then don't," The Gorgon snapped. "Being a writer is all about having something to say. And it'd better be interesting. If you don't have anything interesting to say, don't become a writer. Become something useful. Like a doctor."

"Thank you," I whispered.

The Gorgon held out her hand for my mother's book. For a moment, I thought about snatching it away and running out of there, but I was too intimidated. The Gorgon scrawled her name in sharp, tiny handwriting.

"Thank you for coming, Carrie," Ms. Detooten said as the book was handed back to me.

My mouth was dry. I nodded my head dumbly as I stumbled outside.

I was too weak to pick up my bike. I sat on the curb instead, trying to recover my ego. I waited as poisonous waves of shame crashed over me, and when they passed, I stood up, feeling as if I'd lost a dimension. I got on my bike and rode home.

"How'd it go?" my mother whispered later, when she was awake. I sat on the chair next to her bed, holding her hand.

My mother always took good care of her hands. If you only looked at her hands, you would never know she was sick.

I shrugged. "They didn't have the book I wanted."

My mother nodded. "Maybe next time."

I never told my mother how I'd gone to see her hero, Mary Gordon Howard. I never told her Mary Gordon Howard had signed her book. I certainly didn't tell her that Mary Gordon Howard was no feminist. How can you be a feminist when you treat other women like dirt? Then you're just a mean girl like Donna LaDonna. I never told anyone about the incident at all. But it stayed with me, like a terrible beating you can push out of your mind but never quite forget.

I still feel a flicker of shame when I think about it. I wanted Mary Gordon Howard to rescue me.

But that was a long time ago. I'm not that girl anymore. I don't need to feel ashamed. I turn over and squish my pillow under my cheek, thinking about my date with Sebastian.

And I don't need to be rescued anymore, either.

CHAPTER ELEVEN

Competition

"I hear Donna LaDonna is seeing Sebastian Kydd," Lali says, adjusting her goggles.

What? I dip my toe into the water as I tug on the straps of my Speedo, trying to compose myself. "Really," I say casually. "How'd you hear that?"

"She told the two Jens and they're telling everyone."

"Maybe she's making it up," I say, stretching my legs.

"Why would she do that?"

I get up on the block next to her and shrug.

"On your mark. Get set. *Go!*" Coach Nipsie says.

As we're both airborne, I suddenly shout, "I went on a date with Sebastian Kydd."

I catch a glimpse of her shocked expression as she belly flops into the pool.

The water's cold, barely seventy-five degrees. I swim one lap, turn, and when I see Lali coming up behind me, start pounding the water.

Lali's a better swimmer than I am, but I'm the better diver. For almost eight years now, we've been competing with each other and against each other. We've gotten up at four a.m., swallowed weird concoctions of raw eggs to make us stronger, spent weeks at swimming camp, given each other wedgies, made up funny victory dances, and painted our faces with the school colors. We've been screamed at by coaches, berated by mothers, and made little kids cry. We're considered a bad combination, but so far, no one's been able to separate us.

We swim an exhausting eight-lap medley. Lali passes me on the sixth lap, and when I hit the wall, she's standing above me, dripping water into my lane. "Nice way to freak out the competition," she says as we high-five.

"Except it's true," I say, grabbing my towel and rubbing my head.

"*What?*"

"Last night. He came to my house. We went to a museum. Then we went to his house and made out."

"Uh-huh." She flexes her foot and pulls it up to her thigh.

"And he spent a summer living in Rome. And"—I look around to make sure no one is listening—"he bites his nails."

"Right, Bradley."

"Lali," I whisper. "I'm *serious*."

She stops stretching her leg and looks at me. For a second, I think she's angry. Then she grins and blurts out, "Come on, Carrie. Why would Sebastian Kydd go out with *you*?"

For a moment, we're both stunned into one of those terrible awkward moments when a friend has gone too far and you wonder if ugly words will be exchanged. You'll say something nasty and defensive. She'll say something hurtful and cruel. You wonder if you'll ever speak again.

But maybe she didn't mean it. So you give her another chance. "Why wouldn't he?" I ask, trying to make light of it.

"It's only because of Donna LaDonna," she says, backtracking. "I mean, if he's seeing her . . . you wouldn't think he'd start seeing someone else, too."

"Maybe he isn't seeing her," I say, my throat tight. I'd been looking forward to telling Lali everything about the date, turning over each little thing he said and did, but now I can't.

What if he *is* seeing Donna LaDonna? I'll look like a complete and utter fool.

"Bradshaw!" Coach Nipsie shouts. "What the hell is wrong with you today? You're up on the planks."

"Sorry," I say to Lali, as if somehow it's all my fault. I grab my towel and head to the diving boards.

"And I need you to nail the half gainer with a full twist for the meet on Thursday," Coach Nipsie calls out.

Great.

I climb the rungs to the board and pause, trying to visualize my dive. But all I can see is Donna LaDonna and Sebastian together that night at The Emerald. Maybe Lali is right. Why would he bother chasing me if he's still seeing Donna LaDonna? On the other hand, maybe he isn't seeing her and Lali's just trying to mess me up. But why would she do that?

"Bradshaw!" Coach Nipsie warns. "I don't have all day."

Right. I take four steps, come down hard on my left foot, and pop straight up. As soon as I'm in the air, I know the dive is going to be a disaster. My arms and legs flail to the side as I land on the back of my head.

"Come on, Bradshaw. You're not even trying," Coach Nipsie reprimands.

Usually, I'm pretty tough, but tears well up in my eyes. I can't tell if it's from the pain in my head or the humiliation to my ego, but either way, they both hurt. I glance toward Lali, hoping for sympathy, but she isn't paying attention. She's seated in the bleachers, and next to her, about a foot away, is Sebastian.

Why does he keep popping up unexpectedly? I'm not prepared for this.

I get back on the board. I don't dare look at him, but I can feel him watching. My second attempt is a little better, and when I get out of the water, Lali and Sebastian have started talking. Lali looks up at me and raises her fist. "Go, Bradley!"

"Thanks." I wave. Sebastian catches my eye and winks.

My third dive is actually pretty good, but Lali and Sebastian are too engaged in their animated conversation to notice.

"Hey," I say, squeezing water out of my hair as I stride over.

"Oh, hi," Lali says, as if she's seeing me for the first time that day. Now that Sebastian is here, I figure she must be feeling pretty cheesy about what she said.

"Did it hurt?" Sebastian asks as I sit down next to him. He pats the top of my head and says sweetly, "Your noggin. It looked like it took some damage there."

I glance at Lali, whose eyes are the size of eggs. "Nah." I shrug. "Happens all the time. It's nothing."

"We were just talking about the night we painted the barn," Lali says.

"That was hysterical," I say, in an attempt to behave as if all of this is normal, as if I'm not even surprised to find Sebastian waiting for me.

"You want a ride home?" he asks.

"Sure." He follows me to the locker room door, and for some reason, I'm relieved. I suddenly realize I don't want to leave him alone with Lali.

I want him all to myself. He's too new to share.

And then I feel like a crap heel. Lali is my best friend.

I slip out to the parking lot through the gym instead of the pool, my hair still wet, my jeans clinging uncomfortably to my thighs. I'm halfway across the asphalt when a beige Toyota pulls up beside me and stops. The window rolls down and Jen S sticks her head out. "Hey, Carrie," she says, all casual. "Where are you going?"

"Nowhere."

Jen P leans across her. "Want to go to the Hamburger Shack?"

I give them a deliberately skeptical look. They've never asked me to go to the Hamburger Shack before—hell, they've never asked me to go anywhere. Do they really think I'm that dumb?

"Can't," I say vaguely.

"Why not?"

"I have to go home."

"You have time for a hamburger," Jen S says. It might be my imagination, but I detect a slight threat in her tone.

Sebastian honks his horn.

I jump. Jen S and Jen P exchange another look. "Get in," Jen P urges.

"Really, guys. Thanks. Some other time."

Jen S glares at me. And this time there is no mistaking the hostility in her voice. "Suit yourself," she says as she rolls up the window. And then they just sit there, watching as I walk up to Sebastian's car and get in.

"Hi," he says, leaning over to kiss me.

I pull away. "Better not. We're being watched." I point out the beige Toyota. "The two Jens."

"Who cares?" he says, and kisses me again. I go along with it but break away after a few seconds. "The Jens," I say pointedly. "They're best friends with Donna LaDonna."

"And?"

"Well, obviously they're going to tell her. About you and

me," I say cautiously, not wanting to be presumptuous.

He frowns, turns the key in the ignition, and slams the stick into second gear. The car leaps forward with a screech. I peek out the back window. The Toyota has pulled right up behind. I slump down in the seat. "I can't believe this," I mutter. "They're following us."

"Oh, for Christ's sake," he says, looking into the rearview mirror. "Maybe it's time someone taught them a lesson."

The engine roars like a wild animal as he puts the car into fourth gear. We take a sharp turn onto the highway and hit seventy-five. I turn around to check the progress of the Toyota. "I think we're losing them."

"Why would they do this? What is wrong with these girls?"

"Boredom. They don't have anything better to do."

"Well, they'd better find someone else to tail."

"Or what? You're going to beat them up?" I giggle.

"Something like that." He rubs my leg and smiles. We take a sharp turn off the highway and onto Main Street. As we approach my house, he slows down.

"Not here." I panic. "They'll see your car in the driveway."

"Where then?"

I consider for a moment. "The library."

No one will think to look for us there, except maybe The Mouse, who knows that the Castlebury Public Library is my favorite secret place. It's housed in a white brick mansion, built in the early 1900s, when Castlebury was a booming mill town and had millionaires who wanted to show off their wealth by building grand mansions on the Connecticut River. But hardly anyone has the money to keep them up now, so they've all been turned into public properties or nursing homes.

Sebastian whips into the driveway and parks behind the building. I hop out and peek around the side. The beige Toyota is slowly making its way down Main Street, past the library. Inside the car, the two Jens are swiveling their heads around like swizzle sticks, trying to find us.

I bend over, laughing. Every time I try to straighten up, I look at Sebastian and burst out into hysterics. I stumble around the parking lot and fall to the ground, holding my stomach.

"Carrie?" he says. "Is it really *that* funny?"

"Yes," I cry. And I collapse into another wave of laughter while Sebastian looks at me, gives up, and lights a cigarette.

"Here," he says, handing it to me.

I get up, holding on to him for support. "It is funny, isn't it?"

"It's hilarious."

"How come you're not laughing?"

"I am. But I like watching you laugh more."

"Really?"

"Yeah. It makes me happy." He puts his arm around me and we go inside.

I lead him up to the fourth floor. Hardly anyone comes up here because all the books are on engineering and botany and obscure scientific research that most people don't want to bother trekking up four flights to read. In the middle of the room is an old chintz-covered couch.

We're at least half an hour into an intense make-out session when we're startled by a loud angry voice.

"Hello, Sebastian. I was wondering where you'd run off to."

Sebastian is on top of me. I look over his shoulder and see Donna LaDonna looming over us, like an angry Valkyrie. Her arms are crossed, emphasizing her formidable chest. If breasts could kill, I'd be dead.

"You're disgusting," she sneers at Sebastian before she focuses her attention on me. "And *you*, Carrie Bradshaw. You're even *worse*."

"I don't get it," I say in a small voice.

Sebastian looks guilty. "Carrie, I'm sorry. I had no idea she would react that way."

How could he have "no idea"? I wonder, my anger growing. It's going to be all over the school tomorrow. And I'm the one who's going to look like either a fool or a bitch.

Sebastian has one hand on the wheel, tapping the fake wood inlay with a ragged nail, as if he's as perplexed by this as I am. I'm probably supposed to yell at him, but he looks so cute and innocent, I can't quite muster the energy.

I look at him hard, folding my arms. "*Are* you seeing her?"

"It's complicated."

"How?"

"It's not that simple."

"It's like being a little bit pregnant. You either are or you're not."

"I'm not, but she *thinks* I am."

And whose fault is that? "Can't you tell her you're not seeing her?"

"It's not so easy. She *needs* me."

Now I really have had enough. How can any self-respecting girl respond to this nonsense? Am I supposed to say, "No, please, I need you too"? And what's up with this old-fashioned "neediness" stuff, anyway?

He pulls into my driveway and parks the car. "Carrie—"

"I should probably go." There's a bit of an edge to my voice. But what else am I supposed to do? What if he does like Donna LaDonna better and he's only using me to make her jealous?

I get out of the car and slam the door.

I race up the walk. I'm nearly at the door when I hear the quick, satisfying tread of his footsteps behind me.

He grabs my arm. "Don't go," he says. I allow him to turn me around, put his hands in my hair. "Don't go," he whispers. He tilts my face up to his. "Maybe *I* need *you*."

CHAPTER TWELVE

You Can't Always Get What You Want

"Maggie, what's wrong?"

"Nothing," she says coldly.

"Are you angry at me?" I gasp.

She stops, turns, and glares. And there it is: The international girl face for "I'm mad at you, and you should know why, but I'm not going to explain it."

"What did *I* do?"

"It's what you didn't do."

"Okay, what *didn't* I do?"

"You tell me," she says, and starts walking.

I run through a variety of scenarios but can't come up with a clue.

"Mags." I chase after her down the hall. "I'm sorry I didn't do something. But I honestly don't know what that something is."

"Sebastian," she snaps.

"Huh?"

"You and Sebastian. I come to school this morning and everyone knows all about it. Everyone except *me*. And I'm *supposed* to be one of your best friends."

We're nearly at the door to assembly, where I will have to walk in knowing that I'm going to have to face the hostility of Donna LaDonna's friends, as well as a small army of kids who aren't her friends, but want to be.

"Maggie," I plead. "It just happened. I didn't exactly have time to call you. I was planning to tell you first thing this morning."

"Lali knew," she says, not buying my explanation.

"Lali was there. We were at the pool when he came by to pick me up."

"So?"

"Come on, Magwitch. I don't need you mad at me as well."

"We'll see." She pulls open the door to the auditorium. "We'll talk about it later."

"Okay." I sigh as she heads off. I skittle along the back wall and hurry down the aisle to my assigned seat, trying to attract as little attention as possible. When I finally reach my row, I stop, startled by the realization that something is terribly wrong. I check the letter "B" to make sure I haven't made a mistake.

I haven't. But my seat is now occupied by Donna LaDonna.

I look around for Sebastian, but he's not there. Coward. I have no choice. I'm going to have to brazen it out.

"Excuse me," I say, making my way past Susie Beck, who has worn purple every day of her life for the last two years; Ralph

Bomenski, a frail, white-skinned boy whose father owns a gas station and makes Ralphie work there in all kinds of weather; and Ellen Brack, who is six feet tall and is giving off the impression that she'd prefer to disappear—a sentiment I understand completely.

Donna LaDonna is oblivious to my progress. Her hair is like a giant dandelion seed, obstructing her view. She's talking with great animation to Tommy Brewster. It's the longest conversation I've ever witnessed between them. Nonetheless, it makes sense, as Tommy is part of her clique. Her voice is so loud you can practically hear her from three rows away.

"Some people don't know their place," she says. "It's all about pecking order. Do you know what happens to chickens that don't stay in their place?"

"No," Tommy says dumbly. He's noticed me, but quickly returns his eyes to their proper spot—on Donna LaDonna's face.

"They get pecked to death. By the other chickens," Donna says ominously.

Okay. Enough. I can't stand here forever. Poor Ellen Brack's knees are up to her ears. There simply isn't enough room for both of us.

"Excuse me," I say politely.

No response. Donna LaDonna continues her tirade. "And on top of that, she's trying to steal another girl's boyfriend."

Really? Donna LaDonna has stolen just about every one of her friends' boyfriends at one time or another, simply to remind them that she can.

"Notice I said *trying*. Because the most pathetic thing about it is that she hasn't succeeded. He called me last night and told me what a"—Donna suddenly leans forward and whispers in Tommy's ear so I can't make out the word—"she is."

Tommy laughs uproariously.

Sebastian called her?

No way. I can't let her get to me.

"Excuse me," I say again. But this time it's much louder and with much more authority. If she doesn't turn around, she's going to look like a complete idiot.

She turns. Her eyes slide over me like slow-burning acid. "Carrie," she says. "Since you seem to be a person who likes to change the rules, I thought we'd change our seats today."

Clever, I think. Unfortunately, not allowed.

"Why don't we switch seats another day?" I suggest.

"Oooooh," she says mockingly. "Are you afraid of getting in trouble? A Goody Two-shoes like you? Don't want to ruin your precious record, do you?"

Tommy throws back his head as if this, too, is hilariously funny. Jeez. He would laugh at a stick if someone told him to.

"All right," I say. "If you won't move, I guess I'll have to sit on top of you."

Childish, yes. But effective.

"You wouldn't dare."

"Oh really?" And I lift my handbag as if I'm about to place it on her head.

"I'm sorry, Tommy," she says, getting to her feet. "But some people are simply too juvenile to bother with." She brushes past me on her way out, deliberately stepping on my foot. I pretend not to notice. But even when she's gone, there's no relief. My heart is thumping like an entire brass band. My hands are shaking.

Did Sebastian *really* call her?

And where is Sebastian anyway?

I manage to get through assembly by berating myself for my behavior. What was I thinking? Why did I piss off the most powerful girl in the school over a guy? Because I got the opportunity, that's why. And I took it. I couldn't help myself. Which makes me a not-very-logical and perhaps not-very-nice person as well. I'm really going to get into trouble for this one. And I probably deserve it.

What if *everyone* is mad at me for the rest of the year?

If they are, I'll write a book about them. I'll send it into the summer writing program at The New School, and this time I'll get in. Then I'll move to New York and make new friends and show them all.

But right as we're shuffling out of assembly, Lali finds me. "I'm proud of you," she says. "I can't believe you stood up to Donna LaDonna."

"Eh, it was nothing." I shrug.

"I was watching the whole time. I was afraid you were going to start crying or something. But you didn't."

I'm not exactly a crybaby. Never have been. But still.

The Mouse joins us. "I was thinking. . . Maybe you and me

and Danny and Sebastian could go on a double date when Danny comes up to visit."

"Sure," I say, wishing she hadn't said this in front of Lali. With Maggie mad at me, the last thing I need is for Lali to feel left out as well. "Maybe we can all go out. In a group," I say pointedly, adding, for Lali's sake, "Since when did we start needing boyfriends to have fun?"

"You're right," The Mouse says, catching my drift. "You know what they say: A woman needs a man about as much as a fish needs a bicycle."

We all nod in agreement. A fish may not need a bicycle, but it sure as hell needs friends.

"Ow!" Someone pokes me in the back. I turn, expecting to see one of Donna LaDonna's lieutenants. Instead, it's Sebastian, holding a pencil and laughing.

"How are you?" he asks.

"Fine," I say, heavy on the sarcasm. "Donna LaDonna was sitting in my seat when I got to assembly."

"Uh-huh," he says noncommittally.

"I didn't see *you* in assembly."

"That's because *I* wasn't there."

"Where were you?" I can't believe I just said that. When did I turn into his mother?

"Does it matter?" he asks.

"There was a scene. With Donna LaDonna."

"Nice."

"It was ugly. Now she really hates me."

"You know my motto," he says, playfully tapping me on the nose with his pencil. "Avoid female trouble at all costs. What are you doing this afternoon? Skip swim practice and let's go somewhere."

"What about Donna LaDonna?" It's the closest I can come to asking if he called her.

"What about her? You want her to come too?"

I glare at him.

"Then forget about her. She's not important," he says as we take our seats in calculus.

He's right, I think, opening my book to the chapter on rogue integers. Donna LaDonna is not important. Calculus is, along with rogue integers. You never know when a rogue integer is going to show up and ruin your entire equation. Perhaps that's how Donna LaDonna feels about me. I am a rogue integer and I must be stopped.

"Carrie?"

"Yes, Mr. Douglas?"

"Could you come up here and finish this equation?"

"Sure." I pick up a piece of chalk and stare at the numbers on the blackboard. Who could ever imagine that calculus would be easier than dating?

"So the long knives are out," Walt says, referring to the assembly incident with a certain degree of satisfaction. He lights a cigarette and tilts back his head, blowing smoke into the rafters of the dairy barn.

"I knew he liked you," The Mouse says triumphantly.

"Mags?" I ask.

Maggie shrugs and looks away. She's still not talking to me.

She grinds her cigarette under her shoe, picks up her books, and walks off.

"What's eating her?" The Mouse asks.

"She's mad at me because I didn't tell her about Sebastian."

"That's stupid," The Mouse says. She looks at Walt. "Are you sure she's not mad at you?"

"I've done absolutely nothing. I am blame-free," Walt insists.

Walt has taken the breakup awfully well. It's been two days since Walt and Maggie had their "talk," and their relationship seems to be nearly the same as it was before, save for the fact that Maggie is now officially dating Peter.

"Maybe Maggie's mad at you because you're not more upset," I add.

"She said she thought we made better friends than lovers. I agreed," Walt says. "You don't get to make a decision and then be angry about it when the other person agrees with you."

"No," says The Mouse. "Because that would require a certain degree of logic. It's not a criticism," she says quickly, catching the warning expression on my face. "But it's true. Maggie isn't the most logical person."

"But she is the nicest." I'm thinking I'd better go after her, when Sebastian appears.

"Let's get out of here," he says. "I just got accosted by Tommy Brewster who kept asking me something about chickens."

"You guys are too cute," Walt says, shaking his head. "Just like Bonnie and Clyde."

"What should we do?" Sebastian asks.

"I don't know. What do you want to do?" Now that we're in Sebastian's car, I suddenly feel insecure. We've seen each other three days in a row. What does it mean? Are we dating?

"We could go to my house."

"Or maybe we *should* do something." If we go to his house, all we'll do is make out. I don't want to be the girl who only has sex with him. I want more. I want to be his *girlfriend*.

But how the hell do I do that?

"Okay," he says, resting his hand on my leg and sliding it up my thigh, "Where do *you* want to go?"

"Don't know," I say glumly.

"The movies?"

"Yeah." I perk up.

"There's a great Clint Eastwood retrospective at the Chesterfield Theatre."

"Perfect." I'm not sure I know exactly who Clint Eastwood is, but having agreed, I don't know how to admit it. "What's the movie about?"

He looks at me and grins. "Come on," he says, as if he can't believe I would ask such a question. "And it's not *a* movie. It's movies—plural. *The Good, The Bad and The Ugly* and *The Outlaw Josey Wales*."

"Fantastic," I say, with what I hope is enough enthusiasm to cover up my ignorance. Hey, it's not my fault. I don't have any brothers, so I'm completely ignorant about guy culture. I sit back in the seat and smile, determined to approach this date as an anthropological adventure.

"This is great," Sebastian says, nodding his head as he becomes more and more excited about his plan. "Really great. And you know what?"

"What?"

"You're great. I've been dying to check out this retrospective forever and I can't think of any other girl who would go with me."

"Oh," I say, pleased.

"Normally girls don't like Clint Eastwood. But you're different, you know?" He takes his eyes off the road for a second and looks at me. His expression is so earnest, I can almost picture my heart melting into a little pool of sticky sweet syrup. "I mean, it's kind of like you're more than a girl." He hesitates, searching for the perfect description. "It's like—you're a guy in a girl's body."

"What?"

"Take it easy. I didn't say you looked like a guy. I meant you think like a guy. You know. You're kind of practical but tough. And you're not afraid to have adventures."

"Listen, buster. Just because someone is a girl doesn't mean she can't be tough and practical and have adventures. That's the way most girls *are*—until they get around guys. Then guys make them act all stupid."

"You know what they say—all guys are assholes and all women are crazy."

I take off my shoe and hit him.

Four hours later, we stumble out of the theater. My lips are raw from kissing, and I feel slightly woozy. My hair is matted and I'm sure I've got mascara smudged all over my face. As we step out from the darkness into the light, Sebastian grabs me, kisses me again, and pushes back my hair.

"So what'd you think?"

"Pretty good. I love the part where Clint Eastwood shoots Eli Wallach down from the noose."

"Yeah," he says, putting his arm around me. "That's my favorite part too."

I pat my hair, trying to make myself look slightly respectable and not like I've been making out with a guy in a movie theater for half the day. "How do I look?"

Sebastian steps back and grins appraisingly. "You look just like Tuco."

I swat his butt. Tuco is the name of the Eli Wallach character, aka "the Ugly."

"I think that's what I'm going to call you from now on," he says, laughing. "Tuco. Little Tuco. What do you think?"

"I'm gonna kill you," I say, and chase him all the way across the parking lot to the car.

CHAPTER THIRTEEN

Creatures of Love

I lay low for the next couple of days, steering clear of Donna LaDonna by skipping assembly and avoiding the cafeteria during lunch. On the third day, Walt tracks me down in the library, where I'm hiding in the self-help section of the stacks, secretly reading *Linda Goodman's Love Signs* in a futile attempt to discern if Sebastian and I have a future. Problem is, I don't know his birthday. I can only hope he's an Aries and not a Scorpio.

"Astrology? Oh no. Not you, Carrie," Walt says.

I shut the book and put it back on the shelf. "What's wrong with astrology?"

"It's dumb," Walt says snidely. "Thinking you can predict your life from your birth sign. Do you know how many people are born each day? Two million five hundred and ninety-nine. How can two million five hundred and ninety-nine people have anything in common?"

"Has anyone mentioned that you've been in a really bad mood lately?"

"What are you talking about? I'm always like this."

"It's the breakup, isn't it?"

"No, it's not."

"Then what is it?"

"Maggie's in tears," he says suddenly.

I sigh. "Is it about me?"

"Not everything's about you, Bradley. Apparently she had some kind of fight with Peter. She sent me to find you. She's in the girls' room by the chemistry lab."

"You don't have to run errands for her."

"I don't care," Walt says, as if the whole situation is pointless. "It's easier than not doing it."

Something is definitely wrong with Walt, I think, as I hurry away to meet Maggie. He's always been slightly sarcastic and cynical, which is what I love about him. But he's never been this world weary, as if everyday life has drained him of the strength to continue.

I open the door to the small lav in the old part of the school that hardly anyone uses because the mirror is mangy and all the fixtures are from about sixty years ago. The writing scratched into the stalls appears to be about sixty years old as well. My favorite is, *For a good time, call Myrtle.* I mean, when was the last time someone named their kid Myrtle?

"Who's there?" Maggie calls out.

"It's me."

"Is anyone with you?"

"No."

"Okay," she says, and comes out of the stall, her face swollen and blotchy from crying.

"Jesus, Maggie," I say as I hand her a paper towel.

She blows her nose and looks at me over the tissue. "I know you're all caught up in Sebastian now, but I need your help."

"Okay," I say cautiously.

"Because I have to go to this doctor. And I can't go alone."

"Of course." I smile, grateful that we seem to have made up. "When?"

"Now."

"Now?"

"Unless you have something better to do."

"I don't. But why now, Maggie?" I ask with growing suspicion. "What kind of doctor?"

"You *know*," she says, lowering her voice. "A doctor for . . . women's stuff."

"Like abortion?" I can't help it. The word comes out in a loud gasp.

Maggie looks panicked. "Don't even say it."

"Are you—?"

"No," she says, in a heated whisper. "But I thought I might be. But then I got my period on Monday."

"So you did it . . . without protection?"

"You don't exactly plan these things, you know," Maggie

says defensively. "And he's always pulled out."

"Oh, Maggie." Even if I haven't had actual sex, I know quite a bit about the theories behind it, the number one fact being that the pull-out method is known not to work. And Maggie should know this too. "Aren't you on the pill?"

"Well, I'm trying to be." She grimaces. "That's why I have to go to this doctor in East Milton."

East Milton is right next to our town, but it's supposedly filled with crime, and nobody goes there. They don't even go through it, under any circumstances. Honestly, I can't believe there's even a doctor's office there. "How did you find this doctor anyway?"

"The Yellow Pages." I can tell by the way she says it that she's lying. "I called up and I got an appointment for twelve thirty today. And you have to go with me. You're the only person I can trust. I mean, I can't exactly go with Walt, can I?"

"Why can't you go with Peter? He's the person who's responsible for all this, right?"

"He's kind of pissed at me," Maggie says. "When he found out I might be pregnant he freaked out and didn't talk to me for twenty-four hours."

There is something about this whole scenario that just isn't making sense. "But, Maggie," I counter, "when I saw you on Sunday afternoon, you said you'd had sex with Peter for the first time—"

"No, I didn't."

"Yes, you did."

"I don't remember." She grabs a handful of toilet paper and puts it over her face.

"It wasn't the first time, was it?" I say. She shakes her head. "You'd slept with him before."

"That night after The Emerald," she admits.

I nod slowly. I walk to the tiny window and look out. "Why didn't you tell me?"

"Oh, Carrie, I couldn't," she cries. "I'm so sorry. I wanted to tell you, but I was scared. I mean, what if people found out? What if Walt found out? Everyone would think I was a slut."

"I would never think you were a slut. I wouldn't think you were a slut if you slept with a hundred men."

This makes her giggle. "Do you think a woman can sleep with a hundred men?"

"I think she could, if she worked really, really hard at it. I mean, you'd have to sleep with a different guy every week. For two years. You practically wouldn't have time for anything but sex."

Maggie throws away the tissue and looks at herself in the mirror as she pats cold water on her face. "That sounds just like Peter. All he thinks about is sex."

No kidding. Hell. Who knew nerdly old Peter was such a stud?

The doctor's office should be fifteen minutes away, but thirty minutes have passed and we still can't find it. So far we've nearly backed into two cars, driven over four curbs, and run over a handful of french fries. Maggie insisted we stop at McDonald's on the way, and when we got our food into the car, she lurched out of the parking lot with so much force all my french fries flew out the window.

Enough! I want to scream. But I can't do that—not when I'm trying to get one of my best friends to a crackpot doctor's office to get a prescription for birth control pills. So when I look at my watch and see that it's past twelve thirty, I gently suggest we stop at a gas station.

"Why?" Maggie asks.

"They have maps."

"We don't need a map."

"What are you, a guy?" I open the glove compartment and look inside in despair. It's empty. "Besides, we need cigarettes."

"My goddamn mother," Maggie says. "She's trying to quit. I hate when she does that."

Luckily, the cigarette issue distracts us from the fact that we are lost, we are in the most dangerous town in Connecticut, and we are losers. Enough to get us to a gas station anyway, where I am forced to flirt with a pimply faced attendant while Maggie takes a nervous leak in the dirty bathroom.

I show the attendant the piece of paper with the address on it. "Oh, sure," he says. "That street is right around the corner." Then he starts making shadow figures on the side of the building.

"You're really good at doing a bunny," I say.

"I know," he says. "I'm going to quit this job soon. Going to do shadow figures at kids' parties."

"I'm sure you'll have a huge clientele." All of a sudden, I'm feeling kind of sentimental toward this sweet, pimply faced guy who wants to do shadow figures at children's parties. He's so different from anyone at Castlebury High. Then Maggie comes out and I hustle her into the car, making my hand into a barking dog shape as we peel out of there.

"What was that about?" Maggie asks. "The hand. Since when do you do shadow puppets?"

Ever since you decided to have sex and didn't tell me, I want to say, but don't. Instead I say, "I've always done them. You just never noticed."

The address for the doctor's office is on a residential street with tiny houses crammed right next to one another. When we get to number 46, Maggie and I look at each other like this can't be right. It's just another house—a small, blue ranch with a red door. Behind the house we discover another door with a sign next to it that reads, DOCTOR'S OFFICE. But now that we've finally found this doctor, Maggie is terrified. "I can't do it," she says, slumping onto the steering wheel. "I can't go in."

I know I should be peeved at her for making me come all the way to East Milton for nothing, but instead, I know exactly how she's feeling. Wanting to cling to the past, wanting to be the way you always were, too scared to move forward into the future. I mean, who knows what's in the future? On the other hand, it's probably too late to go back.

"Look," I say. "I'll go inside and check it out. If it's okay, I'll come back and get you. If I'm not back in five minutes, call the police."

Taped to the door is a piece of paper that says, KNOCK LOUDLY. I knock loudly. I knock so loudly, I nearly bruise my knuckles.

The door opens a crack, and a middle-aged woman wearing a nurse's uniform sticks her head out. "Yes?"

"My friend is here for an appointment."

"For what?" she says.

"Birth control pills?" I whisper.

"Are you the friend?" she demands.

"No," I say, taken aback. "My friend is in the car."

"She'd better come in quickly. Doctor has his hands full today."

"Okay," I say, and nod. My head is like one of those bobble things truckers put on their dashboards.

"Either get your 'friend' or come in," the nurse says.

I turn around and wave to Maggie. And for once in her life, she actually gets out of the car.

We go in. We're in a tiny waiting room that was maybe the breakfast room in the original house. The wallpaper is printed with tea kettles. There are six metal chairs and a fake wooden coffee table with copies of *Highlights* magazine for kids. A girl about our age is sitting on one of the chairs.

"Doctor will be with you soon," the nurse says to Maggie, and leaves the room.

We sit down.

I look over at the girl, who is staring at us with hostility. Her hair is cut in a mullet, short in the front and really long in the back, and she's wearing black eyeliner that swoops up into little wings, like her eyes might fly away from her face. She looks tough and miserable and kind of mean. Actually, she looks like she'd like to beat us up. I try to smile at her, but she glares at me instead and pointedly picks up *Highlights* magazine. Then she puts it down and says, "What are *you* looking at?"

I can't handle another girl fight, so I reply as sweetly as possible, "Nothing."

"Yeah?" she says. "You'd better be looking at nothing."

"I'm looking at nothing. I swear."

And at last, before this can go any further, the door opens and the nurse comes out, escorting another teenage girl by the shoulders. The girl looks quite a bit like her friend, except that she's crying quietly and wiping the tears from her cheeks with the back of her hands.

"You're okay, dear," the nurse says with surprising kindness. "Doctor says it all went fine. No aspirin for the next three days. And no sex for at least two weeks." The girl nods, weeping. Her friend jumps up and puts her hands on the side of the crying girl's face. "C'mon, Sal. It's okay. You're gonna be okay." And with one final scowl in our direction, she leads the girl away.

The nurse shakes her head and looks at Maggie. "Doctor will see you now."

"Maggie," I whisper. "You don't have to do this. We can go someplace else—"

But Maggie stands, her face resolute. "I *have* to do it."

"That's right, dear," the nurse says. "Much better to take precautions. I wish all you girls would take precautions."

And for some reason, she looks directly at me.

Whoa, lady. Take it easy. I'm still a virgin.

But I may not be for much longer. Maybe I should get some pills too. Just in case.

Ten minutes pass and Maggie comes back out, smiling and looking like a weight has been lifted from her shoulders. She thanks the nurse profusely. In fact, she thanks her so much I have to remind her that we ought to get back to school. Outside, she says, "It was so easy. I didn't even have to take off my clothes. He just asked me about the last time I got my period."

"That's great," I say, getting in the car. I can't get the image of the crying girl out of my head. Was she crying because she was sad or relieved? Or just scared? Either way, it was pretty awful. I open the window a crack and light up a cigarette. "Mags," I say. "How did you hear about that place? Really?"

"Peter told me about it."

"How did he know?"

"Donna LaDonna told him," she whispers.

I nod, blowing smoke into the cold air. I am so not ready for all this.

CHAPTER FOURTEEN

Hang in There

"Missy!" I say, knocking on the bathroom door. "Missy, I need to get in there."

Silence. "I'm busy," she finally says.

"Doing what?"

"None of your business."

"Missy, please. Sebastian's going to be here in thirty minutes."

"So? He can wait."

No, he can't, I think. Or rather, I can't. I can't wait to get out of the house. I can't wait to get out of *here*.

I've been telling myself this all week. The "getting out of here" part is unspecified, though. Maybe I simply want to get away from my life.

For the past two weeks, ever since the library incident, the two Jens have been stalking me. They poke their heads into swim practice and make mooing noises when I dive.

They've followed me to the mall, the supermarket, and even the drugstore, where they had the exciting experience of watching me buy tampons. And yesterday, I found a card in my locker. On the front was a cartoon drawing of a basset hound with a thermometer in his mouth and a hot-water bottle on his head. Inside, someone had written "Don't" before "Get Well Soon," followed by, "Wish you were dead."

"Donna would never do something like that," Peter protested.

Maggie, The Mouse, and I glared at him.

Peter held up his hands. "You wanted my opinion, that's my opinion."

"Who else would do it?" Maggie asked. "She's the one who has the biggest reason."

"Not necessarily," Peter said. "Look, Carrie. I don't want to hurt your feelings, but I can promise you, Donna LaDonna doesn't even know who you are."

"She does now," The Mouse countered.

Maggie was aghast. "Why wouldn't she know Carrie?"

"I'm not saying she doesn't literally know who Carrie Bradshaw is. But Carrie Bradshaw is definitely not high on her list of concerns."

"Thanks a lot," I said to Peter. I was really beginning to hate him.

And then I was furious at Maggie for going out with him. And then I was furious at The Mouse for being friends with him. And now I'm furious at my sister Missy for hogging the bathroom.

"I'm coming in," I say threateningly. I try the door. It's unlocked. Inside, Missy is standing in the tub with Nair on her legs.

"Do you mind?" she says, yanking the shower curtain closed.

"Do *you* mind?" I ask, going to the mirror. "You've been in here for twenty minutes. I need to get ready."

"What is *wrong* with you?"

"Nothing," I snarl.

"You'd better get out of that mood or Sebastian isn't going to want to be with you either."

I storm out of the bathroom. Back in my room, I pick up *The Consensus*, open it to the title page, and glare at Mary Gordon Howard's tiny signature. It's like the writing of a witch. I kick the book under the bed. I lie down and put my hands over my face.

I wouldn't have even remembered the damn book and that damn Mary Gordon Howard if I hadn't spent the last hour searching for my special handbag—the one from France that my mother left me. She felt guilty buying it because it was so expensive. Even though she paid for it with her own money and she always said every woman ought to have one really good handbag and one really good pair of shoes.

The handbag is one of my most treasured possessions. I treat it like a jewel, only taking it out on special occasions, and always returning it to its cloth pouch and then to its original box. I keep the box in the back of my closet. Except this time, when I went to get it out, it wasn't there. Instead, I found *The Consensus*, which I'd also hidden in the back of my closet. The last time I used the bag was six months ago, when Lali and I took a trip to Boston. She kept eyeing the bag and asking if she could borrow it sometime, and I said "yes," even though the thought of Lali with my mother's bag gave me the creeps. You would think it would have given her the creeps too—enough for her to know better than to ask. After the trip, I specifically remember putting the bag away properly, because I decided I wouldn't use it again until I went to New York. But then Sebastian suggested dinner at this fancy French restaurant in Hartford called The Brownstone, and if that isn't a special occasion, I don't know what is.

And now the bag is missing. My whole world is falling apart.

Dorrit, I think suddenly. She's gone from pilfering earrings to stealing my handbag.

I tear into her room.

Dorrit's been awfully quiet this week. She hasn't been causing her usual amount of turmoil, which is in itself suspicious. Now she's lying on her bed, talking on the phone. On the wall above her is a poster of a cat, swinging from a tree branch. *Hang in there,* reads the caption.

Dorrit puts her hand over the receiver. "Yes?"

"Have you seen my bag?"

She looks away, which makes me guess she is, indeed, guilty. "What handbag? Your leather saddlebag? I think I saw it in the kitchen."

"Mom's bag."

"*I* haven't seen it," she says, with exaggerated innocence. "Don't you keep it locked up in your closet?"

"It's not there."

Dorrit shrugs and tries to go back to her conversation.

"Mind if I search your room?" I ask casually.

"Go ahead," she says. She's crafty. If she were guilty, she'd say, yes, she did mind.

I search her closets, her drawers, and under the bed. Nothing. "See?" Dorrit says in an I-told-you-so tone. But in her second of triumph, her eyes go to the giant stuffed panda bear seated on the rocking chair in the corner of her room. The panda bear that I supposedly gave her as a present when she was born.

"Oh no, Dorrit," I say, shaking my head. "Not Mr. Panda."

"Don't touch him!" she screams, leaping off the bed and dropping the phone. I grab Mr. Panda and run out.

Dorrit follows me. Mr. Panda is suspiciously heavy, I note, as I bear him away to my room.

"Leave him alone," Dorrit demands.

"Why?" I ask. "Has Mr. Panda been up to something naughty?"

"No!"

"I think he has." I feel around the back of the stuffed bear and find a large opening that's been carefully fastened closed with safety pins.

"What's going on?" Missy comes running in, her legs dripping with foam.

"This," I say, unfastening the safety pins.

"Carrie, *don't*," Dorrit cries as I slip my hand into the opening. The first thing I pull out is a silver bracelet I haven't seen for months. The bracelet is followed by a small pipe, the type used to smoke marijuana. "It's not mine. I swear. It's my friend Cheryl's," Dorrit insists. "She asked me to hide it for her."

"Uh-huh," I say, handing Missy the pipe. And then my hand closes around the soft nubby surface of my mother's bag. "Aha!" I exclaim, yanking it out. I place it on the bed, where the three of us stare at it aghast.

It's ruined. The entire front side with the chic little flap where my mother used to keep her checkbook and credit cards is speckled with what looks like pink paint. Which just happens to be exactly the same color as the nail polish on Dorrit's hands.

I'm too shocked to speak.

"Dorrit, how could you?" Missy screams. "That was Mom's bag. Why did you have to ruin Mom's bag? Couldn't you ruin your own bag for a change?"

"Why does Carrie have to have everything of Mom's?" Dorrit screams back.

"I don't," I say, surprising myself with how calm and reasonable I sound.

"Mom left that bag to Carrie. Because she's the oldest," Missy says.

"No she didn't," Dorrit wails. "She left it to her because she liked her the best."

"Dorrit, that isn't true—"

"Yes it is. Mom wanted Carrie to be just like her. Except that now Mom is dead and Carrie is *still alive.*" It's the kind of scream that makes your throat hurt.

Dorrit runs out of the room. And suddenly, I burst into tears.

I'm not a good crier. Some women can supposedly cry prettily, like the girls in *Gone with the Wind*. But I've never seen it in real life. When I cry, my face swells up and my nose runs and I can't breathe.

"What would Mom say?" I ask Missy between sobs.

"Well, I guess she can't say anything *now*," Missy says.

Ha. Gallows humor. I don't know what we'd do without it.

"I mean, yeah," I giggle, between hiccups. "It's only a handbag, right? It's not like it's a person or anything."

"I think we should paint Mr. Panda pink," Missy says. "Teach Dorrit a lesson. She left a bottle of pink polish open under the sink. I almost knocked it over when I went to get the Nair."

I race into the bathroom.

"What are you doing?" Missy squeals as I start my handiwork. When I'm finished, I hold up the bag for inspection.

"It's cool," Missy says, nodding appreciatively.

I turn it over, pleased. It really is kind of cool. "If it's deliberate," I tell her, with a sudden realization, "it's fashion."

"Ohmigod. I *love* your bag," the hostess gushes. She's wearing a black Lycra dress and the top of her hair is teased into spiky meringue waves. "I've never seen anything like it. Is that your name on it? Carrie?"

I nod.

"My name's Eileen," she says. "I'd love to have a bag like that with my name on it."

She picks up two menus and holds them aloft as she leads us to a table for two in front of the fireplace. "Most romantic table in the house," she whispers as she hands over the menus. "Have fun, kids."

"Oh, we will," Sebastian says, unfolding his napkin with a snap.

I hold up the bag. "You like?"

"It's a purse, Carrie," he says.

"This, Sebastian, is no mere *purse*. And you shouldn't call a handbag a purse. A purse was what people used to carry coins in the sixteen hundreds. They used to hide their purse inside their clothes to foil robbers. A bag, on the other hand, is meant to be seen. And this isn't any old bag. It was my mother's . . ." I trail off. He's clearly not interested in the provenance of my bag. Hmph. Men, I think, opening my menu.

"I like who's carrying it, though," he says.

"Thank you." I'm still a little annoyed with him.

"What would you like?"

I guess we're supposed to be all formal, now that we're at a fancy restaurant.

"Haven't decided."

"Waiter?" he says. "Can we have two martinis please? With olives instead of a twist." He leans toward me. "They have the best martinis here."

"I'd like a Singapore Sling."

"Carrie," he says. "You can't have a Singapore Sling."

"Why not?"

"Because it's a martini place. And a Singapore Sling is juvenile." He glances at me over the top of the menu. "And speaking of juvenile, what's wrong with you tonight?"

"Nothing."

"Good. Then try to act normal."

I open my menu and frown.

"The lamb chops are excellent. And so is the French onion soup. It was my favorite thing to eat in France." He looks up and smiles. "Just trying to be helpful."

"Thanks," I say, with slight sarcasm. I immediately apologize. "Sorry." What is wrong with me? Why am I in such a bad mood? I'm never in a bad mood with Sebastian.

"So," he says, taking my hand. "How was *your* week?"

"Terrible," I say as the waiter arrives with our martinis.

"Cheers," he says. "To terrible weeks."

I take a sip of my drink and carefully put it down. "Honestly, Sebastian. This week was pretty bad."

"Because of me?"

"No. Not because of you. I mean, not directly. It's just that Donna LaDonna hates me—"

"Carrie," he says. "If you can't handle the controversy, you shouldn't see me."

"I *can* handle it—"

"Well then."

"Is there always controversy? When you're seeing someone?"

He leans back and gives me a smug look. "Usually."

Aha. Sebastian is a guy who loves drama. But I love drama too. So maybe we're perfect for each other. Must discuss this aspect with The Mouse, I think, making a mental note.

"So are the French onion soup and lamb chops good for you?" he asks as he gives our order to the waiter.

"Perfect," I say, smiling at him over the rim of my martini.

And there's the problem: I don't want French onion soup. I've had onions and cheese my whole life. I wanted to try something exotic and sophisticated, like escargot. And now it's too late. Why do I always do what Sebastian wants?

As I lift my glass, a woman with coiffed red hair, a red dress, and bare legs knocks into me, spilling half of my drink. "I'm sorry, sweetheart," she says, slurring her words. She steps back, taking in what appears to be a romantic scene between me and Sebastian. "Young love," she twitters, staggering away as I mop up the mess with my napkin.

"What was *that* about?"

"Some middle-aged drunk." Sebastian shrugs.

"She can't help being middle-aged, you know."

"Yeah. But there's nothing worse than a woman over a certain age who's had too much to drink."

"Where do you pick up these rules?"

"Come on, Carrie. Everyone knows that women are lousy drunks."

"And men are better?"

"Why are we having this discussion?"

"I guess you think women are lousy drivers and scientists, too."

"There are exceptions. Your friend, The Mouse."

Excuse me?

Our onion soup arrives, the top bubbling with melted cheese. "Be careful," he says. "It's hot."

I sigh, blowing on a spoonful of gooey cheese. "I still want to go to France someday."

"I'll take you there," he says, just like that, cool as can be. "Maybe we could go this summer."

He leans forward, suddenly aroused by the thought. "We'll start in Paris. Then we'll take the train to Bordeaux. That's wine country. Then we'll swing down to the South of France. Cannes, Saint-Tropez . . ."

I picture the Eiffel Tower. A stucco villa on a hill. Speedboats. Bikinis. Sebastian's eyes, serious, soulful, staring into mine. "I love you, Carrie," he whispers in my fantasy. "Will you marry me?"

I was still hoping to go to New York this summer, but if

Sebastian wants to take me to France, I'm there.

"Hello?"

"Huh?" I look up and see a blond woman wearing a headband and a gummy smile.

"I had to ask. Where did you get that bag?"

"Do you mind?" Sebastian says pointedly, to the blonde. He plucks the bag off the table and puts it on the floor.

The woman walks away as Sebastian orders another round of drinks. But the mood is broken, and when our lamb chops come, we eat in silence.

"Hey," I say. "We're like an old married couple."

"How so?" he asks in a flat voice.

"You know. Eating dinner and not talking. That's my worst fear. It makes me sad every time I see one of those couples at a restaurant, barely looking at each other. I mean, why bother going out, right? If you have nothing to say, why not stay home?"

"Maybe the food's better at a restaurant."

"That's funny." I put down my fork, carefully wipe my mouth, and look around the room. "Sebastian, what's wrong?"

"What's wrong with you?"

"Nothing."

"Well then," he says.

"Something is wrong."

"I'm eating, okay? Can't I eat my lamb chops without you nagging me the whole time?"

I shrink with embarrassment. I'm two inches tall. I widen

my eyes and force myself not to blink. I refuse to cry. But wow, that hurt. "Sure," I say casually.

Are we having a fight? How on earth did this happen?

I pick at my lamb for a bit; then I put down my knife and fork. "I give up."

"You don't like the lamb."

"No. I love the lamb. But you're mad at me about something."

"I'm not mad."

"You sure seem mad to me."

Now he puts down his utensils. "Why do girls always do that? They always ask 'What's wrong?' Maybe nothing's wrong. Maybe a guy is just trying to eat."

"You're right," I say quietly, standing up.

For a second, he looks anxious. "Where are you going?"

"Ladies' room."

I use the toilet, wash my hands, and peer closely at my face in the mirror. Why am I being like this? Maybe there is something wrong with me.

And suddenly, I realize I'm scared.

If something happened and I lost Sebastian, I'd die. If he changed his mind and went back to Donna LaDonna, I'd double die.

On top of that, tomorrow night I have that date with George. I wanted to get out of it but my father wouldn't let me. "It would be rude," he said.

"But I don't like him," I replied, as sulky as a child.

"He's a very nice guy, and there's no reason to be unkind."

"It would be unkind to lead him on."

"Carrie," my father said, and sighed. "I want you to be careful with Sebastian."

"What's wrong with Sebastian?"

"You're spending a lot of time with him. And a father has instincts about these things. About other men."

Then I was angry at my father too. But I didn't have the guts to cancel on George, either.

What if Sebastian finds out about the date with George and breaks up with me?

I'll kill my father. I really will.

Why don't I have any control over my life?

I'm about to reach for my bag, when I remember I don't have it. It's under the table where Sebastian hid it. I take a deep breath. I order myself to buck up, put on a smiley face, get back out there, and act like everything is fine.

When I return, our plates have been cleared. "So," I begin with false cheeriness.

"Do you want dessert?" Sebastian asks.

"Do you?"

"I asked you first. Can you please make a decision?"

"Sure. Let's have dessert." Why is this so excruciating? Chinese fingernail torture sounds more appealing.

"Two cheesecakes," he says to the waitress, ordering for me again.

"Sebastian—"

"Yes?" He looks like thunder.

"Are you still angry?"

"Look, Carrie. I spend all this time planning a date and taking you out to a really nice restaurant and all you do is pick on me."

"Huh?" I say, caught off guard.

"I feel like I can't do anything right."

For a second, I sit frozen in horror. What am I doing?

He's right, of course. I'm the one who's being a jerk, and for what? Am I so scared of losing him that I'm trying to push him away before he can break up with me?

He said he wanted to take me to France, for Christ's sake. What more do I want?

"Sebastian?" I ask in a tiny voice.

"Yes?"

"I'm sorry."

"It's okay." He pats my hand. "Everyone makes mistakes."

I nod, sinking further into my chair, but Sebastian's mood is suddenly restored. He pulls my chair around next to his, and, in full view of the entire restaurant, kisses me.

"I've been wanting to do this all night," he whispers.

"Me too," I murmur. Or at least, I thought I did. But after a few seconds, I break away. I'm still a bit angry and confused. But I take another sip of my martini and push the angry feelings down, right to the bottom of my soles, where hopefully, they won't cause any more trouble.

CHAPTER FIFTEEN

Little Criminals

"Wow," George says.

"Wow what?" I ask, coming into the kitchen. George and my father are comparing notes on Brown like they're old pals.

"That bag," George says. "I love it."

"You do?" Hmph. After my roller-coaster date with Sebastian, which ended with us making out in his car in my driveway until my father switched the outdoor lights on and off, the last person I want to see is George.

"I was thinking," I say to George now. "Instead of driving all the way to this inn, why don't we go to The Brownstone? It's closer, and the food's really good." I'm being cruel, taking George to the same restaurant as Sebastian. But love has made me evil.

George, of course, has no idea. He's annoyingly agreeable. "Wherever you want to go is fine with me."

"Have fun," my father says hopefully.

We get into the car, and George leans over for a kiss. I turn my head and his kiss lands on the side of my mouth. "How have you been?" he asks.

"Crazy." I'm about to tell him all about my wild two weeks with Sebastian and how I'm being stalked by Donna LaDonna and the two Jens, and the nasty card in my locker, but I stop myself. George doesn't need to know about Sebastian yet. Instead I say, "I had to take a friend of mine to this doctor to get birth control pills, and there was a girl who'd obviously had an abortion and—"

He nods, keeping his eyes on the highway. "Growing up in the city, I always used to wonder what people did in small towns. But I guess people manage to get into trouble, no matter where they live."

"Ha. Have you ever read *Peyton Place*?"

"I mostly read biographies. When I'm not reading for class."

I nod. We've only been together for ten minutes, but already it's so awkward I can't imagine how I'll get through the evening. "Is that what they call it?" I ask tentatively. "'The city?' Not 'New York' or 'Manhattan'?"

"Yeah," he says, with a little laugh. "I know it sounds arrogant. Like New York is the only city on earth. But New Yorkers are a little arrogant. And they do think Manhattan is the center of the universe. Most New Yorkers couldn't imagine living anywhere else." He glances over at me. "Does that sound terrible? Do I sound like an asshole?"

"Not at all. I wish I lived in Manhattan." I want to say "the city," but I'm afraid I'll sound affected.

"Have you ever been?" he asks.

"Not really. Once or twice when I was little. We went on a school trip to the planetarium and looked at stars."

"I practically grew up in the planetarium. And the Museum of Natural History. I used to know everything about dinosaurs. And I loved the Central Park Zoo. My family's house is on Fifth Avenue, and when I was a kid, I'd hear the lions roaring at night. Pretty cool, huh?"

"Very cool," I say, hugging myself. I'm strangely cold and jittery. I have a sudden premonition: I'm going to live in Manhattan. I'm going to hear the lions roaring in Central Park. I don't know how I'm going to get there, but I will.

"Your family lives in a house?" I ask stupidly. "I thought everyone in New York lived in apartments."

"It *is* an apartment," George says. "A classic eight, as a matter of fact. And there are actual houses—townhouses and brownstones. But everyone in the city calls their apartment a house. Don't ask me why. Another affectation, I suppose." He gives me a sidelong glance. "You should visit me. My mother spends the entire summer at her house in Southampton, so the apartment is practically empty. It has four bedrooms," he adds quickly so I don't get the wrong idea.

"Sure. That would be great." And if I could get into that damn writing program, it would be even better.

Unless I go to France with Sebastian instead.

"Hey," he says. "I've missed you, you know?"

"You shouldn't miss me, George," I say with coy irritation.

"You don't even know me."

"I know you enough to miss you. To think about you, anyway. Is that all right?"

I should tell him I already have a boyfriend—but it's too soon. I hardly even know him. I smile and say nothing.

"Carrie!" Eileen, the hostess at The Brownstone, greets me like I'm an old friend, looks George up and down, and nods approvingly.

George is amused. "They know you here?" he asks, taking my arm as Eileen leads us to a table.

I nod mysteriously.

"What's good here?" he asks, picking up the menu.

"The martinis." I smile. "And the French onion soup is pretty good. And the lamb chops."

George grins. "Yes to the martini and no to the French onion soup. It's one of those dishes Americans think is French, but no self-respecting French person would ever order."

I frown, wondering once again how I'm going to make it through this dinner. George orders the escargot and the cassoulet, which is what I wanted to order last night but didn't, because Sebastian wouldn't let me.

"I want to know all about you," George says, taking my hand from across the table.

I slip it away, hiding my resistance by acting like I simply have to have another sip of my martini. How does a person explain everything about themselves anyway? "What do you want to know?"

"For starters, can I expect to see you at Brown next fall?"

I lower my eyes. "My father wants me to go. But I've always wanted to live in Manhattan." And before I know it, I'm telling him all about my dream of becoming a writer and how I tried to get into the summer writing program and was rejected.

He doesn't find this shocking or embarrassing. "I've known a few writers in my life," he says slyly. "Rejection is part of the process. At least at first. Plenty of writers don't even get published until they've written two or three books."

"Really?" I feel a soaring hope.

"Oh, sure," he says with authority. "Publishing is full of stories about the manuscript that got rejected by twenty publishers before someone took a chance on it and turned it into a huge bestseller."

Just like me, I think. I'm masquerading as a regular girl, but somewhere inside me there's a star, waiting for someone to give me a chance.

"Hey," he says. "If you want, I'd be happy to read some of your stuff. Maybe I can help you."

"Would you?" I ask, astonished. No one's ever offered to help me before. No one's even encouraged me. I take in George's gentle brown sloping eyes. He's so nice. And damn it, I do want to get into that writing program. I want to live in "the city." And I want to visit George and hear the lions roaring in Central Park.

I suddenly want my future to begin.

"Wouldn't it be cool if you were a writer and I was an editor at *The New York Times*?"

Yes! I want to shout. There's only one problem. I have a boyfriend. I can't be a louse. I have to let George know now. Otherwise, it isn't fair.

"George. I have to tell you something—"

I'm about to spill my secret, when Eileen approaches the table with a self-important look on her face. "Carrie?" she says. "You have a phone call."

"I do?" I squeak, looking from George to Eileen. "Who would be calling me?"

"You'd better find out." George stands as I get up from the table.

"Hello?" I say into the phone. I have a wild thought that it's Sebastian. He's tracked me down, discovered I'm on a date with another guy, and he's furious. Instead, it's Missy.

"Carrie?" she asks in a terrified voice that immediately makes me imagine my father or Dorrit has been killed in an accident. "You'd better come home right away."

My knees nearly buckle beneath me. "What happened?" I ask in a hoarse whisper.

"It's Dorrit. She's at the police station." Missy pauses before delivering the final blow. "She's been *arrested*."

"I don't know about you," says a strange woman clutching an old fur coat over what appears to be a pair of silk pajamas, "but I'm finished. Through. Ready to wash my hands of her."

My father, who is sitting next to her on a molded plastic chair, nods bleakly.

"I've been doing this for too long," the woman continues, blinking rapidly. "Four boys, and I had to keep trying for a girl. Then I got her. Now I have to say I wish I didn't. No matter what anyone says, girls are more trouble than boys. Do you have any sons, Mr., er—"

"Bradshaw," my father says sharply. "And no, I don't have any sons, just three daughters."

The woman nods and pats my father on the knee. "You poor man," she says. This, apparently, is the mother of Dorrit's notorious pot-smoking friend, Cheryl.

"Really," my father says, shifting in his seat to get away from her. His glasses slide to the tip of his nose. "In general," he says, launching into one of his theories on child rearing, "a preference for children of one sex over the other, especially when it's so baldly expressed by the parent, often results in a *lack* in the child, an inherent *lack*—"

"Dad!" I say, skittering across the floor to rescue him.

He pushes his glasses up his nose, stands, and opens his arms. "Carrie!"

"Mr. Bradshaw," George says.

"George."

"George?" Cheryl's mother stands, batting her eyes like butterfly wings. "I'm Connie."

"Ah." George nods, as if somehow this makes sense. Connie is now clinging to George's arm. "I'm Cheryl's mother. And really, she's not a bad girl—"

"I'm sure she isn't," George says kindly.

Oh jeez. Is Cheryl's mother flirting with George now?

I motion my father aside. I keep picturing the small marijuana pipe I found in Mr. Panda. "Was it—" I can't bring myself to say the word "drugs" aloud.

"Gum," my father says wearily.

"Gum? She was arrested for stealing gum?"

"Apparently it's her third offense. She was caught shoplifting twice before, but the police let her go. This time, she wasn't so lucky."

"Mr. Bradshaw? I'm Chip Marone, the arresting officer," says a shiny-faced young man in a uniform.

Marone—the cop from the barn.

"Can I see my daughter, please?"

"We have to fingerprint her. And take a mug shot."

"For stealing *gum*?" I blurt out. I can't help myself.

My father blanches. "She's going to have a record? My thirteen-year-old daughter is going to have a record like a common criminal?"

"Those are the rules," Marone says.

I nudge my father. "Excuse me. But we're really good friends with the Kandesies—"

"It's a small town," Marone says, rubbing his cheeks. "A lot of people know the Kandesies—"

"But Lali is like one of the family. And we've known them forever. Right, Dad?"

"Now, look here, Carrie," my father says. "You can't go asking people to bend the rules. It isn't right."

"But—"

"Maybe we could call them. The Kandesies," George says. "Just to make sure."

"I can assure you. My little Cheryl has never been in trouble before," Connie says, squeezing George's arm for support as she blinks at Marone.

Marone has clearly had enough. "I'll see what I can do," he mutters, and picks up the phone behind the desk. "Right," he says into the receiver. "Okay. No problem." He hangs up the phone and glowers.

"Community service." Dorrit gasps.

"You'll be lucky to get off that easily," says my father.

George, my father, Dorrit, and I are gathered in the den, discussing the situation. Marone agreed to release Dorrit and Cheryl with the caveat that they have to see the judge on Wednesday, who will probably sentence them to community service to pay for their crimes.

"I hope you like picking up trash," George says playfully, poking Dorrit in the ribs. She giggles. The two are sitting on the couch. My father told Dorrit she should go to bed, but she refused.

"Have you ever been arrested?" Dorrit asks George.

"Dorrit!"

"What?" she says, staring at me blankly.

"As a matter of fact I have. But my crime was much worse

than yours. I jumped a subway turnstile and ran right into a cop."

Dorrit gazes up at George, her eyes filled with admiration. "What happened then?"

"He called my father. And boy, was my dad pissed. I had to spend every afternoon in his office, rearranging his business books in alphabetical order and filing all his bank statements."

"Really?" Dorrit's eyes widen in awe.

"So the moral of the story is, always pay the fare."

"You hear that, Dorrit?" my father says. He stands, but his shoulders are stooped and he suddenly looks exhausted. "I'm going to bed. You too, Dorrit."

"But—"

"Now," he says quietly.

Dorrit gives George one last, longing look and runs upstairs.

"Good night, kids," my father says.

I absentmindedly smooth my skirt. "Sorry about that. My father, Dorrit—"

"It's okay," George says, taking my hand again. "I understand. No family is perfect. Including mine."

"Really?" I try to maneuver my hand out from under his, but I can't. I attempt to change the subject instead.

"Dorrit seemed to like you."

"I'm good with kids," he says, leaning in for a kiss. "Always have been."

"George." I twist my head away. "I'm—uh—really exhausted—"

He sighs. "I get it. Time to go home. But I'll see you again soon, right?"

"Sure."

He pulls me to my feet and wraps his arms around my waist. I bury my face in his chest in an attempt to avoid what's inevitably coming next.

"Carrie?" He strokes my hair.

It feels nice, but I can't let this go any further. "I'm so tired," I moan.

"Okay." He steps back, lifts my head, and brushes my lips with his. "I'll call you tomorrow."

CHAPTER SIXTEEN

How Far Will You Go?

"What's the holdup?" Sebastian asks.

"Have to fix my makeup," I say.

He runs his hand up my arm and tries to kiss me. "You don't need makeup."

"Stop," I hiss. "Not in the house."

"You don't have a problem doing this in my house."

"You don't have two younger sisters. One of whom—"

"I know. Was arrested for shoplifting gum," he says with disdain. "Which ranks pretty low in the annals of criminal activity. It's right down there with lighting firecrackers in neighbors' mailboxes."

"And thus began your own life of crime," I say, gently closing the bathroom door in his face.

He knocks.

"Yeeeees?"

"Hurry up."

"Hurrying," I say. "Hurrying and scurrying." Which is not true. I'm stalling.

I'm waiting for George to call. Two weeks have passed since Dorrit's arrest, but true to form, George called me the next day and the day after that, and then I asked him if he really meant it when he said he would read one of my stories and he said yes. So I sent it to him and now I haven't heard from him for five days, except for yesterday when he left a message with Dorrit saying he'd call me today between six and seven. Damn him. If he'd called at six, Sebastian wouldn't be here, hovering. It's nearly seven. Sebastian will be furious if I get a phone call just before we're about to go.

I unscrew a tube of mascara and lean forward, applying the wand to my lashes. It's the second coat, and my lashes twist into jagged little spikes. I'm about to apply a third, when the phone rings.

"Phone!" Missy shouts.

"Phone!" Dorrit yells.

"Phone!" I scream, bursting out of the bathroom like a lit firecracker.

"Huh?" Sebastian says, sticking his head out my bedroom door.

"Could be Dorrit's probation officer."

"Dorrit has a probation officer? For stealing gum?" Sebastian says, but I can't stop to explain.

I grab the phone in my father's room just before Dorrit reaches it. "Hello?"

"Carrie? George here."

"Oh, hi," I say breathlessly, closing the door. *What did you think of my story? I need to know. Now.*

"How are you?" George asks. "How's Dorrit?"

"She's fine." *Did you read it? Did you hate it? If you hated it I'm going to kill myself.*

"Is she doing her community service?"

"Yes, George." The agony is killing me.

"What did they assign her to?"

Who cares? "Picking up litter on the side of the road."

"Ah. The old litter routine. Works every time."

"George." I hesitate. "Did you read my story?"

"Yes, Carrie. As a matter of fact, I did."

"And?"

A long silence during which I contemplate the practicalities of slitting my wrists with a safety razor.

"You're definitely a writer."

I am? I'm a writer? I imagine running around the room, jumping up and down and shouting, "I'm a writer, I'm a writer!"

"And you have talent."

"Ah." I fall back onto the bed in ecstasy.

"But—"

I sit right up again, clutching the phone in terror.

"Well, really, Carrie. This story about a girl who lives in a trailer park in Key West, Florida, and works in a Dairy Queen . . . Have you ever been to Key West?"

"For your information, I have. Several times," I say primly.

"Did you live in a trailer? Did you work at the Dairy Queen?"

"No. But why can't I pretend I did?"

"You've got plenty of imagination," George says. "But I know a thing or two about these writing programs. They're looking for something that smacks of personal experience and authenticity."

"I don't get it," I mutter.

"Do you know how many stories they're sent about a kid who dies? It doesn't ring true. You need to write what you know."

"But I don't know anything!"

"Sure you do. And if you can't think of something, find it."

My joy dissipates like a morning mist.

"Carrie?" Sebastian knocks on the door.

"Can I call you tomorrow?" I ask quickly, cupping my hand around the receiver. "I have to go to this party for the swim team."

"I'll call you. We'll make a plan to get together, okay?"

"Sure." I put down the phone and hang my head in despair.

My career as a writer is over. Finished before it's even begun.

"Carrie," Sebastian's voice, louder and more annoyed, comes from the other side of the door.

"Ready," I say, opening it.

"Who was that?"

"Someone from Brown."

"Are you going to go there?"

"I have to get in. Officially. But yeah. I guess I probably will."

I feel like I'm being suffocated by thick green slime.

"What are you going to do about college?" I ask suddenly. Strange how I haven't asked him about this before.

"I'm going to take a year off," he says. "Last night, I was looking at the essay portion of my application to Amherst when it hit me. I don't want to do this. I don't want to be part of the system. That probably shocks you, doesn't it?"

"No. It's your life."

"Yeah, but how are you going to feel about having a deadbeat boyfriend?"

"You're not a deadbeat. You're smart. Really smart."

"I'm a regular genius," he says. And after another second: "Do we have to go to this party?"

"Yes," I insist. "Lali has it every year. If we don't show up, she'll be really hurt."

"You're the boss," he says. I follow him out of the house, wishing we didn't have to go to the party, either. *Write what you know.* That was the best George could come up with? A cliché? Damn him. Damn everything. Why is it all so goddamned hard?

"If it wasn't difficult, everyone would do it," Peter says, holding court to a small group of kids who are clustered around the couch. Peter has just been accepted to Harvard, early decision, and everyone is impressed. "Bioengineering is the hope of the future," he continues as I drift away and find Maggie sitting in the corner with The Mouse.

The Mouse looks like she's being held hostage. "Honestly, Maggie," she says, "this is great for Peter. It makes us all look good if someone from Castlebury gets into Harvard."

"It doesn't have anything to do with us," Maggie counters.

"I can't believe Peter got into Harvard," Lali says, pausing on her way to the kitchen. "Isn't it great?"

"No," Maggie says firmly. Everyone is thrilled for Peter—everyone, it seems, but Maggie.

I understand her despair. Maggie is one of the millions of kids out there who have no idea what they want to do with their lives—like Sebastian, I suppose, and Lali. When someone close to you figures it out, it pulls you up short in front of your own wall of indecision.

"Harvard is only an hour and a half away," I say soothingly, trying to distract Maggie from what's really bothering her.

"It doesn't matter how far it is," she says glumly. "Harvard is not any old college. If you go to Harvard, you become someone who went to Harvard. For the rest of your life, it's what people say about you: *He* went to Harvard—"

Maybe it's because I'll never go to Harvard and I'm jealous, but I hate all this elitist talk. Who you are shouldn't be defined by where you go to college. It probably is, though.

"And if Peter is always going to be the guy who went to Harvard," Maggie continues, "I'm always going to be the girl who *didn't*."

The Mouse and I exchange glances. "If you don't mind, I'm going to get a beer," The Mouse says.

"What does she care?" Maggie says, looking after her. "She's going to Yale. She'll be the girl who went to Yale. Sometimes I think Peter and The Mouse should date. They'd be perfect for each other." There's an unexpected bitterness in her voice.

"The Mouse is dating someone," I say gently. "Remember?"

"Right," she says. "Some guy who doesn't live around here." She waves her arm in dismissal. She's drunk, I realize.

"Let's go for a walk."

"It's cold outside," she protests.

"It's good for us."

On our way out, we pass Sebastian and Lali in the kitchen. Lali has put Sebastian to work, placing mini hot dogs from the oven onto a plate. "We'll be right back," I call out.

"Sure." Lali barely glances in our direction. She says something to Sebastian and he laughs.

For a second I feel uneasy. Then I try to look on the bright side. At least my boyfriend and my best friend are getting along.

When we get outside, Maggie grabs my arm and whispers, "How far would you go to get what you wanted?"

"Huh?" I say. It's freezing. Our breath envelops us like summer clouds.

"What if you really, really, really wanted something and

you didn't know how to get it—or you did know how to get it but you weren't sure you should do it. How far would you go?"

For a second, I wonder if she's talking about Lali and Sebastian. Then I realize she's talking about Peter.

"Let's go into the barn," I suggest. "It's warmer."

The Kandesies keep a few cows, mostly for show, in an old barn behind the house. Above the cows is a hayloft, where Lali and I have retreated hundreds of times to spill our most important secrets. The loft is fragrant and warm, due to the heat from the cows below. I perch on a hay bale. "Maggie, what's wrong?" I say, wondering how many times I've asked her this question in the last three months. It's becoming disturbingly repetitive.

She takes out a pack of cigarettes.

"Don't." I stop her. "You can't smoke up here. You could start a fire."

"Let's go outside, then."

"It's cold. And you can't grab a cigarette every time you feel uncomfortable, Mags. It's becoming a crutch."

"So?" Maggie looks evil.

"What did you mean before—about how far you would go?" I ask. "You're not thinking about Peter, are you? You're not thinking about . . . are you taking the birth control pills?"

"Of course." She looks away. "When I remember."

"Mags." I leap toward her. "Are you insane?"

"No. I don't think so."

I slide in next to her and fall back on a bale of hay, gathering my arguments. I stare up at the ceiling, which nature has decorated with swags of cobwebs, like a Halloween extravaganza. Nature and instinct versus morality and logic. That's how my father would put this dilemma.

"Mags," I begin. "I know you're worried about losing him. But what you're thinking about doing is not the way to keep him."

"Why not?" she asks stubbornly.

"Because it's wrong. You don't want to be the girl who forced a guy to be with her by getting pregnant."

"Women do it all the time."

"That doesn't make it right."

"My mother did it," she says. "No one's supposed to know. But I counted backward, and my oldest sister was born six months after my parents were married."

"That was years ago. They didn't even have the pill back then."

"Maybe it would be better if they didn't now."

"Maggie, what are you saying? You don't want to have a baby at eighteen. Babies are a huge pain. All they do is eat and poop. You want to be changing diapers while everyone you know is out having fun? And what about Peter? It could ruin his life. That doesn't seem very nice, does it?"

"I don't care," she says. And then she starts crying.

I put my face close to hers. "You're not pregnant *now*, are you?"

"No!" she says fiercely.

"Come on, Mags. You don't even like dolls."

"I know," she says, wiping her eyes.

"And Peter is crazy about you. He may be going to Harvard, but it doesn't mean he's going anywhere."

"I didn't get into Boston University," she says suddenly. "That's right. I got a rejection letter from them yesterday when Peter got his acceptance to Harvard."

"Oh, Mags."

"And pretty soon, everyone will be leaving. You, The Mouse, Walt—"

"You'll get in someplace else," I say encouragingly.

"What if I don't?"

Good question. And one I haven't faced squarely until now. What if nothing works out the way it's supposed to? On the other hand, if it doesn't, what are you supposed to do? You can't just sit there.

"I miss Walt," she says.

"I do too," I say, hugging my knees to my chest. "Where is Walt anyway?"

"Don't ask me. I've hardly seen him for three weeks. That's not like Walt."

"No, it isn't," I agree, thinking about how cynical Walt's been lately. "Come on. Let's call him."

Back in the house, the party is in full swing. Sebastian is dancing with Lali, which annoys me slightly, but I have more important things to worry about than my best friend and my boyfriend. I pick up the phone and dial Walt's number.

"Hello?" his mother answers.

"Is Walt there?" I ask, yelling over the noise of the party.

"Who is this?" she asks suspiciously.

"Carrie Bradshaw."

"He's out, Carrie."

"Do you know where he is?"

"He said he was meeting up with you," she snaps, and hangs up the phone.

Weird, I think, shaking my head. Definitely weird.

Meanwhile, Maggie has commandeered the party by standing on the couch and doing a striptease. Everyone is hooting and clapping, save for Peter, who is trying to appear as if he's enjoying it, but is actually mortified. I can't let Mags go down alone, not in the state she's in.

I kick off my shoes and jump onto the couch next to her.

Yes, I'm aware that nobody really wants to see me doing a striptease, but people are used to me making a fool of myself. I'm wearing white cotton tights under a cheap sequined skirt that I bought at a discount store, and I begin pulling them off at the toe. Within seconds, Lali has joined us on the couch, running her hands up and down her body while elbowing Maggie and me to the side. I'm standing on one foot, and I fall over the back of the couch, taking Maggie with me.

Maggie and I are lying on the ground, laughing hysterically. "Are you okay?" Peter asks, bending over Maggie.

"I'm fine," she giggles. And she is. Now that Peter is paying attention to her, everything is great. For the moment, anyway.

"Carrie Bradshaw, you're a bad influence," Peter chides as he leads Maggie away.

"And you're an uptight prig," I mutter, fixing my tights as I get to my feet.

I look over at Peter, who is pouring Maggie a whiskey, a tender yet smug expression on his face.

How far would *you* go to get what you wanted?

And that's when it hits me. I could write for the school newspaper. It would give me material to send into The New School. And it would be—ugh—*real*.

No, scolds a voice in my head. *Not* The Nutmeg. *That really is going too far. Besides, if you write for* The Nutmeg, *you're a hypocrite. You never hesitate to tell anyone who will listen that you hate* The Nutmeg—*including Peter, who's the editor.*

Yes, but what choice do you have? asks another voice. *Do you really want to do nothing, letting life just happen to you like you're some kind of loser? If you don't at least try to write for* The Nutmeg, *you'll probably never get into that writing program.*

Hating myself, I head over to the bar, pour myself a vodka cranberry juice, and sidle up to Maggie and Peter. "Hi, guys," I say casually, taking a sip of my drink. "So Petey-boy," I begin. "I was thinking I might want to write for that newspaper of yours after all."

He takes a sip of his drink and looks at me, irritated. "It's not *my* newspaper."

"You know what I mean."

"No, I don't. And it's very difficult to communicate with a person who can't be precise. That's what writing is all about. Precision."

And "authenticity." And "writing what you know." Two other things I apparently lack. I give Peter a look. If this is what getting into Harvard does to a person, maybe Harvard should be banned.

"I know it's technically not your newspaper, Peter," I say, matching his tone. "But you are the editor. I was merely deferring to what I assumed was your authority. But if you're not in charge—"

He glances at Maggie who gives him a quizzical look. "I didn't mean *that*," he says. "I mean, if you want to write for the paper, it's fine with me. But you have to check with our advisor, Ms. Smidgens."

"No problem," I say sweetly.

"Oh, good," Maggie says. "I really want you guys to be friends."

Peter and I eye each other. Never going to happen. But we'll pretend, for Maggie's sake.

CHAPTER SEVENTEEN

Bait and Switch

"Walt!" I say, catching up to him in the hall. He stops and wipes a lock of hair off his forehead. Walt's hair has gotten a little longer than usual, and he's sweating slightly.

"Where were you on Saturday night? We were all expecting you at Lali's party."

"Couldn't make it," he says.

"Why? What else did you have to do in this town?" I try to make it sound like a joke, but Walt doesn't take it as one.

"Believe it or not, I actually have other friends."

"You do?"

"There is life outside of Castlebury High."

"Come on," I say, nudging him. "I was kidding. We miss you."

"Yeah, I miss you guys too," he says, shifting his books from one arm to another. "I had to take an extra shift at the Hamburger Shack. Which means I have to spend all my free time studying."

"That's a drag." We've reached the teachers' lounge, where I pause before going in. "Walt, is everything okay? Really?"

"Sure," he says. "Why would you even ask?"

"Don't know."

"See ya," he says. And as he walks away, I realize he's lying—about the extra shift at the Hamburger Shack, anyway. I took Missy and Dorrit there two nights last week, and Walt wasn't working either time.

Must find out what's up with Walt, I think, making a mental note as I ease open the door to the lounge.

Inside are Ms. Smidgens, *The Nutmeg* advisor, along with Ms. Pizchiek, who teaches homemaking and typing. They're both smoking and talking about how they might get their colors done at the G. Fox department store in Hartford. "Susie says it changed her life," Ms. Pizchiek says. "All her life she was wearing blues, and it turned out she should have been wearing orange."

"Orange is for pumpkins," Ms. Smidgens says, which makes me kind of like her a little because I agree. "This whole color analysis craze is a crock. It's only another way to part unsuspecting fools and their money." And is probably useless if your skin is gray from smoking three packs of cigarettes a day.

"Oh, but it's fun," Ms. Pizchiek counters, with no dampening of enthusiasm. "We get a group of gals together on a Saturday morning and then have lunch afterward—" She suddenly looks up and sees me standing in the doorway.

"Yes?" she asks curtly. The teachers' lounge is strictly off-limits for students.

"I need to talk to Ms. Smidgens."

Ms. Smidgens must be really bored with Ms. Pizchiek, because instead of turning me away, she says, "Carrie Bradshaw, right? Well, come in. And close the door behind you."

I smile as I attempt to hold my breath. Even though I smoke sometimes, being in a closed environment with two women who are puffing away like chimneys makes me want to wave my hand in front of my face. But that would be rude, so I try breathing through my mouth instead.

"I was wondering—" I begin.

"I get it. You want to work on the newspaper," Ms. Smidgens says. "Happens every year. Sometime after the first quarter some senior comes to me and suddenly wants in on *The Nutmeg*. I take it you need to build up your extracurricular activities, right?"

"No," I say, hoping the smoke won't make me sick.

"Then why?" Smidgens asks.

"I think I could bring some fresh perspective to the paper."

This is obviously the wrong thing to say, because she says, "Oh, really?" like she's heard it a million times before.

"I think I'm a pretty good writer," I say cautiously, refusing to give up.

Ms. Smidgens is not impressed. "Everyone wants to write.

We need people to do layout." Now she's really trying to get rid of me, but I don't go. I just stand there, holding my breath with my eyes bugging out of my head. My face must scare her a little, because she relents. "I suppose if you did layout, we could let you try writing something. The editorial committee meets three times a week—Mondays, Wednesdays, and Fridays at four. If you miss more than one meeting a week, you're out."

"Okay," I mumble, nodding vigorously.

"So we'll see you this afternoon at four."

I give her a little wave and skittle out of there.

"I bet Peter's going to dump Maggie," Lali says, removing her clothes. She stretches, naked, before sliding into her Speedo. I've always admired Lali's lack of modesty when it comes to her body. I've never been able to let go of my insecurity about being naked, and I have to contort my arms and legs to maintain a level of dignity when getting changed.

"No way." I tuck my butt as I remove my underwear. "He's in love with her."

"He's in lust with her," Lali corrects. "Sebastian told me Peter was asking him all about the other women he's been with. Specifically, Donna LaDonna. Does that sound like a guy who's madly in love to you?"

Hearing the name Donna LaDonna still makes me cringe. It's been weeks since she launched her smear campaign, and while it's been reduced to dirty looks in the hall, I suspect it's merely bubbling under the surface, ready to erupt at any moment. Perhaps it's part of Donna's plan to seduce Peter and wreak havoc.

"Sebastian told you?" I frown. "That's funny. He didn't tell · me. If Peter told Sebastian he was interested in Donna, Sebastian would have definitely mentioned it."

"Maybe he doesn't tell you everything," Lali says casually.

What's that supposed to mean? I wonder, giving her a look. But she seems to be completely unaware of any breach of friendship etiquette, bending over and shaking out her arms.

"Do you think we should tell Maggie?"

"I'm not going to tell her," Lali says.

"He hasn't done anything, has he? So maybe it was just talk. Besides, Peter's always boasting about how he's friends with Donna."

"Didn't Sebastian date her?" Lali asks.

Another strange comment. Lali knows he did. It's like she's using every excuse to bring up Sebastian's name.

Sure enough, the next thing she says is, "By the way, Aztec Two-Step is playing at the Shaboo Inn in a few weeks. I thought maybe you, me, and Sebastian could go together. I mean, *we* could go, just the two of us, but since you always seem to be with Sebastian, I thought you'd probably want him to come too. Plus, he's a really good dancer."

At one time, I would have loved the idea of going to see our favorite band with Sebastian, but it suddenly makes me uncomfortable. On the other hand, how can I refuse without making it sound like something's wrong? "Sounds fun," I say.

"It'll be a blast," Lali agrees quickly.

"I'll ask him this afternoon." I twist my hair and wedge it under my swim cap.

"Oh, don't worry about it," Lali says, as if it's no big deal. "I'll ask him when I see him." She strides out of the locker room.

I have a disturbing vision of Lali dancing with Sebastian at her party.

I take my place on the block next to her. "You don't have to worry about telling Sebastian. He's picking me up at four. I'll ask him then."

She looks over at me and shrugs. "Whatever."

As my feet leave the block, I remember I have the newspaper meeting at four. My body stiffens, and I hit the water like a board. I'm momentarily stunned by the impact, but then habit takes over and I start swimming.

Crap. I forgot to tell Sebastian about the meeting. What if I'm gone by the time he turns up? Then Lali will get her clutches on him for sure.

I'm so distracted by the thought that I totally screw up my swan dive, which is the easiest dive in my repertoire.

"What's wrong with you, Bradshaw?" Coach Nipsie demands. "You'd better get your shit together by the meet on Friday."

"I will," I say, wiping my face with a towel.

"You're spending too much time with your boyfriend," he scolds. "It's throwing off your concentration."

I look over at Lali, who is observing this exchange. For a second, I catch a tiny smile on her face, and then it's gone.

"I thought we were going to the Fox Run Mall," Sebastian says. He looks away, irritated.

"I'm sorry." I reach out to touch his arm but he takes a step back.

"Don't. You're all wet."

"I just got out of the pool."

"I can see that," he says, frowning.

"I'll only go for an hour."

"Why do you want to work for that lousy newspaper anyway?"

How can I explain? I'm trying to have a future? Sebastian won't understand. He's trying to do everything he can not to have one.

"Come on," I say pleadingly.

"I don't want to go to the Fox Run Mall alone."

Lali strolls by, twisting her towel and snapping it into the air. "I'll go with you," she volunteers.

"Great," he says. He smiles at me. "We'll meet you later, okay?"

"Sure." It all seems innocent enough. So why does his use of the word "we" make me shudder?

I consider ditching the newspaper meeting and going after him.

I even start to follow him out the door, but when I get outside, I pause. Am I going to be like this all my life? Committing to something that seems important and then tossing it aside for a guy? *Weak. Very weak, Bradley,* I hear The Mouse scolding me in my head.

I go to the newspaper meeting.

Due to my indecision, I'm a little late. The staff is already seated around a large art table, with the exception of Ms. Smidgens, who is by the window, covertly smoking a cigarette. Since she's not absorbed in the conversation, she's the first to see me come in.

"Carrie Bradshaw," she says. "You decided to grace us with your presence after all."

Peter looks up and we lock eyes. Bastard, I think, remembering what Lali just told me about Peter and Donna LaDonna. If Peter gives me any trouble about joining the *Nutmeg* staff, I'll remind him about what he said to Sebastian.

"Does everyone here know Carrie? Carrie Bradshaw?" he asks. "She's a senior. And I guess she's . . . uh . . . decided to join the newspaper."

The rest of the kids look at me blankly.

Besides Peter, I recognize three seniors. The other four kids are juniors and sophomores, plus one girl who looks so young, she must be a freshman. All in all, a not terribly promising group.

"Let's get back to our discussion," Peter says as I take a seat at the end of the table. "Upcoming article suggestions?"

The young girl, who has black hair and bad skin, and is one of those I'm-going-to-be-successful-if-it-kills-me types, raises her hand. "I think we should do a story about the cafeteria food. Where it comes from, and why it's so bad."

"We already covered that," Peter says wearily. "We do that story in nearly every issue. Doesn't make any difference."

"Oh, but it does," says a nerdly kid with the requisite safety glasses. "Two years ago the school agreed to allow healthy vending machines in the cafeteria. So at least we can get sunflower seeds."

Aha. So that's the reason we have a group of students who are constantly nibbling sunflower seeds like a colony of gerbils.

"How about gym?" says a girl whose hair is pulled back into a tight braid. "Why don't we lobby for a workout video instead of basketball?"

"I don't think many guys want to do aerobics in gym," Peter says drily.

"Isn't it stupid to write about things that people can do at home anyway?" points out the nerdly kid. "It would be like forcing everyone to take laundry."

"And it is all about *choice*, right?" says the freshman. "Which reminds me. I think we should do the story about the cheerleader discrimination suit."

"Oh, that." Peter sighs. "Carrie, what do you think?"

"Didn't someone try to pass the cheerleader antidiscrimination act last year and it failed?"

"We won't give up," insists the freshman girl. "The cheerleading team discriminates against ugly people. It's unconstitutional."

"Is it?" Peter asks.

"I think there should be a law against ugly girls in general," the nerdly kid says, and begins panting loudly in what appears to pass for a laugh.

Peter gives him a dirty look and turns to the freshman. "Gayle, I thought we discussed this. You can't use the school newspaper to further the causes of your family. We all know your sister wants to be a cheerleader and that Donna LaDonna has rejected her twice. If she wasn't your sister, you might have something. But she is. So it makes it look like the newspaper is trying to force the cheerleading squad to take her. It goes against every journalistic convention—"

"How?" I ask, suddenly interested. Especially as it sounds like Peter is trying to protect Donna LaDonna. "Isn't the whole point of journalism to make people aware of the wrongdoings in the world? And wrongdoings do begin at home. They begin right here at Castlebury High."

"She's right!" exclaims the nerdly guy, thumping his fist on the table.

"Okay, Carrie," Peter says, annoyed. "You take the story."

"Oh no. Can't do that," Ms. Smidgens says, stepping in. "I know Carrie's a senior, but as a new member of the paper, she has to do layout."

I shrug pleasantly, as if I don't mind at all.

A few minutes later, Gayle and I are relegated to a corner of the room to move around sections of type on a large piece of lined paper. The job is unbearably tedious, and I look over at Gayle, who is frowning, either in concentration or anger. She's at the apex of the worst stage of being a teenage girl, meaning she has blemishes, greasy hair, and a face that hasn't yet caught up to her nose.

"Typical, isn't it?" I say. "They always make the girls do the most unimportant job."

"If they don't make me a reporter next year, I'm going to start a petition," she says fiercely.

"Hmmmm. I've always thought there were two ways of getting what you wanted in life. Forcing people to give it to you, or making them want to give it to you. Seems the latter is usually the better choice. I bet if you talked to Ms. Smidgens, she'd help you out. She seems pretty reasonable."

"*She's* not so bad. It's Peter."

"That so?"

"He refuses to give me a chance."

Suspecting, perhaps, that we're talking about him, Peter strolls over. "Carrie, you don't have to do this."

"Oh, I don't mind," I say airily. "I *love* arts and crafts."

"You do?" Gayle asks when Peter walks away.

"Are you kidding? My worst nightmare was those relief maps. And I failed sewing when I was in the Girl Scouts."

Little Gayle giggles. "Me too. I mean, I want to be Barbara Walters when I grow up, even if everyone does make fun of her. I wonder if she ever had to do this?"

"Probably. And probably a lot of other worse things as well."

"You think?" Gayle asks, encouraged.

"I *know*," I say, just for the hell of it. We work in silence for another minute, and then I ask, "What's this thing with your sister and Donna LaDonna?"

She looks at me suspiciously. "Do you know my sister?"

"Sure." It's a bit of a lie. I don't really know her, but I'm aware of who she is. Gayle's sister has to be a senior named Ramona who looks just like Gayle, albeit a slightly less pimply and more refined version. I never paid that much attention to her because she moved here during our freshman year and immediately made other friends.

"She's a really good gymnast," Gayle says. "I mean, she was, back in New Jersey. When she was thirteen, she was the all-around state champion."

I'm surprised. "Why isn't she on the gymnastics team, then?"

"She grew. She got hips. And boobs. Something happened with her center of gravity."

"I see."

"But she's still really good at doing splits and cartwheels and all the things cheerleaders do. She tried out for the cheerleading squad and was sure she'd make it because she's so much better than the other girls, like Donna LaDonna, who can't even do a full split. But she wasn't even picked for

Junior Varsity. She tried out again, last year, and afterward, Donna LaDonna went up to her and told her right to her face that she wasn't going to make it because she wasn't pretty enough."

"She came right out and said it?" I gasp, astonished.

Gayle nods. "She said, and I quote, 'You're not pretty enough to make the squad, so don't waste your time and ours.'"

"Wow. What did your sister do?"

"She told the principal."

I nod, thinking maybe this is typical Ramona behavior, always tattling to an adult, and that's why they didn't want her on the team. But still. "What did the principal say?"

"He said he couldn't get involved in 'girl stuff.' And my sister said it was discrimination, pure and simple. Discrimination against girls who don't have straight hair and tiny noses and perfect boobs. And he laughed."

"He's a bastard. Everyone knows that."

"But it doesn't make it right. So my sister has been trying to get this discrimination suit going."

"And you're going to write about it."

"I would, except Peter won't let me do it. And Donna LaDonna won't talk to me. I mean, I'm a freshman. And then she put the word out that if anyone talks about it *at all*, they'll have to deal with her."

"Really?"

"And who wants to go up against Donna LaDonna? Let's face it." Gayle sighs. "She runs the school."

"Or thinks she does, anyway."

At that moment, Peter returns. "I'm going to meet Maggie at the Fox Run Mall. You want to come?"

"Sure," I say, gathering my things. "I'm meeting Sebastian there anyway."

"Bye, Carrie," Gayle says. "It was nice to meet you. And don't worry. I won't try to talk to you if I see you in the hall."

"Don't be silly, Gayle. You come up and talk to me anytime you like."

"Gayle probably told you all about Donna LaDonna and her sister, Ramona," Peter says as we cross the parking lot to a rusty yellow station wagon.

"Mmmhmmm," I murmur.

"It's all a bunch of BS. No one is interested in that boring girl talk."

"Is that how you think of it? As boring girl talk?"

"Yeah. Isn't that what it is?"

I open the passenger door, knock a bunch of papers to the floor, and get in. "Funny. I always thought you were more evolved when it came to women."

"What do you mean?" Peter pumps the gas and turns the key. It takes a few tries to get the engine going.

"I never figured you for a guy who can't stand the sound of women's voices. You know, those guys who tell their girlfriends to shut up when they're trying to tell them something."

"Who told you I was that kind of guy? Maggie? I'm not that kind of guy, I promise you."

"Why won't you let Gayle do her story, then? Or is this really about Donna LaDonna?"

"It has nothing to do with her," he says, clumsily changing gears.

"How well do you know her? Honestly?"

"Why?"

I shrug. "I heard you were talking about her at Lali's party."

"So?"

"So Maggie is a really good friend of mine. And she's a great girl. I don't want to see her get hurt."

"Who says she's going to get hurt?"

"She'd better not get hurt. That's all."

We drive a little farther, and then Peter says, "You don't have to do it."

"What?"

"Be nice to Gayle. She's a pain in the ass. Once you talk to her, you can't get rid of her."

"She seems okay to me." I give him a dirty look, remembering how he wouldn't even take Maggie to the clinic to get the birth control pills.

And apparently, he's feeling guilty. "If you want to write a story for the paper, you can," he says. "I guess I sort of owe you anyway."

"For going with Maggie to the clinic? I guess you do."

"Isn't it better for girls to do those things together anyway?"

"I don't know," I say, with a dark edge to my voice. "What

if Maggie had been pregnant?"

"That's what I'm trying to *avoid*. I should get points for being a good boyfriend and making her take the pill," he says, as if he deserves a pat on the back.

Why is it always about the guy? "I think Maggie is smart enough to know she should be on the pill."

"Hey. I didn't mean to imply—"

"Forget about it," I say, annoyed. I have a sudden image of that girl at the clinic, crying and crying because she'd just had an abortion. The guy who got her pregnant wasn't with her, either. I should tell Peter about *her*, but I don't know where to begin.

"Anyway, it was really decent of you," he concedes. "Maggie told me you were great."

"And this surprises you?"

"I don't know, Carrie," he stammers. "I mean—I always thought you were kind of . . . silly."

"Silly?"

"I mean, you're always making jokes. I could never understand what you were doing in our AP classes."

"Why? Because I'm funny? A girl can't be funny and smart?"

"I wasn't saying you're not smart—"

"Or is it because I'm not going to Harvard? Maggie keeps telling me you're a great guy. But I don't see it. Or maybe you've only become a major asshole in the last three days."

"Whoa. Take it easy. You don't have to get so mad. Why do

girls always take things so personally?" he asks.

I sit there with my arms crossed, saying nothing. Peter starts to get uncomfortable, shifting his butt around on the driver's seat. "So, um, really," he says. "You should write a piece for the newspaper. Maybe a profile of a teacher or something. That's always good."

I put my feet up on his dashboard. "I'll think about it," I say.

I'm still stewing when we pull into the parking lot of the Fox Run Mall. I'm so mad, I'm not sure I can even be friends with Maggie while she's dating this jerk.

I get out of the car and kind of slam the door, which is pretty rude, but I can't help it. "I'll meet you guys inside, okay?"

"Okay," he says, looking nervous. "We'll be at Mrs. Fields."

I nod and then I walk around the parking lot and fish through my bag until I find a cigarette, which I light up. And just as I'm smoking and starting to feel normal again, the yellow Corvette peels into the parking lot and squeals into a space about ten feet away. It's Sebastian. And Lali.

They're laughing and giggling as they get out of the car.

My stomach drops. Where have they been for the past hour and a half?

"Hey, babe," Sebastian says, giving me a quick peck on the lips. "We were hungry, so we went to the Hamburger Shack."

"Did you see Walt?"

"Uh-huh," Lali says. Sebastian links his arm through mine, then holds out his other arm for Lali. Thus entwined, the three of us go into the mall.

My only consolation is that I know Sebastian isn't lying about the Hamburger Shack. When he kissed me, his breath smelled of onions and peppers, mixed with the sharp scent of cigarettes.

CHAPTER EIGHTEEN

Cliques Are Made to Be Broken

"What do you think?" I ask The Mouse, tapping my pen on the table.

"Attacking Donna LaDonna in your first piece for *The Nutmeg*? Risky, Bradley. Especially as you haven't gotten her side yet."

"Not for lack of trying." I counter, which isn't exactly true. I did follow her around for a bit, but I didn't really try to confront her. What I actually did was drive by her house three times. The LaDonnas live on the top of a hill in a big new house, which is also strikingly ugly. It has two columns, one wall made of brick, one wall made of stucco, and the others of wood, as if the person designing the house couldn't decide what they wanted and chose everything instead. Sort of the way Donna LaDonna is about boys, I figure.

On two occasions, the house was deserted, but the third time, I saw Tommy Brewster coming out, followed by Donna.

Just before Tommy got into his car, he made a lunge for her, like he was trying to kiss her, but she pushed him away with her index finger and laughed. While Tommy was still in the driveway, fuming, another car pulled up—a blue Mercedes—and a tall, really good-looking guy got out, walked right past Tommy, and put his arm around Donna's waist. Then they went inside without a backward glance.

When it comes to guys, Donna clearly leads a very interesting life.

"Why not start with something less controversial than Donna LaDonna?" The Mouse asks now. "Get people used to the idea that you're writing for the paper."

"But if I don't write about Donna, I have nothing to write about," I complain. I put my feet up on the table and tip my chair back. "The great thing about Donna is that everyone is scared of her. I mean, what else about high school inspires such universal distress?"

"Cliques."

"Cliques? We're not even in a clique."

"In the sense that we've been hanging out with pretty much the same people for the last ten years, maybe we are."

"I always thought of us as the anti-clique."

"An anti-clique is a clique, isn't it?" asks The Mouse.

"Maybe there's a story here," I muse, leaning all the way back in my chair. When I'm nearly perpendicular, the legs slide out and I fall over, knocking down several books in the process. I land with the chair on top of my head, and when

I peek around the seat, little Gayle is bending over me.

Someone has got to tell this girl about Clearasil.

"Carrie?" she gasps. "Are you all right?" She glances around wildly as she picks several books up off the floor. "You'd better get up before the librarian finds you. If she does, she'll kick you out."

The Mouse bursts out laughing.

"I don't get it," Gayle says, her arms wrapped around a pile of books. Her eyes fill with tears.

"Sweetie," I say. "We're not making fun of you. It's just that we're seniors. We don't care if the librarian kicks us out."

"If she tried, we'd probably give her the finger," The Mouse adds. We look at each other and snicker.

"Oh. Well." Gayle nervously pinches her lip. I pull out the chair next to me. "Have a seat."

"Really?"

"This is Roberta Castells," I say as Gayle cautiously sits. "Also known as 'Mighty Mouse.' Or 'The Mouse' for short."

"Hello," Gayle says shyly. "I know all about you. You're a legend. They say you're the smartest girl in school. I wish I could do something like that. Be the smartest. I know I'm never going to be the prettiest."

The two Jens come into the library, sniffing around like bloodhounds. They spot us and take a seat two tables away.

"See those girls?" I indicate the Jens with my head. "Do you think they're pretty?"

"The two Jens? They're beautiful."

"Now," I say. "They're beautiful *now*. But in two years—"

"They're going to look really, really old. They're going to look like they're *forty*," The Mouse says.

Little Gayle covers her mouth. "Why? What happened to them?"

"They're going to peak in high school," I explain.

"What?"

"That's right," The Mouse agrees, nodding. "And after high school, it's all downhill. Babies. Cheating husbands. Dead-end jobs. You don't want to peak in high school. If you do, the rest of your life is a disaster."

"I never thought of it that way." And she looks over at the two Jens like they're freaky aliens from another planet.

"Speaking of which," I ask, "what do *you* hate most about high school?"

"Um, the food?"

"Not good enough. Cafeteria stories are boring. And you can't say Donna LaDonna, either."

"I guess I'd have to say cliques."

"Cliques." I nod and raise an eyebrow at The Mouse. "Why?"

"Because they make you insecure. Like you always know if you're not in a clique because those people don't talk to you. And sometimes if you are in a clique, it's like being in *Lord of the Flies*. You always wonder if you're the one who's going to get killed." She puts her hand over her mouth again. "Did I say too much?"

"No, no. Keep talking." I turn over my notebook, open it to a blank page, and start scribbling.

"So this story I'm doing for *The Nutmeg* is coming out really well," I say, taking a batch of chocolate chip cookies from the oven.

Sebastian turns another page of *Time* magazine. "What's it about again?"

I've already told him at least a dozen times. "Cliques. I've interviewed about ten people so far, and I've gotten some really interesting stories."

"Hmm," Sebastian says, clearly not interested. I press on, nonetheless. "Walt said that while cliques provide protection, they can also stunt your growth as a person. What do you think?"

"What I think," Sebastian says, not looking up from his magazine, "is that Walt has issues."

"What kind of issues?"

"Do you really care?" He looks at me over the rim of his Ray-Ban-style reading glasses. Whenever Sebastian wears his reading glasses, my heart melts. He has a flaw. He doesn't have perfect vision. It's just so darn cute.

"Of course I do."

"Then trust me and leave it alone," he says, and goes back to his magazine.

I remove the warm cookies from the pan and gently place them on a plate. I put the plate in front of Sebastian and sit down across from him. He absentmindedly takes a cookie and bites into it.

"What are you reading?" I ask.

"More about the recession," he says, flipping the page. "No point in looking for a job now, that's for sure. Hell, there's probably no point in going to college. We're all going to be stuck living in our parents' basements for the rest of our lives."

I suddenly grab his wrist. "What do you know about Walt?"

"I saw him." He shrugs.

"Where?"

"At a place you don't know and don't want to know about."

What is he talking about? "What kind of place?"

He removes his glasses. "Forget it. I'm bored. Let's go to the Fox Run Mall."

"I'm not bored. I want to hear more about Walt."

"And I don't want to talk about it," he says, rising to his feet.

Hmph. I pick up a cookie and shove half of it into my mouth. "I can't go to the mall. I want to work on my piece." When he looks confused, I add, "For *The Nutmeg*."

He shrugs. "Suit yourself. But I'm not going to sit here while you're writing."

"But I want it to be *good*."

"Fine," he says. "I'll see you later."

"Wait!" I grab my coat and run after him.

He puts his arm around my waist, and we do a funny walk we invented one night at The Emerald, and we walk like that all the way out to the car.

But when we pull out of the driveway, I look back at my house and feel enveloped in a fog of guilt. I shouldn't be doing this. I ought to be working on my piece. How can I become a writer if I don't have discipline?

But Lali has a new job at the mall, working at The Gap, and if left to his own devices, Sebastian is sure to stop by to see her, and the two of them will be alone again, without me. I feel lousy thinking I can't trust Lali with Sebastian, but lately, the two of them have become increasingly buddy-buddy. Every time I see them joking or high-fiving each other, I have a bad premonition. It's like the sound of a clock ticking, except the ticks get further and further apart, until there's no ticking at all—only silence.

Cynthia Viande stands on the stage in front of assembly and holds up a copy of *The Nutmeg*. "And this week, we have a story from Carrie Bradshaw about cliques."

There's a tepid round of applause, and then everyone gets up.

"You got your piece in, Bradley. Good job," The Mouse says, hurrying over.

"Can't wait to read it," a few kids murmur, rolling their eyes as they pass by.

"Glad that's over, huh?" Sebastian interrupts, giving The Mouse a wink.

"What do you mean?" I ask.

"*The Nutmeg*," he says to The Mouse. "Was she bugging you with these endless ace reporter questions?"

The Mouse looks surprised. "No."

I flush with embarrassment.

"Anyway, it's done," Sebastian says, and smiles.

The Mouse gives me a curious look, but I shrug it off as if to say "Guys—what can you do?"

"Well, *I* thought it was *great*," The Mouse says.

"Here she comes," Maggie cries out. "Here comes our star."

"Oh, come on, Magwitch. It was only a stupid story in *The Nutmeg*." But still, I'm pleased. I slide in next to her at the picnic table in the barn. The ground is frozen and there's a damp chill in the air that will last, on and off now, for months. I'm sporting a knit cap with a long tail that ends in a pom-pom. Maggie, who deals with winter by pretending it doesn't exist and refusing to wear a hat or gloves, except when she's skiing, is rubbing her hands together in between taking drags off a cigarette that she and Peter are passing back and forth. Lali is wearing men's construction boots, which seem to be all the rage.

"Give me a drag of that cigarette," Lali says to Maggie, which is strange, because Lali rarely smokes.

"The piece was good," Peter says grudgingly.

"Everything Carrie does is good," Lali says. Smoke curls

out of her nostrils. "Isn't that right? Carrie always *has* to succeed."

Is she being intentionally hostile? Or just Lali-ish? I can't tell. She's staring at me boldly, as if daring me to find out.

"I don't always succeed," I counter. I slip one of Maggie's mother's cigarettes from the pack. Apparently Maggie's mom has given up on quitting. "In fact, I usually fail," I say, trying to make a joke of it. I light up and take a drag, holding the smoke in my mouth and then exhaling several perfect smoke rings. "But every now and then I get lucky."

"Come on," Lali says, with an edgy skepticism. "You're writing for *The Nutmeg*, you've got about four diving trophies, and you stole Sebastian away from Donna LaDonna. Sounds to me like you get everything you want."

For a moment, there's a painful silence. "I don't know about that," The Mouse says. "Do any of us ever get what we really want?"

"You do," Maggie says. "You and Peter."

"*And* Lali. And *you*, Maggie," I insist. "Besides, I didn't exactly steal Sebastian from Donna LaDonna. He said he wasn't seeing her. And even if he were—well, it's not exactly like she's a friend of mine. It's not like I owe her or anything."

"Try telling her that," Lali mutters as she grinds the cigarette butt under her boot.

"Who cares about Donna LaDonna?" Maggie says loudly. She looks at Peter. "I am so sick of her. I don't want to hear anyone mention her name ever again."

"Agreed," Peter says reluctantly.

"Well," I say.

Peter glances away as he lights a cigarette, then turns to me. "So you know Smidgens expects you to write another story for the newspaper now."

"That's fine."

"What are you going to write about?" Lali asks. She takes another cigarette from the pack, looks at it, and puts it behind her ear.

"I guess I'll have to think of something," I say, wondering once again why she's being so strange.

CHAPTER NINETEEN

Ch-ch-ch-changes

"Maggie, this isn't *right*," I hiss. School has just ended, and The Mouse, Maggie, and I are hiding in Maggie's Cadillac.

"Okay. What about Lali?" The Mouse asks, changing the subject. "Didn't you think she was weird this morning up at the barn?"

"She's jealous," Maggie says.

"That's what I think," The Mouse agrees.

"She's a very jealous person," Maggie adds.

"No, she isn't," I protest. "Lali's confident, that's all. People take it the wrong way."

"I don't know, Bradley," The Mouse says. "I'd be careful if I were you."

"Okay, guys. There he is. Everyone duck!" Maggie commands as we hit the floor.

"This is so wrong," I mutter.

"You're the one who wants to be the writer," Maggie says.

"You should *want* to find out."

"I do, but not like this. Why can't we just ask him?"

"Because he won't tell us," Maggie replies.

"Mouse? What do you think?"

"I don't care," The Mouse says from the backseat. "I'm only along for the ride." She sticks her head up and looks out the rear window. "He's in the car! He's leaving the parking lot! Hurry, or we'll lose him."

So much for The Mouse's lack of involvement, I think.

Maggie bolts up, puts the car into gear, and steps on the gas. She drives the wrong way out of the parking lot, and when we reach a dead end she continues right over the grass.

"Jesus Christ!" The Mouse exclaims, clutching onto the front seat as Maggie makes a sharp turn to the left. In seconds, we're two cars behind Walt's orange hatchback.

"Not too obvious, Mags," I remark drily.

"Oh, Walt will never notice," she says obliquely. "Walt never notices anything when he's driving."

Poor Walt. Why did I ever agree to Maggie's harebrained scheme to follow him? For the same reason I took her to get the birth control pills. I can't say no to anyone. Not to Maggie, not to Sebastian, and not to Lali, either.

Lali got those damn tickets for Aztec Two-Step, and now we're all set to go the weekend after Christmas vacation.

But that's still weeks away. And besides, I have to admit I'm dying to know where Walt is sneaking off to after school.

"I'll bet he has a new girlfriend," Maggie says. "And I'll bet she's older. Like Mrs. Robinson. She's probably somebody's mother. That's why he's being so sneaky."

"Maybe he really is studying."

Maggie gives me a look. "Come on. You know how smart Walt is. He's never had to study. Even when he says he's studying, he's always doing something else. Like reading about eighteenth-century chamber pots."

"Walt is into antiques?" The Mouse asks, surprised.

"He knows everything about them," Maggie says proudly. "We used to have this plan: We were going to move to Vermont. Walt was going to have an antique store and I was going to raise sheep and spin the fleece into wool and knit sweaters."

"How . . . quaint," The Mouse says, catching my eye.

"I was going to grow vegetables, too," Maggie adds. "And have a farm stand in the summer. We were going to become vegetarians."

And look at what happened to that scheme, I think, as we pass through town in pursuit of Walt.

He drives past the Fox Run Mall and continues down Main Street. At one of the two lights in town, his car makes a left and heads toward the river.

"I knew it," Maggie says, gripping the steering wheel. "He has a secret assignation."

"In the woods?" The Mouse scoffs. "There's nothing down there but trees and empty fields."

"Maybe he killed someone accidentally. And he's buried

the body and now he's going back to make sure it hasn't risen to the surface." I light up a cigarette and sit back, wondering how far this can possibly go.

The road leads straight to the river, but instead of continuing on the dirt track, Walt makes another sharp turn under the highway. "He's heading for East Milton," Maggie shouts, stating the obvious.

"What's in East Milton?" The Mouse asks.

"A doctor's office."

"Carrie!" Maggie exclaims.

"Maybe he has a job as a male nurse," I say innocently.

"Carrie, will you please shut up?" Maggie snaps. "This is *serious*."

"He could be a male nurse. It's going to be a very chic profession in the next ten years."

"All the doctors will be women, and all the nurses will be men," The Mouse says.

"I would not want a male nurse." Maggie shudders. "I would not want any man I did not know touching my body."

"What about a one-night stand?" I ask, razzing her. "I mean, what if you went out and you met a guy and you thought you were madly in love with him and you had sex with him like three hours later?"

"I'm crazy about Peter, okay?"

"Anyway, it might not count," says The Mouse. "If you knew him for three hours, you'd kind of know him, wouldn't you?"

"It would have to be like the zipless fuck in *Fear of Flying*."

"Please, do not say 'fuck.' I hate that word. It's 'making love,'" Maggie says.

"What's the difference between 'making love' and 'fucking' anyway? I mean, *really*?" I ask.

"Fucking is just intercourse. Making love is intercourse plus all the other stuff," The Mouse says.

"I can't believe you haven't had sex with Sebastian yet," Maggie declares.

"Well . . ."

Maggie turns around to look at The Mouse in disbelief, which causes her to nearly drive off the road. When we recover, Maggie says, "You're still a virgin," as if it's some kind of crime.

"I don't like to think of myself as a 'virgin.' I prefer to think of myself as 'sexually incomplete.' You know. Like I haven't finished the course yet."

"But why?" Maggie asks. "It's not even a big deal. You think it's a big deal until you do it. And then you think, 'God, why did I wait so long?'"

"Come on, Maggie. Everyone has their own timetable. Maybe Carrie isn't ready," The Mouse says.

"All I can say is that if you don't do it with Sebastian soon, somebody else will," Maggie intones ominously.

"If that happens, it means Sebastian wasn't the right guy for her," The Mouse insists.

"Besides, I think they already have," I quip. "Done it with

Sebastian in the past, anyway. And, hey, I've only been seeing the guy for two months."

"I was only seeing Peter for two *days* when we did it," Maggie says. "Of course, our circumstances were special. Peter had been in love with me for years."

"Maggie. About Peter—" The Mouse begins.

I want to caution her that now is probably not the time to bring up the truth about Peter, but it's too late.

"I think 'high school' and 'college' are two separate categories for him. When he goes to Harvard, he's going to leave Castlebury behind. He has to. Otherwise, he won't succeed."

"Why not?" Maggie challenges.

"Mags," I say, giving The Mouse a look. "Mouse isn't talking about you, *per se*. She only means that he's going to have to study a lot, and he might not have as much time for a relationship. Right, Mouse?"

"Sure. All of our lives are going to be different. We're all going to have to change."

"I, for one, am not going to change," Maggie says, resolute. "No matter what happens, I'm always going to be me. I think that's the way people should behave. Decently."

I agree. "No matter what happens, we should all swear that we'll always be ourselves at all times."

"Do we have a choice?" The Mouse asks drily.

"Where *are* we?" I ask, looking around.

"Good question," The Mouse mutters. We're on a rutted asphalt road that appears to be in the middle of nowhere.

On either side are rocky fields, dotted with a few rundown houses. We pass an auto repair shop and a yellow house with a sign that reads SUNSHINE DOLL REPAIR, DOLLS LARGE AND SMALL. Ahead of us, Walt suddenly swerves into a small driveway next to a long, white, industrial-looking building.

The building has a large metal door and small, blacked-out windows; it looks deserted.

"What is this place?" Maggie asks, as we slowly drive past.

The Mouse sits back and folds her arms. "It doesn't look good, that's for sure."

We go a little further, until Maggie finds a place to turn around. "A place you don't want to know about," I say aloud, echoing Sebastian's warning.

"What?" Maggie asks.

"Nothing," I say quickly, as The Mouse and I exchange a look. The Mouse taps Maggie on the shoulder. "I think we should go home. You're not going to like this."

"Like *what*?" Maggie says. "It's a building. And it's our duty as friends to find out what Walt is up to."

"Or not." The Mouse shrugs.

Maggie ignores her, following the driveway around to the back where we find a lot hidden from the street. It contains several cars, including Walt's.

A secret back entrance is flanked by neon signs that say

things like VIDEOS, TOYS, and—as if that isn't enough—LIVE SEX.

"I don't get it." Maggie glares at the hot purple and blue signs.

"It's a porn place."

"Maggie, you really don't want to be here," The Mouse warns again.

"Why not?" Maggie asks. "Do you think I can't handle it?"

"No, I don't."

"*I* can't handle it," I say in sympathy. "And it's not even my ex-boyfriend in there."

"I don't care." Maggie parks the car next to a Dumpster, grabs a pack of cigarettes, and gets out. "If you guys want to come, fine. Otherwise you can stay in the car."

Now there's a change. I lean across the seat and call to her from the window. "Mags, you don't know what's in there."

"I'm going to find out."

"You're going to confront Walt? What's he going to think when he finds out you've spied on him?"

Maggie walks away. The Mouse and I look at each other, get out of the car, and follow her.

"Come on, Magwitch. It's bad form, following someone around like this. Especially if he's trying to keep it a secret. Let's go."

"No!"

"Okay," I say, backing off. I point to the Dumpster. "We'll

hide behind there. We'll wait a few minutes and if nothing happens, we'll go home."

Maggie takes another look at the entrance. Her eyes narrow. "Fine."

We skittle behind the Dumpster. It's freezing now, and I wrap my arms around my chest, jumping up and down to keep warm.

"Will you stop that?" Maggie hisses. "Someone's coming." I dive into a bush next to the Dumpster, scramble around for a bit, and sit back on my heels.

A souped-up Mustang screeches into the lot. Black Sabbath blares from the car as the door opens and the driver gets out. He's a large muscular guy, and when he glances around surreptitiously, I recognize Randy Sandler, who was two years ahead of us and the quarterback on the football team.

"Ohmigod. Randy Sandler just went in."

"Randy Sandler?" The Mouse asks. She and Maggie crawl over to join me.

"This is my fault," Maggie says. "If I hadn't stopped seeing Walt, he wouldn't need to come here for sex. He must be suffering from a terrible case of blue balls."

"Blue balls is a myth," I whisper loudly. "It's one of those lies men tell women to get them to have sex."

"I don't believe it. Poor Walt," Maggie groans.

"Shhhh," The Mouse commands as the door swings open.

Randy Sandler appears again, but this time he's not alone.

Walt comes out behind him, blinking in the light. He and Randy exchange a few words and laugh, then they both get into Randy's car. The engine roars to life, but before they pull away, Randy leans over and kisses Walt on the mouth. After a minute or so, they separate; then Walt pulls down the vanity mirror and smoothes his hair.

For a moment, there's silence, save for the thumping of the muffler. Then the car pulls away as we squat, motionless, listening to the sound of the engine until it fades into a low peep.

"Well." Maggie stands up and brushes herself off. "That's that, I guess."

"Hey," The Mouse says gently. "You know what? It's all for the best. You're with Peter, and now Walt is with Randy."

"It's like *A Midsummer Night's Dream*," I add hopefully, "where everyone ends up with the person they're supposed to be with."

"Uh-huh," Maggie says blankly as she heads for the car.

"And you have to admit, Randy Sandler is pretty good-looking. He was one of the best-looking guys on the football team."

"Yeah," I say. "Think about how many girls would be jealous if they knew that Randy was—"

"Gay?" Maggie suddenly screams. "That Randy and Walt are gay? And they're lying to everyone about it?" She yanks open the car door. "It's great. Just great. Thinking for two years that some guy is in love with you and then finding out

that he doesn't even like girls? And all the time you were with him he's been thinking about"—she pauses, takes a breath, and shrieks—"some other *guy*!"

"Maggie, take it easy," The Mouse says.

"I will not take it easy. Why should I?" Maggie starts the engine, then shuts it off and buries her face in her hands. "We were going to move to Vermont. We were going to have an antique store. And a farm stand. And I believed him. And all that time he was lying."

"I'm sure he wasn't," The Mouse says. "He probably had no idea. Then when you guys broke up—"

"He loved you, Mags. He really loved you. Everyone knows that," I say.

"And now *everyone* is going to know how stupid I was. Do you have any idea how utterly dumb I feel right now? I mean, could I *be* any dumber?"

"Maggie." I shake her arm a little. "How were you supposed to know? I mean, a person's sexuality is . . . kind of their own business, right?"

"Not when they hurt other people."

"Walt would never hurt you on purpose," I say, trying to reason with her. "And besides, Mag. This is about Walt. It's not really about you."

Oops. There's an expression of fury I've never seen on Maggie's face before. "Oh yeah?" she snarls. "Then why don't you trying being *me* for a change?" And she bursts into tears.

CHAPTER TWENTY

Slippery Slopes

"These are supposed to be the best days of our lives," I say mournfully.

"Oh, Carrie." George stretches his lips into a smile. "Where do you get these overly sentimental ideas? If you took a survey, you'd find half the adult population hated their high school years and would never want to go back."

"But I don't want to be one of them."

"No danger of that. You've got too much joie de vivre. And you seem to be a great forgiver of human nature."

"I guess I figured out a while ago that most people can't help what they do," I say, encouraged by his interest. "And what they do doesn't usually have anything to do with *you*. I mean, people kind of instinctually do what's best for them at the time and think about the consequences later, right?"

George laughs, but this, I realize with a pang, is a nearly perfect description of my own behavior.

A gust of wind blows a fine dust of snow from the tops of the trees into our faces. I shiver. "You cold?" George slides his arm around my shoulders and pulls me closer.

I nod, inhaling the sharp air. I take in the snow and the pine trees and the cute log-hewn lodges and try to pretend I'm someplace far, far away, like Switzerland.

The Mouse and I forced Maggie to make a pact that we would never tell anyone what we saw that day in East Milton, because it's Walt's business and his to handle how he sees fit. Maggie agreed not to tell anyone—including Peter—but it didn't prevent her from turning into an emotional wreck. She skipped two days of school and spent them in bed; on the third day, when she finally appeared in assembly, her face was puffy and she was wearing sunglasses. Then she wore nothing but black for the rest of the week. The Mouse and I did everything we could—making sure one of us was with her during breaks and even getting food for her at the cafeteria so she didn't have to stand in line—but you'd think the love of her life had died. Which is slightly annoying, because if you look at it from a logical point of view, all that really happened was she dated a guy for two years, broke up with him, and then they both found someone else. Does it really matter if that "someone" is a guy or a girl? But Maggie refuses to see it that way. She insists it's all her fault—she wasn't "woman enough" for Walt.

So when George called and offered to take me skiing, I jumped at the chance to get away from my own life for a few hours.

And the minute I saw his steady, happy face, I found myself telling him all about my problems with Walt and Maggie, and how my piece came out in *The Nutmeg* and my best friend was weird about it. I told him everything, save for the fact that I happen to have a boyfriend. I will tell him today, when the moment is right. But in the meantime, it's such a relief to unburden myself that I don't want to spoil the fun.

I know I'm being selfish. On the other hand, George does seem to find my stories highly entertaining. "You can use all of this in your writing," he said during the drive to the mountain.

"I couldn't," I countered. "If I put any of this in *The Nutmeg*, I'd be run out of school."

"You're experiencing every writer's dilemma. Art versus protecting those you know—and love."

"Not me," I said. "I'd never want to hurt someone for the sake of my writing. I wouldn't be able to live with myself afterward."

"You'll warm up as soon as we get moving," George says now.

"*If* we get moving," I remind him. I peer over the railing of the chairlift to the trail below. It's a wide path bordered by pine trees, where several skiers in candy-colored suits weave across the snow like sewing needles, leaving tracks of thread behind. From this vantage point, they don't appear to be exceptional athletes. If they can do it, why not me?

"You scared?" George asks.

"Nah," I say boldly, even though I've skied a total of three times in my life, and only in Lali's backyard.

"Remember to keep the tips of your skis up. Let the back of the seat push you off."

"Sure," I say, clutching the side of the chairlift. We're nearly at the top, and I've just admitted that I've never actually ridden in a chairlift before.

"All you have to do is get off," George says in amusement. "If you don't, they have to shut down the entire lift and the other skiers get angry."

"Don't want to piss off those snow bunnies," I mutter, bracing for the worst. Within seconds, however, I'm gliding smoothly down a little hill and the chairlift is behind me. "Wow, that was easy," I say, turning back to George. At which point I promptly fall over.

"Not bad for a beginner," George says, helping me up. "You'll see. You'll pick it up in no time. I can tell you're a natural."

George is just so *nice*.

We tackle the bunny slope first, where I manage to master the snowplow and the turn. After a couple of runs, I've worked up my confidence and we move on to the intermediate slope.

"Like it?" George asks on our fourth trip up the chairlift.

"Love it," I exclaim. "It's so much fun."

"You're fun," George says. He leans in for a kiss, and I allow him a quick peck, suddenly feeling like a sleazebag. What would Sebastian think if he saw me here with George?

"George—" I begin, deciding to tell him about Sebastian now, before this goes any further, but he cuts me off.

"Ever since I met you, I've been trying to figure out who you remind me of. And finally, I have."

"Who?" I ask, full of curiosity.

"My great-aunt," he says proudly.

"Your great-aunt?" I ask, with mock outrage. "Do I look that old?"

"It's not how you look. It's your spirit. She has the same fun-loving spirit you do. She's the kind of person other people love to be around." And then he drops the bomb: "She's a writer."

"A writer?" I gasp. "An actual writer?"

He nods. "She was very famous in her time. But she's about eighty now—"

"What's her name?"

"Not going to tell you," he says cunningly. "Not yet. But I'll take you to visit her sometime."

"Tell me!" I demand, playfully swatting his arm.

"Nope. I want it to be a surprise."

George is just full of surprises today. I'm actually having a good time.

"I can't wait for you to meet her. You two are going to love each other."

"I can't wait to meet her, either," I gush with enthusiasm.

Wow. A real writer. I've never met one, with the exception of Mary Gordon Howard.

We slide off the chairlift and pause at the top of the run. And then I take a look down the mountain. It's steep. Really steep. "I'd like to get down this hill, first, though," I add, clutching my ski poles.

"You'll be fine," he says reassuringly. "Take it slow and do lots of turns."

I do pretty well at the top of the hill. But when we get to the first drop-off, I'm suddenly terrified. I stop, dizzy with panic. "I can't do this." I grimace. "Can I take off my skis and walk down?"

"If you do, you'll look like a total wimp," George says. "Come on, kiddo. I'll go ahead of you. Follow me and do everything I do and you'll be fine."

George pushes off. I bend my knees, picturing myself on crutches, when a young woman glides past. I only catch a glimpse of her profile, but she looks oddly familiar. Then I register the fact that she's incredibly stunning, with long, straight blond hair, a rabbit-fur headband, and a white one-piece ski suit with silver stars up the side. I'm not the only one who's noticed her though.

"Amelia!" George cries out.

This gorgeous Amelia girl, who looks like she belongs in an ad for some fresh outdoorsy toothpaste, slides smoothly to a stop, lifts her goggles, and beams. "George!" she exclaims.

"Hey!" George says, and skis after her.

So much for helping the skiing impaired.

He slides up next to her, kisses her on both cheeks, exchanges a few words, and then looks uphill. "Carrie!" he cries, waving. "Come on. I want you to meet a friend of mine."

"Nice to meet you," I yell from afar.

"Come down," George shouts.

"We can't come to you so you'll have to come to us," adds the Amelia person, who is beginning to irritate me with her easy perfection. She's obviously one of those expert-types who learned to ski before she could walk.

Here goes nothing. Gripping my knees, I push off on my poles.

Fantastic. I'm heading straight for them. There's only one problem: I can't stop.

"Watch out!" I scream. By some miracle of nature, I don't actually ram right into Amelia, only scraping the tops of her skis. I do, however, grab her arm to stop myself, at which point I fall over and pull her down on top of me.

For a few seconds, we just lie there, our heads inches apart. Once again, I have a sickening feeling that I *know* Amelia. Maybe she's an actress or something?

And then we're surrounded. What nobody tells you about skiing is, if you fall down, within seconds you will be rescued by several people, all of whom are much better skiers than you are and filled with all kinds of advice, and shortly thereafter, the ski patrol will arrive with a stretcher.

"I'm fine," I keep insisting. "It was nothing."

Amelia is back up and ready to go—she only tipped over, after all—but I, on the other hand, am not. I'm petrified, envisioning another headlong plunge down the mountain. But then I'm informed—happily, for me—that my ski went and crashed into a tree all on its own. Said ski is now slightly cracked—"Better your ski than your head!" George keeps saying over and over—so I will not be attempting the Bradshaw skidoo after all.

Unfortunately, the only way I can get down the mountain now is by stretcher. This is horrendously embarrassing and excessively dramatic. I lift my mittened paw and wave weakly at George and Amelia as they lower their goggles, plant their poles, and leap into the abyss.

"Done much skiing?" asks the ski patrol guy as he tightens a strap across my chest.

"Not really."

"You shouldn't be on the intermediate slope," he scolds. "We try to emphasize safety here. Skiers should never take runs that are above their abilities."

"It's the number one cause of accidents," adds a second. "You were lucky this time. Try this again, and you're not only a danger to yourself, but a danger to other skiers."

Well, *excuuuuuse* me.

Now I feel like a complete crap heel.

George—good old, faithful George—is waiting at the bottom. "Are you really okay?" he asks, bending over the stretcher.

"I'm fine. My ego is bruised, but my body seems to be intact." And, apparently, ready for more humiliation.

"Good," he says, taking my arm. "I told Amelia we'd meet her in the lodge for an Irish coffee. She's an old friend of mine from Brown. Don't worry," he adds, taking in my expression. "She's not competition. She's a couple of years *older*."

We clomp into the lodge, which is steamy and loud, filled with happy people boasting about the great day they had on the slopes. Amelia is seated near the fireplace; having removed her jacket, she's in a tight-fitting silver top and has managed to brush her hair and put on lipstick, which makes her now look like she's in an ad for hair spray.

"Amelia, this is Carrie," George says. "I don't think you've been properly introduced."

"No, we haven't," Amelia says warmly, shaking my hand. "In any case, it's not your fault. George should never have taken you on that run. He's a very dangerous man to be around."

"He is?" I ask, settling into a chair.

"Remember that white-water-rafting trip?" she asks, then turns to me and adds, "Colorado," as if I, too, should be familiar with the incident.

"You were not scared," George insists.

"I was. I was terrified to death."

"Now I know you're joking." George points his finger at her for emphasis and pats my hand. "Amelia isn't afraid of anything."

"That's not true. I'm afraid of not getting into law school."

Oh boy. So this Amelia is beautiful *and* smart. "Where are you from, Carrie?" she asks, in an attempt to include me in the conversation.

"Castlebury. But you've probably never heard of it. It's this tiny farm town on the river—"

"Oh, I know all about it." She smiles sympathetically. "I grew up there."

I suddenly feel queasy.

"What's your last name again?" she asks curiously.

"Bradshaw," George says, signaling the waitress.

Amelia raises her brows in recognition. "I'm Amelia Kydd. I think you're dating my brother."

"Huh?" George says, looking from Amelia to me.

My face reddens. "Sebastian?" I croak. I recall Sebastian talking about an older sister and how fantastic she was, but she was supposed to be away at college in California.

"He talks about you all the time."

"He does?" I murmur. I sneak a look at George. His face is intensely blank, save for a bright red patch on each cheek.

He determinedly ignores me. "I want to know everything you've been up to since I last saw you," he says to Amelia.

I break out in a sweat, wishing I'd broken my leg after all.

We ride most of the way home in silence.

Yes, I should have told George I had a boyfriend. I should have told him the first night we had dinner. But then Dorrit was arrested and there was no time. I should have told him on the phone, but let's face it, he was helping me with my writing and I didn't want to screw that up. And I would have told him today, but we ran into Amelia. Who happens to be Sebastian's sister. I suppose I could argue it's not entirely my fault, because George never asked if I had a boyfriend. On the other hand, maybe you're not supposed to ask if a person is seeing someone else if they agree to go out with you—and continue to see you. Maybe dating is like the honor system: If you're otherwise engaged, it's your moral duty to let the other person know right away.

Problem is, people don't always play by the rules.

How am I going to explain this to George? And what about Sebastian? I spend half my time worrying that Sebastian is going to cheat on me, while the person I should be concerned about is myself.

I peek at George. He's frowning, concentrating on the road as if his life depends on it.

"George," I beseech him. "I'm so sorry. Honestly. I kept meaning to tell you—"

"As a matter of fact, I happen to be seeing other women as well," he says coldly.

"Okay."

"But what I don't appreciate is being put into a situation that makes me look like an asshole."

"You're not an asshole. And I really, really like you—"

"But you like Sebastian Kydd better," he snaps. "Don't worry. I get it."

We pull into my driveway. "Can we at least be friends?" I plead, making a last-ditch effort to rectify the situation.

He stares straight ahead. "Sure, Carrie Bradshaw. Tell you what. Why don't you give me a ring when you and Sebastian break up? Your little fling with Sebastian won't last long. Count on it."

For a moment, I sit there, stung. "If you want to be that way, fine. But I didn't mean to hurt you. And I said I was sorry." I'm about to get out of the car, when he grabs my wrist.

"I'm sorry, Carrie," he says, instantly contrite. "I didn't mean to be harsh. But you do know why Sebastian got kicked out of school, right?"

"For selling drugs?" I ask stiffly.

"Oh, Carrie." He sighs. "Sebastian doesn't have the guts to be a drug dealer. He got kicked out for cheating."

I say nothing. Then I'm suddenly angry. "Thanks, George," I say, getting out of the car. "Thanks for a great day."

I stand in the driveway, watching him go. I guess I won't be visiting George in New York after all. And I certainly won't be meeting his great-aunt, the writer. Whoever she is.

Dorrit comes out of the house and joins me. "Where's George going?" she asks plaintively. "Why didn't he come in?"

"I don't think we're going to be seeing any more of George Carter," I say with a mixture of finality and relief.

I leave Dorrit standing in the driveway looking extremely disappointed.

CHAPTER TWENTY-ONE

The Hall

The judges hold up their scores: Four-point-three. Four-point-one. Three-point-nine. There's a collective groan from the stands.

That puts me in second-to-last place.

I grab a towel and drop it over my head, rubbing my hair. Coach Nipsie is standing to the side, arms crossed, staring at the scoreboard. "Concentration, Bradshaw," he mutters.

I take my place in the bleachers, next to Lali. "Bad luck," she says. Lali is doing great in this meet. She won her heat, making her the favorite to win the two-hundred-meter freestyle. "You've still got one more dive," she says encouragingly.

I nod, scanning the bleachers on the other side of the pool for Sebastian. He's on the third riser, next to Walt and Maggie.

"Do you have your period?" Lali asks.

Maybe because we spend so much time together, Lali and I are usually on the same cycle. I wish I could blame my performance on hormones, but I can't. I've been spending too much time with Sebastian, and it shows. "Nope," I say glumly. "Do you?"

"Got it last week," Lali says. She looks across the pool, spots Sebastian, and waves. He waves back. "Sebastian's watching," Lali says as I get up to do my final dive. "Don't screw up."

I sigh, trying to focus as I climb the ladder. I stand at the ready, arms by my side, palms facing backward, when I have an unsettling but startlingly clear revelation: I don't want to do this anymore.

I take four steps and hop, launching my body straight into the air, but instead of flying, I'm suddenly falling. For a split-second I see myself hurtling off a cliff, wondering what will happen when I hit bottom. Will I wake up, or will I be dead?

I enter the water with my knees bent, followed by an ugly splash.

I'm finished. I head to the locker room, peel off my suit, and step into the shower.

I always knew someday I'd leave diving behind. It was never going to be my future—I knew I'd never be good enough to dive on a college team. But it wasn't just the actual sport that made it fun. It was the raucous bus trips to other schools, the ongoing backgammon games we'd play in between heats, the excitement of knowing you're going to win and then pulling it off. There were bad days too, when I knew I was off. I'd chastise myself, vow to try harder, and move on. But today, my lousy diving feels like more than a lousy day. It feels unavoidable, like I've reached the limits of my abilities.

I'm done.

I get out of the shower and wrap myself in a towel. I wipe a patch of steam off the mirror and stare at my face. I don't look any different. But I feel different.

This isn't me. I shake out my hair and flip the ends under, wondering how I'd look with a shorter haircut. Lali just cut her hair, feathering the top and spritzing it with a can of hair spray she keeps in her locker. Lali never worried much about her hair before, and when I commented on it, she said, "We're at the age when we need to start thinking about how we look to guys," which I thought was probably a joke.

"What guys?" I asked, and she responded, "All guys," and then she looked me up and down and smiled.

Was she referring to Sebastian?

If I quit swim team, I could spend more time with him.

It's been two weeks since the skiing incident with George. For days I was petrified Sebastian's sister, Amelia, would tell him she met me with George, but so far, Sebastian hasn't mentioned it. Which means she either hasn't told him, or she has, and he doesn't care. I even tried to get to the bottom of it by asking him about his sister, but all he said was, "She's really cool," and "Maybe you'll meet her someday."

Then I tried asking him why he left prep school to come to Castlebury High. I didn't want to believe what George told me was true—after all, why would Sebastian need to cheat when he was smart enough to take courses like calculus?—but he only laughed and said, "I needed a change."

George, I decided, was simply jealous.

Having been granted a reprieve on the George front, I've been determined to be a better girlfriend to Sebastian. Unfortunately, so far it means putting aside most of my normal activities. Like swimming.

Nearly every other day, Sebastian tries to get me to ditch practice by tempting me with an alternative plan. "Let's go to the Mystic Aquarium and look at killer whales."

"I have swim team. And then I have to study."

"The aquarium is very educational."

"I don't think looking at killer whales is going to help me get into college."

"You're so boring," he'd say, in a way that made it clear if I didn't want to hang out with him, some other girl would. "Skip practice and we'll go see *Urban Cowboy*," he said one afternoon. "We can make out in the movie theater." I agreed to this outing. It was a miserable day and the last place I wanted to be was in a cold pool—but I felt guilty through the entire movie and Sebastian annoyed the hell out of me when he kept putting my hand inside the front of his jeans to squeeze his penis. Sebastian was a lot more advanced than I was when it came to sex—he often made casual references to various "girlfriends" he'd dated at prep school—but the girlfriends never seemed to last more than a few weeks or so.

"What happened to them?" I asked.

"They were crazy," he said matter-of-factly, as if craziness was an inevitable by-product of dating him.

Now I jerk open my locker, pause, and wonder if I've been cursed with the same affliction.

My locker is empty.

I shut it and check the number. It's my locker, all right. I open it again, thinking I've made a mistake, but it's still empty. I check the lockers to the left and the right. They're empty too. I wrap the towel around my waist and sit down on the bench. Where the hell is my stuff? And then it hits me: Donna LaDonna and the two Jens.

I'd spotted them at the beginning of the meet, sitting on the edge of a bleacher, snickering, but I didn't think much about it. Actually, I did think something about it, but I never thought they'd go this far. Especially since Donna apparently does have a new boyfriend—the guy I saw her with outside her house. The two Jens have been busy spreading rumors about him, telling anyone who will listen that he's an older guy who goes to Boston University but is also a famous male model who's in an ad for Paco Rabanne. Shortly thereafter, a page ripped from a magazine, featuring a photograph of a guy holding a bottle of aftershave, appeared taped to Donna LaDonna's locker. The image stayed put for several days, until Lali couldn't take it anymore and scribbled a thought bubble coming out of the model's head that read: *I AM M-T AND STOOPID.*

Donna probably thought I did it, and now she's out for revenge.

Enough. I yank open the door to the pool, about to stride out, when I realize a race is in progress and Lali is swimming. I can't stroll out in the middle of a meet wearing only a towel. I peer around the door into the bleachers. Donna LaDonna and the two Jens are gone. Sebastian is absorbed in the race, raising his fist when Lali flips her legs over her head two feet from the wall and shoots into first place. Walt is looking around as though planning his escape, while next to him, Maggie is yawning.

Maggie. I've got to get to Maggie.

I hurry to the end of the locker room and scoot out the door that leads to the hallway, then skittle across the hall and through an entrance to the outside. It's freezing and I'm barefoot, but so far, no one has seen me. I scurry around the building to the back wall and slip through a door that opens right under the bleachers. I creep under the tangle of legs and grab Maggie's foot. She jumps and looks around.

"Mags," I hiss.

"Carrie?" she says, peering down through the slats. "What are you doing here? And where are your clothes?"

"Give me your coat," I implore.

"Why?"

"Maggie, please." I tug her coat off the seat next to her.

"Don't ask. Meet me in the locker room and I'll explain."

I grab the coat and make a run for it.

"Carrie?" she says, a few minutes later, her voice echoing through the empty locker room.

"Over here." I'm searching through the dirty towel bin, thinking maybe Donna dumped my clothes. I find a gross pair of gym shorts, a dirty sock, and a yellow bandanna. "Donna LaDonna took my clothes," I say, giving up.

Maggie's eyes narrow. "How do you know?"

"Come on, Mags." I wrap her coat around my shoulders. I'm still cold from my run outside. "Who else would do it?"

She plops down on a bench. "This has to stop."

"Tell me about it."

"No. Really, Carrie. It *has* to *stop*."

"What am *I* supposed to do?"

"*You're* not supposed to do anything. Make Sebastian do something. Make him tell her to end it."

"It's not really his fault."

"Actually, it is. Have you forgotten how Sebastian led Donna LaDonna on and then dumped her for you?"

"He told her he wasn't serious and he'd just moved back and was going to see other people."

"Well, obviously. After all, he got what he wanted."

"Right," I say. My hatred for Donna LaDonna feels like a physical object—round and hard—lodged in my belly.

"And he should be defending you. Against her."

"What if he won't?"

"Then you should break up with him."

"But I don't want to break up with him."

"All I know is that Peter would defend me," Maggie says vehemently.

Is Maggie doing this on purpose? Trying to get me to break up with Sebastian? Is there some kind of conspiracy going on that I don't know about? "Having to have a guy defend you—it's so old-fashioned," I say sharply. "Shouldn't we be able to defend ourselves?"

"I want a guy who will stick up for me," Maggie says stubbornly. "It's like a friend. Would you put up with a friend who wouldn't stick up for you?"

"No," I agree reluctantly.

"Okay then." The door to the locker room swings open and Lali comes running in followed by several teammates. They're high-fiving and snapping one another with wet towels.

"Where were you?" she asks, peeling off her suit. "I won."

"Knew you would," I say, slapping her outstretched palm.

"Seriously, though. You disappeared. You're not upset, are you? About choking on your dives?"

"Nah. I'm fine." I have too many other things to be upset about now. "You don't have an extra pair of shoes, do you?"

"Well, *I* think it's hilarious," Lali declares. "I laughed so hard, I nearly peed in my pants."

"Uh-huh," I say with stiff sarcasm. "I'm still laughing."

"You have to admit. It *is* pretty funny," Sebastian says.

"I don't have to admit a thing," I say, crossing my arms as we pull into my driveway. A burning fury suddenly overtakes me. "And I don't think it's funny *at all*." I open the door, get out, and slam it as hard as I can. I run into the house, imagining Lali and Sebastian sitting in the car in shock. Then they'll look at each other and burst out laughing.

At me.

I race up the stairs to my room. "What's going on?" Missy asks as this whirlwind passes her.

"Nothing!"

"Thought you were going to the dance."

"I *am*." I slam the door to my bedroom.

"Jesus," Dorrit says from the other side.

I'm *over it*. Finished. Done. I open my closet and start throwing shoes across the room.

"Carrie?" Missy knocks on the door. "Can I come in?"

"If you don't mind having your eye blackened by flying footwear!"

"What's wrong?" Missy cries, entering the room.

"I am so sick of going out with my boyfriend and having my best friend always tagging along. I am so sick of the two of them making fun of me. And I'm so sick of these *little idiot girls*"—I really scream this part, as loud as I can—"following me around and making my life *hell*." I heave a high-heeled shoe that belonged to my grandmother with such force that the heel actually penetrates the spine of a book.

Missy is unfazed. She sits cross-legged on the bed and nods her head thoughtfully. "I'm glad you brought this up. I've been wanting to talk to you about this for a while. I think Lali is trying to undermine your relationship with Sebastian."

"No kidding," I snarl, yanking back the curtain and peering out the window. They're still out there. Sitting in the car, laughing.

But what can I do? If I go out there and confront them, I'm going to look insecure. If I say nothing, they'll continue.

Missy folds her hands under her chin. "You know what the problem is? Mom never taught us any feminine wiles."

"Was she supposed to?"

"I mean, here we are, knowing nothing about boys. Nothing about how to get them or how to keep them."

"Because when Mom met Dad, they immediately fell in love and he asked her to marry him right away," I say mournfully. "She didn't have to try. She didn't have to scheme. She didn't have to deal with a Lali. Or a Donna LaDonna. Or the two Jens. She probably thought we'd be just like her. Some guy would come along and instantly fall in love with us and we'd never have to worry."

"I know." Missy nods. "I think, when it comes to men, we're doomed."

CHAPTER TWENTY-TWO

Dancing Fools

"What do you think?" The Mouse asks shyly, dipping her finger into a pot of gloss and dabbing it onto her lips.

"He's adorable, Mouse. He really is."

The Mouse has finally made good on her promise to introduce us to her mysterious Washington boyfriend, Danny Chai, and has brought him to the dance. He's a tall, delicate boy with black hair, glasses, and lovely manners, who found a place for our coats and got us two glasses of punch, to which he cleverly added vodka from a flask hidden in his jacket pocket. I've never seen The Mouse insecure, but she keeps dragging me to the bathroom, checking to make sure her hair is still in place and her shirt is properly tucked into her jeans.

"And it's adorable that you're wearing lip gloss," I add teasingly.

"Is it too much?" she asks in alarm.

"No. It looks great. It's just that I've never seen you wear lip gloss before."

She looks in the mirror, considering. "Maybe I should take it off. I don't want him to think I'm trying too hard."

"Mouse, he's not going to think you're trying too hard. All he's going to think is that you're beautiful."

"Carrie," she whispers, like a little kid with a secret. "I think I really, really like him. I think he could be the one."

"That's fantastic." I give her a hug. "You deserve someone great."

"So do you, Bradley." She hesitates. "What about Sebastian?" she asks casually.

I shrug, pretending to search for something in my bag. How can I explain? I'm crazy about Sebastian in a way that feels overwhelming and amazing and disturbing and probably unhealthy. And at first, being with Sebastian was like being in the middle of the best dream I'd ever had—but now it mostly feels exhausting. I'm up one minute and down the next, questioning what I say and do. Even questioning my sanity.

"Bradley?"

"I don't know," I say, thinking about how Lali and Sebastian were laughing about how Donna LaDonna and the two Jens stole my clothes. "Sometimes I think—"

"What?" The Mouse asks sharply.

I shake my head. I can't do it. I can't tell The Mouse that sometimes I think my boyfriend likes my best friend better than me. It's too paranoid and creepy.

"I think Lali needs a boyfriend," The Mouse says. "Doesn't Sebastian have a friend he could fix her up with?"

There's my solution. If Lali had a boyfriend, she'd be too preoccupied with him to keep tagging along with me and Sebastian. And it's not like I ever discouraged her from hanging out with us. I guess I feel a little guilty that I have a boyfriend and she doesn't. I don't want her to feel abandoned. I don't want to be one of those girls who forgets about her friends as soon as some guy comes along.

"I'll work on it," I say, feeling some of my old confidence coming back.

But it's immediately deflated when I pull open the door to the gym. Disco music is blaring from the speakers, and I spot the top of Sebastian's head, bobbing and weaving as the crowd hoots and claps. He's doing the Hustle, but with whom? My throat tightens. I figure he's dancing with Lali, but then Lali comes up and grabs my arm.

"I think you need a drink."

"I have a drink," I say, indicating my vodka-laced punch.

"You need another one."

I wriggle away toward the crowd. "Bradley! You don't want to see this." Lali sounds alarmed as I push my way to the center.

Sebastian is dancing with Donna LaDonna.

I'm immediately overcome by a desire to storm up to him and throw my drink in his face. I can picture it, my hand shooting forward, sloshing the sticky sweet liquid all over his pale skin, his shocked expression followed by frantic pawing. But Lali stops me.

"Don't do it, Bradley. Don't give them the satisfaction." She spins around and spots The Mouse and Danny. The Mouse is whispering angrily into Danny's ear, no doubt explaining the horror of the situation.

"Excuse me," Lali says, inserting herself between them. "Do you mind if we borrow your boyfriend?"

And before poor Danny can protest, Lali takes his arm and leads him onto the dance floor, grabbing my wrist in the process. We sandwich Danny between us, shimmying up and down his legs, spinning him around, and generally causing the sort of mayhem that results in Danny's glasses flying off his face. Poor Danny. Unfortunately, I can't really worry about him because I'm too busy trying to ignore Sebastian and Donna LaDonna.

Our antics get the crowd's attention, and as Lali and I do-si-do Danny across the floor, Donna LaDonna retreats to the edge, sporting a tight smile. Suddenly, Sebastian is behind me, his hands around my waist. I twirl around and with my lips close to his ear, hiss, "Fuck you."

"Huh?" He's startled. Then amused, thinking I can't be serious.

"I mean it. Fuck you."

I can't believe I just said that.

For a moment, I'm high on my anger, the buzz in my head drowning out all other sound. Then the impact of what I've said penetrates like a sting, and I'm horrified and embarrassed. I don't think I've ever said "fuck you" to anyone, except maybe once or twice in passing, muttered under my breath, but never in a face-to-face confrontation. Those words, gigantic and ugly, sit between us like two enormous boulders, and now I can't see my way around them.

It's too late to say "I'm sorry." And I don't want to, because I'm not sorry. He was dancing with Donna LaDonna. In front of everyone.

It's inexcusable, isn't it?

His face is hard, his eyes narrowed, like a child who's been caught out, whose first instinct is to deny any wrongdoing and blame his accuser.

"How could you?" I say, more shrilly than I intended, and loud enough for the small group of people around us to overhear.

"You're crazy," he says, and takes a step back.

I'm suddenly aware of ripples of movement through the crowd—nudging and nodding, faces curling into curious smiles. I'm frozen with indecision. If I move toward him he might push me away. If I walk away, it will probably be the end of our relationship.

"Sebastian—"

"What?" He sneers.

"Forget it." And before he can say more, I storm off.

I'm immediately surrounded by my friends.

"What happened?"

"What did he say?"

"Why was he dancing with Donna LaDonna?"

"I'm going to beat the crap out of him." That's Lali.

"No. Don't make it worse."

"Are you going to break up with him?" Maggie asks.

"Does she have a choice?" Lali says.

I'm numb. "Was I wrong?" I turn to The Mouse.

"Not at all. He's acting like a shit."

"What should I do?"

"Don't go up to him, no matter what you do," Danny says, stepping in. "Ignore him. Let him come to you. Otherwise you look desperate."

This Danny—he's very wise. Even so, I can't help scanning the gym for Sebastian.

He's gone.

My heart freezes. "Maybe I should go home," I say, full of uncertainty.

The Mouse and Danny exchange a look. "We'll take you," The Mouse says firmly.

"Lali?" I ask.

"Maybe you *should* go home, Bradley," she agrees. "You've had a really rotten day."

Thanks. "If Sebastian—"

"Don't worry. I'll take care of him," she says, and punches her fist into her hand.

I allow The Mouse and Danny to lead me away.

Sebastian's car is still in the parking lot, exactly where we left it an hour ago, when we were somewhat happily in love.

How is this possible? How can a three-month relationship

end in less than fifteen minutes? But the world can change in seconds. There are sudden car accidents. And deaths. They say you're lucky if you know someone is going to die, because that way you have time to say good-bye.

My knees buckle. I stumble to the curb and collapse in a heap.

"Carrie! Are you okay?"

I nod miserably. "Maybe I shouldn't go. Maybe I should stay and confront him."

The Mouse and Danny exchange another glance, as if they already have some kind of secret ESP couple thing between them.

"I don't think it's a good idea," Danny says soothingly. "He's probably drunk. And you're a little drunk yourself. You don't want to have a confrontation with him when he's drunk."

"Why not?" I ask, wondering where The Mouse found this guy.

"Because when a guy's drunk, all he can think about is winning. And not losing face."

"Walt," I say. "I want to see Walt."

For once, Walt actually is working at the Hamburger Shack.

"Are you sure you're okay?" The Mouse asks again.

"I'm fine," I say breezily, knowing she wants to be alone with Danny.

Danny walks me to the entrance. As we say good-bye, he looks into my eyes with what appears to be a deep, sympathetic understanding, and suddenly, I envy The Mouse. A girl could be comfortable with a guy like Danny. She wouldn't have to wonder if he was going to flirt with her best friend or dance with her worst enemy. I wonder if I'll ever find a guy like that. And if I do, whether I'll be smart enough to want him.

"Hey," Walt says as I saunter up to the counter. It's nearly nine thirty, almost closing time, and he's cleaning up, putting chopped onions and peppers into a Tupperware container. "I hope you're not here for food."

"I came to see you," I insist, then suddenly realize I'm starving. "A cheeseburger might be nice, though."

Walt looks at the clock. "I need to be out of here—"

"Walt, *please*."

He looks at me strangely, but unwraps a hamburger patty and puts it on the grill. "Where's your *boyfriend*?" he asks, as if "boyfriend" is barely a word worth saying.

"We broke up."

"Nice," Walt says. "Sounds like your week's been about as good as mine."

"Why?" I pull a few napkins from the metal holder. "Did you break up with someone too?"

He turns his head sharply. "What's that supposed to mean?"

"Nothing," I say, feigning innocence. "Come on, Walt. We used to be best friends. We used to tell each other everything."

"Not everything, Carrie."

"Well, lots of things, anyway."

"That was before you dumped me for Maggie," he says

sarcastically. Then he adds quickly, "Don't be upset. I'm not. I expected that when Maggie and I divorced, everyone would take sides. Maggie got all our friends."

This makes me laugh. "I've missed you."

"Yeah. I guess I've sort of missed you too." He flips the hamburger, puts a prewrapped piece of cheese on top, opens a bun, and places the two pieces on either side.

"You want onions and peppers?"

"Sure." I fool around with the bottles of mustard and ketchup, until I can't stand the guilt any longer. "Walt. I have something to tell you. It's really horrible, and you're probably going to want to kill me, but don't, okay?"

He lifts the hamburger onto the bottom of the bun. "Lemme guess. Maggie is pregnant."

"She is?" I ask in shock.

"How would *I* know?" he asks, sliding the cheeseburger onto a plastic plate and pushing it toward me.

I stare down at the burger. "Walt. I *know.*"

"So she is pregnant," he says, resigned, as if this was always going to be a foregone conclusion.

"Not about Maggie." I take a bite of the burger. "About you."

He wipes the counter with a cloth. "I can assure you I'm not pregnant."

"Come on, Walt." I hesitate, holding the burger between my hands like a shield. If I'm going to tell him, I have to do it now. "Don't be mad, please. But you've been acting so strangely. I thought you were in some kind of trouble.

And then Sebastian—"

"What about Sebastian?" he asks, his voice tightening.

"He said he'd seen you—at that place. And then The Mouse and I—we spied on you."

There. I've said it. And I will not tell him Maggie was there. I mean, I will tell him, eventually. After he digests this information.

Walt breaks out into a nervous laugh. "And what did you see?"

I'm so relieved he's not angry I take another bite of the cheeseburger. "You," I say with my mouth full. "And Randy Sandler."

He freezes, and then yanks his apron over his head. "That's just great," he says bitterly. "How many other people know besides you now?"

"No one," I insist. "We didn't tell anyone. We wouldn't. I mean, it's your business, not ours, right?"

"Apparently it is your business." He throws the apron into the sink and stalks out the swinging door in back.

I sigh. Can this evening get any worse?

I grab my coat and run after him. He's standing behind the restaurant, trying to light up a cigarette. "Walt, I'm *sorry.*"

He shakes his head as he inhales, holds the smoke in his lungs, and slowly releases it. "It was going to come out anyway." He takes another drag. "Although I was hoping I could keep it a secret until I go to college and get away from my father."

"Why? What's he going to do?"

"Ground me. Or send me to one of those shrinks who are supposed to convert you back to straightdom. Or maybe he'll send me to a priest, who will tell me what a sinner I am. Wouldn't that be ironic?"

"I feel horrible."

"Why should you feel bad? You're not gay." He exhales a stream of smoke and looks up at the sky. "Anyway, I doubt this is going to come as much of a surprise. He already calls me a homo and a fag—oh, and he likes to refer to me as sissy pants behind my back."

"Your own father?"

"Yeah, Carrie, my own father," he says, grinding the cigarette butt under his shoe. "Fuck him," he says suddenly. "He doesn't deserve my respect. If he's embarrassed, it's his problem." He looks at his watch. "I take it you're not going back to the dance."

"I can't."

"Randy's picking me up. We're going to go someplace. You want to come?"

Randy arrives about five minutes later in his souped-up Mustang. He and Walt have a hushed conversation, then Walt motions for me to get into the car.

Ten minutes later, I'm wedged into the tiny backseat as we head south on Route 91. The music is blaring and I can't quite get over the fact that I'm out with macho Randy Sandler, the ex-quarterback of the Castlebury High football team, who is now Walt's boyfriend. I guess I don't know as much about people as I thought I did. I have a lot to learn, but it's kind of exciting.

"Where are we going?" I yell over the music.

"P-Town," Walt shouts.

"Provincetown?"

"We need to go to another state to have fun," Randy says. "How fucked up is that?"

Yikes. Provincetown is on Cape Cod, at least an hour away. I probably shouldn't be doing this. I'm going to get into trouble. But then I remember Donna LaDonna and Sebastian and all the rest of my lousy life, and I think—*what the hell?* I'm always trying to be good, and where has it gotten me?

Nowhere.

"You cool with that?" Randy shouts.

"I'm cool with anything."

"So this guy, Sebastian Kydd, was dancing with your worst enemy?" Randy shouts over the music.

"Yes." I strain to make myself heard.

"And he saw us. At Chuckie's," Walt yells to Randy.

"Maybe *he's* gay," I scream.

"I think I know this guy," Randy shouts, nodding at Walt. "Tall, blond hair, looks like some asshole from a Ralph Lauren ad?"

"That's him!" I cry.

"He's hot," Randy says. "But not gay. I've seen him renting porn tapes. Jugs—that kind of thing."

Porn? Jugs? Who *is* Sebastian? "Great!" I scream.

"Forget about that asshole," Randy yells. "You're about to meet two hundred guys who are gonna *love* you."

CHAPTER TWENTY-THREE

The Assumption of X

"Carrie?" Missy asks.

"Wake up!" Dorrit shouts in my ear.

I moan as visions of twisting pelvises swirl through my head.

"Carrie? Are you alive?"

"Mng." I gulp.

"Uh-oh," Dorrit says as I throw back the covers.

"Get away." I leap out of bed, run to the bathroom, and get sick.

When I look up, Missy and Dorrit are there. Dorrit's lips are curled into an evil, triumphant smile, like the Grinch who thinks he's stolen Christmas.

"Does Dad know?" I ask.

"That you got home at three a.m.? I don't think so," Missy whispers.

"Don't tell him," I say warningly, glaring at Dorrit.

"Sebastian's downstairs," she says sweetly.

Huh?

He's seated at the dining room table across from my father. "If you assume that X equals minus-Y to the tenth degree," my father says, scribbling an equation on the back of an envelope, "then it's obvious that Z becomes a random integer." He pushes the envelope toward Sebastian, who glances at it politely.

"Hello," I say, with a little wave.

"Morning," my father says. His manner indicates he's considering questioning me about my ragged appearance, but apparently his equation is more interesting. "You see, Sebastian?" He continues tapping his pencil on the X. "The danger here is in the assumption of X—"

I skittle by and hurry into the kitchen, where I dig around for an old jar of instant coffee, dump half of it into a mug, and wait for the water to boil. The phrase "a watched pot never boils" comes into my head. But that isn't true. With the application of proper heat, the water will boil eventually, whether someone is watching or not. Which somehow seems very relevant to this situation. Or maybe it's just that my brain feels like its boiling.

I take my mug into the dining room and sit down. My father has moved on from calculus to grilling Sebastian about his future. "Where did you say you were going to college?" he asks in an uptight voice—a tip-off that Sebastian has failed to impress him with his knowledge of assumptive integers.

"I didn't." Sebastian smiles and pats my leg possessively, which is sure to make my father insane. I squeeze his hand to make him stop. "I thought I'd take a year off," Sebastian says. "Travel the world. Check out the Himalayas—that kind of thing."

My father looks skeptical as I take a sip of my coffee. It's still too hot and has the consistency of sludge.

"I'm not ready to get boxed in," Sebastian continues, as if this explains his lack of ambition.

"You must have some money, then."

"Dad!" I exclaim.

"Actually, I do. My grandmother died and left me and my sister her estate."

"Aha." My father nods. "I get it. You're a very lucky young man. I'll bet if you're ever in trouble, you always manage to get out of it."

"I don't know about that, sir," Sebastian says politely. "But I am lucky." He looks at me and puts his hand over mine. "I've been lucky enough to meet your daughter, anyway."

I suppose this should thrill me, but it only makes me want to puke again. What new game is he playing now?

My father gives me a look, as if he can't believe this guy, but I can only manage a sickly smile.

"So anyway," Sebastian says, clapping his hands together. "I was wondering if you wanted to go ice skating."

Ice skating?

"Hurry up and finish your coffee." He stands and shakes my father's hand. "Nice to see you, Mr. Bradshaw."

"Nice to see *you*," my father says. I can tell he doesn't know what to make of him, because then he pats Sebastian on the shoulder.

Men are so *weird*.

Am I supposed to start this conversation or is he? Or are we going to pretend nothing happened last night?

"How's Donna LaDonna? Do you think you can get her to give me my clothes back?"

The suddenness of my attack startles him. His skate slides out beneath him and for a moment, he flails. "Ha. You're one to talk."

He steadies himself and we glide along silently, while I mull this over.

It's *my* fault?

What did I do? I pull my cap down over my ears as a boy on hockey skates hurtles toward us, laughing over his shoulder at his friends, completely unaware of the dozens of other people skating on the pond. Sebastian grabs the kid's shoulders as we're about to collide and pushes him off in the other direction. "Watch it!" he says.

"You watch it!" the kid growls.

I skate away to the side, where several sawhorses have been set up around a patch of dangerous ice. Black water laps at the edges of a ragged hole.

"You were the one who disappeared last night," Sebastian points out, a note of smug triumph in his voice.

I give him a half-dirty, half-astonished look.

"I was looking for you everywhere. And then Lali told me you'd left. Really, Carrie," he says, shaking his head. "That was rude."

"And it wasn't rude of you to dance with Donna LaDonna?"

"It was a dance. That's what people do at a dance. They *dance*." He takes a pack of cigarettes from inside his leather jacket.

"No kidding. But they don't dance with their girlfriend's worst enemy. Who also stole her clothes!"

"Carrie," he says patiently. "Donna LaDonna did not steal your clothes."

"Then who did?"

"Lali."

"What?"

"I had a long talk with Lali after you left." He holds a cigarette between his thumb and forefinger as he lights up. "She meant it as a joke."

I suddenly feel queasy. Or queasier, as the cold air has done little to alleviate my hangover.

"Don't be mad. She was afraid to tell you because you made such a big deal out of it. I told her I would tell you and she asked me not to because she didn't want you to be angry." He pauses, smokes some more, and flicks the cigarette butt into the patch of dark water, where it sizzles like a defective firecracker before floating gently under the ice. "We both know how sensitive you are."

"So now I'm sensitive?"

"Come on. I mean, with what happened to your mother—"

"Has Lali been talking to you about my mother, too?"

"No," he says defensively. "I mean, maybe she mentioned it a couple of times. But what's the big deal? Everybody knows—"

I think I'm going to be sick again.

Don't bring my mother into this. Not today. I can't handle it. Without speaking, I pick up a splinter of wood and toss it into the watery hole.

"Are you *crying*?" he asks, half smirking and half sympathetic.

"Of course not."

"You *are*." He sounds almost gleeful. "You act all cool on the outside, like nothing bothers you, but inside you really care. You're a romantic. You want someone to love you."

Doesn't everyone? I'm about to speak, but something about his expression stops me. There's a flicker of hostility mixed with a searching compassion. Is he offering me love, or throwing it back in my face?

I falter, thinking I'll always remember how he looked at that moment because I can't fathom his intent. *"Why?"* I ask. "Why would Lali take my clothes?"

"Because she thought you were being a pain in the ass."

"How?"

"I don't know. She said you two are always playing practical jokes on each other. She said you gave her Ex-Lax gum before a meet."

"We were *twelve*."

"So?"

"*So*—"

"Are you going to break up with me now?" he asks suddenly.

"Oh, God." I pull my knit cap over my face. That's why he was at my house this morning. That's why he took me ice skating. He wants to break up with me but he's afraid to do it, so he wants me to break up with him. It's why he was dancing with Donna LaDonna last night, too. He's going to behave as badly as possible until I have no other choice.

Not that I haven't been considering it for the past twelve hours.

While I was dancing with Walt and Randy at the club in Provincetown, the idea of "dumping the bastard" was like rocket fuel, shooting me into a stratosphere of uncaring bliss. I danced harder and harder, pounding out my aggressions, wondering why I needed Sebastian when I could have *this*— this carnival of sweaty bodies that flicker and flash like fireflies—*this* is *fun*.

"Fuck Sebastian," I'd screamed, waving my arms over my head like a crazed worshiper at a revival meeting.

Randy, strutting beside me, replied, "Honey, it all happens for a *reason*."

But now I'm not so sure. Do I really want to break up with him? I'll miss him. And surely I'll be bored without him. How can you change your feelings in a day?

And maybe—just maybe—Sebastian is the one who's terrified. Maybe he's scared of disappointing a girl, of not being good enough, so he pushes her away before she can find out that he's not this incredible, special guy that he pretends to be. When he said I was cool on the outside but wanted love on the inside—maybe that wasn't about me. Maybe he was secretly referring to *himself*.

"I don't know. Do I have to decide right now?" I peel my hat back, looking up at him.

And this, apparently, is the right thing to say, because he looks at me and laughs. "You're crazy."

"So are you."

"Are you sure you don't want to break up with me?"

"Only because you're so sure I want to. I'm not that easy, you know?"

"Oh, I *know*." He takes my hand as we skate across the pond.

"I want to do it, but I *can't*," I whisper.

"Why not?"

We're in his room. "Are you scared?" he asks.

"A little." I roll onto my elbow. "I don't know."

"It doesn't always hurt. Some girls really love it the first time they do it."

"Yeah. Like Maggie."

"See? All your friends are doing it. Don't you feel stupid being the only one who isn't?"

No. "Yes."

"Then why can't you do it with me?"

"Maybe it doesn't have anything to do with you."

"Of course it does," he says, sitting up and pulling on his socks. "Otherwise you would do it."

"But I haven't done it with *anyone.*" I crawl after him and put my arms around his shoulders. "Please don't be mad at me. I just can't do it . . . today. I'll do it another day, I promise."

"That's what you always say."

"But this time I *mean* it."

"Okay," he says warningly. "But you can't expect me to wait much longer."

He pulls on his jeans and I flop back onto the bed, giggling.

"What's so funny?" he demands.

I can barely get the words out. "You could always watch a porn video instead. Jugs!"

"How do you know about that?" he asks in a fury.

I cover my face with his pillow. "Haven't you figured it out? I know *everything.*"

CHAPTER TWENTY-FOUR

The Circus Comes to Town

"Two more days," Walt says, taking a toke on the joint. "Two more days of freedom, and then it's over."

"What about the summer?" Maggie asks.

"Ah yes. Maggie's long summer," Walt murmurs. "Tanning by the pool, basting herself with baby oil—"

"Putting Sun-In in her hair—"

"You put Sun-In in your hair," Maggie says, rolling over.

"True," I concede.

"This is boring." Lali gets up off the couch. "Bunch of deadheads. Give me a hit of that."

"I thought you'd never ask," The Mouse says, handing her the joint.

"Are you sure you want to smoke?" I ask teasingly. "The last time you ate an entire pound of bacon. Remember?"

"It was three strips!" she exclaims. "God, Carrie. Why are you always making things up?"

"Because it's fun?"

The six of us—Walt, Maggie, The Mouse, Lali, Peter, and I—are hanging out in the old playroom above The Mouse's garage. It's New Year's Eve, and we're smugly congratulating ourselves on being too cool to bother going out to a party. Not that there's a party we'd want to go to anyway. There's a dance for old people at the country club—"Deadly," according to The Mouse—there's a movie night at the library—"Middle-brow conservatives who want to pretend they're intellectuals," according to Walt—and a fancy dinner party at Cynthia Viande's where the girls wear long dresses and the boys rent tuxes and they supposedly drink Baby Champs and pretend to be grown-ups. But it's limited to twenty of Cynthia's nearest and dearest friends, if you can categorize the two Jens and Donna LaDonna as bosom buddies. None of us have made the cut, with the exception of Peter, who was only asked at the last minute because Cynthia needed an "extra man." In order to spare Peter this indignity, we decided to gather at The Mouse's to smoke pot, drink White Russians, and pretend we're not losers.

"Hey," Peter says to Maggie, tapping on his bottle of beer. "The extra man needs another brewskie."

"The extra man can get it himself," Maggie says, giggling. "Isn't that what an extra man is for? To do all the extra work?"

"What about an extra woman?" Lali asks, passing the joint to me. "How come no one wants an extra woman?"

"Because an extra woman is a mistress."

"Or a third wheel," adds The Mouse.

I cough and slide off the old easy chair where I've been stationed for the last hour. "Anybody want another drink?" I ask, giving The Mouse a look. She shrugs, knowing exactly what she's said.

If Lali is offended, she doesn't show it. "I'll have another. And make it a double."

"Coming right up." A bag of ice, plastic cups, and various alcoholic potions sit atop an ancient card table. I begin mixing two drinks, filling Lali's cup with vodka. It's slightly evil, but I've been feeling slightly evil toward Lali ever since Sebastian informed me that she took my clothes. We laughed it off, but there's a quiet tension between us, like the shadow of a cloud on a beautiful summer day. You look up and suddenly realize you're in for a thunderstorm.

"When is Sebastian coming back?" Lali asks with deliberate casualness, which may be a reaction to The Mouse's "third wheel" comment after all. She knows Sebastian returns from his family vacation tomorrow. And she also knows that on Sunday, we have those tickets to see Aztec Two-Step at the Shaboo Inn. She hasn't been able to stop talking about it. Until now.

"Tomorrow," I say, as if it's no big deal. What Lali doesn't need to know is how desperately I've been counting the days until his return. I keep playing our reunion over and over again in my head. He'll pull up to my house in his yellow Corvette. I'll run to him and he'll sweep me into his arms and kiss me passionately, murmuring, "I love you." But when I imagine the scene, instead of picturing me, I see Julie Christie in *Dr. Zhivago* instead. I'm in my early twenties, I have dark hair, and I'm wearing a white ermine hat.

"What time is it?" Walt asks suddenly.

"Ten fifteen."

"I don't know if I can make it till midnight," Maggie groans contentedly.

"You have to," I insist. "Just because we're losers doesn't mean we have to be lightweights."

"Speak for yourself." Walt picks up the bottle of vodka and takes a swig.

"Walt, that's gross," Maggie scolds.

"You didn't think it was gross when we swapped spit," he says.

"Hey!" Peter jumps to his feet, making boxing motions in the direction of Walt's head.

"Take it easy, homeboy." Walt looks at me and takes another gulp of vodka.

"Do you want a glass?"

"Nope." He places the bottle back on the table and claps his hands. "Okay, everybody," he says loudly. "I have an announcement to make."

Crap. This is it. The moment we've all been waiting for. I glance at The Mouse and Maggie. The Mouse is making tiny nods of encouragement, smiling kindly the way you would at a five-year-old who has just shown you a stick figure drawing of his family. Maggie has covered her mouth with her hands and is looking wildly from me to The Mouse, as if hoping someone will tell her what to do.

"You got into Penn," Peter says.

"Nope."

I move behind Walt and glare at Maggie, making a face as I put my finger to my lips.

"Hey—what's going on?" Lali says, catching me. "I know. You're taking over as the manager of the Hamburger Shack."

"A pox on you," Walt replies. It's a phrase he's never used before but probably picked up from Randy.

"This surprise is much better," he continues, swaying slightly from side to side. "I was going to wait until midnight, but I'll probably be passed out by then." He looks around the room to make sure he has our complete attention. Then he casually drops the bomb:

"For those of you who haven't figured it out, I'm now officially gay."

For a moment, it's quiet, as we all ponder how to react to this information, given our previous knowledge of it or lack thereof.

It's broken by a low chortling sound. "That's it?" Lali declares. "You're gay? That's *news*?"

"Thank you very much," Walt says with faux indignation.

"Congratulations, man," Peter says. He crosses the room and hugs Walt gingerly, patting him on the back. "When did you find out?" he asks, as if Walt has just announced he's having a baby.

"When did you find out you were straight, Peter?" I ask, giggling.

"Well," Maggie says coyly. "We knew it all along."

Actually, "we" didn't. But luckily, ten days after "we," meaning Maggie, found out, she got all caught up in planning a camping trip with Peter, and completely forgot about Walt's insult to her womanhood. I raise my cup. "To Walt," I cheer.

"To Walt!"

"And to us," I add. "To nineteen eighty—"

There's a loud knock on the door.

"Shit." The Mouse grabs the marijuana paraphernalia and shoves it under the cushions of the couch. Peter hides the vodka bottle behind a chair. We run our fingers through our hair and dust the ash off our fronts.

"Come in," The Mouse says.

It's her father, Mr. Castells. Even though he's kind of old, I'm always struck by how handsome he is. The Mouse says that when he was young, he was known as the Cary Grant of Cuba.

"I hope you're having a good time," he says politely, striding into the room. I can tell by his manner that this is not a social call. "Carrie?" he asks. "Your father is on the phone. He needs to speak with you immediately."

"Apparently they have an old car that nobody uses. They didn't realize it was missing until I called," my father says. His face is white. He's in shock—probably terrified.

"Dad, I'm sure it will be *fine*," I say, praying he won't notice that he now has two juvenile delinquents for daughters—Dorrit, the runaway, and me, the stoner. Except I feel frighteningly sober and clearheaded. "How far could they get? Neither one of them has a license. How can Cheryl even know how to drive?"

"I know nothing about these people other than the fact that Cheryl's mother has been married three times."

I nod, staring at the road ahead. Despite its being New Year's Eve, the streets are dark and mostly deserted. I'm convinced that somehow this new crisis with Dorrit is my fault. I should have been paying more attention. But how was I to know? She said she was going to the library for the movie event—my father even dropped her off at four and waited until she met her friend Maura, who we've known for years. Maura's mother was going to pick them up at seven and drop Dorrit off at home on her way to a party. But when she arrived at the library, Maura told her mother that Dorrit had gone to the mall and was going to get a ride home from me. When she wasn't home by nine, my father started to panic. He tried calling Maura's mother, but there was no answer until after ten. He called Cheryl's house, guessing Dorrit might have snuck off with her, but Cheryl's little brother said his sister wasn't home and his parents were at The Emerald. So my father called The Emerald, and Cheryl's mother and stepfather went back to their house and found the car missing. And now we're on our way to Cheryl's house to try to figure out what to do.

"Dad, I'm sorry."

He says nothing, only shakes his head.

"She's probably at the mall. Or the golf course. Or maybe the meadows."

"I don't think so," he says. "She took fifty dollars from my sock drawer."

I avert my eyes as we turn off Main Street and drive past The Emerald, as if I've never even noticed the place. We continue a bit farther onto a narrow road crowded with nearly identical houses and stop in front of a Colonial with peeling paint and a recently remodeled front porch. Light pokes around the edges of the drawn blinds, and as we examine the house, a man peers out, glaring. His face appears bright red, but it could be the lighting.

"I should have known," my father says grimly. "Mack Kelter."

"Who's he?"

"Local contractor," my father says, as if this explains everything. He pulls into the driveway, behind a truck. At the side of the house is a rundown two-car garage. One of the doors is open, the inside illuminated by a bare bulb.

"What does that mean?" I ask.

"Mack Kelter is what's known as a shady character." My father unbuckles his seat belt and takes off his glasses, delaying the inevitable encounter. "Your mother refused to deal with him. She had a few run-ins with him over some building construction. One evening we found Mack Kelter standing in our driveway with a crowbar."

I'm shocked I don't remember this. Or maybe I do. I have a vague recollection of hysteria and of us three girls being told to hide in the basement. "Did you call the police?"

"No. Your mother went out and confronted him. I was scared to death, but she wasn't. You know Mom," he says, getting teary. "She was a little thing but tough as hell. No one messed with Mimi."

"I know. And she never had to raise her voice," I add miserably, recounting my line from our familial stories about my mother.

"It was something in her manner. . . She was a lady, through and through, and men knew it," my father says, doing his part. He sighs. "She had a few words with Mack Kelter, and he skulked away with his tail between his legs."

That was my mother—a Lady with a capital L. *A Lady*. Even when I was little, I knew I'd never be one, not like my mother. I was too rough and tumble. I wanted to go every place my parents said was bad, like New York City. I made Missy and Dorrit burn their Barbie dolls in a bonfire. I told my cousins there was no such thing as Santa Claus. I suspect my mother always knew I wouldn't make it as a lady, that I'd never be like her. But it never seemed to matter.

"Do you think Dorrit knows about Mack Kelter? And what Mom thought of him?" If she does, it could explain something about Dorrit's behavior. "Dad, I think Dorrit needs to see a shrink."

I've made this suggestion several times before, but my father always resists. He comes from a generation that thinks shrinks are bad. Even in this dire circumstance, my father still won't have it.

"Not now, Carrie," he says. And looking as if he's going to an execution, he gets out of the car.

The door opens before we can knock, and Mack Kelter stands in the entrance, blocking our passage. He's handsome in a kind of dirty way that makes you feel slightly ashamed even looking at him.

"Bradshaw?" He smirks. "Yeah," he says, answering his own question. "Come in."

I hope he doesn't have any crowbars lying around.

"In there." He motions toward the living room with a bottle of beer. We sidle in tentatively, not knowing what to expect. Along one wall is an enormous television set, flanked by two speakers. There's a brick fireplace, a scattering of toys on the white shag rug, two small yellow poodles with runny eyes, and a long modular couch. Sprawled across it with what appears to be a gin and tonic in one hand and an ice pack in the other is Cheryl's mother, Connie.

"My little baby," she wails when she sees us. She puts down her drink and holds out her hands, which we have no choice but to take. "My little girl. She's just a little girl," she sobs.

"She's not that little," Mack Kelter scoffs.

"What if they've been kidnapped?" Connie blinks rapidly. "What if they're lying in a ditch somewhere—"

"Put a lid on it, Connie," Mack Kelter says. "They took the car. They went drinking. When Cheryl gets back, she's going to get a walloping. That's all."

My father, meanwhile, has politely managed to extract his hand from Connie's and is standing stiffly, as if trying to pretend he is not in this situation. "Have you called the police?"

"Why do we want them involved?" Mack Kelter asks. "They'll only cause trouble. Besides, they don't investigate missing persons until they've been gone for at least twenty-four hours."

"By which time they could be dead!" Connie cries out. She puts her hand on her heart, gasping for air. "And this is my reward for a life of misery. I've got a juvenile delinquent for a daughter and a deadbeat drunk for a husband."

"You want one upside the head?" Mack Kelter asks. "I told you to zip it."

My father and I glance at each other in horror.

"I think we ought to look for them." I check my watch. "It's ten forty-five. They've been gone for about three hours—"

"They could be all the way to Boston by now," Connie exclaims. She looks over at her husband.

"I'm heading back to The Emerald," he announces. He takes in our shocked expressions and grins. "Hey—she's not my kid. And there's a man called Jack Daniel's waiting for me at the bar."

My father, Connie, and I drive all around town looking for Dorrit and Cheryl. We check out the meadows, the country club, and several little bars Connie knows about, although why she thinks anyone would serve alcohol to thirteen-year-olds is a mystery to both me and my dad. But we keep searching anyway, to no avail. At two a.m., we finally give up.

"Did you find her?" Missy squeals hopefully as we walk into the house.

"Nope."

"What are we going to do?"

"What can we do?"

"How could this happen?" Missy wails.

"I don't know. If she's not back by six a.m., we're going to the police."

We stand there in terrified silence, and then I tiptoe across the floor and peek into the den where my father has retired to suffer alone. He's sitting on the couch, slowly turning the pages of the old photo album my mother started when she and my father became engaged.

I return to the kitchen, ready to fortify myself for a long night, taking bread and cheese and mayonnaise from the refrigerator to make a sandwich.

The phone rings.

The sound is loud and jarring and somehow expected. I drop the bread and grab it.

"Carrie?" says a male voice.

"George?" I ask in shock. And then I'm disappointed. And angry. Why is George calling now—way past midnight on New Year's Eve? He must be drunk. "George, this is *not* the time—"

He cuts me off. "I have someone here who wants to talk to you."

"Who?"

"Happy New Year," Dorrit says, giggling into the phone.

CHAPTER TWENTY-FIVE

Lockdown at Bralcatraz

All morning I've been avoiding the phone.

I know I have to do the right thing. And the sooner you do the right thing, the better. You get it over with, and you don't have to worry about it anymore. But who does that in real life? Instead, you procrastinate and think about it and put it off and think about it some more until that one little pebble grows into a giant block inside your head. It's only, I remind myself, a phone call. But I have so many other important things to do first.

Like cleaning out the space above the garage, which is where I am now, wearing a down coat, fuzzy gloves, and a mink stole. The mink belonged to my grandmother, and it's one of those really creepy ones where the heads and tiny paws of the little minks are attached at each end. I put the two heads together and make them talk to each other.

"Hello."

"How are you?"

"Not so good. Someone took my tail and back legs."

"Eh—who needs a tail, anyway?"

I found the old stole when I was digging through a box filled with my grandmother's things, which, with the exception of the stole, have turned out to be a treasure trove of fantastic old hats with net veils and feathers. I put one of the hats on my head and pull the veil down over my nose. I picture myself walking down Fifth Avenue, stopping in front of Tiffany on my way to lunch at the Plaza.

With the hat still on my head, I push aside a few more boxes. I'm looking for something, but I don't know what. I'll know what it is when I find it though.

My nose is assaulted by the sharp musty smell of old paperbacks as I lift open the flaps on a box bearing the fuzzy imprint of Del Monte canned corn. My grandmother always described herself as "a great reader," and prided herself on reading five books a week, although her choice of reading material consisted largely of romances and Greek mythology. On the summer weekends we'd spend at her cottage by the shore, I'd be right behind her, devouring those romance novels like candy, thinking, I could do this someday. I'd turn the books over and study the photographs of the authors with their teased hairdos, lying on pink chaises or propped up in four-poster beds. Those lady authoresses, I knew, were fantastically rich, and unlike the female characters in their books, made their own money without needing a man to rescue them. The idea of becoming one of these lady writers filled me with a secret excitement that was nearly sexual, but also terrifying: If a woman could take care of herself, would she still need a man? Would she even want one? And if she didn't want a man, what kind of woman would she be? Would she even be a woman? Because it seemed if you were a woman, the only thing you were really supposed to want was a man.

I guess I was about eight then. Maybe ten. Even twelve. Inhaling the scent of those old paperbacks is like inhaling the little girl of my childhood. I've learned one thing since then: No matter what happens, I'll probably always want a guy.

Is there something pitiful about that?

I close the box and move on to another. And suddenly, I find it: a rectangular white box with yellowed corners, a dry cleaner's box for men's shirts. I lift the cover, take out an old composition book, and turn to the first page. *The Adventures of Pinky Weatherton* is printed in my sloppy young hand.

Good old Pinky! I invented her when I was six. Pinky was a spy with special powers: She could shrink herself down to the size of a thimble, and she could breathe underwater. Pinky always seemed to be getting washed down the drain in the sink, and then she'd swim through the pipes and pop up in someone's bathtub.

I carefully take out the contents of the box, laying them on the floor. Besides Pinky, there are drawings and homemade cards, diaries with metal locks (I never managed to write more than a few entries in any of them, although I remember chastising myself for my lack of discipline, knowing even then that writers were supposed to keep journals), and at the bottom, my attempts at stories, crudely typed on my mother's Royale typewriter. It's like a surprise party, suddenly coming into a room filled with all your friends. But it's also the sign, I decide, picking up the box and carrying it down the stairs. It's the sign that I really do have to call George.

"You need to call George" were the first words out of my father's mouth this morning.

"I will, Dad. Don't worry about it." It made me kind of angry. I'd vowed never to talk to George again, not after what he'd said about Sebastian. Even if I did end up at Brown, which was looking more and more likely as I hadn't managed to come up with a viable alternative, I planned to avoid him. And yet, once again he had managed to insert himself into our lives—my life—and it wasn't right. I didn't want him there. I knew my feelings were wrong—it wasn't George's fault—but I was convinced he was still somehow to blame. If he hadn't paid so much attention to Dorrit when she was arrested, if he hadn't been so *nice*, then Dorrit would have never developed a crush on him. It was only one of those mewling irrational crushes that young teenage girls develop for pretty-boy singers, but why George? He was cute enough, but certainly not pretty. He wasn't even dangerous.

Maybe it wasn't danger Dorrit was looking for but stability.

And perhaps there was an element of competition. Dorrit had grown bolder with each infraction, starting with stealing earrings and lip gloss, and moving on to my mother's bag. Maybe it made sense that George was her final conquest.

Back in the house, my father is in exactly the same position I left him in two hours ago, seated at the little desk where we keep the mail, staring down at a blank piece of paper with a pencil in his hand.

"Did you call George yet?" he asks, looking up.

"I'm going to. Right now."

"You owe him a phone call. What would have happened if George hadn't been there? And now I need to find a way to repay him."

I have a terrible thought: Perhaps I should offer myself as repayment, like one of those heroines in my grandmother's romance novels whose family forces her to marry a man she doesn't love. And then Sebastian will have to rescue me. Except he can't, because my father has forbidden any of us to leave the house without adult supervision. We're not even allowed to talk on the phone unless we clear it with my father first. I thump up the stairs to my room, hating my father, Dorrit, and most of all, George.

I shove the box of stories under the bed and pick up the phone. Maybe George is still asleep. Or out. At least I can say I tried. He answers on the second ring.

"How are you holding up?" he asks.

"I'm okay."

"And Dorrit?"

"Locked in her room." I pause. "Anyway, I want to thank

you. We couldn't have managed without you." I do my best to sound sincere on this last statement, but I don't quite succeed. George doesn't seem to notice, however.

"No problem," he says, full of good cheer. "These things happen. Glad I could help."

"Thanks again." Having done my duty, I'm about to ring off when I make a fatal mistake. "George," I ask. "Why did she pick you?"

He laughs. "That almost sounds like an insult."

"It isn't. You're a great guy—"

"Am I?" he asks eagerly.

"Well, sure," I say, trying to figure out how to get out of this trap. "But she's thirteen. It seems so extreme to steal a car and drive all the way to Providence—"

I hear a telltale ping indicating my father has picked up the extension below and is listening in.

"I've been meaning to talk to you about that," George says, lowering his voice. "I could come by next week."

"I'll have to check with my father," I sigh, knowing my father will say "yes," and surprised he hasn't already broken into the conversation.

When George and I hang up, I head downstairs to confront my father. "Are you going to listen in on every conversation I have from now on?"

"I'm sorry, Carrie, but yes. And I'm not listening in. I'm monitoring."

"Great," I say sarcastically.

"And if you were thinking about seeing Sebastian later, forget it," he adds. "I don't want that little S-H-I-T anywhere near this house."

"But, Dad—"

"I'm sorry, Carrie."

"He's my boyfriend!"

"That's the way it is," he says, unmoved by my obvious distress. "No boys. And that means no Sebastian, either."

"What is this? Alcatraz?"

My father says nothing.

Arrggghhh.

My anger is like some rudimentary, single-celled beast, an exploding virus of fury that paralyzes rational thought and blinds me to everything except one single goal. . .

"I'm going to *kill* you!" I scream, rushing upstairs to Dorrit's room. I leap on top of her, but she's prepared, having raised her legs into a defensive position. I know that somewhere in the world, in truly perfect families, sisters don't fight. But we're not one of them. We used to be regular pugilists, kicking and twisting arms and chasing each other with shovels and rakes and locking each other in the car or out of the house, shaking each other out of trees, hiding in closets or under the bed or running each other down like rabbits. "I'm going to kill you," I scream again, raising a pillow over my head as Dorrit kicks my groin.

I try to get the pillow over her face, but she squirms away, landing on the floor. She gets up and tries to jump on my back. I buck like a horse but she won't let go. I struggle to stand up and we both fall over. We land on the bed with me lying on top of her.

Then the dam of emotion bursts and we're laughing hysterically. "It's not funny," I insist, tears running down my face. "You've ruined my life. You deserve to die."

"What's going on?" Missy says, appearing in the doorway. Dorrit points at her, which is not funny either, but manages to send us into another round of hysterics all the same. "Stop laughing," Missy scolds. "I just talked to Dad. He's thinking of sending Dorrit to reform school."

"Will I have to wear a uniform?" Dorrit shrieks with laughter.

"Dad's serious this time." Missy frowns. "He says he's not kidding. We're in big trouble. All of us. We're not even allowed to have friends anymore."

"We're in Bralcatraz," I say.

"Ha," Dorrit says dismissively. She gets off the bed and looks at herself in the mirror, twisting a strand of blue hair in front of her face. "He'll get over it. He always does," she says viciously.

"Dorrit—"

"I don't even know why he's the one left," she says. "*He* should be dead. And Mom should be alive." She glares defiantly at Missy and me, at our shocked expressions. It's a sentiment we've all felt but never expressed.

"And I don't care if I do go to reform school," she adds. "Anything would be better than being stuck in this family."

CHAPTER TWENTY-SIX

The S-H-I-I Hits the Fan

A horn honks in the driveway, breaking the silence. Please let it be The Mouse, I pray.

Missy, Dorrit, my father, and I are gathered at the table, pretending to eat dinner in a futile attempt at normalcy. At the sound of the horn, my father goes to the window, pulls back the curtain, and peers out. "It's Roberta," he confirms. I jump up and grab my coat and my painted Carrie bag, which are standing at the ready.

"Not so fast. We need to go over this one more time," my father says as Dorrit rolls her eyes. "You're going to see *The Importance of Being Earnest* at the Hartford Stage. You will call during the intermission. You will be home at eleven o'clock."

"Eleven or *so*," I say, slipping my arms into the sleeves of the coat.

"I'll be waiting up for you." He glances at Missy and Dorrit. They have their heads down, pretending to eat, pretending they don't know where I'm really going.

"Sure, Dad." I wrap my grandmother's old mink stole around my neck. I wouldn't normally wear it, but I figure it's the kind of thing one would wear to the theater, and I need to keep up my act.

I walk quickly to the car, feeling like I have a target on my back.

I lied. But not entirely. The Mouse and I *are* going to a show, just not to one at the Hartford Stage. We're meeting up with Lali and Sebastian at the Aztec Two-Step concert. Not exactly how I pictured my reunion with Sebastian, but it doesn't matter. Every molecule in my body is pulsating in anticipation.

A blast of hot, dry air hits me as I swing open the door of the Gremlin. The Mouse gives me a triumphant look as I carefully buckle my seat belt, knowing my father is watching. "Any trouble?" she asks.

"Nope. He doesn't suspect a thing." When we're safely out of the driveway and on the highway, I laugh, giddy with excitement, nervously checking my lipstick in the tiny mirror tucked into the visor. "I can't believe we pulled it off," I squeal. "Mouse, you're the best."

"Hey," she says. "What are friends for?"

I lean back, smiling like a madwoman.

When Sebastian called yesterday at three and my father told him I wasn't available, things got ugly at Chez Bradshaw. I screamed and threatened to tear out my hair, but it didn't make any difference. My father unplugged all the phones and barricaded himself in his bedroom. Then my sisters and I came up with a plan to take the car, but my father had outsmarted us and hidden the keys. We tried to break into his room, but then we thought we heard him crying, so we went into the den and huddled on the couch like three terrified orphans. Finally, my father came in and Missy broke down and said, "Dad, I'm sorry," and started to sob. My father said, "It's not your fault. I just love my girls so much." And we all agreed to try to be better in the future. All I could really think about, though, was Sebastian and how to get in touch with him. The reality of him being minutes away and not being able to see him made me feel like I had a rat in my stomach, gnawing away at my insides.

Eventually, I went upstairs and took out the box of my old stories, and tried to soothe myself by imagining a better life, when I would live in New York and write books and have a completely different existence. I pictured my future like a jewel buried deep inside of me, where it couldn't be taken away even if I was stuck in Bralcatraz for the rest of my life.

Then my father came softly into the room.

"I don't mean to be so hard on you," he said.

I had my opening if I could remain reasonable and calm. "It's okay, Dad."

"I'm only trying to be fair. If I let you and Missy out, I'll have to let Dorrit out too. And what if she runs away again?"

"Sure, Dad," I said soothingly.

"It's not forever. Just for a week or two. Until I can figure out what to do."

"I understand."

"You see, Carrie," he said, sitting on the edge of the bed, "it's all about systems. And what we don't have in this household is a system. If we apply a system for success to the actions of human beings . . . if we take the human being down to its most basic molecular equation . . . after all, we are only molecules and electrons, and electrons are governed by a rigid set of rules. Well," he said, standing up as if he actually had found a solution to our problems. "I knew I could count on you. I appreciate it. I really do."

He hugged me awkwardly and said what he always does in these situations: "Remember, I don't just love you. I *like* you."

"I like you too, Dad," I said, scheming. "Dad? Can I make one phone call?" And before he could object, I added quickly, "I need to call The Mouse. I was supposed to meet her." I guess he really did feel bad, because he relented.

This morning, when things had calmed down and my father agreed to restore phone service—although he was still insisting on answering every call himself—The Mouse rang and spoke to him while I listened in on the extension.

"I know Carrie's not supposed to go out, but we've had these tickets for months. They're for the Hartford Stage and they don't give refunds. And it's part of our English Literature class. We don't have to go, but if we miss it, it might affect our grade."

And now—freedom. Puffing along in the Gremlin, the radio turned up full blast, The Mouse and I screaming along to the B-52s. My head is buzzing with the daringness of my escape. I am ready to rock the house. I am, I think, invincible.

Or not. Halfway to our secret destination, I start to worry. What if Sebastian is late? What if he doesn't show at all? And why do I feel the need to entertain the worst possible scenario? If you think a bad thought, can you make it come true? Or is it a warning?

But the yellow Corvette is there, parked in the dirt driveway.

I fling open the door to the club. He's sitting at the bar, and I vaguely register that Lali is there too. "Hey!" I shout. Lali spots me first. There's an odd slackness in her face, the muscles flattening in disappointment. Something's wrong. Then he turns and she whispers something in his ear.

He's deeply tanned and the aura of a carefree summer boy still clings to him like a salty sweet veneer. He nods at me, his smile tight, which is not the reaction I expected to see from the love of my life after we've been separated for two weeks. But perhaps he's like a dog that's been left alone by its master—it will take time for him to get used to me again.

"Hi," I exclaim. My voice sounds too loud and too

enthusiastic. I put my arms around him and jump up and down.

"Whoa," he says, and kisses me on the cheek. "Are you okay?"

"Of course."

"What about Dorrit?" Lali asks.

"Oh, that," I say with a wave. "It's nothing. All fine. I'm just so happy to be here." I take the bar stool next to him and order a beer.

"Where's The Mouse?" he asks.

The Mouse? What about me? "She's in the bathroom. So when did you get back?" I ask eagerly, although I know when he got back—he called me.

"Yesterday afternoon." He scratches his arm.

"I'm sorry I couldn't talk—but The Mouse called and told you, right? What happened with Dorrit?"

Lali and Sebastian exchange a look. "Actually," he begins, "when your father hung up on me I called Lali. She told me something had happened to Dorrit on Friday night."

"So we went to The Emerald," Lali says, finishing his sentence.

"I knew you were indisposed," he adds quickly, tapping my nose with his finger. "I didn't want to sit at home with my parents another night."

A rock tears through my insides and comes to rest in the pit of my stomach. "So how was the vacation?"

"Boring," he says.

I catch Lali's expression over his shoulder. She looks sick. Did something happen last night? Did Lali and Sebastian ...? *No.* She's my best friend. He's my boyfriend. They *should* be friends. Don't act jealous, I berate myself. It will only make you look weak.

"Hi, all." The Mouse comes up to the bar. Sebastian envelops her in a bear hug. "Mouse!" he exclaims.

"Hey." She pats him on the back, as confused by his effusive behavior as I am. Sebastian has never been this friendly before.

I gulp my beer. Am I crazy, or is something very odd going on?

"I have to go to the bathroom." I hop off my barstool and look at Lali. "Want to come?"

She hesitates, glances at Sebastian, and puts down her beer. "Sure."

"Is it my imagination or is Sebastian acting weird?" I ask from the stall.

"I haven't noticed anything."

"Come on. He's being really strange." When I come out of the stall, Lali is standing by the sink, staring at herself in the discolored mirror as she fluffs her hair.

She won't look at me. "Maybe it's because he's been away."

"Do you think something happened? While he was on vacation? Maybe he met another girl."

"Maybe."

This is not the proper response. The correct answer is: no.

No way. He's crazy about you. Or something along those lines.

"So you guys went to The Emerald last night," I say.

"Yeah."

"Did he mention anything about another girl?"

"No." She fusses with a strand of hair on the back of her neck.

"How long were you there?"

"I don't know. We had a drink. He wanted to get out of the house. I did too. So—"

"Yeah." I nod, desperate to know more. Which songs they listened to and what they drank and whether or not they danced. I want to probe her, get inside her brain and find out exactly what happened. But I can't. I don't want to hear something I know I can't handle.

When we return, The Mouse is deep in conversation with Sebastian. "What are you guys talking about?" I ask.

"You," Sebastian says, turning to me with uncharacteristic seriousness.

"What about me?" I laugh lightly.

"How hard it is for you," he says.

Not this again. "It's not *that* hard," I say dismissively. I finish my beer and order another. Then I order a shot.

"Let's all have shots," Sebastian says.

The thought of alcohol lightens the mood. We lift our shot glasses and clink—to the new year, to the summer ahead, to our futures. Sebastian smokes a cigarette with his arm around my shoulder. The Mouse talks to Lali. I lean in to Sebastian, sharing his cigarette. "Is anything wrong?"

"What do you mean?" He takes a drag of his cigarette, turning his head away, a note of aggression in his tone.

"I don't know. You're acting sort of funny."

"Really? I think you're the one who's acting weird."

"Me?"

"Yeah," he says. He stares at me wide-eyed.

I back down. "Maybe I am. All the stuff with Dorrit—"

"Mmmm." He averts his glance as he stubs out his cigarette.

"Anyway, I'm not going to let it affect me. I want to have fun." And I drag him onto the dance floor.

Then I have too much fun. The band comes on, and we all sing along. The alcohol works its magic and I suddenly don't care about anything anymore. I take off my stole and make the mink heads drink beer. Other people gather around to join in the fun. Nine o'clock comes and goes and I don't even notice until it's too late.

At ten fifteen, The Mouse points to her watch. "Bradley, we should go."

"I don't want to go."

"Two more songs," she warns. "Then we're going."

"Okay." I grab my beer and push through the crowd to the front of the stage, catching the eye of the lead singer, who smiles at me, amused. He's cute. Really cute. He has the smooth face and curly hair of a guy in a Renaissance painting. Lali has had a crush on him since we were fourteen. We'd

play his records while Lali stared longingly at his photograph. When the song ends, he leans over and asks what I want to hear. "'Cosmos Lady'!" I shout.

The song begins. The lead singer keeps looking at me, his mouth moving above the microphone as the music rises up, enveloping me like a puffy cloud of helium. Then it's only the music and the singer and his full, soft lips, and suddenly, it's like I'm back at the club in Provincetown with Walt and Randy, wild and free. Listening to the music isn't enough. I must participate. I must . . . *sing*.

On the stage. In front of everyone.

And then it's like I've willed it to happen, because the singer holds out his hand. I take it and he pulls me onto the stage, making room for me next to the microphone. And there I am, singing my heart out, and before I know it, the song is over and the crowd is laughing and clapping. The singer leans into the mike and says, "That was—" and I shout, "Carrie Bradshaw," my name echoing like a blast.

"Let's have a round of applause for . . . *Carrie Bradshaw*," he says.

I give the audience a little wave, stumble off the stage, and wobble through the crowd, giddy with the silliness of my behavior. *I am,* I think.

I am . . . *here*.

"I cannot believe you just did that," Lali says, aghast, when I reach the bar. I look from Lali to The Mouse to Sebastian, and with a shaking hand, pick up my beer.

"Why?" As the beer trickles down my throat, I can feel my confidence going with it. "Was it bad?"

"Not exactly bad," Sebastian says.

"Bradley, you were great," The Mouse exclaims.

I look at Sebastian accusingly.

"I didn't know you could sing," he says, defensive again. "I'm surprised, that's all."

"Oh, Carrie's always singing," Lali says, her voice toxic. "She sang in the school play in third grade."

"We'd better go," says The Mouse.

"Party's over." Sebastian leans over and kisses me briefly on the lips.

"Are you guys going?" I ask.

Lali and Sebastian exchange yet another mysterious look before Lali's eyes slide away. "In a minute."

"Come on, Bradley. Your father doesn't need any more trouble," The Mouse says, handing me my stole.

"Sure." I wrap the mink around my neck. "Well—" I begin awkwardly.

"Well," Sebastian says. "I'll see you tomorrow, okay?"

"Yeah." I turn and follow The Mouse.

But then, in the parking lot, I'm suddenly overcome with remorse. "Maybe I shouldn't have done that."

"Done what?"

"Got up on the stage. Maybe Sebastian didn't like it."

"If he didn't, it's his problem. I thought it was funny," The Mouse says firmly. We get into the car and she starts the ignition. We're backing out when I bang my hand on the dashboard. "Stop the car."

"What?" she says, hitting the brakes.

I scoot out of the car. "Something's wrong. I need to apologize. Sebastian is pissed off. I can't go home feeling like this."

"Carrie, don't!" The Mouse shouts, but it's too late.

I pause inside the door, scanning the club. My eyes sweep the bar, and suddenly, I'm confused. They're not here. How could they have managed to leave before we did? I take a few steps closer, and that's when I realize I'm wrong. They are here. They're still at the bar. But I didn't recognize them at first because their faces are pressed together, bodies entwined, making out like they're the last people left on earth.

This can't be. I must be seeing things. I've had too much to drink.

"Hey," I call out. My eyes aren't fooling me: They are making out. But my mind still hasn't processed the reality of the scene. "Hey," I say again. *"Hey!"*

Their eyes swivel in my direction, and then, reluctantly it seems, they release their mouths. For a moment, everything is still, as if we're frozen in a glass snow globe. And then I feel myself nod. *Yes,* says a voice in my head. *You knew this was going to happen. You knew this was inevitable.*

And then I hear myself speak. "Did you think I wouldn't find out?" I start to turn, and out of the corner of my eye, I see Lali jump off the barstool, her mouth forming my name, while Sebastian reaches out and grabs her wrist.

I walk through the room and out the door. I don't look back.

The Gremlin is idling outside the entrance. I get in and slam the door. "Let's go."

Halfway home, I ask The Mouse to stop the car again. She pulls over to the side of the road where I get out and am sick several times.

The downstairs lights are blazing when we finally creep into my driveway. I walk resolutely up the path and into the house, stopping at the door to the den. My father is sitting on the couch, reading a magazine. He looks up, closes the magazine, and places it carefully on the coffee table.

"I'm glad you're home," he says.

"Me too." I'm grateful he doesn't scold me about not calling at nine.

"How was the play?"

"Fine." I picture a house of cards, each card imprinted with the words, "What if?" The cards begin to tumble, breaking apart and collapsing into a pile of ash.

What if Dorrit hadn't run away? What if I'd been able to see Sebastian last night? What if I hadn't gotten up on the stage and made a fool of myself?

What if I'd given Sebastian what he wanted? What if I'd had sex with him?

"Good night, Dad."

"Good night, Carrie."

CHAPTER TWENTY-SEVEN

The Girl Who . . .

A coffin. Except it isn't really a coffin. It's more like a boat. And it's leaving. I have to get on it, but the people keep blocking my way. I can't get around them and one of the people is Mary Gordon Howard. She grabs my coat sleeve and pulls me back. She jeers. "You'll never get over it. You'll be scarred for life. No man will ever love you—"

No. *Noooooooooo.*

Wake up. Feel like crap. Remember something bad happened last night.

Remember what it is.

Deny it is true.

Know it *is* true.

Wonder what to do. Freak out and call Lali and Sebastian and scream? Or dump a bucket of pigs' blood on them à la movie *Carrie* (but where would I obtain said blood, and besides, too gross). Or feign a serious illness, attempt suicide (*then* they'll be sorry, but why give them the satisfaction?), or pretend nothing happened at all. Act like Sebastian and I are still together and the Lali incident was merely a weird aberration in a long and happy romance.

Five minutes pass. Think odd thoughts. Such as: In life, there are only four kinds of girls:

The girl who played with fire.

The girl who opened Pandora's Box.

The girl who gave Adam the apple.

And the girl whose best friend stole her boyfriend.

No. He cannot like her better than me. He cannot. But of course, he can.

Why? Pound fists on bed, attempt to rend garment (a flannel pajama top that I do not remember putting on), and scream into pillow. Fall back onto bed in shock. Stare at ceiling as terrible realization dawns:

What if no one ever wants to have sex with me? What if I'm a virgin for life?

Scramble out of bed, run downstairs, grab phone. "You don't look so good," Dorrit says.

Snarl, "I'll deal with you later," then scurry, squirrel-like, with phone into room. Carefully shut the door. With trembling hand, dial Lali's number.

"Is Lali there?"

"Carrie?" she asks. She sounds slightly fearful, but not as afraid as I'd hoped. This is a bad sign.

"Please tell me what happened last night didn't happen."

"Um. Well. It did."

"Why?"

"Why?"

"How could you do this?" Agonized cry.

Silence. Then: "I didn't want to tell you—" Pause, as I'm drowning in emotional quicksand. Death appears imminent. "But *I'm* seeing Sebastian now." So simple. So matter-of-fact. So *unarguable*.

This cannot be happening.

"I've been seeing him for a while," she adds.

I knew it. I knew something was going on between the two of them, but I didn't believe it. I still don't believe it. "For how long?" I demand.

"Do you really want to know?"

"Yes," I hiss.

"We've been together since before he went away."

"What?"

"He needs me."

"He told me he needed me too!"

"I guess he changed his mind."

"Or maybe you changed it for him."

"Think whatever you want," she says rudely. "*He* wants *me*."

"No, he doesn't," I spit. "You just want him *more* than you want me."

"What does that mean?"

"Don't you get it? We are no longer friends. We will never be friends ever again. How can I even talk to you?"

Long, dreadful silence. Finally: "I love him, Carrie." Click, followed by a dial tone. I sit on my bed, stunned.

Cannot face assembly. Slink up to dairy barn instead. Maybe I will spend the whole day here. Smoke three cigarettes in a row. It's fucking freezing. Decide to use the word "fucking" at every opportunity.

How could this happen? What does she have that I don't? Okay, have already been over this. Apparently, I am inadequate. Or I deserve this. I took him away from Donna LaDonna and now Lali has taken him away from me. What goes around comes around. And eventually, some other girl will take him away from Lali.

Why was I so stupid? I knew all along I could never keep him. I wasn't interesting enough. Or sexy enough. Or pretty enough. Or smart enough. Or maybe I was too smart?

I put my head in my hands. Sometimes, I acted dumb around him. I'd say, "Oh, what's that?" when I knew perfectly well what he was talking about. It made me feel like I didn't know who I was, or who I was supposed to be. I giggled nervously at things that weren't funny. I would become too aware of my mouth, or how I was moving my hands. I began living with a black hole of insecurity that had moved into my consciousness like an unwanted relative who refused to leave yet constantly criticized the accommodations.

I should be relieved. I feel like I've been in a war.

"Carrie?" Maggie says tentatively. I look up, and there she is with rosy cheeks, hair twisted into two long braids. She holds her mittened hands up to her mouth. "Are you okay?"

"No." My voice is a mere husk.

"The Mouse told me what happened," she whispers.

I nod. Soon everyone will know. I'll be talked about and mocked behind my back. I'll become a joke. The girl who couldn't keep her boyfriend. The girl who wasn't good enough. The girl who was shown up by her best friend. The girl who you can grind under your heel. The girl who *doesn't matter.*

"What are you going to do?" Maggie asks, outraged.

"What *can* I do? She said he said that he needed her."

"She's lying," Maggie exclaims. "She's nothing but a big liar. Always bragging about herself. It's all about her. She stole Sebastian because she's jealous."

"Maybe he really does like her better," I say wearily.

"He can't. And if he does, he's stupid. They're both evil nasty people who deserve each other. Good riddance. He wasn't good enough for you."

But he was. He was all I ever wanted. We belonged together. I will never love another guy the way I loved him.

"You need to do something," Maggie says. "Do something to her. Blow up her truck."

"Oh, Magwitch." I lift my head. "I'm just too *tired.*"

Hide in library during calculus. Furiously read *Star Signs*. Lali's a Leo. Sebastian (Se-bastard) is a Scorpio, which figures. Apparently they will have explosive sex together.

Attempt to decide what I hate most about this situation. The shame and embarrassment? The loss of my boyfriend and my best friend? Or the betrayal? They must have been planning this for weeks. Talking about me and how to get rid of me. Engineering secret assignations. Discussing how to tell me. But they didn't tell me. They didn't have the decency. They simply put it right out there, in my face. Like the only way they could deal with it was to get caught. They didn't think about how I might feel. I was only in the picture as an obstacle, because I don't matter to them. I am *no one* to them.

All those years of friendship . . . Was it all a lie?

I remember once in sixth grade, Lali had a birthday party and didn't invite me. I walked into school one day and Lali wouldn't talk to me, and neither would anyone else. Or so it seemed. Maggie and The Mouse still talked to me. But not Lali or the other girls we hung around with, like Jen P. I didn't know what to do. My mother said I should call Lali, and when I did, Lali's mother said she wasn't home, although I heard Lali and Jen P giggling in the background. "Why are they doing this to me?" I asked my mother.

"I can't explain it," she said helplessly. "It's just one of those things girls do."

"But why?"

She shook her head. "It's jealousy." But I didn't think it

was jealousy. I thought it was more instinctual, like being part of a pack of wild animals that drive one animal out into the wilderness to die.

It was scary, how a girl couldn't live without friends.

"Ignore it," my mother advised. "Act like nothing is wrong. Lali will come around. You'll see."

My mother was right. I did ignore it and Lali's birthday came and went, and sure enough, four days later Lali and I were mysteriously friends again.

For weeks afterward, however, when Lali mentioned her birthday—she had taken six girls to an amusement park—my face would redden in shame at the memory of being shunned. When I finally asked Lali why I wasn't invited, she looked at me in surprise. "But you did come, didn't you?"

I shook my head.

"Oh," she said. "Maybe you were acting like a jerk or something."

"That Lali is a *dope*," my mother said, "dope" being an insult she reserved for those she considered the very lowest form of human being.

I let it go. I figured it was the way of girls. But this—this betrayal—is that the way of girls as well?

"Hey," The Mouse says, discovering me in the stacks. "He wasn't in calculus. And she wasn't in assembly. So they must be feeling really guilty."

"Or maybe they're at some hotel. Fucking."

"You can't let them get to you, Bradley. You can't let them

win. You have to act like you don't care."

"But I *do* care."

"I know. But sometimes, you have to act the opposite of what people expect. They want you to go crazy. They want you to hate them. The more you hate them, the stronger they become."

"I just want to know *why*."

"The cowards," Walt says, putting his tray down next to mine. "They don't even have the guts to show up at school."

I stare down at my plate. The fried chicken suddenly resembles a large insect, the mashed potatoes a nacreous glue. I push it aside. "Why would he do it? From a guy's perspective?"

"She's different. And it's easier. It's always easier at the beginning." Walt pauses. "It might not even have anything to do with you."

Then why does it feel like it does?

I attend the rest of my classes. I'm there physically, but mentally I'm stuck on replay: Lali's shocked expression when I caught her kissing Sebastian and the way Sebastian's mouth turned down in displeasure when he saw I'd come back. Maybe he was hoping to keep both of us on the line.

"She's a little bitch," Maggie says.

"I thought you liked her," I say craftily. I need to know who's really on my side and who isn't.

"I did like her," Maggie says, jerking the wheel of the Cadillac and overshooting the turn, so we're driving on the wrong side of the road. "Until she did this."

"So if she hadn't done it, you would still like her."

"I dunno. I guess so. I was never crazy about her, though. She's kind of arrogant and full of herself. Like everything she does is so great."

"Yeah," I say bitterly. Lali's words, "*He* wants *me*," ring in my head. I open the glove compartment and take out a cigarette. My hand is trembling. "You know what's scary? If she hadn't done this, we'd probably still be friends."

"So?"

"So it's weird, you know? To be friends with someone for so long, and then they do one thing, and it's over. And they weren't a bad person before. Or at least you didn't think they were. So you have to wonder if that bad thing was always there, waiting to come out, or if it was just a one-time thing, and they're still a good person, but you can't trust them."

"Carrie, Lali did do this," Maggie says matter-of-factly. "Which means she is a bad person. You just never saw it before. But you would have realized it, eventually."

She presses on the brakes as the brick facade of Sebastian's house comes into view. Slowly, we drive past. Lali's red truck is parked in the driveway behind Sebastian's yellow Corvette. I crumple like I've been kicked in the stomach.

"Told ya," Maggie says triumphantly. "Can you please act normal now and admit that you hate her guts?"

Day Two: Wake up shaken and angry, having dreamed all night about trying to punch Sebastian in the face and being unable to connect.

Lie in my bed until the last minute. Cannot believe I still have to deal with this. Will it ever be over?

Surely they'll be in school today.

I can't skip assembly and calculus two days in a row.

Arrive at school. Decide I need a cigarette before I can face them.

Apparently, Sebastian feels the same way. He's there, in the barn, sitting at the picnic table with Lali. And Walt.

"Hi," he says casually.

"Oh, good," Walt exclaims nervously. "Do you have a cigarette?"

"No," I reply, my eyes narrowing. "Don't you?"

Lali has yet to acknowledge me.

"Have one of mine," Sebastian says, holding out his pack. I look at him suspiciously as I take a cigarette. He flips open his lighter, the one with the rearing horse etched on the side, and holds out the flame.

"Thanks," I say, inhaling and immediately exhaling a puff of smoke.

What are they doing here? For a second, I have a vague hope that they're going to apologize, that Sebastian is going to say he made a mistake, that what I saw two nights ago wasn't what I thought. But instead, he snakes his arm around

Lali's wrist and holds her hand. Her eyes glide toward me as her lips form an uneasy smile.

It's a test. They're testing me to find out how far they can push me until I explode.

I look away.

"So." Sebastian turns to Walt. "Lali tells me you made a big announcement on New Year's Eve—"

"Oh, *shut up*," Walt declares. He tosses his cigarette and walks out. I raise my arm and drop mine to the ground, stubbing it out with my toe.

Walt is waiting for me outside. "I have one word for you," he says. "Revenge."

CHAPTER TWENTY-EIGHT

Pretty Pictures

A week passes. But every time I see Lali, my heart races and I'm seized by a queer sense of dread, as if my life is in danger. I do my best to avoid her, which means I'm constantly watching out for her, scanning the halls for the top of her feathered hair, looking over my shoulder for her red truck, even bending down to check the shoes beneath the closed doors in the bathroom stalls.

I know Lali so well—her walk, the way she waves her hands next to her face when she's making a point, the defiant incisor that sticks out just a tad too far—I could pick Lali out of a crowd a mile away.

Even so, on two occasions we've inadvertently ended up face-to-face. Each time I gasped and we both quickly looked away, sliding past each other like silent icebergs.

I watch Lali a lot when she's not looking. I don't want to, but I can't help it.

She and Sebastian don't sit with us at lunch anymore.

Half the time, they avoid the cafeteria, and sometimes, walking up the hill to the barn before a break, I'll spot Sebastian's yellow Corvette pulling away from the school grounds with Lali in the passenger seat. When they do eat in the cafeteria, they sit with the two Jens, Donna LaDonna, Cynthia Viande, and Tommy Brewster. Maybe it's where Sebastian always thought he belonged, but couldn't get there with me. Maybe it's why he picked Lali instead.

Meanwhile, Jen P is behaving strangely. The other day, she actually joined us at lunch, giggling and acting like she and I were good friends. "What happened with you and Sebastian?" she asked, all girlish concern. "I thought you guys were so cute together."

The insincerity—the hypocrisy—is spectacular.

Then she asked Maggie and Peter if they wanted to be on the Senior Prom Committee.

"Sure," Peter said, looking to Maggie for approval.

"Why not?" Maggie exclaimed. This from the girl who hates parties, who cannot even get out of the car to go to one.

Sometimes I wonder if I'm beginning to hate *everyone*. The only two people I can stand are The Mouse and Walt.

Walt and I make fun of everyone. We spend all our spare time in the barn. We laugh about how dumb Tommy Brewster is, and how Jen P has a birthmark on her neck, and how stupid it is that Maggie and Peter are on the prom committee. We vow to skip the prom, considering it beneath us, and then decide we might go, but only if we go together and dress as punks.

On Wednesday afternoon, Peter stops by my locker. "Hey," he says, in a voice that makes me suspect he's doing his best to act like he doesn't know what happened between me and Sebastian. "You coming to the newspaper meeting?"

"Why?" I ask, guessing Maggie must have put him up to this.

"Thought you might want to." He shrugs. "It doesn't matter to me either way."

He strolls off as I stare into my locker. I slam the door and run after him. Why should he get off the hook so easily? "What do you think about Sebastian and Lali?" I demand.

"I think that it's high school."

"Meaning?"

"Meaning it doesn't matter. *It's high school*—a frequently unpleasant but relatively short percentage of your life. In five months we'll be out of here. In five months, no one will *care*."

Not "no one." I'll still care.

I follow him up the stairs to the newspaper meeting. No one seems particularly surprised to see me as I take a seat at the counter. Ms. Smidgens nods at me. Apparently, she's abandoned her rigid rules about attendance. The year's half over, and it's probably not worth the effort.

Little Gayle walks in and slides onto the stool next to me. "I'm disappointed," she says.

Jeez. Even freshmen know about me and Sebastian? This is worse than I thought.

"You said you were going to write that story about the cheerleaders. You said you were going to expose Donna LaDonna. You said—"

"I said a lot of things, okay?"

"Why did you say you were going to do it if you had no intention—"

I put my finger to my lips to shush her. "I didn't say I wouldn't do it. I just said I haven't gotten around to doing it."

"But you are going to do it, right?"

"We'll see."

"But—"

I suddenly can't take Gayle's needling. Without thinking, I do something I've never done before but have always wanted to: I gather my books, get up, and leave. Just like that, without saying good-bye to anyone.

It feels good.

I clatter down the stairs and stroll out into the cold, wintry air.

Now what?

The library. It's one of the few places that haven't been spoiled by Sebastian and Lali. Lali never liked going to the library. And on the one occasion I was there with Sebastian, I was *happy*.

Will I ever be happy again?

I don't think so.

A few minutes later, I'm wading through the dirty slush on the front porch. Several people pass me going in. The library seems to be especially busy today. The nice librarian, Ms. Detooten, is standing by the steps. "Hello, Carrie," she says. "I haven't seen you in a while."

"I've been busy," I murmur.

"Are you here for the photography class? It's right upstairs."

Photography class? Why not? I've always been slightly interested in photography.

I head upstairs to check it out.

The room is small and contains about twenty folding chairs. Most of them are already filled with people of various ages—this must be one of those free courses offered to the community to get people into the library. I take a seat in the back. A not-unattractive thirty-ish guy with dark hair and a thin mustache stands behind a table. He looks around the room and smiles.

"Okay, everyone," he begins. "I'm Todd Upsky. I'm a professional photographer here in town. I work for *The Castlebury Citizen*. I consider myself an art photographer but I also do weddings. So if you know someone who's getting married, send them my way."

He grins easily, as if he's made this joke several times before, and the crowd twitters in appreciation.

"This is a twelve-week course," he continues. "We meet once a week. Each week you'll take a photograph, develop it, and we'll discuss what works and what doesn't—"

Suddenly he breaks off and, with a pleasantly surprised expression, stares toward the back of the room.

I swivel my head around. Oh no. It can't be. It's Donna LaDonna, wearing one of those big puffy down coats and rabbit-fur earmuffs.

What the hell is she doing here?

"I'm sorry I'm late," she says breathlessly.

"No problem," Todd Upsky says. His smile is enormous. "Take a seat anywhere. There," he says, pointing to the empty chair next to me.

Crap.

I don't breathe once during the several minutes it takes for Donna LaDonna to remove her coat, pull off her earmuffs, pat her hair, and slide a camera bag under her seat.

This cannot be happening.

"Right, then," Todd Upsky says, clapping his hands together to get everyone's attention. "Who has a camera?"

Several people raise their hands, including Donna.

"Who doesn't?"

I raise my hand, wondering how quickly I can escape.

"Great," he says. "We're going to work in teams. The people who have cameras will pair up with those who don't. You there, miss." He nods at Donna. "Why don't you team up with the girl next to you?"

Girl?

"Our teams will head outside and take a photograph of nature—a tree or a root or anything else that you find interesting or strikes your fancy. You have fifteen minutes," he says.

Donna turns to me, parts her lips, and smiles.

It's like staring straight into the mouth of an alligator.

"Just for the record, I'm enjoying this about as much as you are," I say.

Donna lifts the camera. "Why are you taking this course, anyway?"

"Why are *you*?" I counter. Besides, I think, I'm not sure I am taking this course. Especially now that Donna's taking it.

"In case you haven't realized, I'm going to become a model."

"I thought models were in front of the camera." I pick up a twig and heave it as hard as I can. It twists in the air and lands two feet away.

"The best models know everything about photography. I know you think you're special, but you're not the only one who's going to get out of Castlebury. My cousin says I should be a model. She lives in New York. I sent her some photographs and she's going to send them to Eileen Ford."

"Yeah, right," I say sarcastically. "And I hope all your dreams come true. I hope you become a model and I hope your face is on the cover of every magazine in the country."

"Oh, I plan on it."

"I'm sure you do," I say, my voice sharp with disdain.

Donna takes a picture of a small bush, its limbs bare.

"What's that supposed to mean?"

"Nothing." I hold out my hand for the camera. I've spotted a stump that looks interesting. It seems to sum up my life right now: lifeless, cut off at the knees, and slightly rotten.

"Listen, Miss Priss," she snaps. "If you're trying to imply that I'm not pretty enough—"

"What?" I scoff, flabbergasted that Donna LaDonna is insecure about her looks. Apparently she has a weakness after all.

"Let me just remind you that I've had to take all kinds of bullshit from assholes like you my whole life."

"Oh, really?" I click the shutter and hand the camera back. *She's* had to take bullshit? What about all the bullshit she's dished out? What about all the kids whose lives have been made miserable by Donna LaDonna?

"Excuse me, but I daresay most people believe the opposite is true." When I'm nervous, I use words like "daresay." I definitely read too much.

"Excuse *me*," she responds. "You don't know what the hell you're talking about."

"Ramona Marquart?" I reply.

"Who?"

"The girl who wanted to be on the cheerleading team. The girl you rejected for being too ugly."

"Her?" she asks in surprise.

"Did you ever consider the fact that maybe you destroyed her life?"

She smirks. "You would look at it that way."

"What other way is there?"

"Maybe I saved her from embarrassment. What do you think would have happened if I'd let her get out on the field? People are cruel, in case you haven't noticed. She'd have been a laughingstock. All the guys would have made fun of her. Guys don't come to games to see ugly women."

"You're kidding, right?" I say, as if I don't believe her. But I do. A little. It's a horrible world.

I'm not ready to concede the point, though. "Is that how you plan to live your life? Based on what guys like and who they think is pretty? That's pathetic."

She smiles, sure of herself. "So what? It's the truth. And if there's anyone pathetic here, it's you. Girls who can't get guys always say there's something wrong with girls who *can*. If *you* could get guys, I promise we wouldn't be having this conversation."

"Is that so?"

"I only have two words for you: Sebastian Kydd." She laughs.

I have to grit my teeth to prevent myself from jumping on top of her and punching her in her oh-so-pretty face.

And then *I* laugh. "He dumped you too, remember? He dumped you for me." I grin wickedly. "And I seem to recall that you spent most of the fall making my life miserable because I was seeing Sebastian and you weren't."

"Sebastian Kydd?" She sneers. "You think I give a fuck about Sebastian Kydd? Sure, he's cute. And kind of sexy. And

I had him. Other than that, he's completely useless. Sebastian Kydd has no relevance in my life."

"Then why did you bother—"

She shrugs. "I wanted to make your life miserable because you're a jerk."

I'm a jerk? "I guess we're even. Because I think you're a jerk too."

"Actually, you're worse than a jerk. You're a snob."

Huh?

"If you want to know the truth," she says, "I've hated you since the first day of kindergarten. And I'm not the only one."

"Kindergarten?" I ask in astonishment.

"You were wearing red patent leather Mary Janes. And you thought you were so special. You thought you were better than everyone else. Because you had red shoes and nobody else did."

Okay. I do remember those shoes. My mother bought them as a special treat for me for starting kindergarten. I wore them all the time—I even tried to wear them to bed. But still, they were only shoes. Who would have thought shoes could cause so much jealousy?

"You hate me because of some shoes I wore when I was four?" I say in disbelief.

"It wasn't just the shoes," she counters. "It was your whole attitude. You and your perfect little family. The Bradshaw girls," she says mockingly. "Aren't they cute? And so well-behaved."

If she only knew.

I'm suddenly exhausted. Why do girls carry these grudges for years and years? Do boys do that too?

I think about Lali and shiver.

She looks at me, gives a little exclamation of triumph, and goes inside.

And then I just stand there, wondering what to do. Go home? Call it a day? But if I leave, it means Donna LaDonna has won. She'll have claimed this class as her territory and my absence will mean she's driven me out.

I won't let her win. Even if it requires being stuck with her for an hour once a week.

I mean, can my life really get any worse?

I pull open the heavy door, trudge up the stairs, and take my seat next to her.

For the next thirty minutes, while Todd Upsky talks about f-stops and shutter speeds, we sit next to each other in silence, each desperately pretending that the other one does not exist.

Just like me and Lali.

CHAPTER TWENTY-NINE

The Gorgon

"Why don't you write about it?" George asks.

"No," I say, snapping off the delicate tip of a tree branch. I examine it, rubbing the soft dry wood between my fingers before tossing it back into the woods.

"Why not?"

"Because." I push forward on the path that leads up a steep hill. Behind me, I hear George breathing heavily from the effort. I grab a sapling around the middle and use it to pull me to the top. "I don't want to be a writer so I can write about my life. I want to be a writer to escape from it."

"Then you shouldn't be a writer," George says, puffing.

That's it.

"I am so sick of everyone telling me what I should and shouldn't do. Maybe I don't want to be your idea of a writer. Did you ever think about that?"

"Hey," he says. "Take it easy."

"I will not take it easy. And I will not listen to you, or anybody else. Because you know what? Everyone thinks they know so goddamned much about everything and no one knows fuck all about anything."

"Sorry," he says, his mouth drawn into a prim line of disapproval. "I was only trying to help."

I take a breath. Sebastian would have laughed at me. His laughter would have briefly pissed me off, but then I'd have found it funny too. George, on the other hand, is so damn serious.

He's right, though. He is only trying to help. And Sebastian is gone. He dumped me, just like George said he would.

I should be grateful. George, at least, has had the decency not to say I told you so.

"Remember when I told you I'd introduce you to my great-aunt?" he asks now.

"The one who's a writer?" I say, still slightly miffed.

"That's right. Do you want to meet her?"

"Oh, George." Now I feel guilty.

"I'm going to arrange it for next week. I think it will cheer you up."

I could kick myself. George really is the best. If only I could fall in love with him.

We pass through Hartford and turn onto a wide street lined with maples. The houses are set back from the road—large, white, practically mansions—with columns and decorative tiny paned windows. This is West Hartford, where the wealthy old families live, where, I imagine, they have gardeners to tend to their roses and swimming pools and red-clay tennis courts. It doesn't surprise me that George is taking me here. George's family is rich, after all—he never talks about it, but he must be, living in a four-bedroom apartment on Fifth Avenue with a father who works on Wall Street and a mother who spends her summers in Southampton, wherever that is. We pull into a gravel driveway edged with hedges and park in front of a carriage house with a cupola on top.

"Your great-aunt lives here?"

"I told you she was successful," George says with a mysterious smile.

I experience a jab of panic. It's one thing to imagine someone has money, but quite another to be confronted with the spoils of their loot. A flagstone path leads around the side of the house to a glassed-in conservatory, filled with plants and elaborately wrought garden furniture. George knocks on the door, and then opens it, releasing a cloud of warm, steamy air. "Bunny?" he calls out.

Bunny?

A red-haired middle-aged woman in a gray uniform crosses the room. "Mr. George," she exclaims. "You startled me."

"Hello, Gwyneth. This is my friend Carrie Bradshaw. Is Bunny home?"

"She's expecting you."

We follow Gwyneth down a long hall, past a dining room and a library, and into an enormous living room. There's a fireplace at one end with a marble mantelpiece, above which hangs a painting of a young woman in a pink tulle dress. Her eyes are wide, brown, and authoritative—eyes, I'm sure, I've seen before. But where?

George walks to a brass cart and holds up a bottle of sherry. "Drink?" he asks.

"Should we?" I whisper, still gazing up at the painting.

"Of course. Bunny always likes a bit of sherry. And she gets very angry when people won't drink with her."

"So this—er—Bunny. She's not cute and fluffy?"

"Hardly." George's eyes widen in amusement as he hands me a crystal glass filled with amber fluid. "Some people say she's a monster."

"Who says that?" a booming voice declares. If I didn't know Bunny was a woman, I might have guessed the voice belonged to a man.

"Hello, old thing," George says, moving across the room to greet her.

"And what have we here?" she asks, indicating me. "Who have you dragged to meet me this time?"

The insult is lost on George. He must be used to her nasty sense of humor. "Carrie," he says proudly, "this is my aunt Bunny."

I nod weakly and hold out my hand. "Bu-bu-bu—" I

falter, unable to speak.

Bunny is Mary Gordon Howard.

Mary Gordon Howard arranges herself on the couch like she's a precious piece of china. Physically, she's frailer than I remember, although George did say she was eighty. But her persona is just as terrifying as it was four years ago when she attacked me at the library.

This cannot be happening.

Her hair is white and thick, swept back off her forehead into a bosomy arrangement. But her eyes look weak, the irises a watery brown, as if time has leaked out their color. "So, dear," she says as she takes a sip of sherry and slyly licks the excess from her lips, "George says you want to be a writer."

Oh no. Not this again. My hand shakes as I pick up my glass.

"She doesn't want to be a writer. She *is* a writer," George interjects, beaming with pride. "I've read some of her stories. She has potential—"

"I see," MGH says with a sigh. No doubt, she's heard this too many times. As if by rote, she launches into a lecture: "There are only two kinds of people who make great writers—great *artists*: those from the upper classes, who have access to the finest education—*or* those who have suffered greatly. The middle classes"—she looks at me, disapprovingly—"can sometimes produce a simulacrum of art, but it tends to be middle-brow or slyly commercial and of no real value. It's merely meretricious entertainment."

I nod dazedly. I can see my mother's face, the cheeks sunk right down to the jaw, head shrunken to the size of a baby's.

"I—um—actually, I met you before." My voice is barely audible. "At the library. In Castlebury?"

"Goodness. I do so many of those little readings."

"I asked you to sign a book for my mother. She was dying."

"And did she? Die, that is," she demands.

"Yes. She did."

"Oh, Carrie." George shifts from one foot to another. "What a nice thing to do. Having her book signed by Bunny."

Suddenly, Bunny leans forward and, with a fearful intensity, says, "Ah, yes. I do recall meeting you now. You were wearing yellow ribbons."

"Yes." *How can she possibly remember? Did I make an impact after all?*

"And I believe I told you not to become a writer. Clearly, you haven't taken my advice." Bunny pats her hair in triumph. "I never forget a face."

"Auntie, you're a genius," George exclaims.

I look from one to the other in astonishment. And then I get it: They're playing some kind of sick game.

"Why shouldn't Carrie become a writer?" George laughs. He seems to find everything "Aunt Bunny" says extremely amusing.

Guess what? I can play too.

"She's too pretty," Aunt Bun-Bun responds.

"Excuse me?" I choke on my sherry, which tastes like cough medicine.

Irony of Ironies: too pretty to be a writer but not pretty enough to keep my boyfriend.

"Not pretty enough to be a movie star. Not that kind of pretty," she continues. "But pretty enough to think you can get by in life by using your looks."

"What would I use them *for*?"

"To get a husband," she says, looking at George. Aha. She thinks I'm after her nephew.

This is all too Jane Austen-ish and weird.

"I think Carrie is very pretty," George counters.

"And then, of course, you'll want to have children," MGH says poisonously.

"Aunt Bun," George says, grinning from ear to ear, "how do you know?"

"Because every woman wants children. Unless you are a very great exception. I, myself, never wanted children." She holds out her glass to George, indicating she needs a refill. "If you want to become a very great writer, you cannot have children. Your *books* must be your children!"

I wonder if the Bunny has had too much to drink and it's beginning to show.

And suddenly, I can't help it. The words just slip out of my mouth. "Do books need to be diapered as well?"

My voice drips with sarcasm.

Bunny's jaw drops. Clearly, she isn't used to having her authority challenged. She looks to George, who shrugs as if I'm the most delightful creature in the world.

And then Bunny laughs. She actually guffaws in mirth.

She pats the couch next to her. "What did you say your name was again, dear? Carrie Bradshaw?" She looks up at George and winks. "Come, sit. George keeps telling me I'm turning into a bitter old woman, and I could use some amusement."

The Writer's Life, by Mary Gordon Howard.

I open the cover and read the inscription:

To Carrie Bradshaw. Don't forget to diaper your babies.

I turn the page. Chapter One: The Importance of Keeping a Journal.

Ugh. I put it down and pick up a heavy black book with a leather cover, a gift from George. "I told you she'd love you," he exclaimed in the car on the way home. And then he was so excited by the success of the visit, he insisted on stopping at a stationery store and buying me my very own journal.

I balance Bunny's book on top of the journal and randomly flip through it, landing on Chapter Four: How to Create Character.

Audiences often ask if characters are based on "real people."
Indeed, the impulse of the amateur is to write about "who

one knows." The professional, on the other hand, understands the impossibility of such a task. The "creator" of the character must know more about the character than one could ever possibly know about a "real person." The author must possess complete knowledge: what the character was wearing on Christmas morning when he or she was five, what presents he or she received, who gave them, and how they were given. A "character," therefore, is a "real person" who exists in another plane, a parallel universe based on the author's perception of reality.

When it comes to people—don't write about who you know, but what *you know of human nature.*

CHAPTER THIRTY

Accidents Will Happen

I write a short story about Mary Gordon Howard. Her maid puts poison in her sherry and she dies a long and drawn-out death. It's six pages and it sucks. I stick it in my drawer.

I talk to George a lot on the phone. I take Dorrit to the shrink George found for her in West Hartford.

I feel like I'm marking time.

Dorrit is surly, but she hasn't gotten into any more trouble. "Dad says you're going to Brown," she says one afternoon, when I'm driving her home from her appointment.

"Haven't been accepted yet."

"I hope you are," she says. "All Dad ever wanted was for one of his daughters to go to his alma mater. If you get in, I won't have to worry about it."

"What if I don't want to go to Brown?"

"Then you're stupid," Dorrit says.

"Carrie!" Missy says, running out of the house. "Carrie!"

She's waving a thick envelope. "It's from Brown."

"See?" Dorrit says. Even she's excited.

I tear open the envelope. It's filled with schedules and maps and pamphlets with titles like, *Student Life*. My hands are shaking as I unfold the letter. *Dear Ms. Bradshaw*, it reads. *Congratulations*—

Oh, God. "I'm going to Brown!" I jump up and down and run around the car in glee. Then I stop. It's only forty-five minutes away. My life will be exactly the same, except I'll be in college.

But I'll be at Brown. Which is pretty darn good. It's kind of a big deal.

"Brown," Missy squeals. "Dad will be so happy."

"I know," I say, floating on the moment. Maybe my luck has changed. Maybe my life is finally going in the right direction.

"So, Dad," I say later, after he's hugged me and patted me on the back and said things like, "I always knew you could do it, kid, if you applied yourself," "since I'm going to Brown . . ." I hesitate, wanting to position this in the best possible light. "I was wondering if maybe I could spend the summer in New York."

The question takes him by surprise, but he's too thrilled about Brown to actually analyze it.

"With George?" he asks.

"Not necessarily with George," I say quickly. "But there's this writing program I've been trying to get into—"

"Writing?" he says. "But now that you're going to Brown, you're going to want to be a scientist."

"Dad, I'm not sure—"

"It doesn't matter," he says with a wave, as if shooing the issue away. "The important thing is that you're going to Brown. You don't have to figure out your entire life this very minute."

And then it's the day swim team starts again.

The break is over. I'll have to see Lali.

Six weeks have passed and she's still seeing Sebastian.

I don't have to go. I don't, in fact, have to do anything anymore. I've been accepted to college. My father has sent in a check. I can skip classes, drop swim team, come to school intoxicated, and there's nothing anyone can do. I'm in.

So maybe it's pure perversity that propels me down the hall to the locker rooms.

She's there. Standing in front of the lockers where we always used to change. As if claiming our once-mutual territory for herself, the way she claimed Sebastian. My blood boils. She's the bad person here, the one who's done wrong. She ought to at least have the decency to move to a different part of the locker room.

My head suddenly feels encased in cement.

I drop my gym bag next to hers. She stiffens, sensing my presence the way I can sense hers even when she's at the other end of the hallway. I swing open the door of my locker.

It bangs against hers, nearly slamming her finger.

She pulls her hand back at the last second. She stares at me, surprised, then angry.

I shrug.

We take off our clothes. But now I don't sink into myself the way I usually do, trying to hide my nakedness. She's not looking at me anyway, wriggling herself into her suit and stretching the straps over her shoulders with a snap.

In a moment, she'll be gone. "How's Sebastian?" I ask.

This time, when she looks at me, I see everything I need to know. She is never going to apologize. She is never going to admit she did anything wrong. She is never going to acknowledge that she hurt me. She will not say she misses me or even feels bad. She is going to continue forward, like nothing happened, like we were friends, but we were never *that* close.

"Fine." She walks away, swinging her goggles.

Fine. I put my clothes back on. I don't need to be around her. Let her have swim team. Let her have Sebastian, too. If she needs him badly enough to destroy a friendship, I feel sorry for her.

On my way out, I hear shouting coming from the gym. I peek through the hatched window in the wooden door. Cheerleading practice is in session.

I walk across the polished floor to the bleachers, take a seat in the fourth row, and lean into my hands, wondering why I'm doing this.

The members of the squad are dressed in leotards or T-shirts with leggings, their hair pulled back into ponytails. They wear old-fashioned saddle shoes. The tinny thump of "Bad, Bad, Leroy Brown" echoes from a tape-player in the corner as the line of girls shake their pom-poms, step forward and back, turn right, place a hand on the shoulder of the girl in front of them, and one by one, with varying degrees of gracefulness and skill, slide their legs apart into a split.

The song ends and they jump to their feet, shaking their pom-poms over their heads and shouting, "Go team!"

Honestly? They suck.

The group breaks up. Donna LaDonna uses the white headband she's been wearing around her forehead to wipe her face. She and another cheerleader, a girl named Naomi, head to the bleachers and, without acknowledging my presence, sit two rows ahead.

Donna shakes out her hair. "Becky needs to do something about that B.O.," she says, referring to one of the younger cheerleaders.

"Maybe we should give her a box of deodorant," Naomi says.

"Deodorant's no good. Not for that kind of odor. I'm thinking more along the lines of feminine hygiene." Donna titters, while Naomi cackles at this witty remark. Raising her voice, Donna abruptly changes the subject. "Can you believe Sebastian Kydd is still dating Lali Kandesie?"

"I heard he likes virgins," Naomi says. "Until they're not virgins anymore. Then he dumps them."

"It's like he's providing a service." Donna LaDonna's voice rises even higher, as if she can't contain her amusement. "I wonder who's next? It can't be a pretty girl—all the pretty girls have already had sex. It has to be someone ugly. Like that Ramona girl. The one who tried to be a cheerleader three years in a row? Some people never get the message. It's sad."

Suddenly, she turns around and, with a patently surprised expression, exclaims, "Carrie Bradshaw!" Widening her eyes, she stretches her lips into an exuberant smile. "We were just talking about you. Tell me, how *is* Sebastian? I mean in bed, of course. Is he really as good a fuck as Lali says he is?"

I am expecting this. I've been expecting it all along.

"Gosh, Donna," I say innocently. "Don't you know? Didn't you do it with him an hour after you met? Or was it more like fifteen minutes?"

"Really, Carrie." She narrows her eyes. "I thought you knew me better than that. Sebastian is far too inexperienced for me. I don't *do* boys."

I lean forward and lock my eyes onto hers. "I've always wondered what it would be like to be you." I look around the gym and sigh. "It must be so . . . *exhausting.*"

I gather my things and hop off the bleacher. As I walk toward the door, I hear her shout, "You wish, Carrie Bradshaw. You should be so *lucky.*"

And so should you. You're dead.

Why do I keep doing this? Why do I keep putting myself into these terrible situations where I know I can't win? But

I can't seem to help myself. It's like having been burned once, I got used to the feeling, and now I have to keep burning myself again and again. Just to prove to myself that I'm still alive. To remind myself that I can still *feel*.

Dorrit's shrink said it was better to feel something rather than nothing. And Dorrit had stopped feeling. She was afraid to feel, and then she was afraid of the numbness. So she started acting out.

All very neat and tidy. Tie up your problems with a big bow and maybe you can pretend they're a present.

Outside, near the door that leads directly to the pool, I spot Sebastian Kydd parking his car.

I start running.

Not away from him, like a reasonable person, but toward him.

He's blissfully unaware of what's about to happen, checking his stubble in the rearview mirror.

I grab my heaviest book—calculus—and heave it at his car. The book barely grazes the trunk as it splits open and lands facedown on the pavement, pages akimbo like the legs of a cheerleader. The thud is just loud enough to jar Sebastian out of his self-loving reverie, and he jerks his head around, wondering what—if anything—is happening. I run closer and throw another book at his car. It's a paperback—*The Sun Also Rises*—and it slams the front window. In the next second, he's out of the car, crouched for battle. "What are you doing?"

"What do you think I'm doing?" I yell, trying to fling my

biology book at his head. I nearly lose my grip on the slick paper cover, so I raise the book over my head and charge at him instead.

He stretches his arms protectively across the car. "Don't do it, Carrie," he says warningly. "Don't touch my car. Nobody scratches my baby and gets away with it."

I'm picturing his car shattering into a million pieces of plastic and glass, scattered across the parking lot like the detritus of an explosion, when the ridiculousness of his statement stops me in my tracks. But only momentarily. A roar of blood fills my head as I rush him again. "I don't care about your car. I'm trying to hurt *you*."

I swing my biology book, but he snatches it out of my hands before I can make contact. But somehow *I* keep going, past him, past his car, stumbling across the macadam until I trip over the curb and come to rest in a heap on the frozen grass. I'm followed by my biology book, which lands with a thump a few feet away.

I am not proud of my behavior. But I've gone too far now and there's no turning back.

"How dare you?" I cry, scrambling to my feet.

"Stop it! *Stop it*," he shouts, grabbing my wrists. "You're *insane*."

"Tell me why!"

"No," he says, furious. I'm happy to see he's finally pissed off as well.

"You *owe* me."

"I don't owe you a goddamned thing." He thrusts my

arms away as if he can't stand to touch me, while I chase after him, popping back and forth behind him like a jack-in-the-box.

"What's the matter? Are you scared?" I taunt.

"Get away."

"You owe me an explanation."

"You really want to know?" He stops, turns, and gets in my face.

"Yes."

"She's nicer," he says simply.

Nicer?

What the hell does that mean?

"*I'm* nice." I pound my chest with my hands. My nose prickles a warning that tears are not far behind.

"Leave it alone, will you?" he asks, running his hands through his hair.

"I can't. I won't. It's not fair—"

"She's just nicer, okay?"

"What does that mean?" I wail.

"She's not—you know—competitive."

Lali? Not competitive? "She's the most competitive girl I know."

He shakes his head. "She's *nice.*"

Nice—*nice*? Why does he keep using that word? What does it mean? And then it dawns on me. Nice equals sex. She has sex with him. She goes all the way. And I wouldn't.

"I hope you're very happy together." I take a step back. "I

hope you're so happy you get married and have kids. And I hope you stay in this stupid town forever and *rot*—like a couple of wormy apples."

"Thanks," he says sarcastically, heading toward the gym. This time I don't stop him. Instead, I shout dumb words at his back. Words like "maggots" and "mold" and "nacreous."

✧ ✳ CB ✳ ✧

I'm stupid, I know. But I don't care anymore.

I pick up a blank piece of paper and roll it through my mother's old Royale typewriter. After a few minutes, I write: *The trick to being a queen bee isn't necessarily beauty but industriousness. Beauty helps, but without the drive to get to the top and stay on top, beauty will only make you a bee-in-waiting.*

Three hours later, I read through my handiwork. Not bad. Now all I need is a pen name. Something that will show people I mean business, that I'm not one to be messed with. On the other hand, it should also convey a sense of humor— even absurdity. I absentmindedly straighten the pages while I consider.

I reread my title, "The Castlebury Compendium: A guide to the fauna and flora of high school," followed by, "Chapter One: The Queen Bee." I pick up a pen, pressing the clicker in and out, in and out, until finally the name comes to me. *By Pinky Weatherton,* I write, in neat block letters.

CHAPTER THIRTY-ONE

Pinky Jakes Castlebury

"Maggie is making me go to this prom committee meeting with her," Peter says under his breath. "Do you mind putting the paper to bed?"

"No problem. Have a good time. Gayle and I will take care of it."

"Don't tell Smidgens, okay?"

"I won't," I reassure him. "You can trust me completely."

Peter doesn't appear entirely convinced, but he has no choice. Maggie has come into the art department and is standing behind him. "Peter?" she asks.

"Coming."

"Okay, Gayle," I say, when they're safely down the hall. "Time to get to work."

"Aren't you scared of getting in trouble?"

"Nope. A writer must be fearless. A writer has to be like a clawed animal."

"Says who?"

"Mary Gordon Howard."

"Who's she?"

"Doesn't matter. Aren't you glad we're getting revenge on Donna LaDonna?"

"Yes. But what if she doesn't know it's her?"

"Even if she doesn't know, everyone else will, I promise."

Working quickly, Gayle and I remove Peter's story about doing away with the gym requirement for seniors, and replace it with my own story on the queen bee—aka Donna LaDonna. Then Gayle and I walk the mock-up of tomorrow's edition of *The Nutmeg* to the AV room, where several happy nerds will turn it into a newspaper. Peter and Ms. Smidgens will be furious, of course. But what can they do—*fire me*? I don't think so.

I wake up early the next morning. For the first time in a long time I'm actually excited about going to school. I run into the kitchen where my father is frying an egg.

"You're awake," he exclaims.

"Yup," I say, making myself a piece of toast and smearing it with butter.

"You seem happy," he says cautiously, carrying his egg to the table. "Are you happy?"

"Sure, Dad. Why wouldn't I be?"

"I didn't want to bring this up," he says, getting all squirrelly and uncomfortable, "but Missy told me a little bit about what happened with—er—Sebastian, and I don't want to make anything worse but I've been wanting to tell you for weeks that, well, you can't rely on anyone else for your own happiness." He pricks the yolk of his egg, as he nods in agreement with his own wisdom. "I know you think I'm only your old man and I don't know much about what's going on, but I'm a great *observer*. And I've observed your *sorrow* over this incident. I've wanted to help you—believe me, nothing hurts a father more than seeing his own child hurt—but I also know that I can't. When these kinds of things happen, you're alone. I wish it weren't true, but it is. And if you can get through these kinds of things on your own, it makes you stronger as a person. It has a vast impact on your development as a human being to know that you have strengths to fall back on, and—"

"Thanks, Dad," I say, kissing him on top of his head. "I get it."

I go back upstairs and rifle through my closet. I consider wearing something outrageous, like striped leggings and a plaid shirt, but think better of it. I don't want to draw unnecessary attention to myself. I put on a cotton turtleneck, corduroy jeans, and a pair of penny loafers, instead.

Outside, it's one of those unseasonably warm April days that makes you think spring is just around the corner. I decide to take advantage of the weather and walk to school.

By bus, the trip is about four miles. But I know all the shortcuts and by zigzagging through the little streets behind the school I can get there in about twenty-five minutes. My route takes me by Walt's house, a pretty little saltbox with a long hedge in front. The outside of the house is perfectly kept due to Walt's efforts, but I'm always amazed how his entire family fits in that tiny abode. There are five kids and four bedrooms, which means that Walt has always had to share a room with his younger brother, whom he hates.

When I get to Walt's house, however, I spot something unusual. A green camping tent has been erected at the far end of the backyard and a bright orange outdoor electrical cord runs from the house into the tent. Walt, I know, would never allow a tent in the backyard—he'd consider it a blight. I move closer as the flap of the tent opens and Walt himself emerges, pale and unkempt in a rumpled T-shirt and jeans that look as though he's slept in them. He rubs his eyes and glares at a robin that's hopping around, looking for worms. "Go away. Beat it!" he says, walking toward the robin and waving his arms. "Damn birds," he says as it flies away.

"Walt?"

"Huh?" He squints. Walt needs glasses but refuses to wear them, believing that glasses will only make his eyes worse. "Carrie? What are you doing here?"

"What are you doing in that tent?" I ask with equal astonishment.

"It's my new home," he says, with a mixture of irony and sarcasm. "Isn't it fabulous?"

"I don't get it."

"Hold on," he says. "I've got to pee. I'll be right back."

He goes into the house and comes out several minutes later with a mug of coffee. "I'd invite you in, but I promise, you won't find it pleasant inside."

"What's going on?" I follow him into the tent. There's a tarp on the ground, a sleeping bag, a rough army blanket, a pile of clothes, and a small plastic table on which stands an old lamp and an open box of Oreos. Walt paws through the pile of clothes, pulls out a pack of cigarettes, and holds it up. "One of the advantages of not living in the house. No one can tell you not to smoke."

"Ha," I say, sitting cross-legged on the sleeping bag.

I light a cigarette as I try to make sense of this situation. "So you're not living in your house?" I ask.

"Nope," he says. "Moved out a few days ago."

"Isn't it kind of cold for camping?"

"Not today." He rolls over and ashes his cigarette in the corner of the tent. "Anyway, I'm used to it. I love hardship."

"You do?"

He sighs. "What do you think?"

"So why are you out here?"

He inhales deeply. "My father. Richard found out I was gay. Oh yes," he continues, taking in my shocked expression. "My brother read my journal—"

"*You* keep a journal?"

"Of course, Carrie," he says impatiently. "I always have. It's mostly ideas for architecture—clippings of buildings I like and drawings. But there is some personal stuff in there—a few Polaroids of me and Randy—and my dumb brother somehow managed to put two-and-two together and told my parents."

"Crap."

"Yeah." Walt stubs out his cigarette and immediately lights another. "My mother couldn't care less, of course—she has a brother who's gay, although no one ever comes out and says it. They call him a 'confirmed bachelor.' But my father freaked out. He's such an asshole you'd never believe he could be religious, but he is. He thinks being 'homosexual' is a mortal sin or something. Anyway, I'm no longer allowed to go to church, which is a relief, but my father decided he couldn't trust me to sleep in the house. He's afraid I might corrupt my brothers."

"Walt, that's *ridiculous.*"

He shrugs. "Could be worse. At least I'm allowed to use the kitchen and the bathroom."

"Why didn't you tell me?" I ask.

"Like you aren't all wrapped up in your own drama."

"I *am*, but I always have time for other people's dramas."

"Could have fooled me."

"Oh, God. Have I been a shitty friend?"

"Not shitty," Walt says. "Just caught up in your own problems."

I hug my knees and stare bleakly at the rough canvas walls. "I'm sorry, Walt. I had no idea. You can come and live at my house until this blows over. Your father can't stay mad at you forever."

"Wanna bet?" Walt says. "According to him, I'm the devil's spawn. He's disowned me as his son."

"Why don't you leave? Run away?"

"And go where?" he scoffs. "Besides, what's the point? Richard refuses to pay for college, as punishment for my being gay. He's afraid that all I'll do in college is dress up and go to discos or something—so I need to save every penny. I figure I'll live in the tent until September, when I go to RISD." He leans back against the damp pillow. "It's not that bad. I kind of like it here."

"Well, I don't. You're going to stay at my house. I'll sleep in my sister's room and you can have mine—"

"I don't want charity, Carrie."

"But surely, your mother—"

"She never gets in my father's way when he's like this. It only makes things worse."

"I hate straight men," I say.

"Yeah." Walt sighs. "Me too."

I'm so shocked by Walt's situation that it takes me a few minutes to realize something is different about assembly this morning. The auditorium is a little quieter than usual, and when I take my seat next to Tommy Brewster, I notice he's reading *The Nutmeg.* "Have you seen this?" he asks, shaking the paper.

"No," I say casually. "Why?"

"I thought you wrote for this rag."

"I did. Once. But that was months ago."

"Well, you'd better read it now," he says warningly.

"Okay." I shrug. And to further emphasize my lack of involvement in the matter, I get up and walk to the front of the auditorium, where I pick up a copy of *The Nutmeg* from a pile on the corner of the stage. When I turn around, three sophomore girls are waiting behind me. "Can we have a copy?" one of them asks as they bump each other.

"I heard it's all about Donna LaDonna," says another. "Can you believe it? Can you believe anyone would do that?" I hand them three papers and head back to my seat, digging my fingernails into my palm to control my shaking. Crap. What if I get caught? But I won't get caught if I act normal and Gayle keeps her mouth shut.

I have this theory: You can get away with anything as long as you act like you're not doing anything wrong.

I open the paper and pretend to read it, while surreptitiously checking to see if Peter has arrived. He has, and he, too, is absorbed in *The Nutmeg*. His cheeks are beet red and a flush like a flame runs from his cheekbones down to his jaw.

I return to my seat, where Tommy, apparently, has finished reading the article and has worked himself into a froth. "Whoever did this should be kicked out of school." He looks at the front page again, checking the name. "Who is Pinky Weatherton? I've never even heard of him."

Him?

"Me neither." I press my lips together as if I'm stumped as well. I can't believe Tommy actually thinks Pinky Weatherton is a real student—and a guy. But now that Tommy has presented the possibility, I go along with it. "It must be someone new."

"The only new person in this school is Sebastian Kydd. You think he could have done this?"

I fold my arms and look at the ceiling, as if the answer might be lurking there. "Well, he did go out with Donna LaDonna. And didn't she dump him or something? Maybe he thought he'd get revenge."

"That's right," Tommy says, pointing his finger. "I knew there was something creepy about that guy. Did you know he went to private school? I hear his family is rich. Probably looks down on us regular kids. Thinks he's better than we are."

"Uh-huh." I nod enthusiastically.

Tommy pounds his fist into his hand. "We have to do something about this guy. Slash his tires. Or get him kicked out of school. Hey." He suddenly stops and scratches his head. "Didn't *you* go out with him? Didn't I hear—"

"A couple of times," I admit, before he can put the pieces together. "But he turned out to be just like you said. A real creep."

All through calculus class, I feel Peter's eyes boring into the side of my head. Sebastian is there as well, but ever since the incident in the parking lot, I have studiously avoided looking at him or catching his eye. Today, however, I can't help smiling when he walks into class. He gives me a startled look, then smiles back, as if he's relieved I'm not mad at him anymore.

Ha. If he only knew.

I rush out of class as soon as the bell rings, but Peter is right behind me. "How did it happen?" he demands.

"What?" I ask, like I'm kind of annoyed.

"'What?'" He rolls his eyes as if he can't believe I'm playing this game. "The piece in *The Nutmeg*, that's what."

"I have no idea," I say, starting to walk away. "I did exactly what you said. I brought the mock-up to the AV room—"

"You did something," he insists.

"Peter." I sigh. "I honestly do not know what you're talking about."

"Well, you'd better figure it out. Smidgens wants to see me in her office. Now. And you're coming with me."

He grabs my arm, but I twist away. "Are you sure? Do you really want to tell her that you didn't close the paper?"

"Damn," he says, and glares at me. "You'd better think fast, is all I can say."

"No problem." The thought of a scene between Peter and Ms. Smidgens is too tempting to resist. I'm like an arsonist who can't stay away from her own fires.

Ms. Smidgens is sitting behind her desk with *The Nutmeg* propped up in front of her. A good two inches of ash is balanced precariously at the end of her cigarette. "Hello, Peter," she says, bringing the cigarette to her lips as I watch, fascinated, wondering when the ash is going to fall. She drops the cigarette into a pile of butts, the ash still intact. Threads of smoke from still-smoldering cigarettes drift up from a large ceramic bowl.

Peter takes a seat. Smidgens nods at me, clearly not interested in my presence. I sit down anyway.

"So," she says, lighting another cigarette. "Who is Pinky Weatherton?"

Peter stares at her, then jerks his head around and glares at me.

"He's new," I say.

"He?"

"Or she," Peter says. "He or she just moved here."

Ms. Smidgens is not impressed. "Is that so? From where?"

"Um, Missouri?" Peter asks.

"Why can't I find him—or her—on my list of students?"

"He *just* moved here," I say. "Like yesterday. Well, not exactly *yesterday*. Maybe last week or something."

"He probably isn't in the system yet," Peter adds.

"I see." Smidgens holds up *The Nutmeg*. "This Pinky Weatherton happens to be a very good writer. I'd like to see more of his—or her—work in the paper."

"Sure," Peter says hesitantly.

Ms. Smidgens gives Peter an evil smile. She waves her cigarette, about to say more, when suddenly the long column of ash spirals into her cleavage. She jumps, shaking the ash out of her blouse, as Peter and I attempt a hasty exit. We're at the door when she calls out, "Wait."

Slowly, we turn.

"About Pinky," she says, squinting through the smoke. Her lips curl into a nasty smile. "I want to meet him. Or her. And tell this Pinky person to decide on a gender."

"Did you see this?" Maggie asks, plunking *The Nutmeg* onto the cafeteria table.

"Um, yeah," The Mouse says, stirring hot water into her Cup-a-Soup. "The whole school's talking about it."

"How come I didn't know about this until now?" Maggie says, looking at Peter accusingly.

"Because you're really busy with the prom committee?" Peter asks. He slides in between Maggie and The Mouse. Maggie picks up the paper and points to the headline. "And what kind of name is Pinky Weatherton, anyway?"

"Maybe it's a nickname. Like The Mouse," I say.

"But The Mouse isn't Roberta's real name. I mean, she would never sign her papers 'The Mouse.' "

Peter gives me a look, and pats Maggie on the head. "There's no need to concern yourself with the inner workings of *The Nutmeg*. I have it all under control."

"You do?" Maggie looks at him in surprise. "What are you going to do about Donna LaDonna, then? I bet she's pissed as shit."

"Actually," The Mouse says, blowing on the top of her soup, "she seems to be enjoying it."

"Really?" Maggie asks. She swivels around in her chair and looks toward the opposite end of the cafeteria.

The Mouse is right. Donna LaDonna does appear to be lapping up the attention. She's smack in the middle of her usual table, surrounded by her henchmen and her bees-in-waiting who have gathered tightly around her, like she's some kind of movie star who needs protection from her fans. Donna preens, smiling and lowering her chin, seductively raising her shoulders as if all her movements are being captured by an invisible camera. Meanwhile, Lali and Sebastian are mysteriously absent. It isn't until I get up to empty my tray that I finally spot them, huddled together at the end of an empty table in the corner of the cafeteria.

I'm about to walk away, when I'm summoned by Donna LaDonna herself.

"Carrie!" Her voice is as loud as a ringing bell. I turn and she waggles her fingers over Tommy Brewster's head.

"Hi?" I ask, approaching cautiously.

"Did you see the story about me in *The Nutmeg*?" she asks, unabashedly pleased.

"How could I miss it?"

"It's so crazy," she says, as if she can hardly stand the attention. "But I said to Tommy, and to Jen P, that whoever wrote that story must know me really, really well."

"I guess they do," I say mildly.

She blinks her eyes at me, and suddenly, try as I might, I just can't hate her anymore. I tried to take her down, but somehow she's managed to twist it around to her advantage.

Good for her, I think as I walk away.

CHAPTER THIRTY-TWO

The Nerd Prince

"Did you know Walt was living in a tent?" I ask Maggie. Our arms are full of bags of confetti.

"No," Maggie says, in a tone that sounds like she thinks I'm making it up. "Why would he do that?"

"His father found out he was gay and won't let Walt sleep in the house."

Maggie shakes her head. "That Richard. He's such a silly man. But he'd never make Walt sleep outside." She leans toward me and, in a loud whisper, says, "Walt is becoming a huge drama queen. Now that he's . . . you know."

"Gay?"

"Whatever," she says as we enter the gym.

Hmph. So much for trying to be a better friend.

After I discovered Walt in the tent, I decided he was right—I'd been so wrapped up in Sebastian and the subsequent betrayal, I'd hardly noticed what was happening with my friends. Hence my acceptance of Maggie's invitation to help her decorate the gym for the senior prom. It's only this once, I remind myself. And it's a way to spend time with Maggie.

"Oh, good," Jen P says, rushing over. "Confetti. Did you get all twelve bags?"

"Uh-huh." Maggie nods.

Jen P looks critically at the bags in our arms. "I'm not sure it's enough. Do you think we need more?"

Maggie looks defeated—she's never been good at organization—and I'm surprised she's lasted this long in the planning.

"How much confetti do we really need?" I ask.

"Put it over there and we'll figure it out later," Jen P orders, pointing to an area piled with streamers and tissue paper. But as we start to walk away, she follows. "By the way," she says to Maggie. "Did you see that story in *The Nutmeg*? The one about who will be prom king and queen? Pinky Weatherton is right. How can Donna LaDonna be prom queen if she's bringing an outside date? Who wants to look back on their senior prom and not even know the prom king? And of course Cynthia thinks she and Tommy are the front-runners. But I liked the part about *me*—how if I could get a date, I'd be a contender." She takes a breath, nudges Maggie, and continues. "But as Pinky says, you never know. You and Peter could be the dark horses—after all, you have been dating for six months."

I have created a monster, I think, dumping my bags of confetti.

This week in *The Nutmeg*, Pinky Weatherton handicapped everyone's chances for prom king and queen, and now no one can stop talking about it. Every time I turn around, someone is quoting the story. "We should consider every couple who has contributed to the school—and is an example of true love." I don't know why I threw in the "true love" part—but I might have done it so Lali and Sebastian wouldn't dare think they were eligible.

Maggie flushes. "I'd never want to be prom queen. I'd die if I had to get up in front of everyone."

"Really? I'd love it. To each her own, right?" Jen P pats Maggie's shoulder, gives me a sharp look, and walks off.

"Right," I mutter under my breath. I sneak a look at Maggie, who appears perplexed.

Maybe I shouldn't have written that piece after all.

A month has passed since Pinky Weatherton made "his" debut in *The Nutmeg*, and since then, Pinky's been busy, publishing a story a week: "The Clique Climber," about a girl who manages to climb her way to the top by becoming everyone's gofer; "The Nerd Prince," about how a nerdly guy can turn into a hunk in senior year; and "Castlebury Horse Race! Who Will Be Prom King and Queen?" Pinky has also completed another story, called "Boyfriend Stealers and the Guys Who Love Them"—a thinly veiled account of Lali and Sebastian's relationship—which he hasn't turned in yet and which he plans to publish the last week of school.

In the meantime, I made photocopies of all five stories

and sent them in to The New School. George insisted I call to make sure they'd been received. Normally, I'd never do something like that, but George says the world is full of people who all want the same thing, and you have to do a little something extra to make them remember you. I said I could run through the halls naked but he didn't get the joke. So I called. "Yes, Ms. Bradshaw," said a man's deep, sonorous voice on the other end of the line. "We received your stories and will get back to you."

"But when?"

"We'll get back to you," he repeated, and hung up.

I'm never going to get into that program.

"She's just so pushy!" Maggie exclaims now, frowning.

"Jen P? I thought you decided you kind of liked her."

"I did—at first. But she's too friendly, you know?" Maggie slides the bags of confetti into place with her toe. "She's always hanging around. I swear, Carrie, ever since Pinky Weatherton wrote that story about Peter—"

Uh-oh. Not again. "The Nerd Prince?" I ask. "How do you know it was about Peter?"

"Who else could it have been about? What other guy in this school was a nerd and then I came along and turned him into a hot guy?"

"Hmmmm," I say, running through the piece in my mind.

It usually starts in September. If you're a girl, and a senior, you look around and wonder: Will I have a date for the

*prom? And if not, how can I find one? And this is where
the Nerd Prince comes in.*

*He's the guy you overlooked in freshman, sophomore, and
junior year. First he was the short guy with the high voice.
Then he was the taller guy with zits. And then, something
happened. His voice deepened. He got contacts. And all of a
sudden you find yourself sitting next to him in biology, and
you think—hey, I could actually like this guy.*

*And the Nerd Prince has his pluses. Because he hasn't been
corrupted by being the hot guy his whole life, he's grateful.
And because he hasn't been yelled at by coaches or trampled
on by the football team, he's actually kind of nice. You can
trust him. . .*

Maggie folds her arms, glares at Jen P's back, and continues.
"Ever since that story came out about Peter, Jen P has been
after him. You should see the way she looks at
him—"

"Come on, Magwitch. I'm sure that's not true. Besides, Peter
would never like Jen P anyway. He hates those kinds of girls."

She shakes her head. "I don't know, Carrie. He's changed."

"How?"

"It's like he thinks he *deserves* more."

"It doesn't get any better than you, Mags," I say gently.
"He knows that."

"He might, but Jen P doesn't."

And then, as if in illustration of her point, Peter strolls into the gym. Maggie waves, but Peter doesn't see her, possibly due to the fact that Jen P rushes over to him first, laughing and waving her arms. Peter nods and smiles.

"Maggie——" I turn to speak to her, but she's gone.

I find her in the parking lot, sitting in the Cadillac. She's in tears and has locked all the doors. "Maggie!" I tap on the windshield. She shakes her head, lights up a cigarette, and eventually rolls down the window. "Yes?"

"Maggie, come on. They were only talking." *Just like Sebastian and Lali were only talking—at first.* I feel horrible. "Let me in."

She unlocks the doors and I crawl into the backseat. "Sweetie, you're being paranoid." But I'm worried she's not. Is this somehow my fault? If I hadn't written that story about the Nerd Prince . . .

"I hate Pinky Weatherton," she gripes. "If I ever meet him, I'm going to give him a piece of my mind. Now Peter's head is swollen, and he thinks he's God's gift." Suddenly, she spins around. "You work for that *Nutmeg*. You must know Pinky Weatherton."

"Maggie, I don't. I swear."

"Well then," she says, narrowing her eyes in suspicion, "who does?"

"I don't know," I say helplessly. "This Pinky Weatherton person—he gives his stories to Gayle, and Gayle——"

"Who's Gayle?" she demands. "Maybe Gayle is Pinky Weatherton."

"I don't think so, Mags." I examine my cuticles. "Gayle is only a freshman."

"I need to talk to Peter."

"That's a good idea," I say soothingly. "I'm sure Peter can straighten everything out."

"So you're on his side now."

"I'm on *your* side, Maggie. I'm only trying to help."

"Then get him," she commands. "Go into the gym and find him. Tell him I need to see him. Immediately."

"Sure." I hop out of the car and hurry back inside. Jen P is still holding Peter captive, yammering about the importance of helium balloons.

I interrupt and give him the message about Maggie. He looks irritated but follows me out of the gym, waving reluctantly to Jen P and telling her he'll be right back. I watch as he crosses the parking lot, anger building into every step. By the time he reaches the car, he's so pissed off he jerks open the door and slams it behind him.

Maybe it's time for Pinky to move back to Missouri.

CHAPTER THIRTY-THREE

Hold On to Your Panties

The Mouse comes over for dinner on Saturday night. I serve coq au vin, which takes me all day to prepare, but I've recently discovered that cooking is a great way to distract yourself from your problems while providing a sense of accomplishment. You feel like you're doing something useful even though a few hours later you eat all the evidence. Plus, I'm trying to stay home more so I can spend time with Dorrit, who, the shrink says, needs to feel like she's still part of a working family. Once a week now, I make something elaborate and time consuming from the Julia Child cookbook.

My dad, of course, loves The Mouse—she can talk theorems almost as well as he can—and after we talk about math for a while, the conversation turns to college and how excited The Mouse is about going to Yale and me to Brown, and then the conversation somehow turns to boys. The Mouse tells my father all about Danny, and eventually, George's name comes up. "Carrie had a very nice fellow interested in her," my father says pointedly. "But she rejected him."

I sigh. "I haven't rejected George, Dad. We talk all the time on the phone. We're friends."

"When I was a young man, boys and girls weren't 'friends.' If you were 'friends' it meant—"

"I know what it meant, Dad," I interrupt. "But it's not like that now. Boys and girls really can be friends."

"Who's this George?" The Mouse asks. I groan. Every time George calls, which is about once a week, he asks me out on a date and I turn him down, saying I'm not ready. But really, when it comes to George, I don't think I'll ever be ready. Aloud I say, "He's just some guy who goes to Brown."

"He's a very nice young man," my father says. "Exactly the kind of guy a father wishes his daughter would be dating."

"And exactly the kind of guy the daughter knows she should be dating but just can't. Because she's not attracted to him."

My father throws up his hands. "What's the big deal about attraction? Love is what counts."

The Mouse and I look at each other and giggle. If only I were attracted to George, all my problems would be solved. I'd even have a date for the senior prom. I could still ask him, and I know he'd come, but I don't want to give him the wrong idea again. It wouldn't be fair.

"Can we please talk about something else?" And suddenly, as if in answer to my prayers, there's a frantic banging on the back door.

"It's Maggie," Missy shouts.

"Can you please tell Maggie to come in?" my father asks.

"She says she won't. She says she has to talk to Carrie alone. She says it's an emergency."

The Mouse rolls her eyes. "Now what?" I put down my napkin and go to the door.

Maggie's face is puffy with tears, her hair wild as if she's been trying to pull it out by the roots. She motions for me to step outside. I try to give her a hug, but she backs away, shaking with rage. "I knew this was going to happen. I knew it."

"Knew what?" I ask, my voice rising in alarm.

"I can't talk about it here. Not with your father around. Meet me at The Emerald in five minutes."

"But . . ." I look back at the house. "The Mouse is here, and—"

"So bring The Mouse," she snaps. "The Emerald. In five minutes. Be there."

"What the hell is her problem now?" The Mouse asks as we pull in next to Maggie's car. It's empty, meaning Maggie has gone inside alone, which is in itself cause for concern.

"I don't know," I say, feeling defeated. "I think it has something to do with Peter. And that story in *The Nutmeg*. About the Nerd Prince."

The Mouse makes a face. "That wasn't necessarily Peter."

"Maggie thinks it is."

"Typical. Maggie thinks everything is about her."

"I know, but . . ." I'm considering spilling the beans about the true identity of Pinky Weatherton when the door to The Emerald opens and Maggie sticks her head out.

"There you are!" she exclaims grimly, and goes back inside.

She's seated at the bar, drinking what appears to be a vodka with no ice. She gulps back the entire contents of her glass and asks for another. The Mouse orders a Scotch, while I ask for my usual Singapore Sling. I have a feeling this is going to be unpleasant, and I need something tasty to drink.

"Well," Maggie declares. "She got him."

"Who's 'she' and who did she get?" The Mouse asks. I know she doesn't mean to sound sarcastic, but she does, a little.

"Roberta," Maggie scolds. "I promise you, this is not the time."

The Mouse holds up her hands and shrugs. "Just asking."

"But I guess it *is* kind of your fault as well." Maggie takes another slug of vodka. "You're the one who introduced us."

"Peter? Come on, Maggie. You've known him for years. You just never noticed him before. And I don't exactly recall telling you to go after him."

"Yeah," I chime in. "It's not like anyone *made* you have sex with him."

"Just because *you* haven't—"

"I know, I know. I'm a virgin, okay? It's not my fault. I

probably would have slept with Sebastian if Lali hadn't stolen him."

"Really?" The Mouse says.

"Yeah. I mean, why not? Who else am I going to have sex with?" I look around the bar. "I guess I could pick some random guy and do it in the parking lot—"

"Excuse me," Maggie interrupts, banging her glass on the bar. "This is about me, okay? I'm the one in trouble here. I'm the one who's freaking out. I'm the one who's ready to kill myself—"

"Don't do it," The Mouse says. "Too messy—"

"*Stop,*" Maggie shouts.

The Mouse and I look at each other and immediately shut our traps.

"Okay." Maggie takes a deep breath. "It happened. My worst fear. It came true."

The Mouse looks up at the ceiling. "Maggie," she says patiently. "We can't help you unless you tell us what 'it' is."

"Don't you know?" Her voice rises to a wail. "Peter broke up with me. He broke up with me and now he's seeing Jen P."

I nearly fall off my barstool.

"That's right," she snarls. "After we had that big fight on Wednesday afternoon, you know"—she looks at me—"that day when he was flirting with Jen P in the gym. We had a huge screaming match and then we had sex and I thought everything was okay. And then this afternoon, he calls me and says we have to talk."

"Uh-oh—"

"So he comes over and . . ." Maggie's shoulders collapse at the memory. "He—he said he couldn't see me anymore. He said it was *over*."

"But *why*?"

"Because he's interested in Jen P. He wants to date her."

Crap. This *is* my fault. How could I be so stupid? But I never expected anyone to actually take those stories in *The Nutmeg* seriously.

"No way," The Mouse says finally.

"Yes, way," Maggie says. She orders another vodka, takes a sip, and puts it down. She's beginning to slur her words. "He said he asked his mother—his mother, can you believe it?—what she thought, and she said he was too young to be seriously involved with one girl and should 'explore his options.' Have you ever heard anyone even talk like that? And it wasn't his mother's idea, that's for sure. It was *his*. And he was using his mother as an *excuse*."

"That's disgusting. What a wimp." I suck hard on the straw in my glass.

"Peter's not really a wimp," The Mouse says. "He might be a jerk, but—"

"He's a wimp with a good haircut."

"A haircut I made him get!" Maggie exclaims. "I was the one who told him to cut his hair. It's like—I turned him into this cool guy, and now every girl wants him. *I* made him. And this is how he repays me?"

"It's nothing short of egregious."

"Come on, Maggie. It's not your fault. Peter's just a typical guy. The only way to look at men is like they're electrons. They have all these charges sticking out, and they're always looking for a hole where they can put those charges—"

"You mean like a penis?" Maggie says, glaring at me.

"Penis would be an exaggeration," The Mouse says, going along with my theory. "We're not talking about actual matter here. It's more like a crude form of electricity—"

Maggie grits her teeth. "He's taking her to the prom."

I slump onto the bar, wracked with guilt. I should tell Maggie the truth. She'll probably never speak to me again, but . . .

A man sidles toward us and slides onto the barstool next to Maggie.

"You seem kind of upset," he says, lightly touching her arm. "Perhaps I could buy you a drink."

Huh? The Mouse and I look at each other and back at Maggie. "Why not?" She holds up her empty glass. "Fill 'er up."

"Maggie!" I say warningly.

"What? I'm thirsty."

I try giving her a wide-eyed look, meant to convey the fact that we don't know this guy and shouldn't be allowing him to buy us drinks, but she doesn't get the message. "Vodka," she says, smiling flirtatiously. "I'm drinking *vodka*."

"Excuse me," The Mouse says to the guy. "Do we know you?"

"Don't think so," he says, all charm. He isn't exactly old—

maybe twenty-five or so—but he's too old for us. And he's wearing a blue and white striped button-down shirt and a navy blazer with gold buttons. "I'm Jackson," he says, holding out his hand.

Maggie shakes it. "I'm Maggie. And that's Carrie. And The Mouse." She hiccups. "I mean, Roberta."

"Cheers." Jackson raises his glass. "Another round for my new friends," he says to the bartender.

The Mouse and I exchange another look. "Maggie." I tap her on the shoulder. "We should probably get going."

"Not until I finish my drink." She kicks me in the ankle. "Besides, I want to talk to Jackson. So, Jackson," she says, tilting her head, "what are you doing here?"

"I just moved to Castlebury." He seems like a fairly reasonable person—reasonable meaning he doesn't appear to be completely drunk . . . yet. "I'm a banker," he adds.

"Oooooh. A banker," Maggie slurs. "My mother always said I should marry a banker."

"That so?" Jackson slips his hand behind Maggie's back to steady her.

"Maggie," I snap.

"Shhhhh." She puts her finger to her lips. "I'm having fun. Can't a person have a little fun around here?"

She stumbles off her barstool. "Bathroom," she exclaims, and teeters away. After another minute, Jackson excuses himself and also disappears.

"What should we do now?" I ask The Mouse.

"I say we throw her into the back of her car and *you* drive her home."

"Good plan."

But when ten minutes have passed and Maggie still hasn't returned, we start to panic. We check the bathroom, but Maggie isn't there. Next to the restroom is a small hallway with a door that leads to the parking lot. We hurry outside.

"Her car's still here," I say, relieved. "She can't have gone far."

"Maybe she's passed out in the back."

Maggie may be sleeping, but her car, however, appears to be engaged in some kind of violent activity. It's rocking back and forth, and the windows are fogged. "Maggie?" I scream, banging on the back window. *"Maggie?"*

We try the doors. They're all locked, except for one.

I yank it open. Maggie is lying on the backseat with Jackson on top of her. "Shit!" he exclaims.

The Mouse sticks her head in. "What are you doing? Get out! Get out of the car."

Jackson fumbles for the door handle behind his head. He manages to unlock it, and as the door suddenly flies open Jackson falls out onto the pavement.

He is, I note with relief, still basically clothed. And so is Maggie.

The Mouse runs over and gets in his face. "What are you, some kind of pervert?"

"Take it easy," he says, backing away. "It wasn't my idea.

She was the one who wanted to—"

"I don't care," The Mouse roars. She picks up his jacket and throws it at him. "Take your stupid blazer and get out of here before I call the police. And don't you dare come back!" she adds as Jackson, shielding himself with his coat, skittles away.

"What's going on?" Maggie asks dreamily.

"Maggie," I say, patting her face. "Are you okay? Did he—he didn't—"

"Attack me? Naw." She giggles. "I attacked him. Or I tried to anyway. But I couldn't get his pants off. And you know what?" She hiccups. "I liked it. I really, really liked it. A lot."

"Carrie? Are you mad at me?"

"No," I say reassuringly. "Why would I be mad at you, Magwitch?"

"Because I've had more guys than you," she says, with another hiccup and a smile.

"Don't worry. Someday I'll catch up."

"I hope so. Because it's really fun, you know? And it's also like . . . power. Like you have power over these guys."

"Uh-huh," I say cautiously.

"Don't tell Peter, okay?"

"No, I won't tell Peter. It will be our little secret."

"And The Mouse too, right? Will it be her little secret, too?"

"Of course—"

"On second thought"—she holds up one finger—"maybe you should tell Peter. I want him to be jealous. I want him to think about what he's missing." She gasps and puts her hand over her mouth. I pull over to the side of the road. Maggie tumbles out and gets sick while I hold back her hair.

When she gets back in the car, she seems to have sobered up considerably but has also become morose. "I did a dumb thing, didn't I?" she groans.

"Don't worry about it, Mags. We all do dumb things sometimes."

"Oh, God. I'm a slut." She puts her hands over her face. "I almost had sex with two men."

"Come on, Maggie, you're not a slut," I insist. "It doesn't matter how many guys you've slept with. It's about *how* you've slept with them."

"What's that mean?"

"I have no idea. But it sounds good, right?"

I pull carefully into her driveway. Maggie's parents are fast asleep, and I manage to maneuver her up to her room and into her nightgown undetected. I even convince her to drink a glass of water and take a couple of aspirins. She crawls into bed and lies on her back, staring at the ceiling. Then she curls up into the fetal position.

"Sometimes I just want to be a little girl again, you know?"

"Yeah." I sigh. "I know just what you mean." I wait a moment to make sure she's asleep, and then I flip off the light and slip out of the house.

CHAPTER THIRTY-FOUR

Transformation

Dear Ms. Bradshaw, the letter begins. *We are pleased to inform you that a place has become available for the summer writing seminar with National Book Award–winning novelist Viktor Greene. If you wish to attend, please inform us immediately as space is limited.*

The New School.

I got in! *IgotinIgotinIgotin.* Or at least I think I did. Does it specifically *say* I got in? *A place has become available. . .* At the last minute? Did someone drop out? Am I some kind of backup student? *The course is limited. . .* Aha. So that means if I don't take the spot someone else will. They've already got dozens of people lined up, maybe hundreds—

"Daaaaaaad!"

"What?" he asks, startled.

"I have to—I got this letter—New York—"

"Stop jumping up and down and tell me what this is about."

I put my hand on my chest to quell my thumping heart. "I got into that writing program. In New York City. And if I don't say yes right away, they're going to give my space to someone else."

"New York," my father exclaims. "What about Brown?"

"Dad, you don't understand. See? Right here: summer writing course. June twenty-second to August nineteenth. And Brown doesn't start till Labor Day. So there's plenty of time—"

"I don't know, Carrie."

"But, Dad—"

"I thought this writing thing was a hobby."

I look at him, aghast.

"It isn't. I mean, it's just something I really want to do." I can't express how badly I want it. I don't want to scare him.

"We'll think about it, okay?"

"No!" I shout. He'll think about it and think about it and by the time he's thought about it, it will be too late. I shove the letter under his nose. "I have to decide now. Otherwise—"

Finally, he sits down and actually reads it.

"I'm not sure," he says. "New York City in the summer? It could be dangerous."

"Millions of people live there. And they're fine."

"Hmmmm," he says, thinking. "Does George know about this?"

"About my acceptance? Not yet. But he was the one who encouraged me to send in my stories. George is all for it."

"Well—"

"Dad, please."

"If George is going to be there—"

Why should George have anything to do with it? Who cares about George? This is about me, not George. "He's going to be there all summer. He has an internship with *The New York Times*."

"Does he?" My father looks impressed.

"So going to New York for the summer is a very big Brown thing to do."

My father takes off his glasses and pinches the bridge of his nose. "It's a long way away—"

"Two hours."

"It's another world—I hate to think I'm losing you already."

"Dad, you're going to lose me anyway, sooner or later. Why not get it over with sooner? That way you have more time to get used to it."

My father laughs. *Yes*—I'm in.

"I guess two months in New York couldn't hurt," he says, talking himself into it. "Freshman year at Brown is intense. And I know how difficult this year has been for you." He rubs his nose, trying to delay the inevitable. "My daughters—they mean so much to me."

As if on cue, he starts crying.

✧　✳　CB　✳　✧

"You surprise me," Donna LaDonna says a few days later.

"You're a lot tougher than I thought."

"Uh-huh." I squint into the viewfinder. "Turn your head to the right. And try not to look so happy. You're supposed to be bummed out about your life."

"I don't want to look ugly."

I sigh and lift my head. "Just try not to look like a goddamned cheerleader, okay?"

"Okay," she reluctantly agrees. She pulls her knee up to her chin and looks at me from beneath her heavily mascaraed lashes.

"Great." I click the shutter, reminded of Donna LaDonna's "big secret": She hates her eyelashes. Without mascara, they're pale stubby spikes, like the lashes on a dog. It's Donna's biggest fear. Someday, some guy will see her without mascara and run screaming from the room.

Sad. I click off several more shots, then shout, "Got it." I put down the camera as Donna swings her legs off the porch railing. "When are we going to do Marilyn?" she asks as I follow her into the house.

"We can do Marilyn this afternoon. But it means we have to do punk tomorrow."

She heads up the stairs, leaning her head over the side. "I hate punk. It's gross."

"We're going to do you androgynous," I say, trying to make the prospect as appealing as possible. "Like David Bowie. We're going to paint your whole body red."

"You're insane." She shakes her head and storms away to

change, but she isn't angry. I've learned that much about her anyway. Having a hissy fit is Donna LaDonna's way of teasing.

I push aside an open box of cereal and hike myself onto the marble countertop to wait. Donna's house is a smorgasbord of textures—marble, gold, heavy silk drapes—that somehow don't go together and create the impression that one has entered a fun house of bad taste. But in the last few days, I've gotten used to it.

You can get used to anything, I guess, if you've been there enough.

You can even get used to the idea that your ex-best friend is still dating your ex-boyfriend and that they are going to the senior prom together. But it doesn't mean you have to talk to them. Nor does it mean you have to talk about them. Not after you've lived with the fact for four months.

It's just another thing you have to live through.

I pick up the camera and examine the lens. I gently blow away a speck of dust and replace the cover.

"Donna?" I call out. "Hurry up."

"I can't get the zipper up," she yells back.

I sigh and carefully place the camera on the counter. Am I going to have to see her in her underwear again? Donna, I've discovered, is one of those girls who will shed her clothing at the slightest provocation. Actually, that's wrong. She requires no provocation at all, only a minimum amount of privacy. The first thing she did—the first thing she always does, she informed me, when she brought me to her house after school—is take off her clothes.

"I think the human body is beautiful," she said, removing her skirt and sweater and tossing them onto the couch.

I tried not to look but couldn't resist. "Uh-huh. If you have a body like yours."

"Oh, your body isn't *bad*," she said dismissively. "But you could use some curves."

"They don't exactly hand out perfect breasts like candy, you know. I mean, it's not like you can go into a store and buy them."

"You're funny. When I was a kid, my grandmother used to tell us that babies came from a store."

"And boy was she wrong."

I head upstairs to Donna's room, wondering once again, how we ever got to be friends. Or friendly, anyway. We're not really friends. We're too different for that. I'll never completely understand her, and she has no interest in understanding me. But other than that, she's a great girl.

It feels like a million years ago when I walked into that photography class at the library and got paired up with her. I kept going to the class, and so did she, and after the piece came out about the queen bee, her attitude toward me began to thaw. "I still can't figure out f-stops," she said one afternoon. "Every time I see the letter 'f,' I think of the word, 'fuck.' I can't help it."

"Fuck stops," I said. "They're like truck stops but you only go there to have sex."

After that, Donna stopped hating me and decided I was

this wacky, funny, crazy girl instead. And when we were again assigned to work in pairs, Donna picked me as her partner.

This week, we had to come up with a theme and photograph it. Donna and I chose "transformation." Actually, I came up with the idea and Donna eagerly agreed. With Donna's looks, I figured we could dress her up in different outfits and make her into three different women, while I'd take the pictures.

"Donna?" I ask now. Her door is open, but I rap on it anyway, just to be polite. She's bent forward, struggling with the zipper on the black silk vintage dress I found among my mother's old clothes. She swings up her head and puts her hands on her hips. "Carrie, for Christ's sake, you don't have to knock. Will you get over here and help me?"

She turns around, and for a moment, seeing her in my mother's dress feels like the past and future rushing together like two rivers emptying into the sea. I feel marooned—a survivor on a raft with no land in sight.

"Carrie?" Donna demands. "Is something wrong?"

I take a deep breath and shake my head. I have a paddle now, I remind myself. It's time to start rowing into my future.

I step forward and zip up the dress.

"Thanks," she says.

Downstairs, Donna arranges herself seductively on the couch, while I set up the tripod.

"You are funny, you know?" she says.

"Yeah," I say with a smile.

"Not ha-ha funny," she says, leaning back on her elbows.

"A different kind of funny. You're not what you seem."

"How's that?"

"Well, I always thought you were pretty much of a wimp. Kind of a nerd. I mean, you're pretty and all, but you never seemed like you wanted to use it."

"Maybe I wanted to use my brains instead."

"No, it's not that," she says musingly. "I guess I thought I could run right over you. But then I read that piece in *The Nutmeg*. I should have been pissed off, but it made me kind of admire you. I thought, 'This is a girl who can stand up for herself. Who can stand up to *me*.' And there aren't a lot of girls who can do that."

She lifts her head. "I mean, you are Pinky Weatherton, right?"

I open my mouth, full of arguments and explanations as to why I'm not, but then I close it again. I no longer need to pretend. "Yeah," I say simply.

"Hmph. You sure had a lot of people fooled. Aren't you afraid they're going to find out?"

"Doesn't matter. I don't need to write for *The Nutmeg* anymore." I hesitate and then deliver the news. "I got into this special writing program. I'm going to New York City for the summer."

"Well." Donna sounds slightly impressed and also slightly envious. Not to be outdone, she says, "You know I have a cousin who lives in New York?"

"Uh-huh." I nod. "You've told me a million times."

"She's this big deal in advertising. And she has a million

guys after her. And she's really pretty."

"That's nice."

"But I mean, really pretty. And successful. Anyway . . ." She pauses to adjust the dress. "You should meet her."

"Okay."

"No, seriously," she insists. "I'll give you her number. You should call her up and get together. You'll like her. She's even wilder than I am."

I pull into my driveway and stop, confused.

A red truck is parked in front of the garage, and it takes me a second to realize that the truck is Lali's, and that she's come to my house and is waiting for me. Maybe she and Sebastian broke up, I think wildly. Maybe they broke up and she's come to apologize, which means that maybe, just maybe, I can start seeing Sebastian again and Lali and I can be friends. . .

I make a face as I park next to the truck. What am I thinking? I could never go out with Sebastian now. He's ruined, like a favorite sweater with a hideous stain. And my friendship with Lali? Also permanently damaged. So what the hell is she doing here?

I find her sitting on the patio with my sister Missy. Ever polite, Missy is helplessly trying to make small talk, probably as confused as I am about Lali's presence. "And how's your mother?" Missy asks awkwardly.

"Fine," Lali says. "My father bought her a new puppy, so

she's happy."

"That's nice," Missy says, with a glazed smile. She looks away and spots me coming up the walk. "Carrie." She jumps to her feet. "Thank God you're here. I have to practice," she says, making a piano-playing motion with her fingers.

"Nice to see you," Lali says. She stares at Missy's back until she's safely inside. Then she turns to me.

"Well?" I say, crossing my arms.

"How could you?" she demands.

"Huh?" I ask, taken aback. I'm expecting her to beg for forgiveness and instead she's attacking me?

"How could *you*?" I ask, astonished.

And then I notice the rolled-up manuscript in her hand. My heart sinks. I know immediately what it is: my story about her and Sebastian. The one I gave to Gayle weeks ago and told her to hold. The one I was planning to tell her not to bother publishing.

"How could you write this?" Lali asks. I take a step toward her, hesitate, and then gingerly take a seat on the other side of the table. She's playing the tough guy, but her eyes are wide and watery, like she's about to cry.

"What are you talking about?"

"This!" She bangs the pages onto the table. They scatter apart and she quickly gathers them up. "Don't even try to lie about it. You know you wrote it."

"I do?"

She hastily wipes the corner of her eye. "You can't fool

me. There are things in here that only you would know."

Double crap. Now I actually do feel bad. And guilty.

But then I remind myself that she's the one who's responsible for this mess.

I rock back in my chair, sliding my feet onto the table. "How did you get it anyway?"

"Jen P."

Jen P must have been hanging out with Peter in the art department and she found it in Gayle's folder and stole it. "Why would Jen P give it to you?"

"I've known her a long time," she says slowly. "Some people are loyal."

Now she's being really nasty. She's known me a long time too. Perhaps she's chosen to skip that part. "Sounds more like a case of 'like attracts like.' You stole Sebastian and she stole Peter."

"Oh, Carrie." She sighs. "You were always so dumb about boys. You can't steal someone's boyfriend unless he wants to be stolen."

"Is that so?"

"You're so mean," she says, shaking the manuscript. "How could you do this?"

"Because you deserve it?"

"Who are you to say who deserves what? Who do you think you are? *God?* You always think you're just a little bit better than everyone else. You always think something better is going to happen to you. Like this"—she indicates my backyard—"like all this isn't really your life. Like all this is just a stepping-stone to someplace better."

"Maybe it *is*," I counter.

"And maybe it *isn't*."

We stare at each other, shocked into silence by our animosity.

"Well." I toss my head. "Has Sebastian seen it?"

The question seems to further agitate her. She looks away, pressing her fingers over her eyes. She takes a deep breath as if she's making a decision, then leans across the table, her face twisting in pain. *"No."*

"Why not? I would think it would be another useful brick in your we-hate-Carrie-Bradshaw edifice."

"He hasn't seen it and he never will." Her face hardens. "We broke up."

"Really?" My voice cracks. "Why?"

"Because I caught him making out with my little sister."

I gather the pages she's thrown onto the table and tap them up and down until the corners are neatly aligned. Then I giggle. I try to hold it in, but it's impossible. I cover my mouth and a snort comes from my nose. I put my head between my knees, but it's no use. My mouth opens and I emit a whoop of laughter.

"It's not funny!" She makes a motion to get up but bangs her fist on the table instead. "It is not funny," she repeats.

"Oh, but it is." I nod, laughing hysterically. "It's hilarious."

CHAPTER THIRTY-FIVE

A Free Man in Paris

June 20th, I write.

I press my knuckles to my lips and look out the window.

*Amtrak train. Dad, Missy, and Dorrit take me to the
station to wave good-bye. I kept saying Missy and Dorrit
didn't have to come. I kept saying it was no big deal. I kept
saying I was only going for the summer. But we were all
nervous, stumbling over one another in an attempt to get me
out the door. It's not like it's 1893 and I'm going to China
or anything, but we sure as hell acted like it.*

And then we were standing on the rickety platform,
trying to make small talk. "Do you have the address?" my dad
asked for the umpteenth time.

"Yes, Dad. I wrote it down in my address book." Just to
make sure, I take the address book out of my Carrie bag, and

read the entry out loud: "Two forty-five East Forty-seventh Street."

"And money. You have money?"

"Two hundred dollars."

"That's only for an emergency. You won't spend it all in one place?"

"No."

"And you'll call when you get there?"

"I'll try." I'll *try*—but my words are drowned out by the long, slow holler of the approaching train as the speaker crackles to life. "Eleven-oh-three train to Penn Station New York, and Washington, D.C., arriving in *approximately* one minute—"

"Good-bye, good-bye"—hugs all around as the giant locomotive rolls slowly down the tracks, wheels screeching like a hundred crows—"good-bye, good-bye"—as my father heaves my suitcase up the steps and I clap my hat to my head—"good-bye, good-bye"—the train starts with a jerk, the doors close and my heart heaves to the bottom of my stomach—"good-bye, good-bye"—*relief.*

I make my way down the aisle swaying like a drunken sailor. *New York,* I think, as I plop down onto a cracked red leather seat and take out my journal.

Yesterday, I said good-bye to all my friends. Maggie, Walt, The Mouse, and I met at the Hamburger Shack for one final hamburger with sautéed onions and peppers. Walt's not working there anymore. He got a job at a law office, answering phones. His father said that even though he couldn't forgive Walt for being gay, he was willing to overlook it if he was successful. The Mouse is going to her government camp in Washington, and Maggie is going to Hilton Head for the summer, where her sister and brother-in-law have rented a cottage. Maggie's going to help out with their kids, and no doubt hook up with a few lifeguards along the way.

I heard Lali is going to the University of Hartford, where she's planning to study accounting.

But there was one person I still had to see.

I knew I should have let it go.

I couldn't.

I was curious. Or maybe I had to see for myself that it was truly over. I needed proof that he absolutely did not love me and never had.

On Saturday evening around seven, I drove by his house. I didn't expect him to be home. I had worked up this idea in my head that I would leave him a note, saying I was going to New York and I hoped he would have a good summer. I convinced myself it was the right thing to do—the polite thing—and would somehow make me the bigger person.

His car was in the driveway.

I told myself I wouldn't even knock. I would leave the note on the windshield of his car.

But then I heard music coming from the house. The screen door was open, and suddenly I just had to see him one last time.

I knocked.

"Yup?" His voice, slightly annoyed, came from the recesses of the family room.

I knocked again.

"Who is it?" he demanded, this time with more irritation.

"Sebastian?" I called out.

And then he was there, staring at me from behind the screen door. I'd like to say he no longer affected me, that seeing him was a disappointment. But it wasn't true. I felt as strongly about him as I had on that first day I'd seen him in calculus class.

He looked surprised. "What's up?"

"I came to say good-bye."

"Oh." He opened the door and stepped outside. "Where are you going?"

"New York. I got into that writing program," I said in a rush. "I wrote you a note. I was going to leave it on your car, but . . ." I took out the folded piece of paper and handed it to him.

He scanned it quickly. "Well." He nodded. "Good luck."

He crumpled up the note and handed it back to me.

"What are you doing? For the summer, I mean," I asked quickly, suddenly desperate to keep him there, for at least a moment longer.

"France," he said. "Going to France." And then he grinned. "Wanna come?"

I have this theory: If you forgive someone, they can't hurt you anymore.

The train rattles and shakes. We pass hollow buildings scrawled with graffiti, billboards advertising toothpaste and hemorrhoid cream and a smiling girl in a mermaid outfit pointing at the words, "CALL ME!" in capital letters. Then the scenery disappears and we're going through a tunnel.

"New York City," the conductor calls out. "Penn Station."

I close my journal and slip it into my suitcase. The lights inside the car flicker on and off, on and off, and then black out altogether.

And like a newborn child, I enter my future in darkness.

An escalator that goes on forever. And then an enormous space, tiled like a bathroom, and the sharp smell of urine and sweet warm sweat. Penn Station. People everywhere.

I stop and adjust my hat. It's one of my grandmother's old numbers, with a long green plume and a small net. For some reason, I thought it was appropriate. I wanted to arrive in New York wearing a hat.

It was part of my fantasy.

"Watch where you're going!"

"Get out of the way."

"Do you know where you're going?" This from a middle-aged lady wearing a black suit and an even blacker scowl.

"The exit? Taxis?" I ask.

"That way," she says, pointing to yet another escalator that seems to rise straight up into nothingness.

I get on, balancing my suitcase behind me. A man, weaving this way and that, comes up behind me—striped pants, jaunty cap, eyes hidden behind dark green glass in gold-rimmed sunglasses. "Hey, little girl, you look lost."

"I'm not," I say.

"You sure?" he asks. "I got a real sweet place you can stay, real nice place, hot shower and pretty clothes. Let me help you with that bag, honey, that looks real heavy—"

"I have a place to stay. *Thank you.*" He shrugs and walks away with a rolling gait.

"Hey! *Hey,*" someone yells impatiently. "You want a taxi or not? I don't have all day here—"

"Yes, *please,*" I say breathlessly, hauling my suitcase across the sidewalk to a yellow cab. I plunk the suitcase onto the curb, place my Carrie handbag on top of it, and lean into the open window.

"How much?" I ask.

"Where you going?"

I turn around to pick up my bag so I can give him the address.

Huh?

"Just a minute, sir—"

"What's the problem?"

"Nothing." I scramble around my suitcase, looking for my bag. It must have fallen. My heart pounds as I flush in embarrassment and dread.

It's gone.

"Where to?" the cabdriver snaps again.

"Are you going to take this cab or not?" demands a man in a gray suit.

"No—I—er—" He brushes past me, gets in the taxi, and slams the door.

I've been robbed.

I stare into the open maw of Penn Station. No. I cannot go back. Will not.

But I have no money. I don't even have the address of the place I'm staying. I could call George, but I don't have his number either.

Two men walk by, carrying an enormous boom box. A disco song blares from the speakers—"Macho Man."

I pick up my suitcase. A tide of people carries me across Seventh Avenue where I'm deposited in front of a bank of phone booths.

"Excuse me," I call out to various passersby. "Do you have a dime? A dime for a phone call?" I would never do this back in Castlebury—beg—but I figure I'm not in Castlebury anymore.

And I'm desperate.

"I'll give you fifty cents for your hat." A guy with arched eyebrows regards me in amusement.

"My hat?"

"That feather," he says. "It's too much."

"It belonged to my grandmother."

"Of course it did. Fifty cents. Take it or leave it."

"I'll take it."

He places five dimes in my hand.

I drop the first coin into the slot.

"Operator."

"Do you have a number for George Carter?"

"I've got fifteen George Carters. What's the address?"

"Fifth Avenue?"

"I have a William Carter on Fifth Avenue and Seventy-second Street. Would you like the number?"

"Yes."

She gives me the number and I repeat it over and over in my head as I drop my second dime into the slot.

A woman picks up. "Hello?" she asks in a strong German accent.

"Does George Carter live there?"

"Mr. Carter? Yes, he does."

Relief. "Can I talk to him?"

"He's out."

"What?"

"He's out. I don't know when he'll be back. He never tells me."

"But—"

"Do you want to leave a message?"

"Yes," I say, defeated. "Can you tell him Carrie Bradshaw called?"

I hang up the phone and put my hand over my face. Now what? I'm suddenly overwhelmed—exhausted, frightened, and charged with adrenaline. I pick up my suitcase and start walking.

I manage one block; then I have to stop. I sit on top of my suitcase to rest. Crap. I now have thirty cents, some clothes, and my journal.

Suddenly, I get up, open my suitcase, and pull out my journal. Is it possible? I had my journal with me that day at Donna LaDonna's house.

I paw through the pages, past my notes on the queen bee and the Nerd King and Lali and Sebastian—and, finally, there it is, all alone on its own page, written in Donna LaDonna's loopy scrawl and circled three times.

A number. And underneath, a name.

I haul my suitcase to the corner, to another bank of phone booths. My hand shakes as I push my third dime into the slot. I dial the number. The phone rings and rings. Seven times. Nine. Ten. On the twelfth ring, someone picks up.

"You must be awfully desperate to see me." The voice is languid, sexy. Like the owner of the voice has just gotten out of bed.

I gasp, uncertain of what to say.

"*Hello?* Is that you, Charlie?" Teasing. "If you're not going to talk to me—"

"Wait!" I squeak.

"Yes?" The voice becomes suddenly suspicious.

I take a deep breath.

"Samantha Jones?" I ask.

ABOUT THE AUTHOR

Candace Bushnell is the critically acclaimed bestselling author of *Sex and the City*, *Lipstick Jungle*, *One Fifth Avenue*, *4 Blondes*, and *Trading Up*, which have sold millions of copies. *Sex and the City* was the basis for the HBO hit show and film of the same name. *Lipstick Jungle* became a popular television series on NBC. She lives in New York City.